The Wa

"Besides that," ... "I have the hole card. Before your bow-and-lance troops, excellent though I admit they are, can kill me, I'll kill her."

Deshin's voice was distinctly tense now. "You can all go. Just leave me the girl."

"On the contrary. We'll take her along. Tell your men to unstring their bows. Stray arrows might happen otherwise, and we'd hate any accidents."

Reluctantly the order was given. As the Cuirassiers got busy, Cap turned back to face Bey. Keilin caught a hand signal. "And to make doubly sure," said Cap, his voice calm, "we'll take you too." As he spoke Bey launched himself in a terrific spring. The first bodyguard was dead. The other was dying. And the bloody sword pressed against the throat of the Emperor.

"Back! Back off, if you want your Emperor to live," Cap shouted, his voice carrying loudly back into the rain haze.

"Let me go! My men will—"

"Your men will back off and allow us to pass. If they do exactly as I tell them, you'll stay alive."

THE FORLORN

DAVE FREER

BAEN

THE FORLORN

A Baen Books Original

Baen Publishing Enterprises
P.O. Box 1403
Riverdale, NY 10471

ISBN: 0-671-57831-6

Cover art by Larry Elmore

First printing, September 1999

Distributed by Simon & Schuster
1230 Avenue of the Americas
New York, NY 10020

Typeset by Brilliant Press and Windhaven Press
Printed in the United States of America

For Barbs

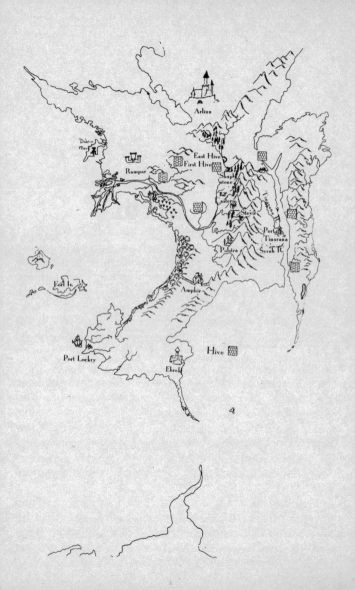

CHAPTER 1

Port Tinarana was like an old, decaying tart, her face lined with a myriad of streets and alleys, inexpertly caked with a crude makeup of overhanging buildings. The alleyways seemed to grow narrower and more choked in filth with the passing of each year. Judging by the ankle-deep slush, this dead end hadn't had the garbage cleared in the last three hundred of those years. And in a few minutes his body would become yet another once-human part of it. He shrank back against the cold, oozing stones of the overhanging wall. The night haze of fog and coal smoke streamered in twisted eddies about the ragged boys. They were vague, almost ethereal, except for the silver-pale lines of low held knives, moving in slow arcs as they closed in.

"Gonna cut you, dink."

"Yeah! Gonna spill your guts, cull. You bin workin' our turf."

Keilin knew there was no use in pleading. They weren't going to listen. They were all bigger than he was, used to using those knives. He touched the stone of his pendant, pressing it into his thin chest. It was

1

always cool, but now it seemed almost burning cold against his skin. His pale eyes darted, trying to assess his best chance. Oh God, for some kind of break . . . They came closer. . . .

"What've you got there, gutter rats?" The voice was coarse, adult and slightly slurred with alcohol.

The advance of the ragged gang stopped. "Piss off, guardsman, if you want to stay healthy." The rat pack's leader was wary, but defiant.

"Huh! Hear that mates! The rats are worried 'bout my health!"

Another rough voice responded. "Soon have their own to worry about, heh heh!" There was the steely rasp of a sword being drawn.

Keilin knew this was no rescue for him. The city guardsmen protected those who paid their dues. To this brethren of thugs he was as much of a louse on the city's underbelly as his attackers were. The dead end the gang had caught him in had now become their trap, too.

"Wait a minute, Sill. Let's see what they've got first. We might even want it instead of a rat." There was a nasal quality to the voice that failed to overlay the lust. With a sharp metallic click the slide of the dark lantern was pulled back. Light spilled out. It revealed four boys in tattered clothing remnants. They were stunted and malnourished, but visibly between the ages of fifteen and the wispy first traces of beard. Their victim was smaller and younger still.

The light was directed at the victim. "Ooh! Pretty one, isn't he!" The nasal voice thickened. Here, in the deep south, a pale skin, green eyes and red hair were rare, as was the hawksbill nose in the middle of it all. Enough of the light washed back for Keilin to see the holder. His belly crawled. Guard-Captain Kemp. It was widely rumored that Kemp got his kicks from pain . . . and that his young victims ended up dead . . . much later.

"Go on, rats. Get lost. It's your lucky night." As the ragged figures scampered past the guardsmen, Keilin saw the Guard-Captain set the dark lantern down and start fumbling with the buttons on his pants. "Hold him for me, boys. Looks like this one'll fight back." Something in his voice indicated that this would simply add spice.

Keilin struggled vainly against the big hands that held him. He was wild with fear, into the realms of panic, too far gone to feel pain from the sudden bitter cold of the jewel on his chest.

"Holy shit!" The rough hands loosened their grip on his arms. Keilin writhed free, pulling up his trousers. Whatever this was, he was going to run, and he'd not get far with them around his ankles. He heard the scraping sound of swords being drawn. Looking up, he saw just how futile this act was. In the lantern light the bull was huge, filling most of the alley. Living in the gut of the city, Keilin barely knew what the animal was, but hearing the beast's bellow, seeing those long horns lowering, he was sure it was very, very angry.

The city guardsman nearest the beast knew equally little about the temper of an old swamp aurochs. If he'd been from the wide, wild marshes of Vie'en, five hundred leagues to the southeast, where the vast beast had been grazing peacefully in the pale morning a few moments before, the fat one would never have been so stupid. But the nearest thing to this beast he'd ever met was an elderly milch cow. So he waved his sword ineffectually at it, as one might a hazel switch, and shouted, "Go on! Shoo!"

The sweeping horn caught him, sheer weight and power punching it through his rib cage, like a spear through wet tissue paper. His bubbling scream was cut off as he was tossed and flung with bone-smashing force to crack against the wall. He bounced off it, to fall beneath the angry hooves.

The guardsman called Sill grabbed Keilin's arm, and pulled the boy across his body, holding him as a human shield. Such a shield was, of course, meaningless to the three-ton beast that was pawing the ragdoll remnants of the guardsman's former companion.

Then Keilin heard a high-pitched thin whine. He knew what came next. It had happened three times before. The guardsmen didn't appear to be able to hear it . . . or didn't know what it meant. With frantic strength the boy lunged forward and bit his captor's lower bicep with all his might. Sill grunted with pain and jerked the boy away; Keilin desperately threw himself downward. The guard's chest, and a tardy lock of Keilin's hair vaporized. So did half the wall behind them, and the door beyond that.

Keilin didn't wait for them to have a second shot at him. He was off, bolting through the new-made way out of the dead end. His one glance backward showed that the Guard-Captain had made his escape through the same hole. The man seemed to have no intention of following him, though. Kemp was just running in blind panic.

Keilin slipped into a narrow multibranched alley, and waited hidden behind a lip of brickwork. No footsteps followed. After a few minutes of swallowed panting and gradually slowing heartbeat, the boy slipped quietly away in a different direction. Finally, as the sky was beginning to pale, and the first sounds of stirring of the city's dayside began, he dropped over a wall, and then shimmied up a drainpipe. This gave access to a narrow ledge surrounding the building at third-floor level. He edged along the dark line of crumbling bricks, and around the corner to a small window.

It wasn't barred . . . most unusual for Port Tinarana. In fact it only appeared to be closed. A fingernail under the edge of the rusty steel and it opened silently, or should have, after the amount of stolen oil that Keilin had lavished on it. Instead, it opened quietly a little way and then . . . stuck. Keilin was standing on a four-inch-wide ledge, trying to apply outward leverage. He cursed in a whisper, using language no fourteen-year-old ought to know: not just because it was obscene, but because it was obscene in an extinct language. Perhaps as a response, the obdurate window flew open abruptly, nearly tumbling him down for perhaps the twentieth time. He *had* fallen once, and the memory of the fear in those stretched-out moments was still with him. He was shaking as he pulled himself into the musty darkness.

His eyes adjusted to the dimness as he closed the window behind him. Relief washed through him as he looked at the familiar cracked washstand from his perch on the toilet cistern. This was one of the port's original buildings, and here, unusually, the plumbing still worked. In most public places the fittings had long since been looted, to become nonfunctioning ornaments in some wealthy merchant's house, or perhaps cut and fitted to the normal bucket and seat arrangement. But here . . . this place was largely forgotten. Those who did remember its existence treated it with superstitious awe. This is the fate of libraries in largely illiterate societies.

After a long drink of the slightly rust-flavored water, Keilin slipped out, through the crowded stack-room, and into the little kitchen the librarians used. He knew that he was in trouble, and needed to think of some way out, but for now he let his familiar rituals carry him. Years back Keilin had worked out that the mistake that most thieves made was to try and attack the food chain at too high a level. If you're hungry, don't try to steal meat pies, or gold for meat pies. Those things are well guarded, and thieves are hunted down. The port grain silos however . . . well, they were poorly defended against rats and pigeons, and easily accessible to a nimble boy. The porridge he made from the mortar-crushed wheat wasn't nearly as appetizing as a meat pie, but Keilin, unlike most of his peers, wasn't malnourished. Also, the grain made good bait for the pigeons he trapped on the roof. Keilin looked down at the porridge and sighed. If he'd not been tempted into trying for peppers, he wouldn't have been spotted and chased into that alley.

He cleaned up meticulously. Everything was left in its exact place. He'd been using the kitchen for three years now without its legitimate owners being any the wiser. By the time they got in, the little alcohol stove would be cold, and any smells lost in the odor of yesterday's curries. He sometimes stole a little of these too . . . but very circumspectly. He went to wash, a ritual he'd taken up when the head librarian had smelt Keilin's far-from-delicate alley bouquet, and had spent the next hour zealously hunting dead rats around his hideout. Keilin had spent the time silently between fear and chagrin. There were no rats in the library, now. But they'd been his main source of food when he'd first taken shelter there.

His mind kept turning back to the previous night. For now, the "Die Hards," the street gang who had caught him first, thought he was dead. But, by tonight, the word would be out. Anyone who denied that the city watch had links with the gangs was just naive. So . . . what passed for the law—the gangs and the watch—would be out to kill him. He didn't know what story the Guard-Captain had come up with to explain his men's sudden demise, but he was willing to bet the truth hadn't figured in it. The man wasn't going to rest easy until Keilin was dead. As for the other gangs . . . they would go along. To keep the peace, any of them that caught him would hand him over to the Die Hards. But the worst was that the whining killers had found him again. He sat down with the book he was currently reading and tried to lose himself in it. Keilin knew that being able to read was all that set him apart from the other scavenging children of the city . . . but this time he couldn't see how it could help him. Gradually the book swallowed him.

He slipped out of his reading-induced trance with a start. Surely it wasn't opening time already? Yes. Those were definitely footsteps on the staircase. Damn. No time for a last visit to the toilet. He'd just have to use the bloody jar again. Moving swiftly but quietly, he went across to the inverted V of an old-fashioned bookstand, which stood against the far wall. In the old days he'd had to lift it, but since then he'd managed to unscrew one of the boards, under the lowest shelf. It had taken him many nights of effort, but it was worth the extra speed it lent to getting into his rat hole. He slipped through the gap with some effort, and pulled the waiting board back into place, just as the two elderly and slightly out of breath librarians reached the top floor. He heard them clatter in the kitchen, as he settled into his nest.

He felt his scraped ribs. He was going to have to do something about that plank. Growing was creating all sorts of problems. Then, as he listened to the librarians discussing the street news, he realized he wasn't going to have to worry about the plank after all.

". . . a black magician!"

"There's no such thing, as you well know, Khabo! Only the ignorant lower classes believe in magic."

"Think what you like, Stannel. Gemme's cousin Shanda saw the dead aurochs herself. Killed seven people it did, before they speared it to death."

"Amazing! Shanda got off her back for long enough to see something outside of her own bedroom! I thought she was *far* too busy for that." Despite the catty comment Stannel was plainly impressed.

"She's thirty years younger than you, old man. If

she'd accepted you, she'd have run off with some sailor by now."

"True. Now, instead, the sailors can come to her. So you say they're offering a reward for this so-called magician?"

"Yes! The Patrician himself has put up five hundred . . . in gold! The brave Guard-Captain who stopped the magician is leading the house-to-house search in person. The boy's to be killed on sight, before he can use his black powers!"

Forgetting his supposed disbelief in magic, Stannel interjected, "I thought they had to light black candles, draw pentacles and . . . you know . . . sacrifice babies and things to do their spells."

"Huh! This one did all that years ago! The Guard-Captain said that the magician was raping a baby girl when they caught him!"

"No! Monster! I hope they're going to make him die slowly."

"It's not safe, I tell you! He blasted his way though six buildings and a man to escape. His kind you kill the minute you see them, preferably before he sees you."

"Speak for yourself! If *I* see him, I'm going to run like hell. What's he look like?"

With a sinking heart Keilin listened to a surprisingly accurate description of himself. Why the hell couldn't Kemp have lied about that too?

"What I don't understand is how come he didn't just blast that Guard-Captain to ash too?"

"Guard-Captain Kemp's a deeply religious man. He believes God protected him against the bolts of the evil and unholy. . . ." The conversation faded off down the stairwell.

Keilin sat there in silence, hands over his face. Holy mother . . . the gangs were after him, the townspeople'd kill him on sight, Kemp was hunting house to house for him, and the whiners . . . and a reward from the Patrician. That one puzzled him though. The citizens of Port T. knew that that bastard never parted with the gold he extracted with infinite care from all his subjects, even the whores, beggars and thieves. And, by all reports, what happened in the cellars beneath the Patrician's palace would make the librarians' idea of black magic look like a Sunday School outing.

There were a few people out there who knew Keilin, but he'd never trusted anyone enough to reveal his hideout to them. He was safe enough here, but if he ventured out . . . well, there were always eyes in the alleys. Sooner or later someone would see him, and then the hunt would be on. He'd never make it back. In the old town alone there were at least a thousand men, and women too, for that matter, who'd slit his throat for a single gold piece, never mind five hundred.

He tried to concentrate on his book again, holding it up to the light coming through the holes he'd made. It was no use. He couldn't divert his mind from Kemp's plot. Hatred twisted at his gut. He'd never killed anyone before, but if he could get that man alone somewhere . . . Still, it was no use dreaming. He must get out, survive, then, one day he could come back and do a little quiet and nasty repayment.

Keilin knew little of the world outside the walls of the port. He'd come here, a fugitive from another dimly remembered city, when he was about seven. He remembered sneaking off the ship in the pale dawn, with his mother. He remembered watching, puzzled and uncomfortable, as his mother had "paid" the bosun for smuggling them off the ship. He remembered in the grim years that followed, as her addiction grew deeper, how his discomfort and resentment had given way to resignation and then acceptance. He stretched his mind back further to misty memories of the city they'd lived in before reaching

Port Tinarana. He could remember the sergeant of
the Caravan Guards, but not his face.

The boy shuddered. His mind wouldn't let him
remember the face. That had been the first time he'd
heard the whining sounds. The caravaneer had been
a kindly man when he was sober. He'd had Keilin's
mother teach the boy to read, and been proud of his
stepson's cleverness. He'd started to teach him to use
a sword. He'd tried to teach Keilin to swim, and kept
Keilin spellbound by telling him tales of far-off places.
If only Keilin could remember more of them, but
most of it was lost in the vagueness of early childhood . . . But he could remember clearly how the man
had changed into a vicious brute when he was drunk.

He'd beaten Keilin's mother . . . slapped her about,
humiliated her, called her a whore and far worse.
Well, she'd had little option once he'd died, but back
then it had been untrue. Keilin hadn't even known
what it meant then. The man had beaten Keilin, too.
That had been bearable. It was when he'd tried to
take Keilin's pendant that it had all happened. Firstly,
his mother had flown to Keilin's aid, screaming like
a fishwife, beating ineffectually at the big man. And
Keilin remembered his own anger and fear, and the
coldness of the amulet. It was his! It was all he had
of his father. His *real* father. Nobody, but nobody,
would take it from him. He'd clung to the dark jewel
with all his strength. His stepfather could have jewels, other jewels, not *his*! He remembered how the
flying tray of baubles had appeared out of nowhere.
He remembered crawling away, and the eerie whine.
He hadn't been scared of it, back then. It had just
seemed strange.

Then he'd been knocked sideways by the drunken
man clumsily and greedily sprawling after the stones.
And the blast of purple fire meant for Keilin had
blown away his stepfather's face. He'd run as fast as
his little legs could carry him, squalling in terror.

When he came cautiously back, his mother hastily gathered him up, with some of the stones, and fled to buy passage for them on an outbound freighter. She would never tell him just what she'd seen that had frightened her into this headlong flight. It never occurred to her that not knowing could be worse.

He felt at the jewel in the amulet. It was cold and oily feeling as always. His inheritance . . . along with two books. The one with the bright pictures which his mother had begged off a drunken highborn trick. *Tales of King Arthur and His Knights of the Round Table.* He'd loved that book. The other, *Geophysical Survey of Planet IV,* had been an incomprehensible thing of lists and strange words. He'd been taught to read from those two books. Before he'd found the library they'd been the only books he'd ever seen. He'd read both of them many times. The latter book had words his mother had said even his great-grandfather had not understood. But he'd been made to read them all, even the strange, burnt-edged pages glued into the back of *Geophysical Survey*—"Log of the Starship *Morningstar*." On the last page someone had scrawled:

"Even if everything else is lost, perhaps this will survive."

Suddenly the hideout seemed too small. He needed air, and space around himself, so that he could see them coming. On the lower floors they'd bricked up the chimney. Here on the top floor they'd just pushed the old-fashioned bookstand against it. He'd noticed it when he'd lifted the bookstand to crawl under it, and realized that it gave the hideout its most essential feature—a bolt hole.

He'd loosened the back planks ages ago, but it had taken him a while to brave the narrow, dark shaft. He'd been tempted to use it as a latrine, but instead had decided that digging out the bottom could give him access to the drains . . . his digging hadn't made much progress yet. He'd broken through into the rubble-filled foundations. There was a weary lot of broken bricks, rocks and concrete fragments to shift before he could get anywhere.

Upwards, however, had proved easier. There had been that tiny circle of sky to aim towards. He'd knocked the chimney pot off one stormy night, and come out into the sheeting rain onto the steep tiled roof.

The roof had a low balustrade. The library was one of the tallest buildings in the city, but, naturally, not as tall as the Patrician's palace. That many-turreted monstrosity hung over the harbor, like some tax-gathering vulture. However, on the landward side of the roof it couldn't even be seen. Instead, there was a view out across the desert, with the thin green line of the Tinarana River and the cultivated lands beside it stretching away to the distant, dusty hinterland. Since Keilin had cut away some of the rotting brick of the chimney below the level of the balustrade, and replaced it with a stolen sheet of tin, he came up here often. Sometimes he came to trap pigeons . . . and sometimes just to gaze out across the vast emptiness, and pretend that he was lord of all he surveyed.

After the sea wind had howled for days, and blown away the miasma of coal and dung smoke from the city hearthfires, he could make out the distant purple mountains. He thought again about the colored illustration that painted his mental picture of mountains. Tall trees around a rushing stream that wove through mossy rocks. Huh! Half of the boys in the city didn't even know there *was* anything beyond the desert. He'd seen the mountains on a map long before he'd come up here . . . That was it! Maps. They'd be watching the harbor. They'd watch the coast road, and the caravan trail. Perhaps there could be another way?

To Keilin the sea was no place of romance. It was

symbolized by the garbage tide he and other scavengers picked at along the littered shore opposite the quays. He had fantasies about those mountains however . . . all those trees, and running water . . . surely that was the place where his dreams could come true? He looked out into the heat haze. He couldn't see the mountains today, but that was where he was going. This afternoon, as soon as the library closed, he'd start looking for a map to get him there. He slipped back down the chimney and into sleep, secure in his optimism.

He got busy as soon as the doors below clicked shut. Gradually the optimism was eaten away as he realized that the atlases were at least three hundred years out of date. The surveyors hadn't been aware that the planet had millennia-long alternating pluvial and dry cycles. The wet cycle had ended nearly two hundred and fifty years ago. The maps also held little in the way of guidance for a boy who would have to travel on foot. He sat peering at an array of them in anger and frustration. Why, they were all rubbish! They showed two rivers crossing the desert, the Tinarana, and the Syrah. The Syrah River was supposed to come out a few miles south of the city. But he'd stared out toward the mountains often enough to know there was no green line into the yellow-brown there, just a dusty valley. And this map showing vegetation types indicated the desert as "dry savannah." He'd had to look the word up. Bloody drivel! Everyone knew that ten miles inland there was only sand and more sand.

He'd have to chance it up the Tinarana. But the caravans only went up to the Thunder Gorge, some hundred and fifty miles away. Above this the river had cut so deeply into the rock of the high plateau that farming with its water was no longer possible. Funny, the maps all showed *that* gorge.

Should he leave tonight? Procrastination, fueled by

fear of the unknown, held him. Tomorrow night would be better. He hated the thought of leaving his refuge. Surely the search would be less intense the longer he waited? And he still had food. He could afford to wait a while.

If he'd gone up to the roof and seen the files of torches as the soldiers moved slowly from house to house, he might have been less tempted to stay. The search was not stopping for nightfall. The curfew might be hurting the Patrician's nightly cut from the dock whores, but it was being strictly enforced. The great chain was raised across the channel. The ranged mangonels were readied. Nothing would leave by sea, and the city gates were closed siege-tight.

Testosterone can cause immense problems. Keilin had snuggled down in the early morning cool, enjoying the security of his lair for the last time. Sleep had claimed him rapidly. Actual sex was outside Keilin's experience, but from his observation of his mother's latter profession he knew a great deal about it. He'd made some detailed studies of the library's dusty elderly medical textbooks, studying the much thumbed sections of otherwise pristine texts with care. But arousal made the pendant stone start to grow colder, and even touching himself made the terrible chill bite at his skin. Fear had always been enough to stop him going any further. But of late his dreams had been getting more and more vivid. Normally the cold jewel on his chest woke him abruptly.

A fold of his ragged shirt betrayed him. It isolated the jewel from contact with his skin and allowed the dream to develop in glorious, if slightly confused, technicolor. It was the instinctive thrusting movements at the moment of release that shook the jewel loose from its cocoon of cloth. It touched his skin, and the cold became suddenly intense. It felt as if it was burning into him. He screamed.

Wakefulness was instantly with him. He clapped

his hand to his mouth. Had anyone below heard him? Peering fearfully through the tiny hole he had drilled with a rusty nail, he realized that it didn't matter if they had heard his scream. Half the city must know exactly where he was now.

The central keep of the Patrician's palace was a hollow tower, a hundred feet tall. Girdling it was a crenellated balcony, constantly guarded. The only way onto its roof was in a roped basket pulled up the center of the tower. Heavy caskets went up, and precious little ever came down. Perched like a single stalk of wheat stubble on the keep's roof was the treasury. Or used to be. Now the dream of every thief in Port Tinarana was bursting through the roof of the library. No one would come up the stairway for a while, because a torrent of coins was running down it.

Coins pushed aside the plank and came spilling into Keilin's hideout. Instinctively he grabbed gold wheels from among the brass and copper, and thrust them into his pockets. He was rich! He was rich! He would . . . His mind checked . . . halted. He would be lucky just to be *alive* in ten minutes' time. A whole sea of money wouldn't help him. If he stayed hiding here they'd find him sooner or later. Perhaps he could still run.

The coins left him no room to get out from under the bookcase, so he lifted it, tipping it over. He ran across the shifting coin floor to the window. Perhaps if he went up to the roof and down the drainpipe . . . His first glance told him that this was a futile hope. It was bright daylight, and people were rushing toward the building. His second, more intent look, made him nearly freeze with horror. Most of the crowd were surging toward the doors of the library. Behind him he could hear the screaming and fighting on the stairs. But what had frightened him was the tableau at the far window.

It was Kemp. A dead lamp-oil seller sprawled on his cart, a sluggish stream of blood still oozing from his back. The Guard-Captain was pouring yet another amphora of glistening yellow lamp oil in through the broken window. Keilin stepped back. He could perhaps mingle with the money-crazed hoard on the stair and escape. At the moment he doubted if they'd notice him if he were green, ten feet tall, with horns on his head. He had to get out before Kemp set fire to the place.

Then his eye was caught by something among the coins and scattered jewels. It was enough to halt him, midflight. For a moment Keilin thought it was his own, and clutched at the jewel around his neck. His pendant was still there . . . was this jewel the same? No, not quite. It *was* the same oily black, with the myriad of shifting colors seemingly within it, but it was smaller, and set on a broad golden ring instead. He hastily stooped and picked it up. And suddenly he heard the high-pitched whine again. It came from the roof. A section of masonry fell in a shower of purple sparks, and a platelike craft dropped through after it. Keilin did not wait to see the hooded passengers. He dived for the shelter of the chimney, a moment before the searing purple blast.

He was falling face-first down the chimney, the newly found jewel still crushed tight in his fist, as cold as his neck amulet had ever been. He didn't see the suddenly materialized marble tombstone that felled the hooded assassins. From their oddly crumpled bodies seeped a puddle of greenish ichor, disappearing into the coins. But he did hear the terrified scream of "FIRE!"

Keilin's scraping, bruising fall was stopped by the first bend in the flue. Disoriented, shaking and frightened, he simply lay still for a few moments. Even surrounded by bricks he could hear the hungry crackling roar of the flames as they ate at the dry paper of thousands upon thousands of books. And above the fire sound there was the thin screaming of humans.

If he went down . . . could he hide under the floor? He could wait until it burnt out, until nightfall. They'd surely think he was dead, and then he could escape. Keilin managed to turn himself the right way up, and began to descend. He reached the small open area underneath the lowest fireplace and curled there miserably, beginning to feel the pain of his rough passage. The fire roared above, and it was growing hotter, harder to breathe. The only relief was the stream of cold, fetid air that poured in on one side of him.

Panic started to rise in him, as the sweat began to prickle at his grazes and cuts. He couldn't stay here. He might as well go up. If it wasn't for the cold air streaming in, he'd have cooked already. Cold air . . . Logic struggled with the fear. It must be coming from somewhere, drawn in to feed the inferno above. If he could follow it, it might lead him out. The rubble lay in the way. If the truth be told, he'd never tried too hard to move it. He had always felt, well, crushed, down here in the blackness. But now he had the need, a dire and desperate need. He put the newfound ring into the thieves' pouch on his ankle, and began pulling at broken blocks and scraps of concrete, shoving them aside with frantic strength, pushing them into the small hollow he'd occupied.

Now that he'd got going he found it wasn't so bad. He could wriggle along quite effectively. In fact the space was growing bigger. Why, he'd almost be able to crawl soon. He followed the airflow. It was cool, damp, and it stank. The city's ancient sewage system was largely unused now. Most of it had long since blocked up, and been abandoned. Instead, folk emptied their stinking buckets into the storm drains. The occasional terrible sea storm would flush these, but it was often a long while between storms. Sometimes the drains became clogged, and well-bribed heroes had to go down and shovel them clear.

Keilin shuddered. When he'd been just eight years old, his mother had "volunteered" him. They'd wanted a small one to get through the remaining space. The price had kept her cloudy-headed for a week. The memory of it gave him nightmares still. Rats he could deal with, but the sea of roaches down in that enclosed place had terrified him. Determinedly he stifled the recall flood and concentrated on the task ahead.

He came to the point where the air rushed in from the big concrete pipe. A thin pipe from the roof above had once joined it here, but corrosion had long ago eaten away the pipe juncture. It was almost certain that the long-dead builders shouldn't have used that handy storm-drainage pipe for disposing of the library's waste water, but, well, there it had been, temptingly close to the foundations. Surely a hand basin's worth of water wasn't going to make that much difference?

The boy felt at the small hole. Stuck. At this point! In frustration he pounded at the edge of it. The concrete crumbled slightly, and small stones fell to splash into the unpleasant liquids that trickled below. The concrete was centuries old, and the pipe juncture had been cut through the steel reinforcing once hidden inside the concrete. Now, exposed to oxygen and often wet, rust had slowly eaten at the steel and the expanding rust had cracked the concrete along the reinforcing lines.

Pounding with a broken slab of tiling, he broke a larger opening. It was still not very wide, but from years of burglary, Keilin knew that where his head and one arm could go, his body could follow. He squirmed through, down into the fetid trickle.

On hands and knees he crawled to where the pipe joined a larger canal. He dared not stop down here in the noisome darkness. The roaches presumed that meat that didn't move was dinner. Ahead he saw light. Distant daylight shone down in a barred pattern through a street grating. Above was the shaft that could take him out of here. He climbed the rusty staples towards it. And stopped. He could hear voices.

He couldn't go up. Not while there was someone out there. But here in the light, the roaches were wary. He hung waiting, waiting for the speakers to move. One voice was high-pitched and lisping. He remembered being herded along to listen to it, just before he ran away from his mother. Only then the man had sounded arrogant, and almost infinitely powerful. Now the voice was wooden, and afraid. ". . . The magicianth dead, I tell you. Nothing could live through that fire!"

The reply was also high-pitched but too full of clicking sibilants to make sense to him, but it was enough to make Keilin begin to retreat.

The Patrician spoke again. His girlish lisping voice, usually so haughty, actually trembled. "I have ordered treble guardth on the wallth and fourfold on the gateth. Thereth patrolth on the coatht roadth. The caravanth have been thtopped. No thips will thail. You can't put your," he hesitated, "men on the gateth. The people would get to hear of it and . . . they'd revolt. I couldn't thtop them. They fear you more than death itthelf!"

Keilin didn't wait for the reply. With infinite care he began to lower himself back down into the dark. He knew now why the Patrician had offered a reward for his capture. Fifteen years ago Port Tinarana had been flooded with a tide of terrified refugees from across the shallow sea. They were fleeing the Morkth and their zombielike troops. These refugee-settlers still made up the bulk of the Port's underclass. Mothers used tales of these Morkth to frighten their children into good behavior. Yet one of these awful creatures plainly had the city's overlord as its inferior partner. It was plain that the Morkth hunted him too.

Why? Why him? Vague fantasies, fuelled by his favorite books, of him being the lost true heir to some great kingdom flitted briefly through his head as he followed the filth stream into the dark. Regretfully he dismissed them. He knew perfectly well who his mother was, and who his father had been. Yes, they'd both claimed to be of Cru blood, but up north, according to his mother, every man and his damned donkey claimed that. Resolutely he put the thoughts away from him and followed the flow of liquid and semisolid dreck. Eventually it had to come out somewhere.

CHAPTER 2

Shael Cimbelyn Xylla-Marie Ensign, Princess Royal of the Tyn States, and holder of a further sheaf of lesser titles, had absolutely no doubts about her near-pure Cru blood. She was indeed the true heir, through her mother, to a kingdom. She was also an only child. Her father, a man who openly bragged of the title "Tyrant," wielded vast power as the absolute ruler of a string of conquered states and principalities. Her own power, as a result, was near absolute too, but it was untrammeled by even the smallest shred of responsibility. She was blessed with perfect features and a good, if immature, figure. She was a spoilt, poisonous little bitch. It is impossible to say what her friends called her, for she had none.

The reams of golden bracelets on her arms tinkled musically as she moved. Their sweet sound failed to enhance the performance of a royal temper tantrum. It was indeed a magnificent theatrical display, otherwise. From a safe distance, say a hundred miles, it had all the elements of a farce, but to those unfortunate enough to be involved in it, it was undoubtedly a tragedy. Five foot two of concentrated ennui and pique was likely to mean at least pain, or even death, to them.

She stormed and ranted at the unfortunate major-domo, her potentially beautiful little face screwed up into a mask of rage. "How *dare* you deny us!" A stamp of a small foot, "We want them! You will get us some, *now!*" she screamed as shrilly as any fishwife. Even in her fury the royal "we" was maintained.

The plump man knelt, shaking with fear. His position had ensured that while the rest of the city starved, he had remained very well larded. Now it seemed that he would have to pay the price for all those meals. "Your Royal Highness!" He wrung his hands. "I can't get you fresh bilberries. You don't even *like* then.!" He held his position because he always remembered her likes and dislikes perfectly.

She ignored the perfect truth of his statement. Her mouth opened in a vixenlike grin, little white teeth clenched. The green eyes narrowed. She pointed out of the diamond-pane windows, across the sprawl of Shapstone City, to the surrounding hills. The voice was cruelly honeyed. "The hills are purple with them. Get us some, *now!*"

She knew as well as he did that the Morkth troops held the city in a vicious siege. They had for the last five months. She knew that those close, purple hills were as unreachable as the moon. But she played a toxic little game with him. The uninitiated would have failed to understand it, but she was, for lack of anything better to practice on, manipulating him. She would reduce him to abject fear and pleading. Then she would forgive him if, of course, he obliged with a few other trifles. The game was partially to relieve her boredom, but partially because this was what she'd been trained to do, from very early childhood.

Yes, she was pampered. Yes, in almost all respects,

she was allowed free rein. But she knew what she was. She was simply a pawn in her father's machinations. He planned to use her to further his Empire dream, and for this he had trained her. She could have her way with all but her instructors. They had shaped her to his design. She knew how to manipulate. She could have written volumes on court intrigue, and how to turn it to her own ends. She'd been taught by the best. She could have seduced an eighty-year-old eunuch if need be. They'd had some very unusual palace guests to teach her the theory of bed arts. Theory only: her virginity had some considerable value in certain circles. However, she'd been taught how to fake that, too. She knew far more than any apothecary about poisons, where to find them, how to make them, and how to administer them. She was an expert with a thin-bladed dagger. She was also sixteen and tired of waiting. She felt her talents were being wasted.

Now for the strike. The pleas would begin in a moment. She turned her face away toward the door, in time to see the second of her ever-present guards stagger and fall. The man who had pressed the razor-tipped spike in through the guard's ear was smiling, sharklike. She'd seen him often enough before, but now she scarcely recognized him. He was a minor courtier, always servile, and exquisitely polite, like so many others. She'd not realized how power and triumph could transform a face. She shrank back.

"Scream and I'll kill you, you little cow." His voice was cruel and deliberate. Blood still dripped from his fingers. Behind him stood several more armed men.

"Try not to, Lord Blis," said a voice from down the passage. The princess was an expert on tone, and this speaker did not sound as if it would concern him greatly if she was mutilated, but not quite dead. "We have her father, but it would be nice to have two little 'gifts' for our great liberators."

The tall, sardonic speaker stepped into the room. The naked and bloody falchion in his hand belied his otherwise foppish appearance. With a single sword-stroke he severed the head of the still kneeling majordomo.

"You promised me *I* could have her!" There was a mixture of fear, chagrin and a dangerous edge of insanity in the guard killer's shrill demand.

"And so you shall, my dear Blis. And so you shall. But only for the next half an hour. The gates are opening now, and I want her alive when our 'friends' arrive. But they won't mind if you've used her first."

The courtier smiled, a dribble of spittle leaking across his thin lips. "Yes, *Emperor* Deshin." He looked at her, his wild eyes hungry. "She'll be . . . alive!" He laughed. "Leave me ten guards. They can take it in turns when I've finished."

The tall man lifted a disdainful lip. "The title is premature, Blis. And I doubt if even the most desperate will use a girl after you've finished with her. Enjoy yourself . . . her body will be worthless to the hive anyway." He looked at her then, his eyes cold with hatred. "You're not going to be raped, little Princess. Rumor has it that you'd enjoy that. Blis has no interest in sex. He can't get it up, so he likes to use knives instead." With this chilling finish, he turned and walked out, ignoring the dangerous glitter in his ally's eyes. The girl wished desperately that she'd not used Count Deshin for one of her little games. But it was too late now. She could hear him selecting guards outside. The door closed.

The thin-lipped Blis dropped the spike, and took a dagger from his highly polished boot. He began to advance, very slowly. "You can scream all you like now. We've secured the palace," he said. His voice, just above a whisper, was full of almost palpable anticipation. He licked his lips, his eyes glowing with an evil inner brightness.

For the first time in her life the Princess knew real fear. Nervously her hands strayed across the golden bangles as she edged further away. The wall was behind her. She tried to press herself into it. She looked around, desperately seeking some avenue of escape. All that she could see was the majordomo's head, the eyes staring vacantly. Bilberries . . .

Blis lunged toward her suddenly, seizing her arm. She screamed in pure panic, and grabbed her own arm with the other hand as she lurched forward. Her fingers closed on a jewel-adorned golden bangle, which abruptly became a lump of dry ice . . .

A bilberry is an innocuous thing on its own. Dusty purple and the size of a fingernail. However, several hundred thousand of them, if they materialize inside someone's body, are more deadly than any toxin can be. Blis didn't even scream. There was no air in his lungs to do so.

For long moments she simply stared at the remains of the man lying in a pool of his own blood into which was slowly seeping a deep purple juice. Then she looked at her own purple and red splattered arms, staggered away, and threw up. For a while she simply wept and shivered. Gradually a measure of emotionally washed-out calm descended on her. She looked at the door. The guard would be expecting sounds of pain. She screamed. It was not difficult to put real anguish into that scream. She tiptoed across and bolted the door as quietly as she could. The door was a heavy oak one, and the bolt a solid bar of steel. It was intended to isolate her apartment from possible assassins, but it would never stop a determined assault with a battering ram. She knew she had very little time.

Her father, on one of those occasions when he had been pleased with her, had said that she had a scalpel mind. She was accustomed to thinking herself far more intelligent than everybody else. It didn't feel that way now. She dithered.

Could she bribe the guards? But if she failed, they'd break in here. She hugged herself in desperate self-pity. Could she hide? If she was not apparent, they'd tear this place apart. Under the bed or in the wardrobes, the only hiding places she could think of, would be the first places they'd search. Could she escape? Her apartments were six stories up. Could she arm herself, at least? She looked across at Blis's dagger, which lay in a pool of swirled purple and red, and retched. It took her a good few more minutes to decide what to do. She tore strips of sheet and knotted them, screaming occasionally for good measure. She would hang the sheet rope out of the window, and *then* hide.

She opened the window, kicking off her jewelled slippers and climbing onto the broad sill. There were bars on the outside. For a moment her heart fell. She'd forgotten those. Careful inspection suggested that she could get through them. She tied the sheet rope to them and dropped it down. It was still a long way short. She'd better just try and see if she could actually squeeze between the bars. Resolutely not looking down, she searched for the best way. The bars were welded into a sort of outwardly bulging box, allowing the window to swing open to the outside. Where the bars were attached to the wall there was just a little more space. She'd just see if her head and shoulders could go through . . .

She was committed, and more than halfway through when the door to her apartments was blown apart in a burst of purple fire. Fear made the rest easy. She was perched on the window ledge outside the bars and out of direct sight when the Morkth burst into what had once been her withdrawing room. A few moments later there were the sounds of combat, but this too lasted only seconds. Then there was silence.

Suddenly, just as she was thinking about going in again she heard more sounds. Running footsteps came to the open window, and then she heard the rasping sibilant speech of the Morkth. The words, as always, were hard to make out. But they definitely included the order to search below. She looked down for the first time since she'd begun to squeeze out between the bars. She could see the streets from here. They were full of fighting. The black-clad Morkthman brigades were everywhere. She didn't want to be down there, even if her frail sheet rope had reached. Perhaps she could go sideways or . . . up. And she'd better make up her mind, quickly. At the moment folk were too busy to look up, but even now searchers were running down the stairs.

Sideways was simply too far for her to reach. But up was plausible. Climbing the bars on this window she could reach the bars of the next, and from the top of them the gutter was within reach. She pulled herself onto the roof just before the Morkth troops spilled into the gardens. A few feet away was a low ornamental curlicue, with a gargoyle at the head of a down pipe. She slithered to lie behind it. Her thin arms were shaking, making the bangles tinkle faintly. Without real fear she could never have done such physical feats. She'd never done any manual labor in her life, and her only muscular training had been for bed arts, which had rather neglected her arms and shoulders. She lay in the gutter behind the stone gargoyle and shivered. It would be more than an hour before she dared to move enough to look out.

When at last she was a little more self-possessed, and able to think rationally and beyond her immediate survival, Shael peeped out cautiously. The picture that presented itself was not an attractive one. There were still patches of fighting, but it was obvious that it was nearly over. The black-clad Morkth troops were herding frightened prisoners along the streets. Sections of the town still burned. She shivered with fear. Would the fire spread? Would they fire the palace?

Resolutely she shrugged off the thought. She must
plan. She must win clear of this place. The fallen city-
state of Shapstone was less than a tenth part of her
father's lands. Even if it had been conquered she
could still go . . . She stopped short. He was dead.
She hadn't loved her father, and he certainly had
never shown the least real affection towards her. She
had never expected any. She was his tool, a valuable
tool, but still a tool, to be married off to his best
advantage. She had never questioned this: It was simply what she was bred for. She now realized that with
his death, she was nothing.

The Tyn States were his creation. If he had fallen,
so had their unity. None of them would welcome the
Tyrant's daughter as a ruler. They were more likely
to kill her in various unpleasant, slow and vengeful
ways. Her mother's people in far-off Arlinn would not
welcome her either. Her father had taken the lady
at swordpoint to be his bride, stepping over the bodies
of several of her kin who had objected. The act that
had resulted in Shael's conception would have been
regarded as rape in any eyes but that of the law. Of
course, when you were the law . . .

Shael knew that in the eyes of the nobles of Arlinn
she was tainted with her father's blood. They would
offer her no refuge. She cast the net of her mind
about for someone else to turn to and drew it back,
empty. Friends, not mere toadies, were something
she'd never had. What need had there ever been?
Relatives were simply other claimants to the throne,
and her father had been singly effective in his purge
of those. The few that had fled to dubious safety in
the lands of exile certainly had no cause to love her.

Where to then? There seemed no answer, except
away from here. Shael was not a likable person, but
as she lay there, with the evening wind blowing cold,
it would have been easy to feel sorry for her. With
goosebumps on her bare arms and tear streaks in her

makeup, she looked far more like a miserable sixteen-year-old than a twenty-four-carat bitch of a princess.

She rationalized that it would be better to wait for the conquerors to get drunk beyond competence before she tried to escape from her hiding place. In reality, which she could not truly hide from herself, she was simply too scared to move from that little patch of safety. She hugged herself and pulled her knees up under her chin. She wished she'd worn something less flimsy and revealing that morning. It was only as she drifted off into an exhausted sleep that the thought slipped into her tired mind: who or what had killed that *animal* Blis? She vaguely tried to focus on this thought spark, but her brain was too soggy to fire up a logical train of thought. Sleep came mercifully.

She awoke cold. Teeth-chatteringly cold. She'd never been this cold in her life. She would *die* for something warm. She was about to call out to her maids when awareness of where she was came flooding back. If she called out now she might really die. Hugging herself and rubbing her bare arms she looked out over the dark city. There were no more burning buildings. There were no sounds of drunken revelry. She could see squads with torches patrolling the streets below in a systematic fashion. These were the zombielike warriors of the Morkth hives. Human bodies without human passions. Soulless, near mindless, killing machines. She watched the regular pattern weaving through the streets, like a formal dance outlined by their torches. Eventually the cold forced her to turn her attention away from the hypnotic ebb and flow of lights. She must get off this roof, out of this cold wind. Could she face going over the edge with that drop reaching for her?

The height had been hard enough to face in the heat of the moment, but now in the dark, and in cold blood, the very idea filled her with terror. But if she stayed . . . she might die of cold. Her stomach growled

at her. It reminded her that it had been a good many
hours since she had emptied it onto the marble floor
of her room. There must be some other way off the
roof. She decided to stand up, and explore the icy
refuge in which she'd interned herself. Standing next
to the gargoyle, with it as a support, was not too bad.
She took the step beyond it on the steeply sloping
slate roof . . . no! The Princess settled for crawling,
with a hand on the gutter. At least that was flat. Even
that small comfort was denied her when it creaked,
and dropped several inches. She pulled away in fear,
the seven stories of darkness dragging at her. Holding her quivering lip between her perfect white teeth,
she moved on, only on the slippery slates now, edging her way round. A slate beneath her knee cracked,
a sudden, sharp sound in the silence. She stayed as
still as fear would let her, tasting the warm saltiness
in her mouth.

When no reaction came after a few cold minutes,
she began to move again, but in reality it was a
pointless exercise. She was no longer looking for a way
out, just moving. Soon even that stopped.

It came on silent wings, with a terrible screech-
ing cry. Her own scream was a feeble, ratlike squeak
in comparison. The feathery soft touch just brushed
her shoulder. She scrambled, almost fell over the
edge, her sweaty hands slipping as her toes felt frantically for some purchase.

And found it. She was no longer above the drop,
but rather just off the edge of the ridge line of the
roof of the south wing of the palace. With immense
relief she dropped and scrambled along the ledge. She
covered several hundred yards before she dared to
stop and look behind her. She could find no sign of
pursuit. Shael would never acknowledge that it could
just have been a hunting owl.

Below her was the great balcony, from which it had
been the tradition of the Grand Dukes of Shapstone

to address their subjects on feast days. It was here that the assassins dispatched by her father had relieved the last of that line of his life, by means of four well-directed crossbow bolts. As the Tyrant had dryly commented afterwards, "height alone is no defense." Right now it was her only defense. But she knew she couldn't stay there forever. At least the balcony would provide a safe place to get off the roof, without too long a fall below her. Perhaps there would be a drainpipe or something to climb down. She left the ridgeline and began her cautious descent.

Which rapidly became an uncontrolled high-speed descent. With two or three loose slates for company she flew clear over the edge, to crash onto the balcony. Half stunned, it took her a moment or two to come to her senses. There was a sound of running feet. She scrambled off her knees, and darted to hide behind some curtains just inside the doorway.

The feet thudded past, through the open door and out onto the balcony. "The sounds came from here." The voice was wooden, with no trace of emotion.

The reply was different. She could hear distaste in the coarse tones. "Slates fallin'. Do whenever th' wind blows." One traitor guardsman, and one Morkth hiver. Her stomach was a knot of fear, but there was a blossoming of hatred, too. The Morkth-man, he was the enemy, but the other was something worse, far more detestable. She could do little to him if they caught her, but at least she would spit in his face. She began working her dry mouth for the material to carry out her resolve.

"We will search anyway." The Morkth-man did not make it a matter of debate.

"Waste o' time. Only the curtains to hide behind here. I'll take t' left side." That was the side she was on. She'd been trained to listen for nuances of voice. He had spoken just a shade faster than natural. Did he know she was there?

She desperately tried to gather spittle for her last
act of defiance. She *would* die like Cru, even if all
she wanted to do was to burst into tears.

He pulled aside the curtain in front of her. And
put his finger to his lips. Then he stepped calmly
away, as if he had seen nothing. She had but seconds
to look at the heavy, brutish face in the lamplight,
but it etched onto her memory. She would never
forget that face. . . . Her knees felt as if they might
give way any moment.

"Nothin' my side." His voice might have betrayed
him to his fellows, but the other guard was unaccustomed to any form of duplicity.

"We must search the other passages." The Morkth-
man was not going to give up easily.

"Aw, come on. The doors are all guarded. Nothin's
gonna get out'v here. Let's go back to our post at the
stairwell." He was telling her where the guards were
stationed. Which stairwell?

"We search." Their footsteps went away up the east
passage.

It was at least warmer here, but she knew it was
no permanent refuge. She had to get out of the
palace, out of Shapstone, somehow. There *was* one
way out of the palace that might not be guarded . . .
and her father's rooms were close. Holding her arms
so that the bangles could not tinkle she fled down
the passage toward the great doors that led into his
palatial apartments. She peered forward. A guard in
Shapstone livery was snoring peacefully to the side
of the doors. She sneaked past him, and cautiously
tried the handle. It was locked, but the valet's door
ten yards further on was not. She slipped inside.

The sounds coming from the great bed indicated
that there was an occupant in the room. In fact there
was little doubt that at least two people were present,
perhaps more. On the other hand, by the moaning
and panting they were otherwise engrossed right now.

Shael moved to leave the walk-in cupboard that was the valet's domain and her bracelets tinkled. Instantly she froze. Obviously the bed's occupants were too busy to notice. Hastily taking a beautifully ironed shirt from one of the shelves she wrapped it around and tucked it under her bracelets. Pleased with the result she did the same on the other side with another shirt. She began her crawl. She had to reach the far room while the bed's occupants were still absorbed. The bedchamber was a substantial room, but well lit, with two small chandeliers on either side. If they looked away from each other they would almost certainly see her. Concentrating on her goal she ignored the panting, urging and pleading from the bed. It was only when she'd reached the far chamber that she risked a look at the huge mirror on the ceiling.

She swallowed a gasp, and quickly moved around the corner. No wonder the tall Count Deshin had hated her power games. They had always included a certain amount of sexual coquetry. It was not the frustration of desire which had angered him, but rather that Deshin really preferred boys. A specific boy, it seemed: a dashing and handsome young captain . . . of her father's secret police. That was the foundation of his successful coup.

The Grand Dukes of Shapstone had not always been satisfied with their wives. Many of them had married for political reasons. Others had been unable to part with their wild days, before assuming the throne, as mere viscounts free to exercise *droit du seigneur*. But bringing one's paramours past the Duchess's chambers was sometimes a risky pastime. Therefore it was necessary to have another route to the Duke's chambers. She knew that many a blindfolded girl had walked that passage, and up the hidden stair. One of her instructors had told her about it in some detail. The captain on that bed *would* know of

the passage. But had he been too occupied with
arranging his lace suspender belt to seal it?

It was dim here. It took her a few steps to ascertain that not only had he not sealed it, he'd left the
hidden door open. His fallen clothes had plainly been
stripped off in haste and on the way. She slipped off
into the welcome darkness and felt her way along.
In a few minutes she was opening the outer concealed
door, and darting away into the gardens, towards the
wicket gate so artfully hidden in the rhododendrons.

She'd won free to the streets. Now, could she get
through the city without being caught? It proved
easier than she'd thought possible. She'd watched the
pattern of patrols from the roof. Their movements
were no more difficult to predict than the steps of
her favorite dances, and thus easy to evade. But the
gates . . .

. . . were thoroughly locked and barred. With distinctly wakeful Morkth-men guards patrolling them.
Could she get over the walls? Unlikely. She knew that
fear had helped her to climb before, but she certainly
didn't feel up to it now. Still, she'd better try to find
a way up onto them. Then she saw her salvation.
Outside the city granaries heavy wagons were being
loaded in the silent, mechanical fashion of the Morkth-
men. Already most of them were piled high with
sacks. She sneaked closer, stumbling over an empty
sack. She picked it up and ran to the last wagon in
the row. The deity who watches over fools and ama-
teurs must have been working overtime for her that
night. The guard had just stepped over to an alley
to relieve himself, a thing even Morkth-men must do,
as she scrabbled and scrambled her way up the cargo
net to the top. She burrowed into the sack and lay
still, holding onto the net and hoping they'd not notice
that the one lumpy sack was outside the net.

A few minutes later she heard the crack of whips,
and then, with a jerk, the steel-cased wheels started

to rumble their way over the cobblestones. Never had the movement of one of her feather-sprung carriages felt as lovely as that slow, rough, bouncing progress. She lay dead still as the wagons rolled away under the gate arch, past the flaring torches, and out into the welcome darkness.

How long could her soft hands survive this? The ropes cut at them, but if she let go on this uneven road she would almost certainly slide and fall. By the paling sky, dawn would be here soon. They'd see her for sure then. Perhaps she should try to get off now? There was a patrol marching behind them. How could she get clear? The train halted abruptly. She risked a peep to see the patrol leader moving past, leaving his men waiting with swords at the ready.

A few moments later he came back. "Sheath swords. One of the wagons has broken a wheel. Come. We must move it from the road."

As soon as they'd filed past, Shael slid out of her sack, scrambled down the netting and ran into the dark shadows among the trees of a small dell. Her protective deity must have gone to answer a call of nature himself just then, because there was a shout behind her.

She ran.

Tripping and falling, tearing through brambles, stumbling down a steep bank and into the stream, up the muddy bank opposite and out into the heather and broken heathlands.

In the woods she'd heard them behind her. Now, although her heart was hammering like a drum in her ears, the sounds seemed further away. It didn't matter any more. They might as well catch her. She simply couldn't run another step. She collapsed into the bushes, and waited, panting.

No sane fugitive would leave the shelter of the woods for open ground. Thus it was that the Morkthmen were peering up every vast-boled tree and sapling instead of following the simple, straight course to their quarry. After a short while Shael realized they were still searching amongst the trees. She got onto hands and knees and crawled away, towards the lip of the dell and over, onto the hillside. Once she was beyond the line of sight she got up and began to walk, painfully. Her feet were unused to such punishment, but she forced herself to go on. She was heading for no specific place, just *away*.

Her lack of decision was probably just as well. She had no real idea where she was. She had always been escorted and taken to places. She had no real notion of distance or direction, for someone else had always taken care of this. She only knew that she was tired and sore, her feet and legs bleeding from a myriad of small cuts and scratches. On top of this she was also hungry, thirsty and cold. The sky was pale now, but the dawn breeze still sliced at her dew-wet legs. If only she'd kept the sack, she thought, she could at least have wrapped it around herself. Then it occurred to her that she did have two large shirts and, once unwrapped from her arms, they made reasonable short dresses on her small frame.

The comfort of the garments, and the first rays of sunlight lifted her spirits considerably. She raised her arms and shook her small fists, jangling her bracelets defiantly. She looked at them and smiled to herself, for the first time since her life had abruptly begun to unravel. On her arms was a small fortune. Perhaps, perhaps she had the means to some power. In Shael's mind power and security were automatically equivalent.

She was still trying to work out the best approach, considering each of her father's generals in turn, when she stumbled upon the stream. She was unsure how one did this rough drinking: usually a servant brought drinks on a silver tray in a container of some kind. She settled for kneeling and scooping water up rather ineffectually with her hands. The water was cold and peat-stained. A day before she would have looked at it, raised an eyebrow and rejected it disdainfully. Now she drank until her side had a stitch in it.

Her vanity was still intact however. Shael was still kneeling, looking at her reflection in the pool when a coldness began creeping down her spine. Small, almost hidden sounds told her there was someone behind her. Slowly she turned. She steeled her face for calmness, but the muscles in her neck were jumping with tension, betraying fear which was mounting towards panic.

Well, he was no Morkth-man. Those were always clean-shaven, both on the head and face, and clad in black. The heavy stubble on his cheeks was the only thing that was black about this man. He was long-haired and his clothes had once been a Tyn States uniform, a lancer's at a guess. He attempted a disarming grin. The blackened stumps of several rotting teeth made it less of a success than it could have been. He touched the hank of limp, greasy hair on his brow, his shifty eyes darting about. "Morning, missy. You alone?"

Her first inclination was to run. Her second, on realizing that this was totally impractical, was to claim a score of companions.

"My . . . my servants are just back there. Lots of them. If you touch me, I'll scream and they'll come." Despite her training her voice belied her.

He was certainly not fooled. He snorted derisively. "Likely bloody story, missy. They're hiding in the grass, belike? Calm down, I'm not gonna hurt you."

She relaxed slightly, even if it was not a credible performance on his part either. This slightly run-to-fat goliath might be physically stronger than she was, but she had other skills. Words . . . and certain *other* talents. She was unaccustomed to being alone. She felt sure she could manipulate him easily. Then he would provide her with company, protection and— most important right now—food.

CHAPTER 3

Humans are the vertebrate equivalent of the cockroach. They can, and will, adapt to nearly anything. The Alpha-Morkth hives pushed this adaptability close to its limits. At this point most humans crack. Some go insane, some try to rebel, and some become catatonic. Still, after more than three hundred years of selection, the Alpha-Morkth had to weed out about seventy percent of each crop of humans they bred. The culls went back into the food supply for the others. The remaining thirty percent were almost all perfect Morkth-men. Almost all . . . but there were always a few exceptions. Adaptation to survive could always be pushed one step further. A few of the humans the Morkth bred had learned not only to survive, but to exploit the system. S'kith 235 was one of those. He was a great danger to the entire hive system. Not only had he learned to exploit it, but also he still had his balls.

The Alpha-Morkth wanted uniformity, absolute obedience, and antlike industry from the humans they bred to replace workers and, reluctantly, warriors of their

own species. The warriors were a problem. A good
fighter needs a certain amount of flexibility in their
response to an enemy. A degree of tactical adaptability
is also needed. A soldier may also have to be deployed
at a variety of tasks, given the chaotic nature of war.
The sheer stupidity bred for in workers was thus
unsuitable, but with too much intelligence and flexibility the warrior Morkth-men could be dangerous to
their creators. The cull rate here was over ninety
percent, and the resultant warrior-breds were still somewhat less effective than wild-human fighters. The selection bias toward strongly left-brain-dominant warriors
failed to adequately deal with the erratic nature of
hand-to-hand combat. It was the main reason for the
hive cities' lack of speed in their advance against the
internecinally squabbling city-states.

In the lower levels of the hive were the small
lightless cells where the Alpha-Morkth kept their
brood-sow humans. It was a place where no male
Morkth-man should ever be found. Even the cleaners down here were microcephalic hormonally-altered
male neuters. S'kith 235 moved calmly along behind
one as it mopped the passage. It would almost certainly not turn around, or react, no matter what noise
he made, but S'kith never took chances. His curiosity was almost equally matched by a secretive caution.
The mopper moved around the corner. Experience
told him that it would be at least twenty-five minutes before it came back.

The grille on the bottom of the cell door was
intended to allow any solid matter to be washed out
after its daily hosing down. The floor within was
curved and sloped towards the door to ensure that
the system worked efficiently. Even the food and
water dispensers were positioned on the back wall,
to assist gravity. S'kith knelt down beside the grille,
and spoke, his voice very low. There could be no
mistake about the eagerness of the whispered reply.

Copulation through a six-inch-wide by five-inch-high steel-barred grille is not easy. It can be done, however, if both participants are very determined. The warrior class are bred for physical strength, agility and speed. They are fed on a well-balanced diet—the protein often coming from the most biologically suitable source: their own species—and are renowned for their stamina. Thus it was that the human cuckoo was able to beat the Alpha-Morkth artificial insemination team five times. Then the sound of the mop bucket being pushed forced him to withdraw and retreat hastily up the passage and onto the internal beam structure which he railed along to reach the next level of the hive. He had another fifteen levels to go before he reached the place where he was supposed to be on guard.

Morkth drone males are nonintelligent. In fact, the brain is reduced to pinhead size. The body, too, is a stunted thing with few functional internal organs. Before maturity they could not survive for an hour outside the caring nurture of the hive. Even their food has to be carefully predigested for their growth period. On maturity the mouth parts meld and change, forming a long tube with vicious extrudable hooks on the end. They crawl up the vast body of the Morkth queen, following pheromone tracers till they reach the soft spot in the chitinous armor, where the great vein pulses close to the surface. Then the sharp snout is forced in through the soft tissues, and the hooks extrude. Sometimes up to a dozen drone males may hang like small, bloated ticks just above the egg vent.

Most of the eggs would be neuter, unmaturing females, the workers and the warriors. The Queen selected which drone male fertilized which egg, depending on the purpose of the egg. She secreted the hormones into her bloodstream which altered the eggs to produce new drones, or new queens. The same hormones in her blood affected the male, altering the fertility and type of gamete he produced. If a drone gene line proved less than viable, the Queen's giant chela would pluck it off, and leave it discarded, to die and be cleared away and eaten by the workers. It was scant wonder that the Morkth found human sex and the emotions associated with it totally incomprehensible. One sex must, logic insisted, be just a source of gametes, nothing more. To the Morkth this was the province of males, but their first human male captive had shown some sign of intelligence by escaping. Therefore females in this species must be the gamete source. It was strange, but then the entire species was strange. Decision was reached. Thereafter the subject was closed. The noises the human sows made were not speech, just instinctive speech imitations. They were fed, watered, washed . . . and bred.

Most of the Morkth-men gene lines were bred stupid. With pain as a punishment, and food as a reward, workers could be trained to perform their tasks regardless of thinking ability. With intelligence-poor gene lines, deprived of almost all sensory stimuli in the dark, small rearing cages, many females producing dim-witted workers had become a pitiful once-human equivalent of the Morkth drones. Brood sows that produced intelligent offspring went to the flesh renderers . . . or, if these offspring had good physical characteristics, the females were used for warrior breeding. The genes for good warrior broodstock also carried other linked characteristics, characteristics that had little to do with the traits the Morkth sought. The harsh selection process had refined and reinforced both the desired and unrequired, carried-along traits. Good warriors of the clockwork type the Morkth liked were powerfully left-brain dominant. This made, purely incidentally, for a natural predilection toward math. . . . They were also good at logic. . . .

Since the Morkth denied that female humans were capable of speech, communication could be easy enough, so long as one did not make too much noise. Noise caused punishment. And punishment meant pain. The Morkth were expert in the administration of pain . . . to other Morkth. Unfortunately, the frail humans died quite easily. The less intelligent and less logical worker brood sows, kept separately from the warrior broodstock, had never realized that they *could* talk, so long as one kept speech quiet and away from high-pitched sounds. Their section of the hive was virtually silent, apart from quiet, purely animal sounds.

It was different, vastly different, in the layer of hive where the warrior brood were kept. Here there was always a susurration of low-pitched cage-to-cage talk. The human mind needs stimulus of some kind. Without stimulus it atrophies. But speech, even only speech, can be enough to keep sanity and, if the selection pressures favor intelligence, can produce far more . . .

The oral tradition had generated a strange and distorted picture of the outside world, passed down from the first captives, but the women had a very real idea of the function and structure of the hive. They had time, endless time, to talk, to theorize, to plot and to scheme, until they became reproductively dysfunctional and were taken away to the rendering rooms. The only other distraction in the tiny cells was one's own body, and the products thereof. The Morkth were unaware that in the eternal semidarkness of their warrior breeders' bare cells they had been fomenting a rebellion for generations now.

This ultimate form of hell had not produced dehumanization, as it had in worker brood sows. Instead it produced a terrible richness, a flowering of poetry, philosophy and mathematics, all directed toward one end: the ultimate destruction of the Morkth. Now they'd found their tool—S'kith 235. And it was even more pleasant than masturbation. It provided a basic human need they'd all been long denied: simple physical contact with another person. For some seven years now the Alpha-Morkth warrior breeding program had been quietly sabotaged. At least eleven thousand new Morkth-men were growing up through the indoctrination classes. Passing unnoticed, yet with a terrifying gene cocktail of high intelligence, intense curiosity and instinctive secretive cunning, virtually from their first reasoning thought. This latter feature was S'kith 235's unique mutation, but he bred true, in more than eighty percent of cases. His male offspring were passing undetected up the layers of the Alpha-Morkth warrior training. All around them other lines were culled. But S'kith 235's children were tailored to survive and flourish in the hive.

It was certain that a reasonable percentage would, like S'kith 235, find a way around the just-post-puberty castration rite of passage, when the Alpha-Morkth collected and selected the semen that was frozen and used for future breeding. And if they had testicles . . . sooner or later they'd find their way down to the breeding cages. His female offspring were already being selected as potential warrior sows. The vertebrate cockroach was adapting yet again. It would beat this system too, before inbreeding weakened the strain.

In the dark, the statisticians calculated again. There was no need. They knew the answer. They simply did it for the sheer satisfaction. The point of break-even probability had long since been reached. They knew that with each S'kith-fathered conception the time of Morkth destruction came closer. They also knew that with each conception the chances of S'kith's capture grew greater. S'kith 235 knew nothing of love. He had little understanding of what the brew of emotions and hormones were that drove him down into this dangerous place, again and again and again. But among the warrior-brood women he was dearly loved. And they were already preparing to mourn him.

It was the twenty percent of his offspring that were culled that were reaching to enmesh S'kith 235. He had manipulated the gene records after the women had pointed out that this would certainly trap him if he did not. After his changes the gene records of his offspring were not what they were supposed to be. Resultantly, when the cull-tissue sample was analyzed, the two did not match. An improbably high number showed a particular chromosome group. A group not in the sperm-bank records. A mutant. A mutation that bred without Morkth supervision. Slowly, slowly, the methodical net of the Morkth was closing in on the Alpha-Morkth guard on the roof of the hive.

There were two possible ways that S'kith 235 could evade certain capture and death at the hands of his masters. A Beta-Morkth raid, or flight. The probability of the former was about 0.2 percent. The Beta-Morkth would simply kill him, it was true; they despised the Alpha's use of humanity. The human race was something to be destroyed utterly, and not consorted with. The probability of S'kith 235 fleeing was even slimmer: The hive was his universe, a conditioning going to the core of his being from his earliest thought. The Alpha-Morkth had attempted to breed the kind of loyalty which was instinctive to them, and constantly reinforced by the pheromones unique to each queen's gene line. At the same time they had done their best to remove all normal human emotional cues: love, family and sex.

They had failed to make S'kith loyal to anything but himself. In humans loyalty is a two-way street, and the hive gave none of the emotional return humans require above such physical things as nutrition. But they had managed to make him terrified of the non-hive world.

The women had known his time was coming. They had not realized that the time was tonight. S'kith stood watch in the darkness on the hive roof. As soon as he saw them come out of the exit port, the Morkth-man knew something was wrong. The mistresses never exposed themselves on the roof of the hive. Besides the safety aspect, they found clear, bright light unpleasant. The gene mistress leading the all-Morkth party was easily recognizable, her high-status patterned chelicerae gleaming in the moonlight. The conclusion was inescapable. They'd found him. S'kith drew his sword and began the ritual of bioenhancement exercises he knew would double his reaction speed, and stop all pain for a few minutes. There was a high physiological cost to this, but he doubted that he would be alive to pay it.

Two hundred zeth-klicks away the Beta-Morkth scanners were watching with their endless robotic patience. They registered the presence of the traitor-kind in an exposed position, and alerted their masters.

The target was tempting: so many Alpha exposed in one fire zone. Clawed hands flickered across the console, calculating the possibility of success, against the use of scarce and irreplaceable resources. The target was declared worthy of one low-impact chemical missile unit. It streaked away on its killing trajectory.

The blast knocked S'kith off his feet. But by the time the debris was starting to fall the warrior training took over. He was up and running. This was a target zone for ordnance: get out, get down. The action seemed to break down barriers within him. Now, he would not, *could* not stop. He hurtled across the broken masonry, swung down from beam to beam, and ran at the gate of the outer hive enclosure.

The gate was intended to prevent entry by human ground troops—a low probability threat here, deep in conquered lands. The hive roof was where Beta-Morkth would attack. The best Morkth-men warriors were put up there. After all, to defend the hive against true Morkth warriors with technologically advanced weapons called for near superhumans. The next best of the crop of Alpha-Morkth bred warriors went to the invasion troops. The gate guards were the bottom of the barrel, adequate for their task, but almost totally rigid in their responses. They were gate guards. Not even an explosion from the hive behind them would turn them. The gate was open, to allow the passage of a worker Morkth-man party. The gate guards would continue to watch for any threat from outside, unless otherwise ordered. S'kith, his body converted into a deadly killing machine by the bioenhancement and pure adrenalin, cut through them like a sharp scythe through wheat stalks.

He was out, and still running. The surviving gate guards stood staring, confused. They watched as S'kith 235 hurtled straight into the flood-full river at the foot of the hill. He was gone, the black of his uniform swallowed by the darkness and the black muddy churn of earth-laden water, and its broken flotsam of branches and logs.

Swimming was not part of a roof guard's training. Drowning, however, was something for which he needed no prior experience. S'kith 235 had, in his frantic thrashings, managed to break the surface several times. He was about to go under for what would have been the last time, when a section of uprooted walnut tree caromed into his back. He managed to grasp its branches with all the strength of a drowning man.

It had taken the last of his energy to haul himself onto the trunk of the long-dead tree. Having roughly wedged himself upright between two branches, his mind slipped into post bioenhancement oblivion.

He regained consciousness to find his clothing being torn away by a scarecrow figure in a long, ragged skirt.

The stirring and opening of his eyes elicited a start and a surprised comment, "Well, damn me if it ain't alive. Mebbe there's more profit in it than just a few bits o' black rag." He was vaguely aware of being dragged, then of a delicious warmth stealing through his limbs.

The Morkth-man drifted in and out of consciousness several times in the next few days. The man who gave him broth and tended the fire, confirmed S'kith 235's beliefs that non-Morkth-bred humans were very alien creatures indeed. Totally misshapen, bulging with fat on his chest, and wide about the hips, and not wearing proper trousers. Long-haired too. Fever and darkness took him down again.

The place was silent when S'kith woke clear-headed at last, some three days after his flight and involuntary escape from the hive. His ribs ached, and his scalp and chin itched furiously. He looked about the place, trying to piece happenings together from a patchwork of memories.

He was in a low cave, crudely fronted with rocks, and a half-drawn curtain of hide. A smoky fire burned at the back of the cave. He was lying under some rough covering on a straw pallet. His clothes were gone, and his hands and ankles were bound. He heard voices, and they were coming closer.

". . . . found him on that spit yonder, more dead 'n alive, jammed in a dead tree, free days ago."

To S'kith there was something familiar about the voice. "Them Morkth-men is good workers. Too dumb t'stop, heh, heh! You gonna give me a goo' price fer 'im then?" There was a wheedling, whining quality to the voice.

Somebody snorted. "Likely not worth a bent copper, Sheela. He's probably so bent 'n buggered by the river I won't find a buyer for him."

"Naw! 'E's in good nick, I promise. Checked him out meself, all over. 'E's well hung too. Fought of keeping 'im for a stud for me old age, I did." The vaguely familiar voice went off into a cackle of laughter.

"He's entire?" The second speaker was incredulous. "Then he's no bloody Morkth-man. Stole the clothes y'showed me, likely enough. Stupid bastard."

"Well, I'll take 'em off, then. I'll not let 'is nuts stand between me an' a goo' price." The hide was pushed aside, and the skirted figure with long hair was suddenly outlined against the background of a river sand spit. The face was prune-wrinkled. It was something that S'kith had never seen before. Morkth-men were killed when they began to age past their prime. The eyes that looked out of the face were sharp, and flickered across his attempt to sit up.

"See, Ser Farno. 'E's in good shape, considering. Now, I'll cut his cods off quickly." The knife that came out of her sleeve was long and wickedly sharp looking. It was a mistake. The sight of the knife triggered defensive reactions. To the Morkth trainers the best form of defense is attack. The old cords that bound his wrists were no match for S'kith's iron-hard muscles. They snapped, and he was moving, propelled by his still-bound legs. The knife wrist was seized, forced down. The blade of his hand struck the knife wielder's neck. There was an audible brittle crack.

Without pausing to look at his fallen victim, S'kith took the knife and sliced his ankles free. Stepping into a crouch, knife extended, he advanced on the other person who had entered the cave with her.

"Keep away from me, you bloody madman! You've killed the old woman! You'll hang for that!" There was real fear in the fat man's voice as he edged back against the wall.

S'kith paused. "Woman? That was . . . a woman?"

Trying to press his way back into a crevice behind him, the man stuttered. "Yeah, I, I know she was an ol' bitch, and as ugly as sin, but you didn't haveta' *kill* her. Just . . . just lemme out, okay?"

"You are sure that was a woman? Are you a woman too?"

"Me!" Squeaked the fat one. "No . . . no really, I'm a man. Just like you. I saw . . . it . . . it . . . it was an *accident*. Honestly! Now I'll just go an' tell the Sheriff . . ." He made a sudden lunge, attempting to reach the mouth of the cave. S'kith cut him down without remorse. He'd killed a woman . . . that was wrong . . . somehow. He'd never wanted to *kill* warrior-brood women. He looked down at the tumbled body. Was this really what they looked like?

He lifted the dead woman's skirt. Yes, undoubtedly. She was physically different from him. So *that* was what it actually looked like. He had never been able to *see* it properly before. His emotions, those strange puzzling feelings, were stirred. If he had known the term he would have said that he was saddened by the killing. So, as it was what the females in the Morkth cells had always wanted of him, he had sex with the body. It was not particularly pleasant, but he felt it was the least he could do. Getting up afterwards he realized he was hungry. So he cut himself some hunks off his male victim, and ate them. He took some of the clothes and dressed. He stropped the knife carefully, and shaved his face and head. Then he cut some more steaks for later, put them into a sack, and set out into a world he felt he did not belong in. The gold from the slave buyer's purse was left scattered in the dirt of the cave floor. He had no idea that it was of any value.

It was nearly four hours later that the hue and cry was raised. The country was up in pursuit of the monster: Rapist, Murderer and Cannibal.

CHAPTER 4

The thin stream of filth spilled out of the broken pipe and onto the sand. Once, the pipe had extended far out into the breakers. But time and storms had eaten at it. Now, at low tide it spilled into a series of filthy pools and then trickled into the sea. Occasional seagulls swooped and picked, their mournful cries echoing in the mouth of the pipe, where a scared, hungry and bitter boy waited. The pipe-mouth circle of sky blue faded, becoming tinted here and there with orange and violet cloud streaks. It would be dark soon, and then he would set out.

The mountains . . . how would he get there? All the roads and trails would be watched. He also had no food, no way of carrying water, and a desert to cross. But he was a city child, to whom the distances on the map meant little, and the realities of crossing the desert meant nothing at all. He would follow the dry valley that the map described as the Syrah River. There would be no patrols, for there was no road there, and surely he would have finished crossing the desert by morning.

The sun sank at last in torn gossamer pink streamers of vague cloud. Keilin stepped out into the purple twilight, stretching his cramped limbs. After a hundred yards or so he stopped and washed his hands, legs and feet in the surf margin. Even half-wet the walk to the mouth of the valley was pleasant. The sand was still warm on the beach, as was the gentle night breeze.

When Keilin reached the rocky point which had been shown as the mouth of the river, he set off inland across the farmlands. He was city bred, but when he stumbled across a melon in a field he did manage to recognize it.

Keilin picked five melons, and carrying them in his shirt, he marched resolutely away from the sea, and onwards into the valley. Soon the fields gave way to short grass. The tussocks became further apart as he went on, and then there was just dry sand crunching underfoot. He walked, and walked, and walked. The moon rose slowly ahead of him. Eventually the boy could go no further. He sat down with his back to a rock. A cold dry wind blew down the valley. Taking a melon out of his shirt, Keilin tried to work out how to get into it without a knife.

Finally he settled for cracking the fruit against a stone. The hard outer peel split, showering him with seeds. Eagerly he scraped these aside and bit into the flesh. It was surprisingly hard, totally lacking in the sweet succulence he'd expected. It had less taste than the paper he had chewed on, on hungry days in the library. There was moisture, but not much. The only melons he'd ever tasted before had been two he'd stolen in the marketplace. Belatedly he remembered the housewives pressing and smelling them. Keilin worked things through in his quick mind: ripe fruit would be on the market, not still in the fields. Doggedly he ate on, resisting the temptation to try the other melons. It filled his belly. It gave some moisture.

It did nothing for his sore feet, but it did lift his spirits considerably.

He had meant to sit for just a few minutes and then press on, but sleep came on silent feet and stole his consciousness. Sheer cold eventually cut through his exhaustion, waking him to stare wide-eyed at the panoply of stars above him. The moon was edging down, and in the darkness and clear sky, Keilin suddenly saw just what a crowded heaven it really was. The smoky sky of Port Tinarana had never allowed him to see one tenth of its icy splendor. Besides, the nights were working time, not stargazing time. He knew what stars were, having read incredulously about them. He'd laughed at the ignorant masses who believed them to be the lights in the windows of God's house. Now it didn't seem so funny. Ah well, perhaps if the mountains didn't offer refuge, he could travel to those stars and find a safe place somewhere.

Stiffly he rose to his feet, and began to walk onward. The night grew still colder as he trudged on. Gradually the sky began to pale in front of him, fading the stars and showing the stark outlines of steep, barren hillsides. Then, when Keilin was sure that he could get no colder and still continue walking, came the miracle of a desert sunrise. Within minutes the colors of the landscape went from grays and blues to sharp reds, yellows and browns, still razor sharp and clear in the night-chilled dry air.

Now that it was light, Keilin could see that the valley bottom was in fact a wide, dry river bed, braided with banks of water-polished and size-sorted stones. Had Keilin been desert-wise, he would have seen that the place was, compared to the surrounding hills, full of life. The sand was patterned with the tracks of insects and birds. There were a few dead-looking tufts of grass and weed stalks among the stones. On the margins of the stream bed were occasional near-leafless bushes, their twigs full of cruel

thorns. Despite the thorns, there were signs that
something grazed on them. Succulent plants, their flat
leaves stonelike, were actually common. But the boy
did not see this. To his city eyes it just looked like
the outskirts of hell. However, the sun at least was
welcome, licking down to warm his numb feet. The
mountains surely could not be far now? He'd lost
some time by sleeping, but surely by midmorning he'd
be there?

Midmorning came . . . and went. The sun he'd
welcomed had built up to scorching strength. Not a
breath of air moved between the red cliffs of the
valley. The cliffs themselves however seemed to shiver.
Keilin's feet felt as though they'd never be cool again.
Each step on the burning surface was a small agony.
He'd learned to avoid dark stones, picking his way
across the lighter ones. There was no sign of any
mountains. Finally, in the meager shade of a water-
cut overhang on the dry river's edge, he stopped. He
ate a body-warmed melon, even sucking the limited
juice from around the pips, and then drifted into an
uneasy sleep. When he woke again it was nearly
sundown, and his mouth and throat were mercilessly
dry. He sucked and chewed at the pulp of the third
melon, dragging out its limited moisture, struggling
to swallow the near tasteless muck, ending up spit-
ting out most of it. Still, he was determined. He
walked on, and kept going all night, although the
terrain became steeper and rougher.

The fourth melon proved a rare bonus. Near ripe,
and far more juicy. The fifth and last had been a
bitter disappointment after it. The boy had had the
sense to find deep shade and sleep in that, but now,
with his supplies exhausted, he began to realize that
he might end before the desert did. He'd woken in
the midafternoon too thirsty to sleep. It had taken
him a while to work out what was different about the
harsh desert light. High above, the sky was patched

with great lumbering castles of white cloud. If only . . .
if only it would rain.

His longing for water chilled the jewel on his chest.
The fear that that cooling caused just seemed to
worsen it. Damn! Damn! Damn! The whiners thought
him dead. He couldn't let them find him again. Not
here. There was no possible place to hide. He forced
himself to be calm, to think it all through. The jewelled pendant was magical. He knew that. It seemed
only to work when he was emotionally stirred up; and
then only for some emotions. Hatred did nothing, but
fear had some effect; however, real potency seemed
related to sex and its brew of emotions and desires.
The things it whisked out of nowhere were not con-
sciously chosen by him, but their nature did seem to
have some connection to the circumstance. The jewels
his first fear had materialized. The mattresses his fall
from the library window had produced. The thought
of the girl on the mattress dragged out a tension-
easing smile. She'd been so preoccupied with her own
body that it had taken her a good few moments to
realize she was no longer in the privacy of her bedroom. That she hadn't screamed the street down was
a miracle of sorts. With one horrified, embarrassed
look at him, she'd stifled her screech, grabbed a sheet
to cover her nudity and left at a blind run. He'd often
wondered if she'd got home, and how she'd explained
the missing mattress. He'd often been tempted to try
and recall her, and wished he'd had more of a chance
to do something on their abrupt meeting. She'd been
the subject of many fantasies, abruptly shut down
because of the cooling of the jewel. He knew experi-
mentation was impossible. When the thing was used,
the whiners always came, trying to kill him.

Well, when he was sure he was going to die anyway, he'd try using the jewel. In the meanwhile he
would keep walking. The mountains couldn't be far
now, could they? As for the jewel, well, if it could

stay cool, perhaps it might help his burning mouth? He pushed it in between his lips.

It was cool. Cool enough to start some saliva rising from an inner well. As soon as the jewel was wet there came the weirdest of sensations. Vastness. Memory. Great seas of it. A terrible war threatening even the existence of life itself. Flight: A huge hand reaching for the stars, and then, when the stars had been almost within grasp, the memory of treachery as black and bitter as gall. Overlying all of this was a powerful, desperate calling. He could see the place: There were endless plains of intense whiteness, and a mountain, no place of trees and streams, but a towering white monolith, ribbed with broken gray rock standing in the middle of the limitless white plains. It was bone-freezing cold, and the air was thin and biting.

Using the pendant's chain he pulled the jewel plug out of his mouth. The feeling was gone, cut off as if by a knife. He was still in the heat of the desert. It must have been some kind of illusion, he decided, eyeing the jewel suspiciously. Yet, despite the warm dry air, he was shivering. And there was a powerful compulsion to go to the white plains, even though he had no idea where they were. Shaking himself, Keilin set off again, thirst gradually washing away other concerns.

Some fifty miles away the clouds hit higher, cooler slopes. Thunderheads began forming, and soon heavy driving rain was washing down the bare hillsides. The first that Keilin knew of it was hearing a distant rumble in the valley. He'd read of lions. Would they live out here? Fear plucked at him, enough to begin to chill the jewel against his chest. But . . . surely there was no water for animals? It was only when the roaring came closer, growing louder and more constant that it dawned on him. It *was* water, lots of it. His moment of relief was overwhelmed by the realization that he had to get out of the middle of the riverbed, fast.

Like a brown wall it came, thundering closer, as Keilin scrambled for the red rocky slopes, running as fast as he could, calling on the last of his reserves. Minutes later he sat panting on a high rock, looking down on the flood. Soon he dared to creep down and drink the muddy water. Perhaps there was hope after all. Perhaps he could reach the cool green valleys in the mountains of his dreams.

"What's yer name, missy?" With a shock the small Princess realized that the shifty looking man was attempting to distract her from his advance. His attempts at surreptitiously edging forward were laughable. Except . . . she didn't want to laugh. Her stomach muscles tensed, and she reached a small hand up to finger her earlobe. It was all she could do not to run, and not for all the will in the world could she stop herself from biting her lower lip before she replied. Her nervousness had given her an instant to think. If he knew who she was he would see her as a valuable trade item, to be guarded every instant. She'd better play some other part.

Her potential role models were rather limited. If she pretended to be an aristocrat's daughter it would suggest she had some value, and might be ransomed. The fellow would certainly tie her up . . . It would have to be someone from the lower orders then. A maid perhaps? She had always been attended by maids. She knew that there were also parlor maids and kitchen maids, but she'd never given much attention to *any* of them. They just were, in the way that air was. You didn't notice what they did, or how they behaved. They were trained to be inobtrusive. If they weren't they . . . went.

She could only think of three women of the lower classes to whom she'd truly paid attention. Firstly, her herbal poisons instructress, who had been positively ancient—at least fifty—and who, despite her resemblance to the bad ones in the fairy tales, one very carefully didn't call a witch. Secondly, the two high-class whores who had taught her about bed arts. She didn't think a young poisoner would be well received, so—she'd be a young whore. After all, she knew the theory, and she'd have him in thrall very rapidly.

She dropped her chin forward, cocked her head sideways, and raised her eyebrows coquettishly, "Bella, handsome. What's yours, then?"

"Hur! Best if yer don't know, sweetie." He was standing over her now. She was aware of just how big and coarse he really was.

He reached for her, and she steeled herself not to shrink. He pulled her to her feet, fondling her breasts as he did so. Shael decided to change roles very rapidly. The theory was one thing; even watching the practical demonstrations from her hidden vantage had been all right. She knew how she was supposed to respond. Her body just wasn't ready to cooperate.

She pulled away from him, struggling to get free of the thick arms, "Please . . . please don't. You'll get a good ransom for me if I'm, uh, not . . . not hurt. Please, can't you just let me go and . . . give me something to eat."

Her reaction only made him hold her more tightly. The struggle seemed to excite him. He laughed, pushing her down onto the thick mat of grass and sedges. "Don't gi' me that crap! It won't hurt you, ducky, and I'll give yer something fine to eat . . . afterwards." His knee forced her thighs apart. He imprisoned both of her frantically clawing little hands in one of his large powerful ones. With the other hand he tore her skirt and underclothes away. His stinking breath was hot on her face. As he fumbled at his own belt, Shael decided that the theory was absolutely and totally unlike the practical experience.

And suddenly anger, wild searing anger, ripped through her, replacing the panic and fear. She was a Royal Princess. She was Cru, dammit, not some peasant trull to be abused like this! His fumbling hand was trying to open her, to guide his blindly thrusting manhood. She spat up into his face. Then again into his half-closed eye, and then, as he turned his face away, she lunged up and bit his neck with all her strength. She felt her teeth meet as he pulled away from her. She tried to roll away from the buffeting slap. "You fuckin' bitch!" It made her head reel, but despite this she knew what she had to do while she had the chance. As he'd slapped her, his one knee had come off the ground. Her leg had slid under it. Her thighs were well-trained and strong, and she lifted her knee with all the force she could muster.

The would-be rapist reeled back, his grasp on her hands slackening, as he put a sheltering hand over his testicles. He'd fallen half sideways, off her. "I'll kill yer for this!" He bellowed in pain. As he spoke, a raking set of claws stabbed at his eyes . . . and she was rolling away. He dived at her, but she had had time to pull her knees up under her chin. There was no science in it, but the double-footed, instinctive kick caught him in the solar plexus. The force of the kick, plus his own momentum, emptied his lungs with an explosive *whuf!* and sprawled him sideways next to her. The stream was beside them. And it was full of rocks. She seized one with both hands, and brought it down on his head as hard as she could. He lay still, blood sluggishly oozing through his dirty hair. For a moment Shael was still too. Then she pounded his head several more times, before dropping the rock, her hands shaking. Only then did she spit out the piece of his flesh that she still had in her mouth.

"That," she said, after a long, long moment, with her voice quivering, "is what you get for trying to rape

the daughter of the Tyrant, you . . . you . . ." Words
failed her. The best she could manage was "pig!"

The anger that had carried her through her furious defense was over now, and the fear was beginning to steal back. She'd been lucky. If . . . if she
hadn't won, he'd probably have killed her . . . afterwards. After a few moments her self-possession came
back. He'd dropped his bag as he'd advanced on her.
She walked over to it and opened it. Looted tawdry
bits of silk; a few scraps of ornamental silver, probably stolen from a temple somewhere; a bone-handled
dagger with a broken tip and . . . a pie. She stood,
pie and knife in hand, when she heard a groan from
behind her.

He was sitting up, blood still running down his
face, which was contorted in a mixture of hatred and
pain. Panic took her. She turned and ran.

She sat down in a brake of tall trees. It was a place
of great natural beauty, the stream falling through a
series of musical, lacy cascades into sunlight and leaf-
shadow dappled pools. At this stage Shael only saw
it as a place to hide. After a panting rest she began
to take stock: What did she have, besides a black eye,
a ripped skirt, a next-to-useless dagger, and a pie that
she'd yet to find a chance to eat? What should she
do now? Shapstone lay far behind. She'd seen no signs
of the Morkth pursuit. But *he* was still after her. She
shuddered. At least . . . she thought he was still after
her. She hadn't seen him behind her for a while.

This side of Shapstone had been sparsely farmed,
mostly just sheep-grazing lands, and the Morkth had
burned the only two cottages she'd seen so far. So
where should she go?

The sharp crack of a breaking stick, audible even
above the water music, cut through her reverie. He
had succeeded in following her. And his face, now
a mask of scratches and dried blood, was flushed with
pursuit . . . and triumph. "Thought I didn't 'ear you,

little Princess!" He spat the last word out. "Those I'm goin' ta sell you to won't care what shape you're in. It'd make a good story for the alehouses. I'll be the man that finally screwed the world's ultimate royal bitch! I'm gonna make *you* suffer!"

Shael shakily held the dagger in front of her. She dropped the pie, her other hand fingering her bangles nervously. Suddenly she was aware of intense cold under her sweating fingers. This was what she'd felt in her apartments when Lord Blis had grabbed her. The picture of that scene leapt through the window of her mind.

The corpses fell and tumbled between them. Almost as an afterthought the majordomo's severed head popped out of thin air, and bounced against the man's legs. The deserter and would-be rapist staggered back. For a moment they stood frozen. Then he swore, his voice rising in sudden fear, "Motherfu—!"

Shael didn't stop to see what would happen next. She was already running when the air was hammered with a terrific booming sound. The leaves shook. Looking over her shoulder she saw a Morkth plate-craft dropping stonelike onto the spot where she'd been a minute before. The terrible purple flare of their weapons drove her to dive deep into a bramble thicket, and to burrow down into it, too frightened even to pull away from the myriad needle points that pressed at her flesh.

It was perhaps half an hour later when she slowly began to extricate herself from the brambles, with much tearing and scratching. The birds were singing again and it seemed as if nothing had ever disturbed the tranquillity of this spot. She crept cautiously back to where she had been.

He would never chase her again. Not with a fist-sized hole seared through his chest. At the same time she could not take any of his garments to replace those he'd torn. The clothes had been very thoroughly taken apart, including every possible stitch and seam. Even his boots had been dismembered. A few coins from a slit-open neck pouch lay beside him. The other bodies too had been similarly searched. The sight of Blis's purple-mottled body was nearly too much for her. She turned away, and looked down at her bracelets. It was that one, she was sure. The one she didn't like very much. It was the old-looking one with its snaky double helix pattern and that chilly black stone, the stone with the oil-on-water surface which seemed to shift as she looked at it.

With sudden insight she realized that this was what the Morkth had been looking for. It was this bracelet that had had such unpredictable magiclike effects. But to use it was to summon the Morkth, too.

She picked up the pie, miraculously still intact, and walked away. There was much to think about, but she wanted to do it elsewhere. An hour later she was seated with her back to the wall of a burned-out shepherd's hut. The place had been fired, but not looted. Looting was not the Morkth way. The roof had burned, as had some of the rude furniture. But the moldy blanket from under the stone shelf had not. She would have something to sleep under tonight. There was food. Now to eat, and then sleep. The thought of food shut out all other ideas, even the horrors of the past twenty-four hours.

Shael bit into the pie with the sort of greed that she had never shown for even the most rare of sweetmeats. The crust was crumbly and rather stale, but the inside was full of tart fruit. She was more than two-thirds through it when she recognized the purple juice dripping off her fingers. She gagged. It had been almost inevitable. Bilberry preserve was common hereabouts.

She was hungry and more pragmatic the next morning, after an amazingly good night's sleep. She'd tossed and turned on the finest feather beds before.

Now a few armfuls of heather and a smelly blanket had seemed wonderful. She brushed away the tiny black ants that had been making the most of her discarded dinner, and ate it herself. Sleep and food had done much to restore her mind's tone. She sat and looked at the bangle, thinking.

It gave her a direction of travel. Here she had what was potentially a source of riches and power, if she could use it where they could not reach her. Her background had taught her more about the Morkth than most humans cared to know. She knew, for instance that there were two factions of Morkth, and that their internecine fight was more bitter than their hatred of humanity. She also knew they struggled with high altitudes and low temperatures. Their attacks were almost always limited to the coastal cities and the fertile lowland plains. Therefore she would go to the mountains. She could see the purple line of them from here.

S'kith too had thought he would aim for the mountains. He had needed a goal, a geographical target of some kind. Now these lower life forms were hounding him in such a fashion that he began to doubt if he would ever reach the blue jaggedness he could see before him.

CHAPTER 5

Slave markets have a peculiar scent. The pheromones of human fear and desolation are concentrated
there. The noses of those engaged in the trade
become blunted to it, just as butchers become used
to the sight of blood: besides it was not a profession
for the overly squeamish. It was the lifeblood of the
city of Castern, and in some way or another it
impacted on all its citizens' lives. Which was why the
townspeople were building the gibbet right in the
middle of the market square. This man would hang
where all the slaves could see him. There'd be no
trap door's sudden drop for this one. No. He was
going to dangle and jangle a bit. His throttling dance
would be something the merchandise would remember. The fine upstanding citizens of Castern wanted
to make a real example of him. He was worse than
a slave who had killed his owner. He was a slave
who'd killed a slave merchant, as well as committed
another murder and a bit of cannibalism and rape.
It was the latter crimes that had had him hunted by
the countryfolk, but in this city it was the former the

citizens had found so heinous. It was the sort of idea one rooted out at all costs.

They'd marched him down, past the lines of cages, to look at the scaffold they were building for him. He had stared long at it, his face expressionless, but then, it always was. Even now, he neither flinched nor wept, nor seemed defiant. As a warning to other watching slaves the exercise was worse than a failure. His captors did not understand that the gallows had no meaning for him. He'd never seen one before, and had no idea of its fell purpose. The mere wooden structure might make his escort shudder, but had no effect on him.

He'd run half the countryside ragged . . . and then been captured by a slip of a farmgirl, armed with no more than a cattle goad. S'kith 235 had stood when she'd told him to stand, had dropped his knife at her word, had allowed her to bind him and lead him like a lamb to the hunting soldiers, and scythe-and-pitchfork-armed countrymen. Now he stood in chains in an iron cage in the middle of the market. Occasionally passers-by would pelt him with rotten fruit or bits of dung. Yet he remained impassive. No signs of emotion moved across his wooden countenance, no matter what they did. They thought him tough beyond belief. They did not realize he was merely emotionally newborn.

S'kith 235 watched the three moving steadily from stall to stall. They were unusual enough to attract the attention of someone with a less intense curiosity than his . . . and he had nothing else to distract him. Most of the buyers who came to the market fitted into more-or-less defined categories. Masters and overseers looking for new laborers, wanting men with strength rather than intellect; haughty matrons in search of domestic staff, generally looking for ugly or disfigured young girls; furtive affluent folk, the young ones still conscience-pricked, the older ones with a terrifying

jaded-hungry look, in their quest for sexual enter-
tainments. Different sections of the market were
dedicated to the different types of merchandise.
Seldom did any buyer wander through more than one
sector. Except these three. They'd started at one end
and had been steadily going through it all.

They were an ill-assorted trio. One of them was
short and broad, the other slim and obviously fem-
inine, even to the Morkth-man's untrained eye, and
the third exceptionally tall and, by the look of the
sun reflecting off his head, bald. From S'kith's point
of view this was something in the fellow's favor. He
found the head and facial hair so overtly displayed
by these mongrel humans repulsive.

They came closer, going through stall after stall.
S'kith continued to watch them. The short one was
truly amazingly broad, nearly as wide as he was high.
The backs of his hands and his bare legs were covered in a thick down of reddish brown hair. As this
extended into a bushy beard and curly hair mop, it
was only the loose, faded-green canvas jerkin and
lederhosen that he wore that stopped folk thinking he
was a small pet bear. That, and the pale weimaraner-
yellow eyes that stared out from under those bushy
brows, intelligent and cold. Across his back was
strapped a great, two-handed, jagged landsknecht's
sword.

The girl's hair was a deep and lustrous black, flowing back over her shoulders. Her eyes, slightly wet-
looking, were faintly slanted, and as dark as the broad
one's were light. Her high cheekbones were faintly
lighter than the otherwise uniform smooth amber skin.
Her soft mouth was set in a small pout above a
determined chin.

But it was not her face that caught most eyes. It
was her body. It was . . . generous. Women were
inclined to say, through slightly pursed lips, that she
had just a bit too much of everything. Their husbands

would agree, but their eyes would be faintly glazed. Despite the potential for marital discord, men found themselves unable to resist watching her walk away. She radiated sexuality the way a fire radiates heat. Her clothes were tight-cut but simple, and irrelevant; as every heterosexual male undressed her with his eyes anyway. She carried a bow and a quiver of black-fletched arrows, to bring down any man-prey out of range of her other weapon.

The third member of the party, however, put off hopeful young men, and made luxury bed-slave merchants reconsider their immediate ideas of midnight acquisition raids. He was tall, head and shoulders above most men. His square-jawed narrow face was scarred here and there, the scars cutting across the age lines on the slightly sunken cheeks. The nose, however, was the dominant feature of his face. Powerful and aquiline, it led one's gaze into the never-still eagle eyes of a man to whom command was second nature. He might be old, a fact betrayed by the bald head and the lines on his face, but he walked with a powerful and dangerous strut. Instinctively, even hardened troublemakers stepped around this man.

S'kith 235 was trained to note weapons as a first step in his assessment of potential enemies. He could see no obvious signs of any about this man. Why then did S'kith *know* that the bald man was so dangerous? On the shoulder of his battered jacket was an embroidered patch. It meant nothing to S'kith, but he noted how folk peered at it, and then backed off, sometimes bowing.

At last they came out of the nearest stall, the proprietor still bowing obsequiously and rubbing his hands. His lacquered tones were tinged with regret. "Great Sirs, magnificent Lady, are you sure none of my fine stock suits your needs?"

The broad man's voice was oddly high. "Not unless you're for sale, you fat rogue. I've a use for you." The

grin full of big yellow snaggle teeth suggested whatever that use was, it wouldn't be pleasant.

"Enough, Beywulf," the tall man commanded, his
voice disapproving. "It's not the most appealing head,
but leave it on his shoulders . . . for now. Come, we've
a few more of these carrions' stalls to check through."

The slave dealer was left wordless as they strode
off.

They walked past the cage. S'kith's eyes followed
them . . . especially her. Her voice was deep, husky,
fitting the body image. "What about the one in the
cage, Cap?"

They stopped, looking in at him. Finally it was the
tall one who spoke. "H'mm. I've never actually tested
one of those. It's an Alpha-Morkth warrior breed. The
hair color is difficult to ascertain, but the physiog-
nomy is plausible. Unfortunately, Leyla, they're cas-
trated at puberty. It would limit their potential."

It was the first of these mongrel humans who had
recognized him for what he was. To the others all
Morkth-men were alike. A flicker of interest drifted
through S'kith's mind, but he refused to let it distract him from staring at the woman.

She snorted. "If he's castrato then *I've* got nuts.
Hey, Morkth-man, have you still got your balls?"

Balls. That was what the warrior brood sows had
called them. Like a hypnotized rabbit S'kith nodded.

The tall thin man raised his eyebrows and slowly
held out his hand. The broad Beywulf reached into
a pouch at his waist, and produced an orb of dark
stuff, which he placed in the outstretched hand.

"Look, Morkth-man." He held the ball-like thing
aloft, demonstrating. "Put your finger in this hole.
Keep it there while I count to five."

Mutely he did as he was told, still staring at the
woman. She looked at the tall man questioningly. He
looked at the orb, and then with a hiss of indrawn
breath, he nodded. Quite calmly she untied her waist

sash, the front of her dress falling open. Taking the
flaps in either hand, she pulled it wide open, exposing
her nakedness to his devouring eyes. S'kith stared,
his mouth falling open. Somehow he instinctively
knew this was how women *should* look. Then he
reacted with a yelp of pain. The inside of the orb
was suddenly icy, and drawing, compelling. He pulled
his finger away in fright and the cold and the strange
feelings were gone.

"At last!" The tall man's eyes blazed, and a wintry smile played on his thin lips. "Of all the unlikely
ones. The emotional readout is strange though . . . I
hope . . . I think he will do!"

"Hey you! Get away from there." The bulky sergeant came belting out from between the tents, hand
on his sword. Slowly the threesome turned, looking
at him, the girl calmly fastening the waist sash, and
the short man-mountain reaching over his shoulder.
The tall man spoke in an arctic voice. "Are you
addressing me, sirrah?"

Arriving behind their leader at a trot, and fanning
out in a half-circle around the three, came some
twenty-five of the city watch, their pikes at the ready.

Many men would have wilted before the eagle-eyed
man's question, but this sergeant stayed calm. He did,
however, wait to reply until he was sure all his men
were ready. Then he stepped forward, deliberately
pushing into the personal space of the tall man. "Yuss!
I was. And you'll listen to me unless you want to
swing next to your little caged friend."

"Relax, Sergeant. The slave is no friend of mine.
Why is he in a cage? I should like to purchase him."
The tall man spoke calmly, although something about
his voice suggested that he also spoke with great
restraint.

"Huh! Likely bloody story," said the sergeant,
scornful. "You don't know why the murdering cannibal's in the cage? You want to *buy* him? Don't give

me your crap, mister. The whole bloody *country* knows what he's done. I suppose you'd like me to think *you* don't? That you just dropped in from 'eaven, complete with your bloody Cru badge!"

There was an abrupt hissing sound. It happened so fast that even S'kith's warrior reflexes found it difficult to see, and the ordinary city watchmen certainly had no chance to react. The huge jagged blade rested against the sergeant's neck. "Give the word, Cap."

The tall man raised his eyebrows, tilted his head slightly. For a long silent minute he stared at the sergeant, taking in the sheen of sweat leaping out on the fellow's forehead. Then he shook his head. "No, Beywulf. The sergeant didn't *mean* to insult me . . . did you Sergeant?"

"No, no . . . but I'm warning you, hurt me and there'll be trouble. Just get on your way, and we'll say no more of it, my word on it," said the sergeant, his bravado growing with each second of potential reprieve.

"Very well. Remove your sword, Beywulf. The sergeant will tell his men to put up their pikes."

The sergeant was relieved to have the weight of the long blade lifted from his neck. But there was a warm wetness seeping down onto his collar. The sword had been sharp enough to cut just by touching. The sergeant staggered away, back to his men. He moved a healthy distance behind them. But he was a petty-minded soul. He'd given his promise, yes, but he would still let them feel the weight of his authority. "Nar then, come along you three. I said you could be on your way, an' I keep word, but that way is now *outside* the city gates before this murderer hangs. And just to make sure you unnerstand that, we're going to see you along it."

In a fringe of pikes they were marched away. S'kith watched them go, curiosity bubbling in his head. What did "hang" mean?

Sunset came. The scaffold was finished. The traders' stalls and tents were packed up, but the merchandise stood assembled, watching and waiting. Several bonfires were kindled about the square and vendors, selling everything from sweetmeats to abortifacient powders, plied a brisk trade among the growing crowd. A drum began to beat out a slow tattoo. The pickpockets waited, selecting their marks. A brief scuffle, quickly quelled, broke out outside the ale draper's noisome place. Then, at last, five men, one of whom wore a black hood, came to the cage. They led S'kith out and up onto the platform. As he climbed the stairs silence fell like a curtain across the crowd. Only the slow drumbeat continued.

It was only when they led him to the front of the platform, and the hooded man put the thick noose around his neck that S'kith 235 truly understood what they meant by "hang." What a stupid way of sending flesh to the rendering! The struggling would almost certainly spoil the quality, and make it tough. The hooded man adjusted and tightened the noose. S'kith began his bioenhancement exercises. He would resist as long as possible, and at least he would not feel the end.

Then, just as the executioner was about to push S'kith to the edge, an intense ruby beam cut through the darkness and sheared the rope. Except for the pickpockets, who hadn't been watching, the crowd were dazzled. Too dazzled to see the arrows that the marksman on the roof had put into the bonfires. Moments later the fires exploded, scattering burning logs and embers into the crowd.

S'kith had seen the discharges of energy weapons before, although they had been incandescent purple, not a blaze of red. He had known what they were, but he'd thought they were meant for him rather than the rope. That anyone might come to his rescue never occurred to him. Thus it was not surprising that he fought like a kif-crazed dervish against the vast arms that encircled him. Then a skilled hand squeezed his carotid artery, and he knew no more.

He'd been vaguely aware of the bouncing motion for some time. When was it going to stop? He was going to vomit any minute now. He opened an eye warily. The earth was moving past him. He was hanging over the side of some large brown moving thing. A horse . . . he was tied onto a horse. And that was sunlight falling on his face. Sunlight splintered by pine needles. He must have made some sound because someone said, "Our little bundle of joy is awake, I see. Can we call a halt for a few minutes, Cap?"

"I think we can afford a little time, Leyla. By the sound of it, it will do Beywulf's horse no harm to rest a while anyway." The tall man still sounded remote.

They stopped. The trio dismounted, tied their horses and remounts calmly before turning any attention to S'kith. He too waited silently, his mind rapidly paging through possibilities. In the Morkth-man's philosophy he could see no good reason for what they had done.

The tall man reached into his saddlebag, and produced a braided-handled cattle goad. "The closest I could find. Here, Leyla, you'd better hold it. Morkth females give orders and punishments, you know."

The sight of the goad had made S'kith wide-eyed and rigid with fear. She looked at him, a strange almost feral-hungry expression coming into her eyes. "Well, Morkth-man, fancy a little . . . spanky?" She stood legs apart, and fondled the whip suggestively. It brought a guffaw of laughter from Beywulf, who was untying the knots that held S'kith on the horse's back. "Really, Leyla! Haven't you ever got anything else on your mind?"

To S'kith however the whip was totally unfunny. When Beywulf pulled him off the horse and released him, he immediately sank down on his knees and grovelled in front of her. "Command me, Mistress."

This only made Beywulf laugh even louder. With a look of irritation at him, the girl slapped the whip against the palm of her other hand.

"For God's sake don't hit him with it," said the tall man.

"Why ever not? I've hit men with far worse. And," she licked her upper lip, catlike, "some of them even liked it. Called me mistress, too."

"Not this one. He'd die. As far as he's concerned that's a Morkth discipline prod. To other Morkth it causes pain; to humans irredeemable nerve damage. More than a few blows and he'll start having fits, with pain stimuli coming in from each nerve in turn. It just recurs and recurs until the victim dies. Now, tell him to come and sit here and listen to me. You two prepare some food."

S'kith sat with the plate of food on his lap, attempting to use the clumsy wooden spoon which Beywulf had quickly whittled for him. He covertly watched the other three eating, and tried to imitate them. His mind was still boiling with what the man called Cap had told him. His hand unconsciously went down to the stitches on his side.

"Leave them alone, man. Eat your food." Cap said.

"Yeah, Morkth-man, what's up with you? Don't you like my cooking?" Beywulf asked, his voice half-mocking, half-serious.

S'kith's natural caution helped him to bite back his first reaction to the question. The food was, well, hot, and tasted nothing like the Morkth rations he was used to. It did all sorts of things to his taste buds, which were unaccustomed to such stimuli. And none of it was alike. Morkth rations were blended to uniformity. If any ingredients were cooked it was because they were going off. He'd never had warmed food before. His taste buds revelled, but his mind revolted. It wanted the comfort of something familiar.

"Well, Morkthy, what do you think of it then?" asked Beywulf again.

S'kith realized he had to give some kind of reply. "I am sure it is very nutritive," he said at last. "Why is it eaten hot?"

"A beautiful fricassee of a fresh young leveret, done in its own blood and red wine with garlic and wild mushrooms, and homemade spaetzle, and you're sure it's very nutritive, and you ask me why we eat it hot. Well bugger me! Last time I'll waste good vittles on you, you odd fish. Eat your nutrition then . . . while it's hot." The broad Beywulf helped himself to yet another plateful as he spoke.

S'kith kept quiet and ate. These mongrel humans were truly strange, but he was a master at adaptation.

Keilin had walked on determinedly all night. Two hours after the flood wall had come beating down on him, the water had begun to subside. By morning there were only drying puddles on the sand. The hills on either side of him were far bigger now. At last he was coming to some almost-mountains. They still bore no resemblance to the beautiful, forest-clad things he'd seen in the book, but perhaps he would still find those. The air was cooler here too. Going on in the small hours had been agony, but he knew that to stop here was to die of exposure. But the character of the land was changing: There were occasional sparse aromatic-leaved bushes and tufts of coarse grass in the watercourses. He'd walked awhile, until it got too warm, and then found a shaded resting spot among the broken rocks. He lay down, desperately tired. Sleep was slow in coming, he was so hungry, but eventually tiredness carried him beyond the threshold. Till the cool of evening he'd wandered through strange dreams of empty white plains adrift with white flakes.

The eerie pip-pip sound in the dusk nearly made him run for cover. He'd been attempting to stretch his lips down to the scummy water in a narrow crack in the now-dry rapids. Who would have thought that the water would all vanish so quickly?

It was a bird; a speckled, brownish hensized thing. It was looking at him with round, suspicious tea-colored eyes. Keilin had never seen a sand grouse before, but he'd dined off pigeons and seagulls often enough. And before he'd made traps, he'd learned to throw stones with some success.

The boy eyed his kill. Just the sight of it made him hungry. He had no means of cleaning it, or cooking it. And then an errant breeze carried an unexpected scent to him: wood smoke. He turned, questing with his nose. It came from upvalley. He was none too certain about meeting the locals, but perhaps he could steal a firemaker, or even just a live coal. Eventually, in the gathering darkness, he caught the flicker of light from a hidden fire. As quietly as he could Keilin crept closer. At last he could see the small neatly constructed blaze, almost entirely hidden by slabs of sheetrock. There was no one sitting beside it, and no signs of an encampment of any sort.

For a moment Keilin hesitated. But hunger drove him on into the limits of overconfidence. Whoever had lit this fire was plainly off having a leak or still hunting. A dash now, and he could have that small ember-tipped log, and be away in fifteen seconds. He sneaked closer, and then stood up and darted forward—

—to be frozen in his tracks. The voice from behind him suggested that moving would be the last thing he ever did. It was an old voice and, if anything, it sounded amused. Someone came up behind him, and then circled around to face him. The man was undoubtably old, his face folded and lined. However, there was nothing decrepit in his movements. Certainly the black-hafted, bright-bladed spear he held with such assured ease suggested that he should be treated with extreme respect.

"You make enough noise for ten men, boy. Think I'm deaf, do you?" He chuckled, the black finger of the spear reaching towards Keilin's ribs. He stared carefully at the boy. "But mebbe I'm goin' blind. Were you plannin' to brain me with that bird? Where's your weapon, boy?"

Keilin felt his legs wobble under him. The jewel was cold on his chest. "Please," he stammered, "I just wanted a coal . . . just something to start my own fire and cook my supper. I promise . . . I haven't even got a knife!" To his intense shame he felt a tear trickle down his cheek.

It might have embarrassed him, but it plainly eased his captor's mind. "Sit down, boy, afore you fall down," the old man said with rough kindness, lowering the spear, "and don't start blubbering now. I don't mean you any harm, son. Just that a man's inclined to be suspicious o' strangers out here, especially when folk try and sneak up on you. You're welcome to a piece of my fire, if you wants it, and welcome to cook your fowl here if you like." He cast a knowing look at Keilin's nervous upturned face in the firelight. "You don't have much to fear from old Marou, boy. And iffen you don't have the means of makin' fire and you don't even have a knife I'm willin' to bet you don't have the faintest idea how to cook the bird either."

"I do!" said Keilin, stung. "I've cooked heaps of pigeons and gulls. You pluck them, gut them, and cut them up, and broil them!"

"What's gulls? I've et rock pigeons though," said the old fellow, sitting down, his spear across his knees, "Besides, what was you going to cook it in? And it sounds like turrible way to spoil a good sand grouse. No. You just give it to me, sonny, I'll show you how to do it right. Then when we've had a bit of a feed, you can tell me just what you're doin' with nothin' in the middle o' nowhere. It's sounds like it might be a interestin' tale. It gets a mite lonely out here, and I've a fondness for a good story."

He pointed at the fire. "I've a nice plump goanna roasting under them coals, so I won't have to deprive you, sonny. You look short a good few meals, though heaven knows why. It's seldom I've seen the land lookin' so fat."

Mutely Keilin handed over the bird. The deft old hands began plucking, and within a few minutes it was plucked, drawn, had salt rubbed into its skin, had been split, and was grilling on a blackened, battered grid above the scraped-out coals. Keilin had sat silent while all this happened, and the old man seemed content to have it so.

When the sumptuous-smelling bird was getting its skin finally crisped, the old man pushed aside the coals with a stick and pulled out what looked like a long blackened sausage. Using his knife and the stick he lifted it up onto a flat rock. The grilled fowl was speared on the knifepoint and put next to it.

Using the knife hilt the cook carefully tapped the sausage shape. Pieces cracked off, and were flicked away, revealing steaming white flesh, which the old hands salted carefully. A fibrous root was added to the stone table, skinned and rapidly sliced. "There you go, me boy, as fine a feast as the hills'll provide." The old man sounded faintly nervous. "Goanna baked in clay, a nice plump little grilled sand grouse, and a paro root, not even two year old! What more could a man ask for, eh?"

Keilin's mouth was watering. "It smells very good, sir."

The old fellow expanded like a peony in the sun.

Keilin realized he was probably unused to feeding anyone but himself, and had indeed been nervous about the reaction of his surprise guest. "Bless you, son. Don't you be calling old Marou Skyann 'sir.' Dig in, lad. It's prime tucker this. No sense in lettin' it get cold." He scuffled among the rocks and produced a leather wineskin. "Ain't eggsactly wine . . . but it's a rare vintage. Near on two weeks old." He cackled at his own joke, and handed Keilin the skin. The brew inside it was sour, and vaguely alcoholic . . . and wet.

With his throat lubricated, a drumstick in one hand, a piece of goanna in the other, grease on his chin, and the fire warmth licking at him, the boy relaxed for the first time in days.

While Keilin ate with hungry greed, he retained enough common sense to be loudly appreciative of the food. The old man drank the praise in like thirsty ground, and was soon telling him the best way to trap goanna, and where to look for sand grouse in the mornings, which banks the sand martens nested in, and how to steal their eggs without being mobbed by the entire nesting colony. Keilin was warm, he had a full belly and he was unused to alcohol, even a mild brew like this. It was hardly surprising that, when Marou finally said, "Now son, time for that story," his answer was a snore.

The old man looked across at him, and sat silent for a while. Finally he spoke quietly, more to himself than the sleeper. "Don't look much like a claim jumper to me. You're lucky, boy. Five year ago I'd'a killed you just in case. In th' morning I'll feed you th' antidote." Burrowing among the rocks he pulled out a mangy old rug of rabbit pelts, and tossed it over the boy. "Sleep easy, son," he said, a wry smile teasing the wrinkles.

It was just before gray dawn when Keilin found himself poked sharply in the ribs. Opening his eyes he saw the old man prodding him with his spear butt.

"On your feet, boyo. Cain't sleep all day. Move your tail if you want to eat."

Keilin staggered up, rubbing his wide eyes. "I . . . I'm sorry . . . I must have fallen asleep."

The old man cackled. "If you hadn't been snorin' I'd'a thought you was dead, kid. Sleep like that and you will be. Here . . . drink this." He handed Keilin a small mug full of bitter hot brew. The boy gagged at the first mouthful. He found the spear was against his chest. "Drink it!" The voice was deadly. Keilin swallowed.

The old fellow relaxed. The spear point dropped. "All right, boy. Let's go. We've got to get the traps set before it gets light."

Keilin's jaw dropped. "But . . . why? Why did I have to drink that foul stuff first?"

The old man looked discomforted. "You needed it." He set his mouth in a hard, thin line. "Now come on. Let's move. We want to get the traps set."

They were simple drop traps: a wire cage with a door which fell shut behind the bird. At the back of each cage was a mirror. Marou carefully scattered a few seeds outside the cage. Inside it, in front of the mirror, he put a generous pile of seed. "Ol' sand grouse, he's a mighty suspeecious feller. Put the biggest trail o' seed into that cage, an' 'e still won't go in. But when 'e sees that other fowl in there a-pecking away at a big pile o' seed while he's getting mighty thin pickin's . . .

"Now, let's get breakfast. There's a good slope that hasn't bin worked for a good while."

Keilin's stomach rumbled in agreement. He was somewhat less keen when he discovered that breakfast was to be caught by turning over stones on the hillside. "If they've got small claws an' fat stings, leave 'em, son," said his mentor, catching a large-clawed two-inch gleaming bronzy carapaced monster with his old deft hands. He plucked the stinger off, and crunched the beast between strong teeth. Keilin turned pale. As a street brat he'd eaten damn near anything he could scavenge. Fried rat was perfectly acceptable . . . in fact, quite tasty, but . . . raw live scorpion! Gingerly he turned over the next rock. It was still cold, and thus the snake that struck at his foot was a fraction too slow. He dropped the rock with a startled yell. His erstwhile instructor dived behind some rocks and disappeared. Keilin simply couldn't find him. After a few moments, the white head peered out from behind a boulder. "What'n hell was that, son? Mohocks?"

"S-s-snake, under that rock . . ." With shaking hand Keilin pointed.

The old chap bobbed up with glee, rubbing his wrinkled belly. "Great! Why'd ya yell! Y'might frighten it!" He rapidly hobbled over to the rock.

"Watch out! It's a bad one!" said Keilin fearfully.

"Ain't no such animal! Snake's good. Skin's useful too. But him'll be good'n mad after you pissing about with him. You jump away sharpish when you pull the rock over, see."

The fat diamond-backed reptile still twitched occasionally as it dangled from the spear. "Nasty poison, these puffies," said Marou conversationally. "Bite you on th' foot an' you'll lose it . . . if you don't lose th' leg . . . if you live. You swell up like a balloon an' then break out in great big sores that rot away. Them's good eating tho'." Later, once the sections of skinned snake were grilled, Keilin was obliged to admit that it was very tasty indeed.

The old man rubbed his greasy hands on his already greasy fringed trousers. "Now boy . . . that story o' yours."

The sun was high by the time Keilin finished. Marou Skyann pursed his lips as he sat silent, digesting the tale. His old eyes stared at the boy, narrowed, focused and concentrated. He seemed to almost be looking through Keilin. Finally he stood up, spat on his palm and stretched out his hand. Keilin looked at him, puzzled.

"Spit on your hand, boy, an' shake. If you want to become my partner that is. Sounds to me like you need a place to hide. And them mountains you're looking for . . . well they ain't what you think they are."

Thus it was that Keilin became an apprentice turquoise fossicker and trainee desert rat. He eventually learned to enjoy raw scorpions for breakfast. It was a period he was later to describe as one of the happiest of his life. He also changed from a city street-child to a lean, hard young man who could survive off country which, to the untrained eye, would not support a pygmy mouse. In Marou he found both a father figure and a peer, things he'd never had or missed. The only thing from his old life that still called to him were the books.

Shael was footsore, hungry and weary. She'd never realized just how much bigger the world got when it was crossed on foot. If it hadn't been for pure untrammelled luck she'd have starved to death, or been forced to go to one of the marauding bands she had seen and run from. Her future then might have been short indeed. On her second day she had found a farmhouse with its newly dead owners sprawled on the grass outside. But the attackers had fled before looting it. She resolutely turned aside from the dead woman and her spitted son to search hastily for food. She'd found their packs readied for flight. The boy's spare boots were an added blessing, although she thought them most unshapely.

She'd reached the western foothills when she encountered one of the toxins her poisons instructress had neglected to mention. Poison ivy wasn't going to kill her, but her eyes were swollen nearly shut, and her delicate fingers were fat clumsy sausages. She was crying and slightly fevered when the bee wife found her. Few refugees had come this far and the weeping weal-faced girl tore up the buried memories of her own dead daughter.

S'kith 235 was finding life singularly confusing. His basic premises were being overturned. Firstly, the power of this party was not vested in the female. Nor was all the intellect. And the female was not, it seemed, interested in sex, or at least not with him, and not right now.

They'd ridden on for hours, an unfamiliar experience which had increasingly become an agony to the Morkth-man. When they had finally stopped for the night, they had eaten a meal of cold spanish omelette, paper-thin jasper-red slices of ham studded with green peppercorns, and small pearl onions in sherry vinegar. The abrupt taste education had stunned S'kith's overtaxed taste buds. He had been sure that the fire of the things Beywulf termed "peppercorns" was poison. Indeed, he had almost welcomed the surcease this would have been from the experience flood he was struggling to master. The others had eaten the red salty stuff with the fire bits in it with every sign of enjoyment, however. Determinedly S'kith had forced it down. The only positive point seemed to be that at least this time the food was a natural temperature.

Then they'd settled down for sleep. As soon as his secretive nature allowed, S'kith had crept to the woman's bedding-down place. She wasn't there. On his way back to his own newly donated sleeping fur S'kith's keen ears had picked up strange sounds. He'd crept closer. What he saw there made it abundantly plain that he was going to have to adapt to not being the only male with testicles.

The next morning S'kith had to be physically prevented from doing his bioenhancement rituals on being told that he had to get into the saddle again. He was surprised to discover that, except for the places where he was rubbed raw, it wasn't, after the first few minutes, as bad as yesterday. But, in those first few minutes, he did wonder whether he had been rescued, or whether this was just a slower and more painful way of killing him.

Several nights later she had come to his bed. S'kith had then had to come to terms with the fact that he hadn't known much about sex either.

The house was purring like a contented cat. A shaft of dusty sunlight poured lazily through the high window to splash and puddle on the soft colors of the rag rug on the floor next to her. The bed was soft and full of sleepy warmth. For a while Shael just lay there, fearful that opening her half-lidded eyes might shatter the illusion of comfort and security in which her dream had surrounded her. Tendrils of a scent sweeter than all the rare perfumes of Ta'aa—the smell of frying bacon and mushrooms—called to her stomach. It growled at her; it wasn't worried about shattering illusions.

Tentatively she reached out a hand to feel the eiderdown. The dream had painted it so realistically she could touch its softness. She swung her feet out of bed, and splashed them into the pool of sunshine rippling on the rag rug. The dream really had a pleasant solidity. It had to be a dream. Houses didn't hum.

The dream was becoming more complex. Someone for whom the word "round" was the perfect description huffed gently up the stairs. She was short, rounded and plump, with a round face, apple-red round cheeks and a few spare chins underpinning the round, warm chuckle that issued from a cheery mouth. "You're awake, lassie! To be sure, I thought you'd sleep forever. There's some clothes for you set out on that chair there."

Shael did not reply. You don't have to in dreams. She smiled, and stood up, walking across to the chair, supremely unconcerned by her nakedness. On the chair lay a peasant girl's bright frock, embroidered and lovingly adorned with fine stitchery. She looked at it. The round woman picked it up and held it against her. She raised her arms. The round woman looked at her in surprise, but stepped onto the chair—she was considerably shorter than Shael—and dropped the frock over her head. Stepping down from the chair, she busied herself with buttoning and lacing. Then she stepped back, looking at Shael with an odd expression.

It was strange, thought Shael, as the gentle humming sound caressed her. She'd never dreamed of other people crying before. Yet those were definitely tears on the round cheeks.

"Eh, lassie." The voice cracked slightly. "Except for the eyes, you're the image of my Merthly. You're safe now. That Tyrant bastard'll never find *you* here. They're all the same, these dukes, princes and kings: just a bunch of bloody murdering swine to us ordinary folk. 'Tis no wonder you've lost your tongue, wi' the horrible things you've probably seen. But no one will come past th' bees." She gestured toward the window. Shael looked out at a leafy glade set about with white-painted beehives. And the air was alive with their humming.

CHAPTER 6

The three marauders had thought that dawn would be a good time for their raid. The spider-web-thin trip lines had tipped the skep over, virtually on top of them. Shael and Mamma Mae were already up, getting the fire ready to melt the beeswax for the candle molds. It was a task they wanted done before the day grew too hot, and made it unpleasant in the kitchen. The sound of screaming came in through the open window. They ran to bolt and latch the doors and windows. Whoever the bees were after might otherwise run for the house, bringing the angry swarm with them. It was nearly an hour later that the bee master came back to the house, carrying the unconscious man. Baer's normally placid face was grim. He sighed as he put the man down on the settle. "One of t'others with him is dead in the pond. Drowned himself trying to keep down. The other one run off wi' half a hive behind him. I don't like th' look of this, lasses. Them were armed for trouble, but they don't have the ragamuffin look o' hill bandits or deserters. Look you. This one's wearin' a fine golden

ring." For him, it was a mighty long speech. In the
last nine months Shael had seldom heard him use
more than three words in his rare sentences.

Shael was already busy loosening the man's collar.
She looked at the ring on the hand the bee master
was holding up. The fingers were already so swollen
that the gold edges cut deep into the white flesh.
They were not a working man's hands. Too soft and
too white, with the nails clean and exquisitely manicured. It was enough to make her look twice at the
ring with its small engraved claw clutching at a tiny
solitaire diamond. She felt the blood drain from her
face as she stood up, looking carefully at the features
obscured by the black sting points and the beginning
of swelling.

The cry that was torn from her was not just fear:
it was also loaded with misery. "They've found me!"
The beekeeper and his wife stared at her in astonish-
ment. It wasn't what she said. It was just that after
nearly nine months of silence they no longer expected
her to speak.

In the beginning it seemed the easiest way to avoid
talking of her origins until she left. After a week Shael
had decided that if it meant keeping quiet for the
rest of her life she would do it. She had by luck, and
poison ivy, stumbled on a nest of security and happiness she never wanted to leave. The beekeeper and
his wife were simple folk. People who, a month
before, she would have dismissed as nonentities,
whose way of life would have bored her to the
screaming point in minutes. It had taken dispesses-
sion and terror to give her the parents she'd never
had. She felt the tears start behind her eyelids, and
instinctively turned to the reaching arms of Mamma
Mae.

In the early days Shael had stood rigid, both shocked
and aloof, when Mamma Mae hugged her. Why was
this little dumpling woman holding and squeezing her?

After a while she had become accustomed to it, understanding it to be an overflowing of love from someone who, while she had a million cheery words for everything else, had no words for this.

Shael stepped back and looked at the two of them, her eyes wet. She bit her lip. "I will have to go."

She held up her hands, cutting off their protests. "Mamma Mae, Father Baer, I . . . I'm sorry. I didn't know how to tell you. You see . . . that man is Captain Saril Jaine, once of the Tyn secret police. He is . . . *Emperor* Deshin's . . . um . . . closest friend. He . . . could only be looking for me."

She bit her lip again. She knew how their daughter had died, how deep Mae's hatred ran for what Shael's father had done. The Tyrant had spotted Merthly in the local marketplace as his troops moved through, and sent his men to fetch her. There'd not been much a mere beekeeper's wife had been able to do to stop them. Merthly'd been his leman for a while. Then . . . she'd gotten pregnant. She'd let her mother know. Shael had seen the letter with its schoolgirl characters.

They had never heard from her again. But they had heard how she'd died. She'd been strangled, on the Tyrant's orders, when he had discovered she was pregnant. He wanted no byblows born to be used against him. As Princess, Shael had known that it had happened, not once, but often. She'd seen the progression of women through her father's rooms. It had never occurred to her that these were real people, leaving grieving families scattered in the wake of her father's appetites. This was why Shael had kept her silence for those months. Now she would have to tell them they'd sheltered the daughter of their greatest enemy.

"I don't care who you are. I don't care why they want you. If they try to take my second daughter from us, I'll stop them. They'll have to kill me first. You're our girl an' you're staying." The beekeeper was not a voluble man. His wife normally did most of the talking. But grim determination shone from his big honest face. His wife, now suddenly silent, just nodded.

Shael ran to him, and hugged him, something she had never done before. His grimness melted like wax, and he smiled and tousled her hair. It was something of a shock to Shael. No one had *ever* done something like that to her before. A royal tantrum and a flogging for the offender would have followed. It broke the warm illusion, and made her aware of what different worlds they had lived in. She looked up at the big smiling face and realized for the first time in her life, that she could not just put her own concerns first. She had to run from this refuge. Not just to save herself, but for their sake.

She broke away from the enfolding arms. "No. I . . . if I don't go, they won't stop coming. Deshin will just send more men." She sighed. "He's not stupid. He'll send the royal beekeeper. If I stay . . . they'll kill us all. You see I . . . I'm, my name is not Kim, it is really . . ."

"Princess Shael."

She gaped at him. "How . . ."

Mae smiled ruefully at her. "Merthly described you in a letter, lass. Especially the green eyes and all the bangles. We didn't know how to tell you we knew, so we just let it pass. We didn't want to lose you, love."

"But, my father . . . he killed your daughter!" Shael's world was painted with hatreds and vendettas. Sometimes there were compromises of state, but the hatred remained. Shael was not prepared for forgiveness.

"You didn't do it, lass. Your father's sins aren't yours. And by what Merthly said, he treated you like no father should."

Shael's cheeks burned. "I'm sure she also said I was horrible. I always was to his mistresses."

Mae chuckled. "Oh, aye. She also said you was so spoiled you couldn't even dress yourself. She was sorry for you, poor thing." The smile ran away from her face. "She said she'd never let her children be brought up like that. Now, let's be scraping the stings out of this fellow."

"What are you going to do with him?"

"Look after him, and then let him go. We'll hide you, lass, and tell him you ran off," said Baer decisively.

Shael nodded and set to work.

The note on the empty bed was tear-splashed.

"Dear Papa Baer and Mamma Mae,
    Please forgive me. I have to go. Please don't try to follow me. I will come back someday if I can. I wish that you really had been my mother and father. Merthly was right. If I ever have any, I won't let my children be brought up like that either."

It was signed "Love, Kim" the name she had written as her own when they asked her what they should call her. She had taken nothing but the little that she had come with.

"Too slow. I'm too old." The lined face was twisted in pain. The old man clutched at his leg. "Keil, boy," he panted. "Bring me the little bottle from my dilly bag, son."

Keilin didn't wait. He ran as if his heels were on fire. He'd seen the puff adder that had bitten Marou. In the fashion of that particular breed of snake it hadn't slithered off when they came close, but simply gone on lying on the narrow path. The old man had been leading the way, and hadn't even seen it. He'd felt it, but had not been quite quick enough to pull away from the fangs.

By the time Keilin got back, Marou had dragged

himself into the shade of a rocky ledge. The leg was already ballooning, and the old man's face was gray-shaded and beaded with a heavy sweat.

Marou reached for the bottle, unstoppered it with shaky hands. Drank. Shuddered. After a few moments the narcotic began to take effect. He spoke slightly easier, but his voice was high and quavery. "Keil, boy. You been like the son I never had. You know Broken-Chimney Rock?" Keilin nodded. "My stash . . . it's in th' cave with the head-sized piece o' quartz next to the entrance. There's a shelf near the back, high up, goes back a long way. 'Nuff good stuff there t' buy a fair-to-middlin' town. It's all yours, boy."

Keilin found his throat closing up, too tight to speak. He shook his head furiously.

"You see, Keil, I struck it rich maybe twenty-five year ago. Went to live in town. I lasted two whole weeks. Th' town was sick o' me and I was mighty sick of it. So . . . I come back out here. It's bin a good life, but I was gettin' a mite lonely. We had a good year an' a bit, boy. I ain't gonna live through this one. I'm too old. I just wanted to tell you, son, afore I finish the rest of the bottle an' go out peacefullike."

Fear and desperate grief clawed at Keilin. The rapid cooling of the pendant stone went unnoticed. "No! You can't!" It was a cry of utter desolation. With it he felt the jewel like an icy snake biting into his chest . . . and willed. For the first time in his life he used the stone with conscious direction. An entire apothecary's shop, including the apothecary and a furtive looking customer, was translocated abruptly from Port Tinarana into the high desert valley.

The drug had stilled Marou's pain to some extent. It hadn't clouded his sharp old mind. As Keilin ran into the shop, which the shocked owner and his customer were attempting to leave, the old man readied his spear. As Keilin was threatening to push his knife through the terrified-looking apothecary's liver if he didn't immediately provide a treatment for puff-adder bite, there came a sonic boom. The platecraft dropped in on the exact position Keilin had been standing a few seconds before. The deadly black spear was thrown even before the craft had come to a complete halt, toppling one of its two riders. The second fired a deadly purple energy blast at where the old man had been. He was injured and drugged, which is why the bolt actually hit Marou's side, instead of missing completely.

Keilin had spent the last eighteen months being taught to act decisively. He seized the first bottle that came to hand, and flung it through the diamond-shaped window panes at the hooded Morkth gunner.

The furtive customer had been a fence, and the apothecary had been in the very act of assaying some stolen property for him. Gold. With hydrochloric acid. It had been a near-full flask of this that Keilin had snatched up. The flask struck the wind cowl of the platecraft and shattered in a burning rain across the jewelled eyes of the Morkth.

The Morkth do not scream, but a terrible keening and a series of rapid high-pitched clicks accompanied the creature's wild firing. Both the fence and the apothecary attempted to run. It was a mistake. Some of the eye facets were undamaged, and while the Morkth was nearly insane with pain, it still reacted instinctively. The movement was seen, and drew fire. Keilin stood, looking for a weapon. His own black spear lay where he had dropped it, a few yards from Marou. It might as well have been on the moon.

But . . . he could read. And the apothecary's supplies were most punctiliously and clearly labelled. Moving slowly he took the large one labelled ALCOHOL, unstoppered it, and tossed it in a lazy arc through the broken window. It showered over the creature that had staggered away from the platecraft, and was advancing on the building in a mad dance. Keilin followed the

alcohol with the still burning oil-light from the counter.
He did not pause to watch the incandescent chittering
thing that ran off into the desert. He sprinted to the
old man's side. It was plain that he was too late.

Marou's eyes, wide and staring, looked into some
distant place. Beyond speaking, he weakly squeezed
Keilin's hand, and then . . . he was gone. For a long
time the boy just sat there, until the silence was
recaptured by the small sounds of the desert.

At last the boy stood up, gently taking the old hand
and laying it back on the old man's bony chest. He
looked across at the Morkth body still impaled on the
long black spear. "That's what you are all going to be!
I'm going to kill *all* of you. Do you hear me?" His voice
rose to a scream. The transmitter line to Beta-Morkth
HQ was still open. So, indeed, they did hear him. But
they did not believe him. And it was not in the Morkth
warrior's genetic design to know fear anyway.

It was evening, and Keilin leaned on his spear, and
watched as the fire consumed the last of Marou
Skyann. He had dressed the old man in his best fringed
leather shirt, with his broad snakeskin turquoise-studded belt. Marou's black spear Keilin had wrenched
from the Morkth corpse, and laid across the gnarled
hands. Then he had placed the body out on a bier
of dead mountain cedar, which had been carried here
into the desert by the floods. It had been doused with
the apothecary's entire store of flammable oils.

The fire might call other desert prowlers, but Keilin
was beyond caring. He would welcome the opportunity
to kill anyone or anything now. When the flames
finally died he turned his back on the place, picked
up his pack and walked off into the night. He was
going nowhere in particular, just away from here. Pure
chance took his feet upvalley, heading toward the
higher mountains that he'd been aiming towards some
eighteen months before. Unable to focus on any
course of action but that of killing the Morkth, anger

and bitterness gnawed at him. He'd tried focusing his hatred on the pendant stone, to no effect. Only fear or sexual stimulus appeared to make the thing respond. Neither were things he could muster right now.

Eventually he stopped and slept. But not before he had had two startling thoughts: Firstly, he had not heard the high-pitched whine which had always given him warning before. It always appeared that others did not hear the sound. Had he changed in some way? Secondly, he wondered now whether the Morkth were hunting him . . . or the pendant stone. He decided it could be the latter, and smiled grimly to himself. It would make good bait.

For three days he trailed upward into the mountains. Here, where it was colder and the air was crisp, there was even a small trickle of water down on the valley floor. Around it there grew a profusion of plants, but the slopes were still almost barren. He hoped he'd chosen the right valley. Marou had described the route to him, but they'd never come this far from the desert the old man had loved.

Pantherlike, he stalked on upward along the valley lip, keeping just below the skyline. You could see best from here without being too visible yourself. A movement in the valley snagged his eye. It was a party of men.

In eighteen months, other than Marou, the apothecary and his customer, Keilin had only seen one other human, a distant and equally cautious fossicker. The fools in the valley were neither careful nor nervous. Keilin stood motionless awhile. Then he began to follow the hunters. That night, while the fellows slept beside an unhidden fire, Keilin sneaked up and looted half their kill and three of their best pelts. It was a dual exercise, the first half of which was undertaken almost as a public service: it would teach the hunters care. Had this been Marou's territory the old man would have cut every second throat. Secondly, and more importantly, it was also to prove to himself that he could now do what eighteen months before he had been unable to.

When the bellows of outrage and counteraccusations had died away from the camp in the valley below, a revenge party sallied out questing for any signs of the raider. From his nest under the slabs on the ridgeline, Keilin watched without much alarm. When they could find no signs of him, fear began to grow in them. Within the hour they had packed up and were tailing off upvalley. The desert rat followed.

Three days later he was extremely glad he had. They had led him through the pass he'd been seeking. On either side towered white-capped mountains, many thousands of feet higher still. To have crossed those would have been far more difficult. Marou's directions had been vague . . . and had also failed to tell him a great deal.

The western side of the mountains was the wet side. Here mist and rain were as commonplace as the searing heat of the east. The pine forests and heather slopes were a new and alien landscape to Keilin. Much of his hard-garnered desert lore meant nothing here. There weren't even any decent scorpions under the rocks. Just wet white wiggly things. A man couldn't live on trash like that.

Now he sat in the shadow of the pine trees and looked down on the straggling houses below. Part of him longed for the people, the lights and the voices. Part of him curled inwards, away from it, clinging to the security of loneliness. Eventually he steeled himself. He would go down and enquire where the Morkth lands were. After all, he had to start somewhere.

To a child of Port Tinarana the air of Steyir village would have been clear and sweet. To the desert-primed Keilin it was fetid to the point of making him gag. He walked down the dirt track between the ragged-thatched shanties. Fowls scratched in the street, and a mottled pig rooted in a pile of scraps between the houses. The air was full of boiling cabbage and elementary sanitation. According to Marou, at the end of the street was the Margery Tavern, where a few turquoise buyers always hung out. Keilin had decided they would be the best possible sources of information. He and Marou had uncovered a small pipe, with rather inferior nodules a month or so back. The best pieces had gone into the belt Keilin wore, made from the skin of the first snake he and Marou had eaten together, but Keilin still had a few bits of turquoise to trade with. He'd been nowhere near Marou's hoard. Still, what he had should give him some small money, easier and safer to spend than the gold pieces in his ankle pouch, and it would give him an excuse to talk.

The tavern smelled of beer, urine, and also, vaguely, of decay. Keilin entered with caution. There was a small crowd of men getting noisily drunk in the one corner, and a morose-looking individual sitting at the bar. As Keilin came in, the solitary fellow looked up. He brightened visibly at seeing the dry-land-honed youth in desert garb.

"Buy you a drink, youngster?" he asked, as Keilin looked carefully around the dingy room. "How's the diggin's been?"

He took in Keilin's measuring look, "It's all right, digger. You can trust Honest Clarence." He pushed a barstool out. "Sit. Let's see what you've got."

A shadow of a smile flitted across Keilin's face. He'd heard stories about all of the buyers. Honest Clarence . . . the name itself was a joke among the desert prospectors. "My partner mentioned you. He said you weren't to be trusted."

"Naw, couldn't be me. He must be muddlin' me with Square-Deal Tom, or maybe ol' Jep Deep-Pockets," said Honest Clarence, with an attempt at self-righteousness. "Who is your partner anyhow?"

"Marou Skyann."

A look of profound respect came over Clarence's face. "You don't say! Ol' Marou's mind must be wandering. How could he have said somethin' like that about me? Where is the ol' bugger then? Already gone into Lucy's to screw himself silly? Randy ol' sod never had a bath in his life. Lucy's girls mus' be workin' with clothespegs on their noses."

His statements made Keilin suddenly aware that he hadn't actually washed for the better part of a year himself. "Marou's dead," he said shortly. "Puff adder got him."

"Naw! The grand old man of the desert himself, took out by a puffy? I'd have thought the snake'd die of food poisoning first." He chuckled. "If he hadn't been to town. Then the poor beast would've had alcohol poisoning too." He shook his grizzled head. "Hard to believe, boy. Ol' Marou has been coming in every couple of years or so since my father's time. I reckoned he'd still be around for my son, that's Honest Clarence the third, to take to the cleaners."

He sighed. "Beer, digger? Or are you in too much of a hurry to get along to Lucy's place? Want to sell your stones quick, and go and give good money to bad women?"

Keilin felt himself blushing. To hide his confusion he took the few stones out of his pouch and laid them on the bar. Soon they were wrangling. Keilin was sure he got less than the stones were worth, but he also got more than he'd expected. Clarence handed him a handful of silver and copper. "Not the best stones, not Ol' Marou's usual quality at all, but the price is up with the Morkth invasions around Shapstone City cutting off the western fields."

One of the bunch from the far corner staggered past, on his way to part with the beer he'd briefly rented. He bumped into Keilin as the boy stood up. His blurry eyes focused on the desert garb and then on the turquoise-studded belt. "You're one o' them

fucking miners from across the mountains!" He turned
to his mates. "Hey, boys. One of them thieving pricks
is here."

Honest Clarence spoke. His voice was free of the
lazy digger's drawl he'd affected when dealing with
Keilin. "Leave him alone, Tomas. The turquoise
miners are dangerous men, out of your league."

When Keilin had gone into the desert he'd been
a boy. When he came out it never occurred to him
that he was not a man. So he was unprepared for the
next statement. "Maybe so, *Mister* Clarence, but I ain't
'fraid of no fucking kid."

Keilin stepped back, feeling the reassuring smoothness of his spear shaft in his hand. "I don't want
trouble," he said, looking up at the big man who was
drunkenly rocking on the balls of his feet.

If the hunter had been sober, the tone would have
been warning enough for him. But the fool was very
drunk, and only heard the words. "Well you've found
it anyway, you little turd." His friends came staggering
across from their corner, and their breath was hot
behind him, driving him to prove himself. He half-
turned to his drinking companions and said extrava-
gantly, "What do think, boys? I reckon those stones
ona' li'l lizard fucker's belt will make up for the rou-
deer pelts that some shit stole from us other side o'
the pass?"

Clarence snorted. "You stupid buggers. I told you
before you went that most of the diggers'll kill you
if they even see you on their land. If someone only
stole your pelts, likely the thief was one of your own
mates."

"Me mates? Never!" said the hunter. "Prob'ly this
little fucker. So . . . I'll just have that belt . . ." He
reached forward, to find something very sharp pressing into his ribs.

"On the other side of the pass," said Keilin conversationally, "we dig up shriba grubs. Fat, ugly things,

like you. Then we squash them very carefully, 'cause
if you get the juice in a cut, you're going to die. Then
we rub our spear blades in it. Touch the belt my
partner gave me again, and I'll push this spear in so
deep, it won't matter that it's poisoned."

Two of his friends grabbed him and pulled the
wide-eyed hunter away.

"I think," said Honest Clarence, his voice cracking slightly, "that we'd better be going, before that
bunch get any drunker and stupider." As they left,
a voice echoed after them.

"Run, you little desert turd. Run back to the desert.
I'm going to foller you and cut your fucking throat."

"Phew," said Clarence. "You handled yourself well,
youngster. What did you say your name was?"

"I didn't. It's Keilin . . . Skyann."

The jewel buyer looked at him with some surprise.
"Proper chip off the old block you are. Well, young
Skyann, have a good night with Lucy's girls. Tomas'll
pass out in a few minutes, and it'll be at least ten
tomorrow before he even thinks about hunting you
again. I suppose, like the ol' fellow, you'll leave all
the trouble you've made behind you, and be back over
the pass by then. Come an' see me when you're next
in town. Even if you're a damn sight too sharp a
trader, it's been good doing business with you."

"Actually, I'm going west. How far is Shapstone?"

"Matter of four hundred miles or so. But there's
nothing but Morkth there now," Clarence said, his
surprise showing.

"Good." Keilin's face was far grimmer than it had
been when dealing with the hunter.

It was only after the jewel buyer had turned aside
to his own home that Keilin allowed his control to
slip. He felt himself start to shake.

CHAPTER 7

Trees. And bloody rain. Trees to get in your way, and rain to wet you. This was how Keilin would have described the western side of the mountains now. It never occurred to him that this place looked very like the pictures he had once daydreamed over. On the other hand, the homesteads and travellers along the road would have described his thieving passage as a plague. The truth to tell, the boy-man was getting cocky. The Westerners were mud-soft. And there was no Marou to cut him down to size.

He'd spotted the hidden fire quite easily. Yes, whoever it was had bothered to hide deep in the woods, and had built it in a hollow where the light could not be seen, but they'd used pine. He could smell it a mile off. He moved closer, slipping silently from tree to tree. Perhaps a wary target would be more of a challenge.

The sleeper wrapped in the tatty blanket did not stir as Keilin went through the meager possessions in the bag. What?! There was no food. Not a damn crumb. But wait . . . what was this lot? His expert

fingers read the shape and nature of the bangles.
Gold! He was about to relieve the traveller of a few
on principle when his fingers encountered another
thing. A familiar oily coldness. It was so unexpected
that he gave a small gasp. He looked across at the
sleeper whose face was now clearly visible in the
moonlight, to see if he reacted. And saw his victim
was female, young, and by the looks of it, starving.
Also, if the disturbance in the dirt on her face was
anything to judge by, she'd gone to sleep crying.

It pulled at a cord in Keilin's innermost being. He
remembered his own flight and desperation. If she
too had one of the stones, perhaps she was as much
a victim as he was. Also . . . he had a not insubstantial interest in girls. His brain suggested leaving her
and her troubles strictly alone, but his glands called
for a more chivalrous gesture. As Keilin was a physically normal young male, his glands won without any
effort.

He had a generous amount of the country's finest provender, liberated from a wide selection of now
irate citizens, stashed relatively nearby in his kit. Ten
minutes later he was back, building up the fire and
frying some succulent slices of a stolen side of bacon
in a stolen pan.

Her awakening was amusing. Her nose literally
twitched as the food smell plucked at it. A small
tongue licked out catlike across her lips. Its effect on
Keilin's glands was nearly tectonic. However, her
reaction on seeing him failed to live up to Keilin's
romantic expectations.

She sat up, bleary eyed, took one look at him,
scrambled to her feet, and ran. He sat stunned for
a moment before taking off after her. "Oi! Come back!
I won't hurt you!"

He'd run in the hunt after desert gazelle. She'd
had the rapid pursuit of a waddling bee wife for the
last nine months. It was not much of a chase. She

stood, panting, her back to the rough bark of the tree she'd been trying to climb, broken dagger in front of her. "Come . . . one . . . step nearer, I'll . . . kill you." Her eyes were wild enough to suggest she really meant it.

Keilin was thoroughly irritated by the shattering of his illusions. He'd thought she'd be pleased to see someone, especially with dinner. But the fear in her voice drew sympathy from him too. "The bacon's burning, you daft little girl. Stop being so stupid. I just saw you didn't have any food, so I was cooking some for you. I'm going back to see if I can save that bacon." He turned and walked back. Behind him resentment vied with fear and hunger. One should not call a princess, or possibly anyone, a "daft little girl" on first meeting. It never gets a relationship off to a good start.

The bacon was thoroughly burned. He turned it out, scraped the pan a bit, and sliced some fresh pieces. He was aware that he was being watched. When the rashers were beginning to curl, he tossed in a couple of duck eggs that a farmer he'd robbed a day back was still cursing about.

Without lifting his eyes from the pan, he asked, "Got a plate? I usually eat out of the pan myself, so I can't offer you one."

"Why don't you go away, you horrible boy?" came the fierce voice from the trees.

"I'm going, once I've had supper. You can come and eat, or you can sit up a tree."

"Go away. I've got my own food." The words sounded weak against the smell of the frying bacon.

"No, you haven't. I went through your kit while you were sleeping. You can't eat gold bracelets, you know."

"You've stolen my things, and now you're just trying to lure me out with food. You want to rape me." The voice was suspicious, accusing.

Keilin's mind turned back to an alley and Guard-Captain Kemp. His reply was gentler. "If I'd wanted to rob you, I'd have taken what I wanted and left. If I'd wanted to rape you, I'd have put a knife against your throat while you were asleep, not cooked you supper first. Besides, I've got enough money to buy any girls I want," he said with some pride.

Shael's quick mind assimilated all of this. He could have robbed her. He could have killed her. He could have raped her, too. . . . To her now awake and hungry self it made little sense, but he obviously wasn't planning to do her any harm, even if he was appallingly rude and terribly underbred. "I'm coming down. Try anything and I'll kill you."

He laughed. "Yeah! You and what army?" His experience in the field of diplomacy was not legion. He skillfully speared a piece of bacon on the point of his knife, and dropped it into his mouth. He continued to talk with mouth full. "Come and eat. No sense in letting it get cold." He'd gone from thinking her an object for his gallantry to an object for his pity. It showed in his tone. Shael might be hungry enough to accept his charity, but she did not have to like it. She advanced hungrily on the frying pan with an expression on her face that would have made older and wiser men wary. Keilin, however, knew little about people, and even less about girls. He didn't even notice, which did *not* improve matters. He just shoved the pan towards her while he chewed with his mouth open.

She was smaller than he'd first thought. Under the scowl and the dirt layer it was quite a pretty face. Some sense of gallantry began to return to Keilin, as he watched her gobble, daintiness and the manners of a princess forgotten in a sudden desperate hunger. "Here . . . don't eat so fast. Your stomach's not used to food. You'll cast it all up again."

The books Keilin had devoured in the library had

led him to dream of caring and nurturing a delicate damsel, who would fall into his arms with gratitude afterwards. His experiences with his mother after she'd been on a three-day dream-dust binge stood him in better stead with the reality that followed. When Shael had stumbled up and rushed towards the bushes, he'd followed, held her head and rubbed her back. When she'd finished he handed her a leather water skin. She eyed it suspiciously. Keilin could see her hands were shaking on the flask neck. "Just water. Rinse your mouth out."

When she'd done that, he led her back to the fire, and put her blanket over her thin, shivering shoulders. He put more wood on the fire, took a small pot from his kit, and began shaving dried meat into it. He added water and set it in the flames. "How long," he asked conversationally, "since you last ate?"

The damsel in distress was showing scant signs of appreciation. In fact the hostile, shaky voice suggested that she planned to blame the whole of the indignity and discomfort on him. "I don't see what it has got do with *you*." Then she apparently thought better of it. "I've had a few berries and purslane leaves. Nothing else for . . . quite a long time."

He nodded. "I thought so. Marou an' me had a few thin times too. He taught me that you've got to start eating again slowly. Soup is best." He pulled the pot from the center of the flames with a stick, and let it stand in the embers on the edge, so just a fuzz of little bubbles buzzed up steadily from the hot metal. He went to his pack again, and emerged with a battered mug, and a hunk of bread.

A few balancing tricks with a hot pot filled the mug, which he handed her. "Drink it. Slowly. The bread's a bit old, so dunk it in the soup. And don't be stupid enough to wolf it again. I'm not making you more food to upchuck in the bushes." The knight in shining armor was supremely unaware that every time his kindness raised him a step in the princess's estimation, his tongue took him two steps back.

The warm soup and the small pieces of bread curdled uneasily in her stomach. For the moment at least, it seemed they weren't going to come back up. With food, her mind began to function along its normal paths. This boy . . . he could be used. She'd been avoiding human settlement so as to leave no trace of her passage. At first it had just been wise, but fear had prevented her from going to buy food. But this boy, well, *he* could buy her food, and provide some protection too. He was young and not very big . . . not so good for defending her, but also small enough for her to fend off easily. She gave him one of her devastating smiles.

He looked at her across the fire and sighed. "I wish you were my sister." He came from a place and level of society in which incest was unpleasantly normal.

She was stunned. "I'm no relation of yours, you lowborn common boy!"

He shrugged. "Didn't say you were." He lapsed into silence, looking out at the darkness over her shoulder.

At length, having thought the statement over, and reconsidered it in the light of her time with the bee-keepers, she decided that it was perhaps not an insult at all; she had the courage to ask why he wished that she were his sister. His reply did him no good at all.

"I dunno, I always thought if I had a sister then I would have been able to join one of the gangs."

"Why did you have to have a sister to join a gang?"

" 'Cause they didn't let you in if they didn't get one."

There was a dangerous silence. "What did your gang want with the girls?"

He failed to read the signals, concentrating on something else in the darkness. "For the gang bosses to screw, of course, and to rent out."

"You are a despicable, revolting disgusting toad, and you stink!"

He looked at her puzzledly. "Why are you so mad?"

"Do you think, you filthy commoner, that I'd be a . . . a prostitute? I'm a princess, you . . . pig!"

He looked the thin, ragged girl up and down. "Yeah. And I'm the Captain of the Cru. Grab your kit. There's somebody out there and we'd better scram. Move!"

Once again the little princess was silenced. She would cheerfully have refused to go, or have gone elsewhere, but she was too scared of what could be out there in the dark. They left the fire, took up their bags and moved off into the night. Keilin led them unerringly to a trail between the straggling brambles, and up to an area of broken rock slabs. "Slip in here," he whispered, pointing to a rock-edged crack. "I'll leave my gear and go back and see what they're up to."

He'd left his pack . . . so he was planning to come back. Time passed. She had felt safe hidden here among the rocks, but the stillness of the night slowly consumed her confidence. Her stomach hurt. She wasn't sure if it was the soup and bread, or fear. He must have been caught . . . of course he'd lead them to her. He was prepared to sell his own sister, after all. Even though her ears were desperately reaching for sounds, she didn't hear him return.

"Phew, girl, you've got some mean folk looking for you. Pity they couldn't find their own bums in the woods in the dark. I've led them on a merry chase. They're feeling right sorry for themselves now. Next time you steal things make sure you take it from folk who aren't going to try so hard to find you."

She was too relieved at his return to react to his presumption that she was a thief, hunted by those she'd stolen from. "What . . . what did you do?"

He chuckled "They thought they'd sneaked up on your fire. They were a little disappointed to find you weren't there any more. They were about to settle down for the night and track you in the morning, when I threw a stone into the fire, and led them off past our hiding place to that swamp down there. They're muddy and miserable and lost by now."

"I must run. W-which way did they go?" There was an edge of panic in her voice, as she started fumbling for her bag.

"Relax. Only one of them was any kind of woodsman. And he'll be too sick to track anyone for a couple of weeks. I put a little arrow in him, with a dab of shargy on it. The others are city men, and they're not going to find their way out of there for hours. And I stole their gear, and dropped it into one of the pools. They'll sleep cold and wet tonight."

"Where on earth did you get shriba beetle larvae?" she asked, delving into her knowledge of toxins.

"On the other side of the pass. My partner showed me. Move up. It's bloody well starting to rain again."

For the first time in two weeks Shael slept well. Keilin struggled, however. The warm body next to him was having a bad effect on his imagination. It was at least an hour later, when the soft rain had turned to a steady blatter that he suddenly thought, How come she knew just what shargy was? He filed the point away in his memory, meaning to ask her about it in the morning.

The morning, however, brought such an argument about what direction they would take, that he forgot about it. Eventually Keilin prevailed . . . but he had a sneaking feeling that he hadn't won at all. The feeling grew with each passing hour. She was manipulating him, dammit. To the extent that he even began to suspect that he was making a prat of himself.

This boy was nothing but a pain. He didn't do what he was supposed to do. He should have been falling over himself by now to do exactly what she wanted. Instead, every time he opened his mouth he

had something rude or disparaging to say. She'd lost
her temper a couple of times already . . . and then
had to work hard on damage control. She had been
keen on ensuring her safety, encouraging circumspect
behavior. The harder she tried to get him to do so,
the more crazy chances he seemed to want to take.
Last night he'd raided a campfire, stolen the food off
it while the travellers had been beating the bushes
for him. And this morning, when she'd been looking at herself in a pool of water, he'd told her she
was as vain as a two-silver whore. She noticed, however, that he *had* washed himself . . . and the water
in the mountains was bone-chilling cold.

Here he was, going away from Shapstone City, with
a girl who alternated between turning his insides all
stupid with her smiles, and irritating the hell out of
him by making a complete idiot of herself. And every
time he'd made up his mind he'd just had enough
of it, she made him feel desperately sorry for her.
Which was why he was going south and not northwest. She wanted to go to Polstra, the mountain city.
Very well, he would take her there, and then dump
her. But first she was actually going to notice how
good he was. Heroes, after all, had no trouble with
girls . . . at least not in any of the books he'd enjoyed.
Tonight's raid would be spectacular.

If Keilin had been less set on a grandstand performance he might have smelled a rat. Their horses were
too conveniently downwind, the four travellers were
too obviously asleep too early. Their saddlebags hung
too much in plain sight. But tonight he was going to
count coup. He'd brought Shael to a point she considered far too close, in order that she might watch.

Thus she was in a perfect position to observe how
it all went very wrong. The four of them appeared
to be asleep, as Keilin moved into the camp like a
lazy shadow. He pointedly ignored the tempting

saddlebags and moved toward the sleepers. What he was planning to take from underneath the pillow Shael never found out. Keilin let out a startled yowl as a ham-sized hairy fist closed around his arm. A second hand reached out for Keilin's spear.

And missed. If the muscular, shaven-headed one had not neatly twisted the spear out of Keilin's hand someone would have died. As it was, the other huge hairy hand caught his arm before he could reach for a knife. The woman threw a waiting handful of twigs onto the fire, which flamed up. The tall one sat up and looked impassively at the struggling boy, taking in his features, his cold eyes narrowing.

"I think . . . we have caught more than a core section here. I think we may have a psionic too . . . well, well!"

He walked over to Keilin, who was being held easily at the end of an unnaturally long arm's length by Beywulf. "Where is it, boy?" Keilin said nothing, just writhed more energetically. He could feel the jewel chilling against his flesh. "S'kith. Hold his legs. Leyla. Search him." The shaven-headed one too was immensely strong. Keilin kicked out viciously but in seconds he was effectively immobilized. The woman began methodically searching his pockets.

"Notice," said Beywulf cheerfully, "how she starts on the trouser pockets. She'll search your ball bag next, boy."

However, her hands ran up his body, finding the pendant chain and pulling out the jewel. The captain reached out and touched it. It was biting cold. "Well, sod me!"

He looked closely at Keilin. It was not an overly friendly stare. "Evie Lee's hair. Evie Lee's eyes. And the nose . . . I don't need gene typing to guess at your ancestry, boy."

With a quick jerk he snapped the pendant chain. A terrible feeling of abandonment washed over Keilin

for a moment . . . and then more bitter cold sliced
up from the ankle pouch. Keilin forced himself to be
calm. He'd get away . . . he'd kill the man who'd dared
to take it from him. Then a fresh wave of worry
washed over him. What if Kim, hiding just back there
in the trees touched the stone in her bracelet? Would
the Morkth still come?

Keilin was unprepared for the open-handed blow
that rocked his head back. His head reeled and swam.
The tall man's words, uttered through gritted teeth
made little sense. "Something I owed your great-
grandmother. Pity I can't give it to her in person."
Then he appeared to regain control of himself.
"Where is the other one who was with you earlier,
boy? Talk, before I use it as a good excuse to beat
the living shit out of you."

Back in her tree perch Shael watched with horror. She heard the question, and wished she'd thought
to run away as soon as things started to go wrong. . . .
But she'd frozen, and now he would betray her.

"I'm alone." His voice didn't even quaver.

The tall man hit him again, with calculated force.
"Don't *ever* lie to me again, boy. Beywulf here can
track a breeze. He's been following your little ban-
ditry tour for three days now. Talk or get hurt."

"He . . . argued with me. We split up a few hours
ago. He went north." Shael closed her eyes before
the next blow.

"Obstinate little git. Still, I suppose it's in the genes.
Tie him up and finish searching him, S'kith. Beywulf,
you and Leyla, go and find . . . her."

Beywulf put his nose to the ground, and followed
Keilin's back trail like a hound. It took him all of
thirty seconds to find her tree, and drag her out of
it, kicking and squalling.

Meanwhile S'kith's rough hands were searching
Keilin. Skillfully he removed the knife from the boy's
belt, and then the two hidden knives from Keilin's

back and sleeve. His hand moved down the boy's leg, and arrived at the ankle pouch. He touched it, and the remote expression briefly went out of his eyes. Casually the bald-headed man looked at the rest of his party, while apparently checking the soles of Keilin's boots. Their attention was held by Shael's antics. He moved to the other side of Keilin so his back was toward them. And put his finger to his lips. Then he went on searching as if he'd found nothing.

They were put down side-by-side in front of the fire. The one called Cap was looking at them down his long nose, the expression in his eagle eyes cold. "Two little pairs of green eyes." He produced Keilin's pendant from his pocket and touched it to Shael's cheek . . . and snatched it away. "Another flipping one. I search for near on twenty years to find one person the core sections respond to . . . and within a month of finding one, I find another two . . . together. Brother and sister?"

"Yes," said Keilin.

"No!" said Shael, vehemently.

His cold stare washed over them. Finally he spoke. "One of you is still lying to me."

Keilin had less experience at facial schooling. "You, boy? You don't learn, do you? Well, you will."

He turned away briefly, and stared into the darkness. Keilin wondered whether he should try to induce panic in himself, whether the contact between his leg and the signet ring in the ankle pouch was sufficient, and whether he and the girl would be able to survive the Morkth attack that would follow. He tested his bonds. There was no give in them at all.

The tall man turned back to face them again. "We were hunting this," he dangled the broken pendant in front of them. "This is the fourth one I've located. We've been tracking its movement down from the north for two weeks now." Keilin's heart gave a leap. They'd been following Kim. So, it *had* been another jewel on that bracelet. And their captors had made no effort to find their kit. They might be hunting the jewels, just like the Morkth, but they didn't realize that they had not found one, but three. They'd found *his*, but they'd been following *her*. He felt the girl tense up next to him. She'd worked it out too.

Cap continued. "We were going to question you and then kill you." The way it was said, with a chilling lack of any emotion, made it totally believable. "It appears that you're both core-sensitives." He held up the pendant again. "I'm willing to bet you've been manipulated by the backup Compcontrol system." He shrugged. "You may not have been aware of it, but we are working toward the same end. You'll pardon my initial reaction to you. I don't suppose you can help the fact that you are descended from the woman who betrayed the human race to the Morkth."

There was a stunned silence. Then Shael burst out. "That's rubbish. I know my ancestry. I am descended from Queen Lee herself!" Keilin cast his eyes heavenwards. Now she was going to sprout her princess story again. Stupid girl.

Cap nodded, his eyes narrowing. "Evie Lee. So called *Senior* Captain of the colony starship which was *Homo sapiens'* last hope. The treacherous self-centered little bitch who betrayed most of her crew to the Morkth, so she could play at being royalty and have a good time instead of doing her duty." He paused, and then added grimly, "You see, doing her duty would have meant she had to die, so that a hundred million people could live. She betrayed the last hope of our species for her own selfish ends.

"We were supposed to scatter the seeds of the human race on so many planets that the Morkth could never find and eliminate them all. Instead, more than three hundred years later we're all still on one damned colony planet which we share with mankind's worst enemy." His voice was full of a barely controlled fury.

Even Shael quailed before this onslaught, but she came up fighting. "That's simply not true. She only just escaped the command center with her life, when she blew up the transmitter core. Her sub-captain betrayed them. She was little more than a vagabond until she reached Arlinn, and the people recognized her as queen."

The tall man shrugged. "She could hardly tell the truth, could she? As for being a vagabond . . . well, let's rather say she was a promiscuous little tramp. She didn't much care where she got *or* where she dumped her offspring. You, boy, have the look of her command-center lover. The same Sub-Captain Fisher she blamed it on, poor sod. Anyway, what I'm hunting are sections of the supposedly blown-up transmitter core from the starship's control center. Fortunately, it was made to be virtually indestructible. The sections were just scattered across half the continent. This is one of them." He held up Keilin's pendant again. "If I can gather enough of them, then we can take them to the backup Compcontrol in the second landing command center, and reactivate the project."

Despite being tied up, and told that the plan had been to kill him, Keilin was fascinated. He'd seen pictures, and been hypnotized by several stories of starships, back in the library. "You mean . . . my jewel is part of a starship? If you had enough pieces you could fly away from our world to the stars?"

Cap sighed. "It's been a long three hundred years. The ordinary people haven't a clue about reality any more." He pointed upwards. "There is the starship *Morningstar.* Your 'moon.' It's a lot smaller than the moon that used to orbit the world we humans came from. Less than a seventeenth of the size, but still the biggest ship the human race ever made. It's far too big to ever land. And this isn't 'our world' either.

We humans came from Earth, fleeing the Morkth. The terraforming of this place had been started by robot drones nearly fifty years before we even left Sol. Fortunately, there was an atmosphere with oxygen, but no other life except a lot of primitive moss-like stuff before that. I came here with the shipload of construction crews and equipment a year before the *Morningstar* was ready. They built your cities or Evie would have dumped millions of people without any shelter onto an alien world."

"So how did people get down here, sir? I mean . . . that's high, there couldn't have been a ladder. Did they . . . um, have flying ships, or did they lower platforms with ropes or something?"

Cap snorted. "You don't even know what you're talking about, but you've put your finger on the basic problem. We had to get nearly one hundred million evacuees onto that ship, and off again. They had to choose between carrying people or enough fuel to ferry the people down. Trotting up and down into a gravity well is a fuel-expensive process, and the sort of loads we could carry on a shuttle would have meant a couple of lifetimes worth of trips.

"Your 'jewel' as you call it, was the answer. It is part of the matter-transmitter system. We could move passengers up from Earth, frozen, conditioned and ready to be good little settlers, zip-zap. We brought them down here the same way. Easy, although signal attenuation limits the use of the matter transmitter to a couple of thousand miles.

"The only trouble was that we needed a psionic to make the damn thing work. A transmitter system has miles of bloody electronic amplifiers, but triggering the whole thing still needs something else. This 'jewel' of yours. As well as some nanocircuitry, there is an unstable crystal lattice inside it. When you have perfect alignment in that lattice, right down to the atomic level . . . it works. That alignment is right, by

chance, about once in every fifteen thousand attempts.
Yet a stupid psi can make the thing work *every* time,
without even knowing how they're damned well doing
it! So, one decent psionic, and we had no need to
carry loads of fuel and landing craft. We could pack
in a lot more corpsicles instead. We just had a couple
of shuttles for the crew."

He sighed. "We lost those when the Morkth atmo-
spheric craft hit *Morningstar's* principal control center.
Now, the only way back up to the ship is to get the
matter transmitter working again. Even the Morkth
can't get there. The battleship that deployed their
landing craft got taken out kamikaze-style by our one
and only screening cruiser. Anyway, the defenses up
on *Morningstar* should be able to trash the sort of
piddly little ships the Morkth managed to drop. At
least, I hope that's what they think. I presume they
must, as they haven't tried a direct frontal assault on
her. They obviously don't know that the crew are very
dead, and that the ship is in shut-down mode, thanks
to one of Evie's last little tricks."

He ground his fist into his palm. The pendant
swayed wildly. "One live human up there would be
all it takes to get the ship up and running. One human
being . . . and we can't even do that."

Keilin remembered the burned-edged pages in
back of the old book, *Geophysical Survey of Planet
IV*, which his mother said their family had always
had . . . so that was what it had been about. It made
sense now. "Log of the Starship *Morningstar*"! But
the events Cap talked of were different from those
described . . . not totally different, just, well, not *quite*
the same.

Cap held up the pendant. "But if I can get all of
these . . . get into *Morningstar II*, the second control
center, with one psi, and we're away. There is a spare
crew up there, frozen. We can be off looking for a
wormhole nexus before you can say 'knife.' "

He looked at the bemused faces. "Hell! I might as well be talking Greek to you! Just take my word for it. That is a starship up there. It was once an asteroid called Juno. It had two detachable control centers, the size of small mountains themselves. Both of them were deployed, because a Morkth battleship managed to pick us up and follow us in the flight from Earth, despite the fact that Earth threw everything she could spare into that last 'diversionary' attack. Our weakest link was those control centers. Without them to handle planetside matter transmission, we couldn't discharge passengers. Captain Fisher decided it would be safer to have them both down on the planet. It was one of the few orders of his that Evie Lee didn't countermand, although she insisted that the second one, *Morningstar II*, stay in inactive mode."

He ground his teeth. "Computer's awake in there, but nothing else. The bitch had it all planned. She did a data dump at the last minute, programming the thing to exclude anything but her type. But I think I can get around that . . ."

Keilin looked up at the full moon. Half of what the man said was beyond him, but he knew what a spaceship was supposed to look like. There'd been several pictures on book covers. "That's really a spaceship? I thought, I mean in the pictures I saw they were all pointed and, um, shiny *metal*."

"Streamlining's pretty pointless for something that never enters an atmosphere. And a big asteroid had the plus of providing lots of raw material that we didn't have to lift out of the gravity well. Ceres was supposed to be next. I doubt if the engineers got there. You see, we never even got the seventeen years they'd predicted we'd have, before the Morkth invasion hit the solar system. So that is it, above us. Mankind's last hope. A forlorn hope. The good starship *Morningstar*."

Beywulf chuckled and turned to Leyla. "On board the good starship *Venus*
whose figurehead
was a nude in bed
sucking—"

There was no approval in Cap's voice as he interrupted. "That's enough, Beywulf. For all that it's bloody accurate, and that it was a common enough joke among the non-psi crew. The figurehead captain's name was your Evie Lee." The last word was said with overt hatred.

He shook himself, visibly clearing away the excess emotion. "So. I need to collect these transmitter-core sections, and one psionic of sufficient power, and the starship can move on from star to star. We can finally see that it carries out its original mission: to scatter the seeds of Earth far and wide, beyond the reach of Morkth xenophobia." He spoke with such conviction and power that Keilin wanted to be part of it. It was only the bonds that stopped him leaping to his feet and cheering. Being tied up poured cold water on his enthusiasm, allowing him to ask in a fairly steady voice, "What is a psionic, sir? Are you going to find one?"

A wintry smile touched one side of Cap's mouth. "You are one. So is the girl. So is S'kith. A psionic has the ability to do things by mental power alone, like read minds or move things without touching them. Such people are very rare. One in fifty million, perhaps. Which is why Evie Lee's little clique of nutters were able to insist that she was given overall command of the starship, in spite of her having the same capacity for command as I have for childbirth."

Keilin had a retentive mind for details and he was nothing if not stubborn. "Sir. I'm sorry, but you're wrong. I can't do anything just with my mind. If I could I wouldn't be here."

Cap looked at him keenly. "More guts than sense.

You keep arguing with me, boy. The core sections can only be activated by psionics. Did you notice the stone going cold . . . during sex for instance?"

Keilin blushed and very carefully didn't look at the girl next to him. "Er . . . yes."

"Typical of Evie Lee's descendants. She had a couch right there on top of the transmitter chamber. Did any little thing pop out of thin air when you did it?" Cap carefully ignored the guffaw from Beywulf and the snort from Leyla.

Keilin thought of the Patrician's treasury. Hardly a "little thing." Just the biggest flipping phallic symbol in the city. He nodded, hoping he would not be asked for details. To lead off the subject, he added. "The Morkth came just after that too. Every time."

"You're making the thing work . . . even without amplifiers, although you've no chance of getting sufficient range to get someone back up to the ship. The Beta-Morkth have instruments that sense the power flux. They're trying to collect the core sections too. You say this has happened more than once?"

Keilin nodded again. Cap looked at him with a little more respect. "So you and the core section survived a couple of attacks by Beta-Morkth warriors. Not bad, boy." There was grudging approval in his voice.

"I've lived through a couple of attacks myself. You've got a few moments. You've just got to run," said the Princess cooly.

Keilin twisted to look at her, in time to see her going very red in the firelight. "It . . . it had nothing to do with sex! I was scared and it happened."

"Shane Tomo."

She looked puzzled. Cap continued, "It appears that the psionic ability runs in certain families. Shane Tomo was a handsome young blond paranoid manic-obsessive. He was psionically active when he was scared. Which was whenever he wasn't planning a murder. He is the so-called Tyrant's maternal great-great-grandfather. I knew the blond bastard well. He also escaped the crew massacres . . . because he expected them to happen."

He turned to Beywulf. "Cut them loose."

Keilin sat rubbing circulation back into his feet as he listened to Cap speak. He was not sure he could run yet . . . and he hadn't made up his mind if he ought to. The man was using mighty fine noble words and promising them the moon, with the sun and stars thrown into the bargain. Keilin was carried along by the tide of the words, but he still remembered the blows. He was covertly watching Kim, too. At the end of the speech she clapped.

"Very good. I am sure half the peasants in the duchy would rise at your call. However, I am not a fool, or new to power speaking, Cap, or whatever your name is. You offer us any reward we care to name. What authority do you have to do so?" Keilin had never heard her doing the ice princess before. She did it quite convincingly.

For a moment a red light burned in Cap's eyes. Then he laughed. It was a humorless sound. "This is my authority." He touched the badge on his shoulder. "I am, as far as I know, the only crew member that survives. All of you colonists are mine to command. I am First Mate Jacoob Ahrens and, as the surviving senior ranking crew officer, I intend to do just that. Besides," he looked at them with scorn, "what else do you think you can do? A Captain Jaine is hot on your heels, as is a large posse of local folk. They're failing to track you . . . but your raids have been so predictable they know where you are. That's how we found you." He looked at Keilin's stricken face. "Didn't think that far, did you? Too busy showing off, eh? What do you have in your head for brains, boy—cheese?"

"Very well. I accept your offer. I'll join you. I want the Tyn States as my reward," Shael said coolly.

"You can't be one of the Cru!" blurted Keilin. "Why, you'd be *hundreds* of years old then."

"Three hundred and eighty-seven Earth years, to be precise. Longevity treatments for the crew can stretch my lifespan for at least six or seven hundred years, son. I'll make it clear, I might need you, and if need be I'll take you along in chains. And don't think you can run, because Beywulf will track you down. You can, however, try to kill me." The wintry smile that accompanied this final comment suggested that the man didn't think this much of a threat.

Keilin shrugged. "I'd rather come along. I don't like the idea of chains. Can I get my kit?"

CHAPTER 8

They were hunting core sections. So far four, including Keilin's pendant, were already in Cap's hands. Keilin had another one in the ring in the hidden ankle pouch. Kim had another core section set in the bracelet. He wondered if keeping them secret from Cap was wise. Then he remembered S'kith's reaction on finding it and decided it was, for now anyway. He must get together with Kim and thrash out a story. If Cap ever thought it over he might realize that her outburst implied the existence of another core section.

And now they were on their way to Amphir, city of the southern plains, riding through the night to leave behind some of the pursuit Keilin had stirred up. He looked resentfully at Kim. She'd obviously been on a horse before, often. After a few uncertain minutes he asked if he could run instead. The others had laughed, except Cap. He looked thoughtfully at the boy and nodded. "Keep up, or you get back on."

"Aw, come on, Cap, the boy won't last five minutes," Beywulf protested.

"Then he'll just have to get on again, won't he?" said Cap calmly.

So Keilin ran. Old Marou had trained him well. He'd used the boy both as a courser and greyhound in their hunts. On the overall Keilin was a better courser. The stony mountainside they were climbing was too steep and too broken for the horses to do more than walk anyway. Stung by the hairy ape's comments Keilin paced himself carefully. He could keep this up all night if need be.

It wasn't quite all night . . . but pretty close. Dawn was only a few hours off when they bedded down for the night. And before midmorning they were off again. Keilin was obliged to ride for an hour or so the next day, but when he saw how Kim was struggling even to walk after the long ride, he realized that running wasn't too bad. Amphir was far south in the wide plains beyond the mountains. It took them nearly three weeks to reach it, by which stage the party had become familiar with each other, and Keilin could ride. The one and only advantage of riding, he decided, was that he could talk to the other riders without craning his neck.

He had begun to establish relationships with the rest of the party, all except its leader. Cap remained aloof. He was without a doubt the commander of the party, but there was a complex hierarchy under that. Bottom of the pecking order was the Morkth-man. He would literally do anything anyone told him to. He showed no emotion at the occasional taunts. On the other hand he was both strong, and potentially deadly, as Keilin saw in a brief incident with foolishly optimistic bandits along the way. After that Keilin made a careful point of leaving the taunts to other people . . . particularly Kim who, after the first night, treated S'kith as if he was something unpleasant she'd stood in. But then that was only one of the aspects of her behavior Keilin found inexplicable. The fact that S'kith knew Keilin had another core section, and had contrived to hide it was odd, too. The other thing he found bizarre was the Morkth-man's attitude to Beywulf's cooking. The shaven-headed man always treated the meals as if they might bite him, but ate with a strange kind of greed.

Beywulf, the cook, was a bizarre mix between an axe murderer and mine host of the homely tavern. It had taken Keilin a while to realize that his slightly high-pitched voice and crude manner hid an intelligent, complex persona. The only thing that could always distract him from crude jokes and stirring for mayhem was exotic food. When he discovered that Keilin had come from the east coast, he grilled him about the curries and spices of that region. He'd only been there for a week as a bodyguard once long ago, but still his knowledge of the cuisine was a great deal wider than that of a street child's. Marou had been fond of food . . . Beywulf was fanatical. It was infectious. Keilin spent hours dredging his memory for the methods the women of Port Tinarana, and the more exotic refugees from across the gulf, used to enliven their poor diet of fish and lentils. The two of them were even immune to Leyla's put-out-at-being-ignored little barbs about the two housewives swapping recipes again. After her third comment Beywulf finally rose to the bait with a lofty reply, "It is a well known fact that women can't cook. They just have to."

"That just proves how stupid men are!" she returned cattily.

"Couldn't agree with you more. Luckily they're not my species. Now, about preparing that masala . . ."

The species comment lay in Keilin's mind. He brought it up that evening while they were dicing a tough piece of venison, which would later make part of a heavenly meal of herb-scented meatballs in a piquant lemon sauce. He put his fingers at risk by turning to ask Beywulf what he'd meant by it.

"Watch your hands. I mean just what I say. I'm not human . . . or at least I'm only half human. According to Cap I'm a Gene-spliced. I'm a descendant of the military-bred creatures that the humans made to defend themselves against the Morkth. I'm part chimpanzee, part Kodiak bear. I have natural speed, strength and agility that no ordinary human can rival. I also have a decent sense of smell. I'm faster and more deadly than a Morkth warrior-prime. For our services the human race rewarded us generously. They feared us 'better' humans, so . . . I'm sterile or damn near. I've one child by another of my kind. I've had two other cubs . . . they both died. Cap kept my Wolfgang from dying. That is why I have left my inn and my family to go on a quest I have no interest in." There was no mistaking the bitterness in his voice.

Leyla put an arm around his shoulders. "Never mind, you hairy Don Juan. If you hadn't been here I would never have discovered that your kind are perfectly in proportion, *all* over. You're so wide, and so hairy . . . *nearly* all over." This brought a coarse guffaw, and an even more coarse riposte, and the moment was broken.

By Leyla, Keilin was usually hypnotized the way a rabbit is by a snake. She made him make a fool of himself at least five times a day. He desperately wanted to impress her. He dreamed about her at night. Very vivid dreams. His night senses were honed enough to be aware that she amused herself with at least Beywulf and S'kith. He kept hoping . . . but she treated him as if he was a joke and worse . . . as if he were a child.

As for Kim, she was the one person Keilin felt he understood less each passing day. She had become positively fatuous about Cap. And if she told him that she was a princess now . . . he might almost believe her. He even got to half-believing the crap about being descended from Queen Lee. Fat joke, what would a Princess be doing with stolen goods, starving to death on the run? But still she became more stuck-up by the day, behaving like one of those fancy tarts on Deale Street. She expected to be waited on by all of them, especially Keilin. Next thing she'd be fluttering her eyelashes and behaving like one of the really cheap girls down on Dock Street. And all of this while speaking more fancy lah-di-dah than ever.

She hated all of them. Especially that stupid boy. How dare he behave like that. Ignoring her all the time. And he was always hanging around that big slut, like a bee around sugar water. Couldn't he see he was making an absolute idiot of himself? Yet . . . he'd not given her away, when he'd been caught . . .

As for that Morkth-man, creeping to her sleeping place without any trousers on! She blushed thinking about it. She had thought it was Keilin, and had called him closer.

Then there was the big ape-bear. He kept making rude jokes at her. And worse still, he could cook food which was better than the decorated and prettied dishes of her father's court. Of course she thought, loyally, his food wasn't as good as Mamma Mae's solid farm meals, but it *was* different.

Naturally, you had to treat Cap with respect. He was authority, and she was used to living in its shadow. But the rest of them! And now she was going to be involved in a jewel theft from Amphir, of all places. She didn't believe Cap's story about saving the human race from the Morkth, but there were some strange elements of truth in it. Some things he shouldn't have known, secrets only the royal family knew. Still, if she could have distracted Keilin from panting around that bitch-in-permanent-heat, she'd have run. He would be able to get them away, but she didn't think she could do it alone.

❖   ❖   ❖

Amphir. Fabled Amphir, jewel of the plains gap. Place of a thousand exotic smells, many of them unpleasant. The gem trade capital of the world, the city straddled the north-south caravan route and had the only open trail to the eastern coast, too. It was the banking and gem trade capital of the world for one other reason besides its position: its security. As Beywulf pointed out disgustedly, it was so policed that you couldn't even fart without some flatfoot investigating your bowels with a potent laxative. Inevitably, a few jewels had been stolen from there. But Amphir's council, the richest in the world, had a policy. They followed up. They would follow, no matter where or for how long, and extract ten times the weight of any gem from the thief's body. They got to choose just which bit of body they took it from. Sometimes they made a considerable hole in getting to that part.

Keilin stared at the great city with its white onion domes gleaming above the red walls. At some time in its geological history the land had been wrenched and torn here. The red cliffline marched east to west for hundreds of miles. Once there had been a gap in front of them. Now the cliff wall loomed continuous, with Amphir's walls blocking the gap. If you wanted to go through you had to march your caravan through the toll passage. The toll was small. Merely a token payment. Although one that added up, with the numbers that came through it. If the toll had been more than trivial, merchants would have found it worth evading. That would have spelt disaster to the real income of Amphir. With the trade of a whole continent funnelled through it, a vast amount of wealth came through the city. Inevitably, quite a bit of it stayed there. The visible result of this accumulation was huge and imposing to the street-kid-turned-desert-rat. There was a measure of awe in his voice as he asked, "Where is the place we have to rob?"

"We don't exactly know." Cap was matter of fact about it. "And we'll only steal it if we can't buy it."

"What do mean you don't know where it is, you idiots? How do you know there are core sections here at all?" demanded Shael, forgetting respect for a minute. "I mean . . ." she floundered.

"You *mean* you spoke without thinking," said Cap coolly. Cap expected respect. It was plain he did not find its disappearance pleasant. "How I organize this search is my business. I *am* the commander. Don't ever forget that."

As if anyone could, thought Keilin. But the girl was adroit at talking her way out of the difficult situations her too-quick temper got her into. "Yes, I did speak without thinking. I'm sorry. I wasn't referring to you of course, Cap. Could you explain, please?"

Cap snorted. However, she had gauged his ego correctly. "We use the core sections to track other core sections. There is a resonance between them. They are partially self-aware complex computing systems, and they retain contact with central computing. Unfortunately only psis can communicate with them, so I've had to rely on the Morkth-man. Even S'kith can't communicate directly, but he can tell how far, and in what direction the sections lie. He also 'sees' a core section's eye view of the place. That's how we know this section is in Amphir. The red walls and white minarets are very characteristic." He looked at them with sudden intensity. "Come to think of it, you two brats should be able to do the same. Maybe we can get more clues."

He produced a thin-bladed knife. "Wet contact is best. Saliva works to an extent, but blood seems more effective." Next to Keilin, Kim shrank back. Stupid girl. Yes, for a minute he'd thought Cap would bend him over a handy rock and cut his throat. But they were too valuable for that. And S'kith was still alive, wasn't he?

The same thoughts had obviously occurred to Cap. He laughed, not quite without humor. "I'm not going to gut you, and read your bloody entrails, girl. I'm just going to prick your finger, that's all."

"I'm scared of the sight of blood. Especially my own," she said in a small voice.

Cap raised his eyebrows. "And you, boy? Also chicken?"

Keilin fancied that knife's needlelike point not at all, but he couldn't see any way of backing out either. Not without appearing a coward and a fool in front of all of them. Gingerly he held out his hand.

Cap clicked his tongue as he took the boy's hand. "Look at the city." Keilin didn't even feel a prick. But there was bright blood welling from the ball of his thumb. Cap pressed the thumb to the core section he took from his pocket.

For a brief instant he was back in the desert, almost as if it was establishing context. Then the feeling of vastness again, and a feeling of recognition, questioning, drawing information, a feeling of the rightness of shaved scalp, of fear, of loneliness . . . of an erect penis? Suddenly it dawned on him. This was S'kith as he saw himself: The pendant was linking him with S'kith! Then his mind's eye saw the red wall towering upward. A double onion dome above. An expensive shop, with rare carpets and the scent of sweet cinnamony incense. It all faded into the terrible memory of betrayal again.

He was back among them. They were all staring at him, but his eyes quested for S'kith's. Was the normally expressionless man looking worried and . . . jealous? Keilin shook himself, and S'kith's face slipped back to its impassive mask. Keilin sat down, weak-kneed. After a few minutes he described the shop as best he could. But the rest of the experience he left unmentioned. Was there just a trace of relief in S'kith's face?

The next day they would go in search of the place, posing as ordinary merchants. Keilin's main worry was where to hide the ring in his ankle pouch. Beywulf had been to Amphir before and had told them of the procedures they would have to pass through to get in. They'd be searched. Weapons confiscated and held until they left. All possessions, especially jewellery, would be itemized. On their way out they would be checked again. They would have to provide receipts for any changes. The city jewellers each did duty for a day a week on the gate, and since the system's inception, the problem of gem substitution had vanished.

Then Cap announced that Beywulf would be remaining in the caravanserai outside the walls. Plainly he wasn't keen on putting core sections—or possibly other things—under the scrutiny of Amphir's officers. Keilin had already prepared a small slit in his saddle, but after a whispered consultation with Kim he had to enlarge it, to take her bracelet as well.

The next morning they were taken shopping in the vast bazaar that lined the toll passage. Here you could buy and sell everything but jewellery: for that you had to go into the city itself.

Keilin admired his new garb in the mirror. They were finer clothes than he'd ever owned, even if they were second-hand. Huh! The fuss Kim had made about that. You'd think she hadn't been wearing raggedy old boy's clothes since he'd met her by the way she went on about it.

He stepped out of the dressing cubicle, and caught his breath at seeing her. Well! She certainly was a lot prettier in her new dress than in her oversized trews and shirt. Keilin had rather forgotten she was female in the glare of Leyla's sexuality. He rapidly reevaluated his position with her.

How could he! Shael was still fuming. First to take her to some tawdry second-hand clothier, and then when she'd finally found something nice he'd sent her back to find something more dowdy. And now here she was trailing along behind them, pretending to be some kind of servant. So they'd given her the parcels to carry . . . It had been fun watching the boy's eyes nearly pop out when he saw her. She walked a little straighter, and a smile played across her lips. Coldly, Leyla told her to stop looking so cheerful and to slump her shoulders. "This is Amphir. A woman's place here is three paces in the rear, pretending that she worships the ground that those fatuous male pricks walk on." The voice was bitter.

"You sound like you know *all* about it," said the Princess sarcastically.

"I should. I was born here. I'm not happy to be back." The very matter-of-fact way it was said failed to conceal the loathing.

Shael was taken aback. It was the first time she'd considered Leyla as anything but a mattress. She could begin to understand how living in such conditions would affect someone as bounteous and outspoken as the woman by her side. They walked on in silence for a while. The outer walls curved on for miles, lined with elegant residences and expensive shops. "All of this was built by women working in dark little rooms until their eyes went. Men assess jewels, and do bugger-all else. Women work the jewels . . . actually they do *all* the work, but their fathers, and then their husbands get the money. An Amphir woman never owns anything, not even the clothes she wears." Shael noticed that there were no unattended women in the street. Dowdily dressed and veiled women trailed listlessly behind the menfolk. The men would stop and talk. The women waited, eyes downcast, three or four paces behind their keepers.

"And do you know what the worst of it is?" commented Leyla viciously. "The bloody women maintain the system. Mothers teach their daughters that only a harlot would look a man in the eyes, that a woman's place is in the home to nurture and support her man, and her sons; and this is the way women are meant to be in the eyes of God. If they even suspect that a woman is unfaithful, the other women kill her."

"It sounds awful. How did you get out?" Shael asked, finding herself drawn in and curious.

The question seemed to startle Leyla. It was almost as if she'd been unaware of the fact that she'd had an audience. "I don't want to talk about it. Anyway, you're a fine one to talk. You jumped and hopped at your father's bidding, didn't you?"

Shael was both startled and angry. She drew herself up. "I'm a Royal Princess. I ... I *had* to do ... I mean, he was my *father*. It was the law!"

"Of course *that* makes it all right," Leyla said dryly. "Now slump down. You could get stoned here, just for walking like that."

Before Shael could react both Keilin and S'kith froze, looking for a moment like a pair of bird dogs. A waft of cinnamon incense carried above the city bouquet of unusual spices, jewellers' solvents, garbage, and inefficient sewage systems. Looking up, the double onion dome stared out at them ... actually two domes, neatly in line. A little ahead yawned the mouth of Zaran's Opal Emporium, full of cinnamon halitosis.

Without haste or overwhelming signs of interest they ventured in. Underfoot lay soft carpets full of complex patterns and rich hues. In endless display cabinets were opals in various settings. Blue-greens, yellows ... milky-whites, the rarer reds, and at the back, in a carefully sealed glass case, the blacks. Keilin caught his breath. For a moment it had seemed as if an entire tray of core sections lay before him. Except they felt ... flat. A terrible compulsion pulled at him from behind a nondescript curtain on the left. And S'kith moved dreamily towards it, too.

Keilin saw how Leyla pulled Kim across to the curtained-off doorway. He nodded to himself. Clever. Women were probably the only thing that would effectively stop S'kith once he'd set himself a target. Still, the urge to go through that curtain pulled at him, too. It was nearly pushing him beyond the realms of logical behavior. He risked a glance at Kim, and found his foot following the direction of his eyes. She seemed unaffected. He couldn't take this . . . while Cap, disguised in merchant clothes and broad hat, enquired boredly about prices. He had to go . . . S'kith edged forward, too, trying to flank the girls.

Wait . . . Cap had said that he, Keilin, was . . . psionic. He could use his mind to make the stones work. He tried to focus his thoughts on the core section behind the curtain.

The trumpet blast response blared across the room. Keilin looked around, alarmed. S'kith's normally near-expressionless face had a brief flighting of terror across it. Kim's hands were clapped to her ears . . . but the business of the shop continued as usual. And the compulsion to go through that curtain at all costs had disappeared.

". . . my apprentice. I doubt if he'll ever be any good, but one must try. Boy, come and assess these stones. You know what we are seeking." Cap sounded bored and world-weary.

As Keilin peered into the tray of black opals, Cap continued to talk. "He's the son of an old friend who died in a bandit ambush. I took him on for old Kotar's sake, but he'll never have his father's eye for a good stone. Too much of his mother's blood there. Woman thought too much of herself."

"A pity that there's no possibility of getting sons without corrupting them that way. Your friend Kotar probably had the usual travelling-merchant's problem. When you're away from home too often, the women get to making decisions they shouldn't," sympathized the shopman. "Tried it myself a few years ago. Came back and found the woman *giving orders*. I tell you, my strap and I had a fine job to sort her out again."

Keilin noticed that now it was Kim who was holding Leyla's arm. "I don't think any of these will do, master," he said servilely.

For which he received a sharp clip around the earhole. "Dolt of a boy! There are some stones of the first water here. Still ... do you have any others? We have a commission from the Shah of Ebrek to buy suitable black opals for his new throne. It's his sixth, you know. And each more ornate than the last. He'll ruin that principality of his with his taste, or rather lack of taste, for expensive jewellery."

A few more stones as yet unset were produced from a back room. Keilin managed, now that his head had stopped spinning from the casual blow, to surreptitiously indicate they were not core sections. They bought two stones, and left.

The council of war that evening was heated. "Burn the city down. We can loot it at will then," was Leyla's flame-eyed suggestion.

Memories of the terror of being in a burning building came back to Keilin. "No! Just think how many people will be killed."

"Besides, there's no guarantee of success," said Cap. "No, Leyla. You'll have to restrain yourself until it is yours."

"Go in, take them all hostage, take the core section, and use the hostages to get out of the city. Take the rest of the stock and scatter them in the bazaar along the toll passage. That'll keep the flatfeet occupied awhile," Beywulf suggested, eyeing the concept of professional mayhem with relish.

"With what weapons, pray? And the Amphir policy on hostages is that none of them are worth the city's reputation."

"Well, Cap. Do we raise an army and invade the place? Lot of loot on offer."

"Only if all else fails. My idea means killing the gate guards . . ."

Suddenly all the talk of death and murder sickened him. Keilin interrupted, "I'll do it."

The group was silenced. Finally Cap asked, with exaggerated patience, "How?"

"They have built flush against the city wall here . . . on both sides. I can get over. The shop building is easy to get into. There are no bars on most of the windows. Compared to Port Tinarana, the building security is a joke."

"The only bars are on the women's quarters," interrupted Leyla savagely.

"Well, I won't be going there. I know where the core section is. It's in a steel case on the other side of the curtain to the left of the back room."

"A hidden safe," said Cap, "and then what, small dark horse? Are you an expert safecracker as well?"

"No. But I saw that all that money swindled from the trader in the turban was whisked behind that curtain by the short fat one. And he had a key, which he took out of his pocket on the way. I just have to find it, and remove it from him."

"Boy, you're turning into more than just another little psi." It was not entirely praise and approbation. There was a little threat in his voice too. "Just don't you get too cocky for your own good. Talk with Leyla. She'll tell you the internal layout of the non-shop part of the building. Beywulf will go along in case your fat little burgher wakes up."

"Beywulf . . . but he's so big . . ."

The broad hairy face broke into a sardonic smile. "But I can climb better than you, boy," and he jumped up and down, with an arm above his head, going "Ook! OOK!" and scratching his armpit with the other hand.

"That's enough, Beywulf." Cap was not amused. "You'll go tomorrow night. We need to provision and prepare for a hasty retreat."

"Good. I was hoping you did not want me to go tonight," Keilin said slowly. "I'd like to get a few things from the bazaar, and do a careful recce of the jeweller's shop tomorrow." He didn't dare to point out that it wasn't Beywulf's climbing ability that had worried him, but the hairy man's ability to be a silent burglar.

The next night scuds of cloud hid the moon, making the night alternately light and dark. Whenever it was dark Keilin spidered across the rooftops, to freeze in the light periods. Behind him he could hear his somewhat unwelcome assistant grunting along. Frustration made him grit his teeth with annoyance. He could have moved at twice this speed on his own. And he kept expecting that great behemoth to fall through the slates. It was a good thing this wasn't a more ordinary city, but an overprotected, overpoliced and pampered place. Otherwise they'd certainly have been caught by now, or at least attacked for poaching on someone else's territory.

At last they were on the roof next door to the target. And luck was with them. There was a window open on the top story. But there were still voices coming from inside, and a scattering of lights coming from windows in the upper floors. In the shadow of a tall gable they settled down to wait. They had a fine view of the building, and soon found entertainment. The barred windows were visible only from the rooftop, and Keilin and Beywulf spent an entertaining and educative half hour watching the three middle-to-late-teen-age daughters of the house prepare for bed. Keilin found he hadn't noticed the cold at all.

When the candles were finally snuffed Beywulf sighed gustily next to him. "Seems a shame to leave three well-endowed little gems like that to become

those dispirited women one sees sludging about in
this place. Tell you what . . . I'll liberate them, while
you go and collect this pretty that Cap wants." Keilin
smothered a sneeze. Damn. It was colder than he'd
thought, and knowing Beywulf, he was only half-joking
too. Before he could reply his eye was caught by
another dark figure dropping onto the next-door rooftop. Keilin motioned Beywulf to silence. This person
moved with the kind of sneak-thief caution alien to
Beywulf.

Keilin got a second's worth of a good look in an
unexpected shaft of moonlight. The moon reflected
off a shaved head. S'kith was no burglar, but he had
three times the natural talent that Beywulf had. Keilin
called softly as S'kith gathered himself to jump the
last gap. The Morkth-man nearly fell off the roof, but
a few moments later he came to join them.

"What in hell are you doing here, Morkthy?"
Beywulf demanded roughly.

Keilin already knew. "The section below us is
calling him, Bey. He probably couldn't help coming.
It is dragging at me, too."

"Hell's teeth! A pair of bloody nutters. But you took
a chance, S'kith! Cap'll skin you. And aren't you too
far . . ."

The Morkth-man looked doubtfully at them. "They
do not know I have come. And it is not too far. They
are less than two hundred yards away, outside the
wall. Why do you wait?"

"The lights have only just gone off. We've at least
half an hour before it will be safe to move." A strange
kind of understanding for S'kith came over Keilin.
"Bey. I'll go in with S'kith. You cover our backs here."

"Not what the man said," muttered Beywulf.

"Bugger the man. He's not here. And face it, Bey.
S'kith's a natural-born sneaker, which you're not. And
if I don't take him with me he'll probably go in
anyway."

He could see in the change of set in S'kith's shoulders that he'd said the right thing. He made another snap decision. "S'kith. Come and huddle in here and help me warm up. I'm cold and I don't want to sneeze and give us away." Without a word the muscular, bald-headed man slid in next to them. His arms went around Keilin and he held him, not as a lover might . . . but as a mother might hold a child. Keilin did not know why, but he felt this was something of a profound experience for the strange shaven-headed man. So he put an arm around him, too. They waited in silence for the half hour to pass.

"If you hear a noise, come running," said Keilin to Beywulf, as they slipped in through the window.

Keilin and S'kith moved as silently as shadows down the corridors of the sleeping house. No house with people in it is ever completely quiet. There are small sounds. If these stop then the burglar should know fear. Keilin's ears listened carefully to these sounds, as they moved to the master bedroom.

Motioning S'kith to wait, he slipped within. The master's little piggy face was cherubic in snoring repose. The girl sobbing in her sleep at the foot of the bed belied his angelic appearance. She must have been younger than his own daughters . . . Keilin couldn't be truly sure she was asleep as he stealthily searched the pockets of the tossed-aside trousers, and removed the keys from them. She hadn't sobbed for a while. He slipped away . . . waiting for the cry.

It didn't come. They moved downstairs, and into the echoing silence of the showroom. The safe opened with a small creak. It was too dark to see here, but his hands needed no visual guidance. Keilin cursed softly to himself. It was in some heavy gold setting. They moved to a shaft of moonlight, and there with S'kith's knife they pried the claws aside, and roughly substituted one of the black opals which Cap had bought. Suddenly, knowing it was right, Keilin gave the jewel to S'kith. "Go up," he whispered. "I'll put this back and return the key."

Piggy was still doing his whistle snore, but the girl was too quiet. Under those heavy-lidded brows, she was watching him as he dropped the key into the pocket. He knew it, but he was also unsure what to do about it. Should he just hope she'd be too scared to do anything? Or should he risk a scream by threatening her with his knife?

The decision was abruptly taken out of his hands by a terrible crash downstairs. Keilin was out of the room before she could even draw breath. He knew what that noise meant. Bloody Beywulf had come looking for them. The swearing from below told him he was right. Bey came boiling up the main stair as doors flung open all around them. Keilin ran for the window they'd come in by, as people fumbled for tinderboxes and candles. Keilin nearly ran headlong into S'kith, and the occupant of the room. The Amphirian jeweller was advancing on the frozen Morkth-man with a well-used riding crop in hand.

If he'd had a sword instead, the man would simply have died. But S'kith's fear reaction to the whip, combined with the core section he clutched, produced the only kind of refuge the Morkth-man had ever really known. Ripped from the depths of the hive, human brood-sow cell 9003 was still the same as it was the first time . . . the time he'd sneaked down there driven by feelings he simply could not understand . . . and the immense feeling of joy and . . . *release* that had resulted. He still clung to the memory in his new unfamiliar world, a world where he was not only not in control, but barely able to cope. The cell was the same, although the occupants were not. It now contained a new girl, and three Alpha-Morkth of an artificial insemination team.

When the teams go in, they rely on an integral part of the cell's structure. The Morkth had discovered in the course of a myriad experiments on their human subjects that a certain combination of flashes of the visible spectrum, as well as pulsed low-frequency sound, caused uncontrolled neuromuscular spasms in humans, inducing, in effect, a *petit mal* fit, followed by neural overload and a blackout. Under these conditions no escapes had *ever* occurred. Until now. The cell was no longer part of the hive's power net. It wasn't even a complete cell any more. Just the front section, all that S'kith had ever been able to see.

The woman in the cell's eyes had been conditioned to a lifetime in semidarkness. The moonlight was almost too bright for her, unlike the half-blind Morkth and housefolk. She didn't know where she was . . . or care. All she knew was that at last the warriorbrood women's hatred could have solid form. Her hysterical strength outmatched the Morkth worker who had been pulling her legs open. Beywulf came roaring into the fray. He'd been obliged to leave his sword behind for the climb. He substituted it with the master of the house, whom he swung by both legs.

"SHIT! S'kith! Bey! Let's get *out!* Morkth'll be here any moment," shouted Keilin, putting the pieces together as he struggled towards the window.

The Beta-Morkth base for the southwestern quadrant was less than seven seconds off. The warrior crews waited in their craft with the ready-to-strike immobility that their kind could muster for patient hour upon hour. In the last four missions flown, two had been lost completely, crew, craft and all. The last six missions had also failed to retrieve the core section. In the three hundred years and the five missions previous to that, they'd always struck without loss and successfully retrieved the core sections. It was obvious to the Beta that the equation had changed, and stakes were rising. Therefore three platecraft were on standby.

One got away. As Beywulf and Keilin fled across

the rooftops, half-carrying S'kith, Keilin replayed it in his mind. One of the items that stuck out was the child's voice, as in his half asleep state he came out of his room, and loudly asked what the terrible whining noise was. This in the midst of a killing brawl! Then there was that naked woman from S'kith's materialization, with her insane blind ferocity, and tiger smile even as she bled . . . And S'kith throwing the core section to him, before diving into the fray. The Beta-Morkth had been prepared for human weapons when they had arrived. The presence of an Alpha warrior with an energy weapon had torn their strategy, as had the attack by a trained Alpha guard, and a hairy berserker. Still, without the screaming suicide attack of that woman . . . Keilin shook himself. She'd killed two of them, ripping their heads from their torsos before she'd died. Why had she called out a number as it happened? And just what had it done to S'kith?

There'd be time to think about it when . . . *if* they got away. Meanwhile the city guards were champing about frantically, like bugs from a broken termitarium. At least he'd got one more Morkth himself. Strange that a poison which caused eventual loss of consciousness on hot-blooded creatures would produce instant shuddering death in Morkth. It had been on Marou's spear blade, and Keilin had tipped his knife and arrows with it.

CHAPTER 9

"You stupid, clumsy ham-handed bastards!" Cap's anger was not in the least ameliorated by the fact that they had brought him another core section. "You deserve to be bloody court-martialed, or at least flayed for gross insubordination."

Beywulf was probably the only one feeling the edge of his tongue. Keilin was still too unused to riding to be doing anything but concentrating on staying in the saddle at this speed. And S'kith was sunken deep into some private and expressionless misery.

By that evening Keilin felt that even flaying would have been more gentle than that ride. The opal dealer's shop stood beside the south wall, above the fault cliff. They had not dared ride back through the toll passage. Instead they were pushing further south just as fast as their horses would carry them.

At least Cap's temper had cooled by sunset, although the three were still at the top of the fecal list. The tall man grimly produced a core section from his pocket, and looked at Keilin and S'kith. He drew the thin-bladed knife. "I need to know where we are going next." S'kith showed fear, backing away slightly, his eyes growing that dangerous glazed look which foreordained combat. Keilin sighed. "I'll do it. Relax, S'kith."

The vastness was comforting and familiar. Here at least there was a sense of a job well done. Five more core sections lay together in a place of near total darkness, and endless repeated patterns. It was warm and not-quite scented . . . somewhere between a badger's hole and sweet lavender. The emotion ran high in it, too. It had the tinny taste of hatred . . . and fear. Then came the familiar message about betrayal . . . somehow tied to the smell.

"A place. You've got to tie it to a place, dammit," Cap said, his ire rising in a perceptible tide.

Keilin shook his head helplessly. "I've told you all I can," he said. "But . . . there are four sections," he lied conservatively. He could always say it was a mistake. "It's somewhere north of here."

"Great. Why the hell couldn't you mindee types get *that* before we ran south?" Cap said in disgust. "You damn psi are all the same. Bloody *prima donnas* and then next to useless on top of it. S'kith! Come here, damn you!" Instead the Morkth-man curled himself into a ball. Cap stepped over, gripped him by the shoulder and shook him so that his teeth rattled. It was only in acts like this that one got some idea of the power in that tall, spare frame.

But it had no effect on S'kith. He stayed lost in his distress. Cap took out his knife.

"Don't!" said Keilin. He'd not been too sure if this was to be execution or just blood for the core-section contact. Seeing the look his interruption had brought him he decided to play it as the latter. "Cap . . . in his present state, give him a core section and he'll call the Morkth down on us." Cap's eyes narrowed. Finally he nodded and dropped S'kith to sprawl like a rag doll. His eyes caught Kim's horrified ones. "Come here, girl."

Once again Keilin risked life and limb. He didn't dare risk the familiarity of "Cap." "Sir! Let her put it in her mouth. Then she won't be so scared." It earned him another fulminating look, but Cap did allow her to put it into her mouth, instead of using his knife.

For the first time Keilin saw what happened instead of having it happen to him. Her face lost expression. A vague nimbus seemed to dance around her.

And then she was back. Her eyes darted to his face for a brief frightened moment, before answering Cap's query calmly. "The same as Keilin ... with Morkth clickspeech. I think it must be the inside of a hive."

"The inside of a hive ..." said Cap and whistled between his teeth. "I knew it had to come to this sooner or later ... Question is: Which hive? To the north, yes, but which side of the narrow sea?" He sighed. "We'll have to try and get something more out of that jelly of a Morkth-man's brains ... when he's stopped bloody quivering. See that he is kept warm. Try to get him to eat." Although this was directed at both of them, it was loftily ignored by Kim. She waited until Cap had stalked off into the dark and then retreated to her own gear. Keilin was left to try to spoon the thick pea soup into the vacant-eyed man's mouth. He found himself sitting with an arm around the crumpled-in shoulders for a long time.

Finally, the muscular man shook himself, and sat up. He looked at Keilin strangely and then as if tasting an unfamiliar word in half-whisper he said, "Friend?" Keilin looked doubtful for a moment, and then nodded. The man stood up without a word and went across to his sleeping furs. With relief Keilin went to his own. He was just settling down when it occurred to him that he'd better return haughty Miss Muffet's bangle to her. With it, and another small bundle in hand he crept quietly across to her bedroll.

"Go away! If you come near me again, I shall scream," she said in a fierce whisper. "Oh! It's you Keilin . . . I thought . . . I thought it was S'kith . . . again. Don't go . . . I need to talk to you."

"Don't whisper. The sound carries much better than just talking quietly," he said in a low voice. "If you want to shout at me as usual, we'd better sneak away from the camp a bit."

"Oh, you . . . yes we'd better. I always end up wanting to shout at you, no matter how we start," she said, getting up.

Soon they were sitting on a small knoll about two hundred yards from the campfire. They were out on the great sward of the southern plain, under a full moon. The night wind sent waves of silver and darkness washing across it from far horizon to far horizon.

Without intent she reached out and touched his arm. "It's so beautiful."

He nodded. "Like something out of a romance novel."

She snorted. "What do you know about novels? I'll bet you've never even seen one, and couldn't read it if you did." He was about to protest when she continued, "Look, that's not what I brought you here to talk about. Keilin . . . go very carefully with Cap. He's this close to killing you."

"What?! I mean, I know he's got a bad temper . . ." he said, earlier protests about books forgotten.

"I've been taught to read voices. I promise you, you were so close this afternoon I was nearly scared out of my wits. Cap needs to be in control. He doesn't allow others to challenge him. He didn't like your questioning him, and he likes your being right even less," she said.

"But . . . but, I'm *helping* him!" he said helplessly

"Listen to me for once you . . . idiot. Why do you think he was angry when you came back with the core section? It was supposed to be a total disaster with you getting killed. I know. He was all set to dump your kit back in the caravanserai. *I* put it on to the packhorse. Then when you took S'kith as well he was worried as well as mad. Don't do it again!"

"I don't believe this stuff. He's Cru, for heaven's sake. Why would he send Bey with me if he thought I'd get killed?" Keilin said, doubt in his voice.

"Beywulf had orders to give you away, maybe, or even to kill you . . . or Cap didn't trust you on your own. I don't know. All I know is he wasn't expecting you back. He can afford to lose one 'psionic' as he calls us. And you were supposed to be an example to the rest of us. 'We'd better do things his way or else.' Look, just be cautious, and step carefully around him. If you need to get him to do something, let him think it was his idea. Tell him how clever he was to think of it. He doesn't mind then, as long as he gets all the credit," she said.

"Okay. I'll try. But I'm a terrible liar," he promised.

"Then keep your big mouth shut. You only open it to change feet anyway. Now, why did you come creeping to my bed?" There was an edge in her voice at this. It suggested that his answer had better be good.

"I was just bringing your bracelet back."

He was not sure what the look was. Relief? Disappointment? At least he hadn't made her mad at him . . . yet.

"Oh . . . um . . . look, would you keep it? I'm sure someone searched my things." She cocked her head slightly, and tried something different, "Please?"

He grinned. "That's the first you've ever said *that* to me. I thought you saved pleases and thank yous for Cap. Yes, sure. I'll keep it."

She stood up, her chin rising slightly. He scrambled to his feet, too, reaching out and taking her arm. She shook his hand off angrily. "Look, Kim. D-don't go. Oh. Um, er, Bey and I . . . we bought this for you."

She eyed the proffered parcel suspiciously. "What is it?"

"It's that dress. You know, the one Cap made you take back. We thought you might like it."

She said nothing. Just stood there looking at him.

"Look, I'm sorry it's second-hand, but, well, we didn't have much spare money. You don't have to take it."

She did, however. If the moonlight had been brighter Keilin would have seen that the little Princess was close to tears. "Thank you," she said, her voice slightly husky. "I suppose you've never heard me say that to you either."

He grinned "Na. Another first for tonight. But you can thank Bey, too. It was his idea really."

"Beywulf! But he doesn't like me. He's always so rude."

"Only rude to people he likes. He fights with the others. Insult him back. He says you remind him of his daughter. Just about as much of a pain in the ring as she was, too."

"He says that about his own daughter! What does she say about him!"

"She doesn't. She's dead. It's his way of dealing with it, see."

There was a long silence at this. "Cay . . . That core section. It described you both . . ." He was sure she was blushing. He began to glow himself. Then she began to giggle. "It got S'kith right, and it wasn't so far off about you."

She would say no more, and after a few minutes they went silently back to the camp, each lost in words unspoken. But Keilin noticed a change the next morning in her response to Beywulf. She took a second helping of breakfast. Bey snorted, "God, not more, you frowsty little hen. You're getting as broad as an ox cart."

Instead of the usual haughty silence which had

been her response to his heckling, she replied calmly, "I vomited the first lot up. It was full of some ugly ape's hair."

This provoked a snort of laughter, and a swat across the posterior. She jumped. *Nobody* did that to her. Then she noticed that both the ape and Keilin were grinning at her. But it was too much to ask her to ignore it completely. She reached out and dug her nails into Beywulf's arm with all her strength. It was about as yielding as teak. "Don't you *dare* do that to me again, you damned gorilla!" A further snort of laughter.

"Or you'll beat me up, eh? Yes, yer ladyship. I'll be good."

"Good for nothing most likely, you overgrown baboon."

The broad, hairy man drew himself up to his full five-foot-six. "I'll have you know there's not a drop of baboon blood in me. Pure chimpanzee." His face had a look of injured innocence.

"No, the baboon blood is in his cousin Alfeus. The respectable member of the family." This was Leyla, joining in the fray.

"Huh, you just liked his body."

From there on the conversation went rapidly downhill in a cheerful manner. To her amazement Shael found she was enjoying the verbal fencing. Later, when they were going to mount and ride, she asked Beywulf to adjust her stirrups, and thus she found a chance to thank him for the dress. He shrugged it off. "Young Cay's idea. Waste o' good money on a skinny bint like you."

"You're a shameless liar, Beywulf! You said I was getting fat not twenty minutes ago . . . and Keilin said it was your idea," said Shael.

"It's your bottom that's getting so broad. The rest's still skinny. As for the boy, well, he's a good lad, but a bit slow upstairs like," replied Beywulf with a

disarming grin that made him look twenty years
younger.

"Will you stop babbling and mount, Beywulf?
We've a way to go, and I daresay there'll be some
pursuit as well." Cap's interruption prevented any
more comments.

The word "friend" was no sinecure with S'kith. Or
so Keilin found out. S'kith obviously thought it meant
"constant companion," "father confessor," "walking
encyclopaedia," and "mother." He kept making physical contact, too, needing the reassurance of touch. It
made the solitary-natured boy uneasy. However, when
they walked into an ambush late that afternoon, Keilin
discovered it also meant he had a superbly trained
warrior as his utterly devoted personal bodyguard.

Their brief and running brush with bandits in the
north was as nothing compared to this. In the north
they'd been set to rob, and let be. Here, killing came
first, and robbery was an afterthought. The ambushers
always selected small enough parties to annihilate, and
bury deep. They made sure no one ever carried word
to the patrols out of Amphir. This time, however,
they'd bitten off far more than they could chew.

The first arrow had missed Cap, and this, it seemed,
would be their nemesis. The man had always radiated an air of menace. Now Keilin had an opportunity
to see just how deadly he really was. There was a
crimson blaze of an energy discharge. The killing
machine led his group, calling orders as he rode, gal-
vanizing them from a riding party to a fighting unit
in moments. Cap had chosen the weakest flank, and
the long curved blade from his saddlebow sang its way
through blood and bone. In seconds it had stopped
being an ambush and was a just a bloody melee.

The ambush party had been on foot, and the
mounted charge sliced bloodily through them. The
vast two-handed landsknecht's sword smashed through

any defense, its jagged blade ripping off gobbets of
flesh as Beywulf's huge, rearing horse careered
through. On the other flank, keeping close beside
Keilin, the Morkth-man fought with trained clockwork
movements. In front, with weasel-fluid ferocity, Cap's
long curved blade wove an unstoppable ritual dance.
In seconds they'd surged through the skirmish line,
with Leyla calmly turning in the saddle to drop arrows
behind her. Keilin was unaware of using his spear,
but there was bright gore on its tip. It had all been
so quick. He hadn't even had time to be afraid.

Cap laughed rich and free, the sound carrying even
above the hoof thunder. He turned to look at them
and his eagle eyes seemed to glow with an inner
wildfire. Keilin felt the pull, knew that this was a man
that men would follow into hell itself.

Some miles later, with the evening sky fading from
pinks to dark-blue ash, they pulled up. Although they
were sure that they were not being pursued, they
nevertheless made a defensive camp before comparing
wounds. These were slight, but Cap examined them
thoroughly and cleaned and dressed the cuts with
meticulous care. He also insisted they'd merely been
lucky. So he set out on the following days to drill
them into a fighting unit. Keilin discovered discipline.
It didn't fit him very well. The only comfort was that
it suited Kim even less. The only one who thrived
under orders was S'kith. Leyla and Beywulf were
plainly used to a military regimen, and had worked
as a team before.

S'kith had, under Keilin's gentle persuasion, offered
to see what guidance he could give to their next
target. It had left him somewhat wild-eyed again.
"FirstHive. The patterns, they say FirstHive."

"Well, at least we don't have to cross the narrow
sea. But FirstHive. That's bad news," Cap muttered.
"I suppose we'll have to go back along the West
Coast. Other than going back through Amphir, where

I don't think we'd be very welcome, thanks to you gentlemen's bungling, that is the only route still open to us." He looked at Beywulf. "We'll make for Dublin Moss. I'll need an army."

This seemed to both elate and frighten Beywulf. He explained later as Keilin wept and sniffed his way through slicing onions. "It's home. My kind, those of us that there are, are all settled around there. Mind, there's always a few hired out as mercenaries here and there, same as I did as a youth. But it'll be grand to see my folk again." He sighed melancholically.

"You don't sound very happy about it. Won't you at least be seeing your wife and son?"

Beywulf sighed again. "I don't have a wife, Cay. We don't breed too well so . . . um, we tend to try and spread the chances around that two reproductively viables will meet. It's not much good for home life, but with children so few, the whole community spoils 'em. But, aye, it's my boy: He'll be fifteen . . . old enough to join the army Cap'll raise."

"But, why should he? I mean, it sounds like there are so few of your kin anyway you shouldn't be joining anybody's army."

"But we will. We owe a debt. And we always honor our debts. You see, Cap's been our people's physician ever since we had to run from the marines' quarters up in crew territory. He's all that has stood between us and extinction. Every one of the Gene-spliced who can walk will fight at his call."

Keilin kept silent at this. From what he'd heard from S'kith the whole idea of attacking FirstHive was ludicrous. As near ridiculous as the "military exercises" Cap kept putting them through. He had nothing against learning something about the weapons he didn't know, but it did seem rather futile in some ways: He couldn't lift Beywulf's sword—and could barely pull Leyla's bow. His own hunter's bow was a small and weak thing, relying on the poison arrows to make its kill. Cap regarded it with scorn. "All very well for hunting, but no earthly use in combat. The toxin load won't kill quickly enough." Keilin kept quiet about the fact that the poison glazing the arrows' tips killed Morkth quickly all right. He'd learned by now to keep quiet about what he could do. "Like that spear of yours," Cap went on. "Once it's thrown, what have you got? It's all very well for defense, and keeping an unskilled enemy out of swordrange, but no good as an offensive weapon. Well, Bey? What can little lord muck here use from your armory? He hasn't the strength for an axe or a longsword. Saber perhaps?"

Beywulf was rummaging through one of the packhorse's saddlebags. "I've just the thing. He's used to a spear, so this is not a big change." He came up a with canvas-wrapped parcel. Out came three short, broad-bladed spears. The blades were fully two-foot-six long, and sharp enough to cut hair.

"Nice, eh? Ndebele assegais. Picked them up down Estend way. You can throw them . . . but they're essentially a stabbing weapon. Ironwood handle. Beautiful pieces of work." He held out one.

Keilin took the proffered weapon warily. As the heavy silky-smooth wooden shaft slid into his hands that feeling of rightness slipped over him again. The weapon felt as if it were simply part of him.

"He holds it right, anyway," said Bey with a satisfied nod. "Hey, you. The girl with the broad beam and the big mouth. Come and try this saber. It's the lightest thing I've got."

They rode eastward and down off the high plateaus. From the dry, hot, dusty grassland plains into the muggy heat and vicious storms of the lowlands. The ridges they followed downward were covered in coarse blade-edged grasses, with occasional straggly palmettos and ragged tufts of bamboo forest. The valley bottoms, on the other hand, were thick with jungle, and so hung with lianas that they were virtually impassable. Keilin found it unnerving country. He kept feeling they were being followed, but despite carefully studying the hazy distances, he never saw anyone. Yet . . . he was *sure* there was someone behind them. It was all that kept him from rebelling against Cap's constant order barking. He also found that Beywulf, the friendly chef, and Beywulf, the acerbic ex-mercenary sergeant-major and weapons drill instructor, were vastly different people.

Day after day they rode further into the lowlands, the air becoming stickier and thicker. To pass through to the north they had to go down to the coastal plain and thread their way between the swamps. You could ride for a week across the plains of Amphir and see nothing but the occasional betraying dust of a cattle herd. Here in the lowlands, people settled where the landscape forced the trails to go. Settlements popped up at every river fork and jungle crossing. There was virtually no easy way of avoiding the villages and their little terraced pocket-handkerchief fields.

Only Beywulf rejoiced in the villages. He purchased stems of green bananas and pawpaws, m'dumbi bulbs, ground nuts, fresh eggs and smoked monkey flesh: an assemblage with which he experimented to produce exotic dishes. S'kith was unhappy because the women wore very little clothing. The little Princess bemoaned the lack of baths in the villages, and Leyla, still in a militant mood after revisiting her birthplace, muttered about the women working in the fields while the men idled in the shade, smoking long pipes and drinking corn beer. Keilin, for once, found himself in agreement with Cap's reasons for discomfort. The villagers saw them, and could say where they went.

The sea was not the blue which Keilin remembered looking at from his rooftop eyrie in Port Tinarana. Instead, it surged red-brown with the silt of the hillsides. But the smell of salt was enough to distract him, to trigger memories of the security of his bookstand nest and recall the contentment of a good absorbing read. It took the edge off his concentration. He did not spot the scouts in the tangle of brush and palmetto. The rain-laden breeze off the sea meant they were downwind from Beywulf's keen nose. The party rode down a long sand spit between the calm brown lagoon and the churned brown sea. If the lagoon mouth was open it would undoubtably have the usual laconic ferryman, who after a glance at Cap, would give up any attempt to overcharge them.

The race of brown water from the storms in the hills spewed out of the mouth and tangled and frothed with the breakers. The ferry lines hung down, their cut ends dangling and dripping as a coarse mist of raindrops settled on them.

Beywulf sighed. "We've a fine choice. Bloody sharks in that riptide," he pointed to the black shapes visible in a cresting wave, "or going inland and having crocodiles and quicksand in the mangrove swamps."

Cap looked over his shoulder, his eagle eyes squinting into the mizzle. "There is one choice you left out." He pointed. "We might just end up dying right here." In the grayness they could just make out the advancing horsemen. At least two hundred of them in military array across the entire sand spit. "Too many for some petty bandits . . . and too well disciplined. Probably some local baron bent on raising revenues the easy way. Let me try and talk our way out of it."

But as they rode closer it became obvious that it was no local baron. The stiff black horsehair crests on the helmet of the Tyn States Cuirassiers bristled with raindrops. Beside him Keilin heard Kim's sharp intake of breath as a tall man with a finely-carved bloodless face rode out of their midst. His voice was dry, sardonic. "Why," asked the self-proclaimed Emperor, "do you persist in making me travel about in the rain, Princess?"

CHAPTER 10

Keilin looked about, startled. He could only be referring to Leyla, surely. Kim was just a thief . . . wasn't she? One look at her white, frightened face was sufficient to convince him otherwise. "Princess Shael. Hadn't you better induce your lowborn companions to lower their weapons?"

"Why?" she burst out. "Why don't you just leave me alone? What are you going to do with me this time? Give me to another pervert to torture, or just hand me over to the Morkth?"

He waved a languid hand. "That is no way for a future Empress to talk. All that is almost past."

"Empress?! After what you did to me!"

He shrugged. "Part of the exigencies of seizing power, my dear. You, after all, should know that these little excesses are necessary. But now you will be restored to power, influence and comfort. No more struggling to survive with a group of vagabond . . . jewel thieves. Amphir's arm is long, but not long enough to take anything from a reigning Empress."

Keilin turned to watch her, despite the fact that to do so made the rain trickle off his cape and down his back. He saw how her eyes narrowed, and the expression in them changed from fear to challenge. It was not reflected in her voice however. That was cool. "Empress . . . and who, pray, is to be the Emperor?"

Deshin smiled. It was a humorless movement of the lips. "Power games again, Princess. You haven't changed despite all this time of consorting with lower orders. I wonder what use they found for you in their party? You weren't trained to cook, so I must presume you paid your way on your back. *We* are the Emperor of Tynia."

She ignored the innuendo, and replied with a lifted eyebrow. "I see . . . Emperor. And how does your *dear* Saril feel about this . . . marriage?"

The humorless smile was wiped away. "My . . . but we *are* well informed. I'm afraid our marriage will be merely a matter of appearances, Princess. The marriage, however, will put a stop to these ugly little rumors . . . especially when it is blessed with an heir."

"From you! I'd rather die!"

He looked disdainfully at her. "I share your sentiments exactly. No, you would have to find yourself a more . . . willing participant. Select one of these, if you like. I will make no attempt to interfere in your . . . amusements, as long as you are discreet in your use and disposal of them." He paused. "On second thought . . . perhaps you'd better leave disposal to me. You're inclined to be too flamboyant. Killings like the one you carried out on Lord Blis get talked about. What on earth was the toxin you used?"

"Maybe you'll find out. Maybe you should just leave me alone." Shael's voice was more than a little dangerous.

"I've taken steps to prevent any little assassination plans you may have. You see, if I die, a certain somebody is going to be very upset. And he has more experience at killing than you do. He's also," and the thin lips were licked, "very skilled at pain. As for leaving you alone, I'm afraid that won't be practical. You either come with me alive, as my bride-to-be, or you come along as a head on a pole," Deshin said, his voice cold.

Shael's quick mind needed no more prompting. "You need me. You need me for a valid claim on Arlinn."

"Very astute," said Deshin, raising an eyebrow. "Perhaps I underrated your intelligence. But I'll settle for your head if need be. I have sufficient witnesses who will swear the ceremony took place first."

"At this point I think I should intervene." Cap spoke calmly. There was almost a trace of amusement in his voice.

Deshin raised his chin, and attempted to look down his nose at someone who was taller than himself. "Don't interrupt your betters, carrion."

There was a small snort, which might almost have been laughter. "I outrank you six ways to breakfast, you vain little fool. Anyway, I was speaking to the Princess, and not to you." He turned slightly to her while the self proclaimed Emperor fish-mouthed. "I didn't need you getting ideas about running off, but your father, the Tyrant, is free, and has successfully taken control of five of the northwestern states. This pompous ass controls the rest . . . or used to."

"And I have you in the palm of my hand, who-ever you think you are," spat Deshin angrily. "At a word from me, you're dead."

"I see," said Shael slowly, ignoring Deshin. "Arlinn does not rally to my father?"

"Nor does it rise against him. The Tyrant'd be like a nut in a vise then, fighting on two fronts. At the moment our little Emperor here holds the balance of power. But if Arlinn enters the war on the other side, then your father both outnumbers and out-generals him. As your mother's husband, the Tyrant calls for Arlinn's strength. But they evade the Tyrant's call by saying their allegiance is to you, until you are proven dead. This man needs you alive. Dead, you're worthless to him," said Cap.

"How do you know this, Cap?" Shael asked, as a touch of doubt assailed her.

"Heard it from northern merchants in Amphir. I took some care to keep you away from them."

"I've had enough of this." Shael could detect the undertones of fear in Deshin's voice. "I'm tired of standing around in the rain bickering. I came here with a very generous offer. But I can take you in chains if need be. I think the first thing is to deal with this rabble of yours . . ."

Cap smiled again, sharklike, and interrupted, "What do you intend for us, O great Emperor?"

Deshin was too wrapped up in himself to notice the edge of sarcasm. "You'll have to die. I can't afford witnesses. I'll say the girl has been in my custody all along. That should deal with comments on her virginity."

"You are very stupid, little play-acting Emperor." Leyla's voice was still and honeyed.

Before the affronted man could react, Beywulf jockeyed his horse slightly forward, within reach of the emperor. His voice was slightly higher pitched than usual, but otherwise there was no sign of tension. "You say, 'At a word from me, you're dead.' So . . . if you try and utter the wrong one, I'll kill you. If the boy over there doesn't put an arrow in you first. You see, he's got a drawn bow under that cloak."

"I'm wearing a mail shirt, under this garment. It is very uncomfortable but I think I'm quite safe. And my bodyguards can deal with you." Deshin kept his cool with only a slight hesitation.

Cap laughed. "Do you think so indeed! You don't know Beywulf. I've seen that sword cut through a quarter-inch steel gorget and continue on to cut the man in half." As he spoke Bey had drawn the huge sword.

"And the boy is from the desert, Deshin." Shael's voice trembled slightly. "They use thin little poisoned arrows. There is a good chance they'll go right through your mail shirt, if he doesn't hit your face or neck. And his arrows are tipped with curare." Keilin wished she spoke the truth. Actually his cloak hid an assegai, and the man's head would be a hard target.

"Besides that," Cap said from next to Shael, "I have the hole card. Before your bow-and-lance troops, excellent though I admit they are, can kill me, I'll kill her."

Deshin's voice was distinctly tense now. "You can all go. Just leave me the girl."

"On the contrary. We'll take her along. Tell your men to unstring their bows. Stray arrows might happen otherwise, and we'd hate any accidents."

Reluctantly the order was given. As the Cuirassiers got busy, Cap turned back to face Bey. Keilin caught a hand signal. "And to make doubly sure," said Cap, his voice calm, "we'll take you too." As he spoke Bey launched himself in a terrific spring. The first bodyguard was dead. The other was dying. And the bloody sword pressed against the throat of the Emperor.

"Back! Back off, if you want your Emperor to live," Cap shouted, his voice carrying loudly back into the rain haze.

"Let me go! My men will—"

"Your men will back off and allow us to pass. If they do exactly as I tell them, you'll stay alive." There was that kind of certainty in the voice which goes far beyond any form of denial.

They rode through the parting ranks, a grim little

party with blades held against two throats. Leyla had
Deshin's reins, but Shael held her own, sitting straight
and regal, ignoring Cap's blade. But her eye was
caught by a wink from a Cuirassier as they passed.
She knew that face, even if she had had only a second to look at it, back when the guard at Shapstone
palace had "ignored" her presence in the curtains. Just
what had he been trying to say to her?

They had come to the point where the sand spit
became part of the mainland when a shower of arrows
flew out of rain-shrouded scrub. One of them cut
across Leyla's arm and hit Deshin's horse in the hock.
The animal whinnied and reared, almost throwing its
rider, ripping free the reins from Leyla, and bumping into the startled Beywulf. And the Emperor broke
free, hanging low over the horse's neck.

Keilin's assegai flew, as Cap, holding his sword aloft
now, yelled, "Ride!" and kicked his horse to a gal-
lop. In a few moments they were all galloping behind
him. A brief skirmish and they were through, dodging away among the scrub patches and dripping
palmettos in the rain haze.

"To the sea!" Cap cried. They rode neck on neck,
thundering onto the beach and along the tide wash,
and then when they reached a rocky slab, they rode
cautiously into the scrub. They couldn't see anyone
behind them, in the rain curtains, but there were
distant sounds. Cap led them further in, towards the
ridges. He pushed them as hard and fast as the horses
could go until darkness came.

Their camp was as hidden as they could make it,
deep in the liana jungle of the valley bottom. The
rain had stopped but Cap denied them even the
comfort of a small fire. "They're hunting us out there.
It's not worth the chance. We'll leave here before
dawn," he said, in a voice that brooked no argument.
Then he turned to Beywulf, his voice flinty. "Well,
Sergeant-Major, would you care to explain just what

happened back there? Why didn't you kill the little bastard?"

"No excuse, sir. I wasn't prepared for his horse to rear. I didn't think they'd take a chance with their hostage's life." In the dim leaf-shadowed moonlight, Beywulf stood ramrod straight, looking at the middle distance.

"Hmm. That's no excuse, soldier."

"Sir . . ." Keilin said cautiously.

"Don't interrupt me, boy. That was a good throw of yours back there. Pity there wasn't really poison on the thing."

"There was. If it cut him he's going to be unconscious for a day or two at least," Keilin said quietly.

"What! That's better than I'd hoped. I saw it slice nicely into his shoulder. Obviously his mail shirt was more pretty than functional. And I thought it a pity it hadn't killed him! Well done, boy," said Cap, and turned back to Beywulf. "Now let me finish dealing with this bungler."

"Sir, S'kith told me something else you must know," risked Keilin again. "Bey was right, sir. It was not the Emperor's men that shot at us. S'kith and I were at the back, as we're far the worst riders. They were trying to kill the Emperor, not us. There was one hell of a firefight behind us."

At last Keilin had managed to shift Cap's attention. The man actually laughed. "All this for a bloody woman." He looked across to where she was silently unpacking her bedroll. "You're more trouble than you're worth, you know. Any reasons why I shouldn't cut your throat, girl, and get them all off my back?"

A pause. "Because I'm worth something alive. You can buy your way out of trouble using me," she said tiredly. "My father would probably give you a few regiments to attack FirstHive too."

A silence. Keilin could almost hear Cap's mind turning over. "You stay with us, for now," said Cap, and then in an easier tone. "Beywulf, can you rustle us up some food quickly, while I dress Leyla's arm?"

Quietly Bey moved over to the packs. As he passed Keilin, he gave the boy's arm a brief squeeze. Keilin knew what it meant: partly thanks, partly warning.

Before dawn they were away again, moving inland, sticking to the forest margins, avoiding the villages by tedious and hot bushwacking. Once they sighted a party of soldiers, but remained hidden under the trees until they had passed. Keilin had been too tired to think the night before, but now his mind was busy turning over all the revelations of yesterday. His knowledge of politics was slim. In Port Tinarana he'd heard of the Tyrant, yes, but he knew little more. He had heard, and read, more of Arlinn, but he still barely understood the entire thing. He did however know that he'd made a fool of himself. He'd always been wary of talking to girls. He wasn't just wary about princesses, however. He was terrified of them. In Shael's mind, power and authority meant security. In Keilin's mind it meant "avoid at all costs." So he was. With great care. He was also wondering just what had got into him the previous night. Bey was a friend, sure, but when Cap was being like that he was Authority, and Keilin kept his head down and did what he was told. It was a long, hot, hard day, and he had plenty of time to think it all over.

Tired, sweaty, plagued by flies and with the air thick with the coming thunderstorm, camp that evening was not a cheery place. With darkness the flies left, and once the party had plates of food inside them, their spirits began to rise. True, the heavy, starless sky and the breathless air portended yet another wet night, or a night with wet bedding at least, but a few comments were beginning to be made. At last Leyla broached the question on everyone's minds. "Where to from here, Cap?"

He shrugged. "We need to go north, but if we try

it in the midlands we run into real jungle, not just valley-bottom stuff. Cutting our way through it would take three or four months at least, and as like as not some of us'd die in interesting ways before we found our way out. If we found our way out. I tried it . . . once. It's all twisted ravines and impassable rivers, as well as totally confusing forest. I only got out by pure luck."

He took a sip of his coffee. "Thanks to the three bungling burglars we can't go through Amphir. Thanks to our little Princess and her boyfriends the coast trail is closed. Which reminds me, what was all that wordplay about 'Saril,' girl?" asked Cap, fixing her with his eagle gaze.

She shrugged. "He's Deshin's boyfriend."

"Hmm. Interesting . . . and possibly useful to know, in a homophobic society. A lever perhaps?" he asked, questing.

"He does keep it a secret. In most of the Tyn States, it wouldn't be wise to be public about it. It's different in Arlinn, of course," she said.

Cap snorted. "Thanks to bloody Evie Lee. Half of her friends were chutney ferrets. Still, it won't get us north. I suppose we can rope down the cliff between the watchtowers at night, but we couldn't take horses. On foot it would take us too long to get out of Amphir's territory. That only leaves us the option of going by sea to Dublin Moss. It's a bugger of a trip, weatherwise, but I don't see how else we can do it. We'll go further south and then down to Port Lockry."

Keilin dredged his memory, trying to remember the place on the maps he'd pored over. "Back down through the lowlands?" he asked, just the edge of trepidation in his voice.

He was rewarded with a snort of laughter. "Don't like them either, do you? Relax. We go back onto the plateau and then about five days' ride we cut down through some of the finest farming country in the world."

"Cay." His tired eyes jumped open. Only one person whispered like that. He sat up. "Princess. What can I do for you?" The wind was beginning to rip at the tree branches and the air was rapidly chilling. It was going to rain soon.

"Can I sit under some of your blanket? I'm cold." Her voice was timorous. Two days ago Keilin would have been delighted. Now he was wary. "Hadn't you just better go back to your bed, Princess?"

She stamped her foot, forgetting that she was being quiet. Fortunately the wind in the clattering branches effectively masked the sound. "Will you stop treating me as if I've got some disease," she whispered fiercely. "Stop Princessing me too. You know my name."

"I thought I did," he said slowly. "But it seems it isn't Kim after all,"

"Cymbellyn is my second name."

"It's a lovely name, Princess. But you see, I don't even have a second name. I'm a street child. I'm a thief. I ran away from the brothel my mother lived in, because I found out she was going to sell me to a house that specialized in pretty boys. She wanted the money to buy drugs. See, my kind and yours don't mix," Keilin said sadly.

After a long moment's shocked silence he spoke again. "I used to dream about rescuing a princess, and the king making me a noble and giving me his daughter and a fortune. But . . . it isn't like that in real life. If I took you to your father, he'd be glad to have you back. But he'd see that I disappeared sharpish, wouldn't he?"

"Yes." Her voice was very small, and the sudden flash of lightning showed that she was looking at her feet.

"So . . . when we get to Dublin Moss, I'll sneak you away to him. And then I'm going to disappear myself . . . before he helps me along." Big droplets of rain came splattering through the tree-canopy. In the brief lightning starkness he could have sworn she shook her head. But hammer-blows of wind shook and rattled the forest, making speech near impossible, and the raindrops began to come down in earnest now. Keilin bundled his bed roll into an oilcloth saddlebag.

She still stood there, wet faced, and looking lost in the intermittent glare. So Keilin took her elbow and led her to the shelter of a half-fallen tree. They huddled together, under the sloping trunk, sheltering under his cloak. Keilin felt the warmth and softness of her pressing against him. He ground his teeth, and closed his eyes and as felt, even in the ankle-pouch, the core section was growing colder. Storms in these parts were brief but furious. Keilin, for one, was enormously relieved when the rain slackened and the crack and boom of thunder faded to distant rumbling. Yet a small part of him had not wanted the rain to end.

Shafts of leaf-speckled moonlight came spilling down onto them through the ragged edge of the storm clouds as they came out of their makeshift shelter. Her hair was wet and plastered against her skull. It only served to accentuate the high cheekbones and big eyes further. She turned to face him, bit her lip, and tumbled into speech. "I came to sleep with you. To get you to take me to my father."

Keilin was silent for a minute. Then prudence won. "You don't have to. I said I would do that anyway. Now, go back to bed." He pushed her away roughly and immediately turned to the saddlebag and began taking out his bedroll. When, after some studied minutes, he looked up again, she was gone. But it was a long time before he got to sleep that night.

And riding the next day was pure agony. But at least
he didn't have to avoid her as well. She was doing
that with more skill than he had.

The days that followed were hard, pushing both
the horses and riders to their limits. It suited Keilin.
When they stopped he pushed himself still harder,
chopping firewood, fetching water while the others
sat owl-eyed and exhausted. He even forced Beywulf
into weapons drills. By the time Keilin lay down in
the evening, sleep was close to euthanasia.

Once again they'd come down off the plateaus, this
time into country which would lift any man's spirits.
The rolling hills were rich and verdant. The grass was
soft with flowers, the streams clear and laughing. The
farmers were cheery and prosperous. Even the ants
seemed fat and lazy. But Keilin resisted its appeal,
staying locked into a frustrated anger.

Port Lockry was a neat thatch-and-whitewash town,
set in a gap in the sea cliff, built around a well-
constructed harbor mole. From a mile away it looked
the picture of prosperity and comfort. Like all fishing towns it smelt of tar and fish. It also reeked of
fear. People scurried about in little knots of agitation,
talking anxiously. They eyed the hard-ridden, well-
armed group of strangers with suspicion. The party
rode past the smithy, where a queue of townsfolk
waited. By the smoke and din from within, the smith
was working furiously. Keilin saw the plump burgher
at the head of the queue paying over gold, and no
small amount, for the clumsy sword he was receiv-
ing. By the way he was holding it, thought Keilin,
with all the scorn of the newly skilled, it wouldn't
matter that the thing would bend at his first strike.

"We should make for the Silver Anchor, Cap. It's
the best tavern for picking up news of ships with a
berth or two," said Beywulf, hopefulness in his voice.

"No doubt also with the best beer," Cap said dryly.
"Still, I dare say you're right. Might be a good idea

to find out just what is going on around here. Something has got a normally quiet town's fat little folk running around like newly beheaded chickens."

The Silver Anchor was full and noisy, unusual for a sailor's and fisherman's pub at eleven in the morning. Elbowing through a mixture of drunken fishermen and crying-in-their-beer burghers, they fought their way through to the bar. Cap's commanding presence found them service and the attention of the hard-pressed barman. "We'll have four pints and two halves. And we're needful of finding passage on a good ship bound to northern waters. Do you know of any vessels heading up the coast?"

The barman drew the beers from the barrel without a word, and placed the tankards on the scarred and stained bar top. He wiped his hands on his apron. "That'll be six silver," he said, his voice flat.

Keilin took the half pushed at him. A half! Like a child. He was sixteen, dammit. Then he saw the Princess's face and lost some of his own anger in amusement. She was obviously just as displeased at being given a smaller tankard, but, as she'd just taken her first sip, it looked like the thought that she might have to drink *all* of it was vying with her chagrin. In the meanwhile Cap waited, his eyes holding the barman like a fly trapped in a pool of his own beer. Finally Cap said quietly, but in the sort of voice that stopped conversations all around them, "You haven't answered my question, ale draper."

Forty years of working in a dockside tavern had taught him to recognize trouble when it stared him between the eyes. It was one of those things you learned quickly or you didn't survive. This barman had once been a county champion wrestler, and the fact that he welcomed brawls had tended to discourage them. Today he was feeling too old for bruises. And the squat hairy one next to the tall fellow had brawl written all over his wide countenance. But before he could step back and bring the heavy metal-grid shutter slamming down, Cap's long fingers closed on his shirtfront. Without any sign of effort on the tall man's part, he lifted the three-hundred-and-twenty-pound barman, and pulled him half across the bar counter.

"Don't even think about it, friend. Just answer my questions and we'll get along peacefully. What's going on here? Normally every bloody barman in a port town would give you the names of three skippers going anywhere, including hell. Have they stopped giving you kickbacks?" Cap asked, in the sort of voice used when discussing the weather.

There was a faint gargling noise from the barman, and a weak flailing of arms and legs.

"What? Oh," and the viselike hand pushed him back and loosened slightly. But it still remained on the barman's shirtfront.

The barman had a lifetime of experience. This was more than potential bruises. His respectfully toned reply was still faintly choked. "Sorry, sir. I . . . just about every man in this place has asked me to find him or his family a berth . . . on any damn thing that'll float. There's no chance, sir. Not even for all the gold and jewels in Amphir City."

"There's a fair forest of masts out there. Why won't they sail?" Cap asked.

"The Hashvilli!" The barman looked gray just at the mention of the name.

"Hashvilli? Oh, that rabble of pirates and petty slavers from the Ferl Islands. Never used to worry a decent skipper . . . in your father's time that is. I gather they've become something more of a nuisance," said Cap disdainfully.

"Sir! Sir jests! The Hashvilli sea wolves are a scourge on the sea lanes. The Kalmis Navy used to hunt them, keeping the trade route to the north open in return for those extortionate duties at their ports.

I'll admit that when the Tyrant up north swallowed Kalmis, the traders were worried, but at least some of the patrols went on . . . up until last year. Since then there's been nowt to stop the Hashvilli. Eight months or so ago was the last time a vessel made it north and back. The news they brought wasn't good. There's a war in Kalmis between the Tyrant and some new Emperor. And the sea is full of Hashvilli raiders," explained the barman, ignoring calls for beer from the far end of the bar. No one this end was being foolish enough to interrupt.

"Shut up," said Cap to the crowd at large, in his voice of command. Even the drunks were silenced. He turned to the barman again. "Then why the panic today?"

The barman's voice dropped to a near whisper. However, in the newly-won silence they had no trouble hearing him. "Two weeks ago they hit North-haven, forty mile up the coast. Took every able-bodied soul as slaves, impaled the rest. Even a newborn baby. The same again three nights later at Whitesands Bay. But there a few of the farmers got lucky and got away . . . with a Hashvilli prisoner. He talked before they killed him. The Ferl Islands had a drought the year afore last. Bad crop and a lot of starving folk, with no way out except raiding. Then this year, it was a wet winter. The winter crop got the blight. Their wheat turned black in their fields. An' now, there's famine loose there. No food but what the raiders bring home. And there's been no ships going north for dunamany months."

"An' now they're coming here. They'll gut this place like a herring," a panicky voice from the crowd cried. "The *Bess* was out last night long-lining on Fourteen-Mile Bank. They saw 'em at dawn. *Bess*'s skipper dropped the lines and ran, and she got in maybe two hours ago."

Another took up the tale. "The skipper he took

word up to our burgomaster, Johannes the Chandler.
Within twenty minutes our brave Johannes'd chartered
the *Kessaly* to run him an' his family and a couple
of fat chests south." There was some satisfaction in
the tone as he continued: "She was burning off Scarff
Point within twenty minutes."

"The *Garfish* sailed maybe five minutes after. They
made it back though."

Another snorted, "Only just, mind. They were so
badly holed, with four dead an' seven wounded of
a crew of seventeen, that the raiders obviously didn't
expect them to see land. *Garfish's* skipper says the
Hashvilli cut an' run as soon as they could see the
cliffs . . . But they say there's hundreds of masts just
below the horizon."

"Hell's teeth! So what are you folk planning to do
now? Run inland?"

There was a silence. Finally a big man in a striped
seaman's jersey spoke up. His voice was slow and raw
from speaking over a sea wind for half a lifetime. "My
boat's here, mister. So's my life. I'm not going inland.
What could I do there? Beg?" A murmur of agreement went around the room.

"So, you're going to fight."

"Aye!" a belligerent chorus from the fishermen and
sailors. Some of the townsfolk were silent, scared
looking.

"But you don't have a leader, and you're passing
the time in the bar getting soused." Cap's voice was
scathing.

The big seaman pushed his way forward. The
crowd melted back magically. "Look, mister. I don't
like your tone. I don't like your face. And I don't see
what it's got to do with you." He reached out a
contemptuous hand.

And found himself flat on his back. "Get up. Don't
waste your strength fighting me. You'll need it for the
Hashvilli tonight." Cap's voice was icy, commanding.

"I want a ship out of here. Seems to me the only way I can get one is to stop the place from being trashed by a bunch of sea scum. I am an officer of the Crew, and I am taking control of the defense of this town. Any man who wants to challenge me is welcome to try his luck. Barman, this place is closed for the duration. Now, finish up your drinks. I want every man, woman and child that can carry arms, and whatever weapons they have to carry, on the quayside in ten minutes." He raised his tankard. "I give you a toast. Death to the Hashvilli!"

There was a moment of silence. Then every glass and tankard in the house was raised. The tumult was overwhelming.

The quayside meeting had been wary and fearful at first. But within five minutes Cap had them raring to fight, and beginning to believe they could win. Then he split the mob into sections and assigned various duties. Beywulf was set to a weapons inventory, sorting out the usable from the trash, and selecting archers for Leyla and Shael to take in hand. S'kith was demonstrating swordsmanship, assisted by Keilin.

Cap was questioning the skipper and some of the sailors off the *Garfish*, as well as several other senior captains. "You're sure this is where they're bound?"

"Nowhere else to go, sir. There's sea cliff for thirty miles to the southeast and another forty or more northwest," *Garfish*'s skipper replied.

"And coming in here? Where can they beach?" Cap pointed at the harbor.

"Only inside the harbor sir. There's a mean reef just outside the mole. It breaks at low tide, and at high it'll rip the bottom off anything deeper'n a dinghy. I suppose you could jump off onto the moles as you come in, too."

"I see," said Cap slowly. "Tell me . . . what sort of wind do you have most evenings?"

The seamen looked at him in some amusement. "Why, it's allus offshore at this time of year, sir. That's the way it works. Land gets hot and breathes out at night. Then the hills get cold and suck air off the sea in the early morning."

"And what time is the tide? And how soon can they be here after dark?"

"It's rising now, sir. She'll be full at about three. They'll have to tack in an' row the mole. Mebbe ten o'clock? It'll be about full low, then."

"Hmm, right. This is what I want done." He detailed various tasks, and sent a sailor running to fetch Beywulf.

"Lot of bows, but light stuff. And some fair shots, too, from what Leyla says. There's a marsh a few miles away and a lot of the townsfolk go after waterfowl. The swords are rubbish and they've no one worth calling swordsmen either. S'kith'd have killed someone by now if the boy wasn't with him. They'll do one hell of a lot better if they stick to gutting knives. There's hardly a man or woman in the town that hasn't got at least one, an' most of 'em have those ten-inch filleting knives, too."

"Right. I want pikes, fifteen-foot ones. Tell that rascally blacksmith if he makes another so-called sword, I'll gut him. If there aren't enough spearheads, get the seamen to lash knives on poles. Tell S'kith to start them on pike drill instead. I want two hundred men who'll stand. I don't want a single runner, Sergeant-Major. Pick them for steel. Take the skipper of that barque over there and put him and his first mate behind them. He's a murderous old bastard. Tell him to cut the head off the first man who breaks ranks. We want a hundred for each mole, so you'll need to find another sea captain like that. Don't worry about the lightness of those bows. The sea wolves don't have armor. You drown too easily in the stuff. And they won't have to shoot far. Now, I want you to round up a couple of carpenters. Should be easy enough in the boatyards, and make me at least one Brunhilde capable of throwing a hundredweight cask from here into the channel."

Beywulf nodded. "A piece of cake. It's not above a hundred yards."

"Go to it, soldier. Oh, and send a local to me. Somebody who's no use to the militia but who knows his way around. I need to find a couple of masons and some chemicals."

CHAPTER 11

The night was quiet. Too quiet. All that could be heard was the sea's constant crash and whisper. Keilin knew his were not the only ears straining to hear the creak of a rowlock, or any other ship-betraying sound from the sea. He knew that up on the clifftop many anxious eyes were peering seawards, wishing desperately for more moonlight. That didn't stop his stomach twisting itself into knots. What the hell was he doing here? If he slipped off now he could be a good few miles away before morning. His reading had lead him to believe that battles were glorious, and he'd often imagined himself leading the heroic charge. Now it was coming. And he was scared.

Something touched him on the shoulder. He whirled, assegai at the ready. It was Shael.

"Kim! I mean . . . Princess. I'm sorry. I . . . I wasn't expecting you."

There was a glimmer of a smile. "It's all right. Even Beywulf's jumpy. They've spotted them from the clifftops. I . . . just came to say goodbye, Cay, and . . . I'm glad you still think of me as Kim."

"Habit. I'm sorry."

"I'm sorry too. For everything. I absolutely *hate* you. Good luck." She turned and fled.

Keilin was left to reflect about his scant knowledge of what made women tick for the next few minutes. He also spent some time regretting a certain missed opportunity. But he hadn't known he might be going to die quite this soon. Then the first Hashvilli galley came cautiously nosing in between the moles, the rowers putting their muffled oars carefully into the water.

As quietly as possible, men jumped from its sides and spilled like ink across the white stone of the South Mole. Then the second galley arrived, and its reivers leapt off onto the other mole. The third, fourth, and fifth galleys quickly followed, now sacrificing silence for speed. There were nine vessels between the moles, the oarsmen rowing as hard as possible to reach the inner harbor and beach, or run up alongside the quay. The running vanguard surged ahead along the moles and struck against the breastwork and its wall of pikes. In the stilt-mounted pavilion behind the pike line, Leyla waited until the attack was a thick and clustered mass of swearing men hacking against the spear points. Those behind were pushing their leaders onto the thicket of sharp points. Her calmness seemed to spread across the archers. "Aim at the mass, after that, pick your marks." The sound of stretching bows and indrawn breaths was audible in the silence of the pavilion. "Loose."

Across the channel the same scenario was being enacted.

"Like shooting ducks in a barrel," commented one archer as the mass attacking the pike line was suddenly turned into a rout of screaming men. A rending crash, and the sound of splintering timber drowned his words. The lead galley ripped her bottom out on the heavy sharpened logs that had been anchored just below the water line. The next two galleys were only yards behind her. The momentum of the leading galley had borne her onward, until the weight of water in her shattered bow abruptly stopped her. There was no chance for the two behind to avoid collision. The fourth steersman was more alert. He managed to avoid the first three ships in a scream of wood and shattered oars. But the ship's inertia carried her forward, inevitably, onto the waiting logs.

There were fifteen vessels between the moles when the first struck. Of these, eleven had hit either each other or the hidden obstruction. Several of the vessels began to break up. The channel rang with desperate shouts and screams, the sound of rending and tearing wood, and frantic splashings. The few undamaged vessels were unable to move effectively, and men in the water scrambled towards them or the mole embankments. Another four galleys attempted to come in from the sea and their crews jumped, pouring onto the mole.

"Beywulf. Now!" The three catapults sprang and the casks of whale oil and naphtha flew to shatter into the channel. Two minutes later, when the oil was spreading in a greasy sheen across the water, the lit tar-candles in their net-float containers followed. Some went out. Some floated harmlessly amongst the wreckage, emitting clouds of foul black smoke . . . and one spat a fat spark into the naphtha fumes.

The channel erupted into a chaotic inferno. Hashvilli raiders leapt desperately from their burning ships onto the shelterless mole, where the arrow rain fell in heavy sheets. The tide and the night wind carried the wash of flames out and around the harbor mouth, isolating those already on shore from the remaining vessels.

From his duty point, Keilin watched in fascinated horror. Surely they would surrender, or run now? This was butchery, not war. But it seemed not. At the end of the South Mole, beyond the range of all but the heaviest bows, the surviving captains had a hurried council of war. The Hashvilli live close to the sea . . . and they swim like fish. If they could get past the breastwork and tear down the arrow platforms, it would be all over.

Men began pouring into the water outside the moles. How were they to know that the blood of all the domestic livestock of the town had chummed that water for the last two hours? And the deep channel between the outer reef and the mole had always been a favorite hunting ground of the great carcharinids. It was here that the blood and gurry from the whale flensing ran, rather than into the harbor. After the first, and then abruptly the second screaming man was ripped under, the rush for shore became frantic. The cries of "Sharks! Sharks!" were loud enough to carry even above the other horrible sounds of battle. Nothing their captains could do would force those men back into the water.

But those on the North Mole had seen what their companions on the South Mole were doing. The north channel between the reef and the mole was shallow and sandy. Now, at low tide, you could wade neck-deep along it. There was one deep hole, but that was near the shore, behind the breastwork. It too had been chummed, but less successfully here.

Keilin saw them coming, their topknots visible between the waves. Now that it had finally come, he found himself detached and ready. The first axe-wielding raider rushed out of the surf. His face was a grinning mask of hate, and he shouted in triumph. Keilin waited patiently. In the shallow surf gill nets had been spanned in a foot-tangling mess. As the raging marauder splashed forward to meet the boy, he stumbled. Keilin's assegai plunged. Blood gushed into the water.

Thick and fast they came. Soon the bank was full

of struggling, fighting men. Keilin had no time to think, just react.

Then, when the water was black with topknotted heads, a sharp whistle sounded. Teams of fishermen on the quay began the rhythmic hauling they did every day.

A three-hundred-yard seine is heavily weighted with lead balls along the bottom line and sweeps with force along the seabed. A wading man in deep water is less than agile, and the net ripped inwards faster than a man could swim. On the quay the sweating, heaving men pulled as they'd never pulled before. And the topknotted raiders in the water tumbled like skittles as the sweeping lead line knocked their legs out from under them.

The net worked as well for men as for fish. A few clung to the top line and slashed at it vainly. It had been reinforced with light anchor chain, with extra buoys to keep it up. Most of the raiders simply tumbled over each other. Struggling bodies rolled and sprawled along the meshes. The rip of the net dragged them inexorably into the bag. The bag . . . where the head- and foot-lines were sewn into a reinforced pouch that could take seven tons of fish. When the bag slid into the deep hole near the shore the teams slowed, almost stopped. The few men who were not in the net bag scrabbled over the top to freedom. But the rest . . . well, the pieces of old iron tied on to the bag of the net kept it down, and when the net was finally hauled to the edge of the mole, the fishermen methodically speared any bodies that still twitched.

On the South Mole now, the raider captains saw that their only hope was to crack the spear wall. And now they set to it with discipline. The pikes held . . . And then, under the barrage of thrown axes, the channel-side flank folded. Two men turned to run.

Four of the Hashvilli were up. Standing on the

breastwork stones. Cutting at the unprotected heads
below. Making a gap.

With a bellow that echoed above the din, Beywulf
leapt into the fray. The two-handed sword swung in
an unstoppable arc.

The frail flesh and bone of eight legs were no
obstacles. Then he jumped up onto the breastwork.
He hurled back those who would take the weakened
place. Cap bounded up beside him, and turned to
face the panicking pikemen, not the assault.

"Hold, damn you! You bunch of bloody gutless
bastards." Such was the power of that voice that the
wavering spears steadied.

In front of them Beywulf cut a one-man sortie into
the raiders' ranks. And then, having hewed down all
before him, he retreated, scrambling under the spears,
back to safety. In his wake lay carnage. And there
was no eagerness to try again.

The sea wolves were milling about in confusion
when the catapults flung another tub of fire brew.
The catapult crew had attempted to adjust their aim
to help the endangered folk on the mole. They were
partially successful. The barrel struck the inner wall
and shattered into staves. The greasy liquid spewed
out across the white stone. The Hashvilli were a
running, yowling mob even before the mess took
flame. They were jumping from the pier head, sharks
or no sharks, and swimming for the galleys still
offshore.

On the northern mole, the flame wash had eased
enough for another captain to put more men ashore,
before his ship also caught fire, as catapults flung
fresh fuel. The raiders had seized a still-burning mast
spar and used it to ram the pikes aside. It led to a
vicious and wild melee. Gutting knives clashed against
cutlasses and boarding axes.

Keilin flung himself into it.

Cut. Thrust. Parry. With the clockwork strokes of

S'kith guarding his back. But it was all coming apart. Some took to their heels. In two minutes it had gone from strategy to chaos.

Then came Beywulf's familiar battle bellow. At the head of the surge, Cap and Beywulf flung a party of South Mole defenders into the rescue. Somehow the tall man rallied them all. He called order out of confusion, discipline out of chaos. In minutes the tide of the battle was reversed, and the raiders were flung back in full retreat.

Keilin leaned exhaustedly on S'kith, surveying the body wall around them. The Hashvilli were dropping weapons and jumping for flotsam. A flood of top-knotted heads was swimming out to the remaining galleys. And being pushed off and cut at, as the five remaining vessels began hoisting sail, running for the open sea, with a last few arrows from the shore pockmarking the moonlit water behind them.

It was morning. A cold, crisp, unforgiving morning. The bright new sunlight stabbed at his eyes. Keilin wanted to turn over and avoid it, but there was something heavy lying half across his chest. With difficulty his dull aching head ordered his eyes to open again and focus on whatever it was. It was not going to be easy, but it beat trying to move. Moving sent waves of nausea washing up from where his stomach had once been.

Reluctantly he opened his blurred eyes again. It was an arm. And a breast. An extremely large, naked breast. For a few moments, he lay there hypnotized like a rat staring helplessly into the swaying cobra's eyes, watching how the brown nipple moved as the woman breathed. Interest's snake stirred . . . and then nausea jumped up and beat it to death. He struggled out from under the imprisoning arm and thigh. She stirred, and with a small sigh settled back to sleep.

Keilin staggered out. He had to empty his bladder

and oh . . . hell's teeth! He felt dizzy and sick. Flashes of memory from last night kept blurring into his reluctant mind. It had been a night of firsts. First time he'd killed a man. The thought still made him uneasy. He kept remembering the terrible threshing convulsive jerks transmitted up the assegai shaft. He splashed water into the porcelain basin from the cracked jug with faintly shaking hands. Washed his face. First time he'd really ever been drunk. When wariness was all that kept you alive it wasn't something you even considered. He poured water into the glass that stood on the washstand. He was suddenly desperately thirsty, with a strange rising saltiness in his mouth. He drank and looked across at the woman who still snored gently. First time for that too.

She'd rolled over onto her back, and had rather ineffectually pulled the rumpled sheet over her nakedness. He stared at her, trying to clear his memories of last night. She was perhaps twenty or more years older than he was, with faint lines around her closed eyes, and stretch marks on her belly and big breasts. He felt a sudden need for a second and third glass of water, and then . . . a desperate need for that bucket and seat next door.

The sound of his retching woke her up. She brought him a glass of water and a towel, and held him unself-consciously against her breasts while she wiped the beaded sweat off his forehead. "My God, boy hero, you look a lot younger in the morning light." She looked faintly guilty, as well as amused. "I think my sons are older than you are."

He felt his face going hot. "Still, we were both drunk, I guess." She became aware of his embarrassment, of the fact that he was holding his hands in front of his nakedness. Gently she pushed them aside, "And you do wield a beautiful big spear." She rubbed her breast across his cheek. "I see part of you isn't feeling too bad any more . . . It's still very early, and after last night I don't think anyone will be awake for a while. Come back to bed for a bit, before you grab your clothes and slip out of here." She gave a wry smile at his look of surprise. "You heroes'll leave in a haze of glory. I've got to go on living here. At least let me *pretend* to be a respectable captain's lady-o."

Keilin discovered that adrenalin and deep breathing provided the most wonderful hangover cure, and he was actually whistling when he reached the main road. He noticed abruptly that his ankle pouch was missing. He was about to swear and turn around, when another piece of last night's vagueness came back to him. He'd given it to Kim—Shael—before he'd left with Mara. If looks could have killed. . . She'd known exactly where he was going and with what intent. That was why she had come across and demanded her bracelet. He'd solved part of his own problems by simply giving her the pouch. He nervously realized he wasn't going to enjoy asking for it back.

"Hello, youth!" Beywulf's cheerful bellow echoed down the street. "You look like the cat that ate the canary . . . and now you've got indigestion. Well? Did you get lucky last night?"

He looked at Keilin's expression. "Well, well! And it wasn't with our little Princess. I saw her this morning. She's looking likely to curdle milk. Or was it that terrible an experience for her?"

Keilin shook his head, looking at the windows of houses around them.

"Pussycat got your tongue, boyo? What! You mean that's worn out, too!" He guffawed and took Keilin's arm. "Come. Let's go and have some breakfast. Maybe that'll restore you enough to swap lies with me."

Over a hearty meal of red flannel hash and toasted muffins served by a very respectful barkeeper at the Silver Anchor, Keilin caught up on the plans . . . and the happenings of the previous night. "We'll be sailing

on the afternoon tide—if the channel's clear by
then. Or if we can get those girls to part with S'kith."
Keilin discovered that when everybody had got drunk
last night his "friend" had tried alcohol, too, and
decided he very much disliked it.

He'd been trying to keep in the background when
he'd been discovered by the town's three professional
girls. "They tried to get him to drink with them, and
he refused. One of them asked if he'd given up
screwing as well. He pulled his trousers down and
showed her he hadn't." Beywulf laughed. "The pimp
tried to interfere. With his trousers still around his
ankles S'kith threw him into the harbor . . . from over
there." He pointed to the railing outside the tavern.
It was a good twenty yards to the water. "Then he
walked off carrying a girl under either arm, with the
third hanging on to his neck with her legs wrapped
around his waist . . . still with his blooming trousers
down!"

Bey took a deep pull from the foamy pint pot.
"Believe me, lad, he'll be a legend here long after
we've been forgotten."

By ten the town's hangover was forgotten. Men
strained on ropes, heaving wreckage out of the harbor channel. Small boats picked their way between
the straggle of broken masts and tangled rigging
sticking up out of the water, dropping grapples for
shore-based hauling teams. Along the tideline, scavenging men and women disturbed the flocks of
shrieking gulls from their gruesome feasting. But by
noon the gulls had it to themselves again. Every
man, woman and child was hauling on the pulley-
stacked ropes, dragging pieces of vessel out from
between the moles. That channel was the town's
lifeblood artery, and if the danger had gone, the
town was eager to see trade and fish flowing up it
again.

They were working folk in those parts. The channel hadn't been clear by high tide, but by evening it was at least navigable. The only external signs of the Hashvilli raid were the fire-blackened stones of the South Mole. And on the end of the moles a series of tall poles, adorned with topknotted heads. Cap's party could sail on the dawn tide.

For a while Keilin sat and listened to the talk in the Silver Anchor. Cap held court with several of the town's prominent citizens and some of the senior captains. "You've a very defendable site, but you need some kind of warning system. Say a watchtower on that cliff promontory. With pigeons, or a mirror signalling system." Beywulf, sitting picking at a platter of pickled mussels, scallops and sea violets, saw the doubts in the minds of non-military men.

"It'd have great commercial possibilities too," Bey commented amiably. This pricked their interest far more than Cap's military assessment.

"How so, good sir? Tell us more."

"Put a light in. It'd be a great aid to navigation. I've heard safe landings on this coast are a bugger to find in foul weather. You come in close hunting them, and pick up a reef instead. Ships'd find Port Lockry without having to risk coming inshore." He could see the skippers nodding. "It'd bring ships here rather than to Narhoon River or Northaven. Besides," he said with a sly wink to one of the merchants, "knowing the trawlers were coming in with full holds—before everyone else did—'ud make a hell of a difference to the price of cod, wouldn't it?" There was general laughter and agreement.

Keilin slipped away, off down the streets and back to the house he'd left early that morning. Coming to a familiar turning he grimaced. This was where he'd worked out that he didn't have his ankle pouch. Its familiar weight was there now, a little lighter without her bangle in it. He hadn't had to ask for it. She'd thrust it at him, before walking off, without saying a word. She still wasn't speaking to him. Women! He sighed and walked on.

Perhaps because of this his knock was tentative. But here at least he was welcome. It was still night when she woke him up. "It's an hour before dawn. You'd best be going soon." The candlelight was kind to her face, but he could see that the usual smile was gone. Then it came back with all the poignancy of autumn. "But we still have a little time . . ."

Once again he was amazed by the breadth of her gentleness, followed by the depth and frenzied urgency of her need.

Keilin was down on the quayside about half a minute before Beywulf set out to fetch him. He was more than slightly taken aback to discover that Bey knew exactly where to look for him. Considering that the sky was only just turning gray it was surprising to see how many of the townsfolk were there. "By the way," said one of the townsmen, a familiar face from yesterday evening's tavern gathering, the owner of one of the boatyards, "a little, sneaky, blond rat-faced fellow came into town yesterday afternoon asking after you folk. Offered me a fair amount of gold to delay you when he heard you were sailing this morning." He smiled reflectively. "Boatyards are good places for tar, and a fair number of folk contributed the feather pillows. Good voyage to you."

Keilin stood at the rail of the good ship *Starchaser*. He was surprised to see the Princess standing next to him, at first. Then he realized that she'd decided that her silence wouldn't put as many barbs into his flesh as her tongue could.

The three girls who had kissed and hugged and cried over the bemused looking S'kith were waving. "Look at those cheap prostitutes," Shael said, in an arctic and pointed fashion, raising her finely carved nostrils. "You'd think they actually cared. In actual fact they'll be selling their bodies to any disgusting man before midmorning."

"It's probably all they have to sell. Besides, just because they're whores, it doesn't mean they don't have feelings. S'kith's probably the first man that treated them as if they were important and superior to him."

"Hmph!" She snorted in disdain. "You should know. You're familiar with women of that kind. But I don't see your slut come down to the docks to cry over *your* departure!"

He ground his teeth. Finally he spoke, and his voice differed violently from the slightly tentative tone he normally used with her. "She isn't a slut. Don't you *ever* say that about her again. As for crying, I hope she's not. She's got enough to cry about. Her husband and her three sons are eight weeks overdue from their last voyage. She was on the South Mole fighting to see that they had a home to come back to, if they ever come back. And she's worth ten of any princess *I* ever met." He turned on his heel, and left her standing alone and stunned to wordlessness at the rail.

They felt their way carefully out of the channel, pulled by cautious teams of rowers in longboats, and with lines to the moles. Nervous sailors peered over the bow, until the three masted barquentine felt the first rise of the swell of the open sea. A cheer of relief went up, and the bosun's salt-crusted voice bellowed for hands to hoist the sails.

Keilin had few memories of his only other sea voyage. Besides, that had been in the Narrow Sea, where the waves are small. Here, in the open water, were waves that had had a whole third of the globe in which to build up. The *Starchaser* corkscrewed on the great blue-gray swells as she angled across them, the water frothing and bubbling at her bow. Keilin found that relief at getting clear of the harbor was entirely reserved for good sailors. He and Shael, having each decided to avoid the other forever, were abruptly reunited leaning over the stern rail and barking at the seagulls in tandem. An amused and somewhat sadistic cabin boy came and rang the chow bell at them and bellowed, "Brefaaaast! Cooome for brefaaast! Cookie got nice gurry bacon a swimmin' in gurease, an' luvery slimy arf-coooked eggs, sloppin' about your plates!"

Keilin turned, releasing the rail from his desperate clutch. "If you say another word . . . I'll kill you." His gray face was in such deadly earnest that the boy retreated in haste. Shael forgot she was never going to speak to him again, and groaned a heartfelt, "Thank God. Oh Cay . . . I'm going to die!"

He just groaned.

Seasickness doesn't last forever, although to the sufferer it feels as if it is going to. By evening Keilin was feeling totally drained, but at least he felt reassured that surviving until tomorrow would not simply mean more punishment. In the morning he ventured cautiously into the officers' mess, wearing the necklace of onions and garlic cloves given to him by the same grinning cabin boy. The Princess was already seated, eating an insubstantial breakfast of tea and toast. She sniffed when he came to sit down. "Don't you ever wash? You stink . . . but I think your jewellery suits you."

He sat down cautiously. "I think," he said in a loud voice, "I'll have gureasy bacon, and half-coooked slimy eggs." He had the satisfaction of seeing her turn green, when a bellow came from above. "Hands! All hands to your stations!" The ship yawed and shuddered as they changed course. They went up on deck to find out what was happening. The grim-faced mate explained. "Masthead lookout spotted raider sails. We'll run nor'east and try to lose 'em. We usually beat those square-riggers trousers down quartering the wind."

They did, but by late afternoon they saw another raider, and had to beat further east into the darkness. Keilin was up on deck the next day, sitting and sharpening his assegai blade when the yell came from the swaying masthead "Sail. Nor'-nor'east."

"What sail?" came the bellow from the bridge.

"Small craft, sir. Lateen." A few moments later the gray-haired harsh-faced skipper himself was climbing the rigging with his telescope.

"What is it, Captain?" Keilin ventured onto the bridge. He was nervous, but he *knew* he had to find out what had been decided at the masthead. As usual S'kith followed him up.

"Small boat, young man. Maybe a Hashvilli trap. We'll bear away a point or two," the Captain said matter-of-factly, not paying a great deal of attention.

"No. They have no more water, and some of them are dying. They are from Port Lockry," Keilin said in a voice so emotionless it might have come from S'kith. He did not say that, amid the images of thirst and desperation, there was also the image of a face he knew. However, that was why he raised the assegai, until the razor-sharp spearpoint rested on the skipper's breastbone. Behind him he heard the rasp of S'kith's sword coming free. "You will order the crew to make all possible sail and bear for her."

The captain was a tough man, master of his own bridge. He didn't flinch. "This is mutiny, boy. You know what the penalty for that is?" he said, in a voice that showed no sign of quavering.

"I don't want to hurt anyone. But I will kill you if I have to. On that boat there is a Captain Sven Barrow. You are going to rescue him," Keilin said in the kind of voice that brooks no argument.

The stern-faced man reacted far more to this than

at the threatening assegai. He started and actually looked frightened. "Barrow . . . he's months overdue. How do you know about him?"

Keilin sighed. "I just do. I also know that they're dying. Sometimes I know things . . . And I'm never wrong . . ." His voice faded away. He wished he could just explain and be believed without killing. But it was a lot of faith to ask of anyone, and if he had to kill someone to get them rescued, he would.

The sea captain looked at him strangely, almost warily. Then after a long pause he said, "Put down the spear, boy."

Keilin dropped the assegai. The captain's eyes were suddenly very wide. "You knew . . . you knew I was going to fetch them, before you did that. Sven and I were shipmates once."

Keilin nodded nodded. "Yes. I knew. It was . . . right. And I promise, if they're not who I say they are, you can do to me whatever you usually do to people for mutiny."

The normal grim countenance was back. "Believe me, boy, I will. Now take that damn sharp thing off my deck. And don't ever come up here with it again. And take that shaven-haired goon of yours with you."

"I think," said S'kith slowly, in his usual expressionless voice, "that I will stay up here and make sure you keep your word."

"Out!" roared the captain.

S'kith stood impassive. "Better leave him, sir," said Keilin quietly. "And whatever you do, don't threaten him with a weapon of any sort."

It was a thirty-two-foot whaleboat, with a jury-rigged mast and sail. There were seventeen dried-out husks of men in it, some unconscious and one dead. The skeletal captain spoke with difficulty through his cracked lips. "Bloody calms to the north. We outran seven lots of Hashvilli. The eighth got us without any wind, and them with oars, just at dusk." He managed the semblance of a smile, "Sank the bastards. But the old *Hedda* got holed too, and was going down on us."

He sighed. "I lost my youngest boy in the fight. Mara begged me not to take him . . . but he begged harder to come along, I suppose. We've been adrift for six weeks now, and without water for the last three days. Short rations for weeks before that. That cost me my oldest son, too. But I don't think there'd have been a man alive by tomorrow."

He sighed again. "You took a hell of a chance coming to pick us up, Gabe. I'm damn glad you did o' course, but . . ."

"I didn't take a chance at all, Sven. That boy over there knew what you was. Even knew your name, an' where you hail from. Probably knows what your house number is." The captain permitted himself a rare smile. "He was all set to put his pig sticker through me if I didn't go an' fetch you."

The rescued man looked at Keilin, and reached out a hand. "Fey, is he? Had a bosun like that once, got us out of a lot of trouble."

Keilin felt his emotions roiling inside him as he shook the weak hand. "Owe you my life, boy, me an' what's left of the *Hedda*'s crew."

"It's nothing," he muttered, and turned and fled.

Behind him the rescued man said, "Lucky man to have on board, Gabe. I'd listen really careful to what he says. But the fey 'uns are unhappy folk, mostly. That bosun of mine killed himself in the end."

"There's no way I'm venturing my ship further north, mister. Not after what Cap'n Barrow's told me." The captain's iciness was fully a match for Cap's. "I'll refund your charter, or I'll put you ashore anywhere else you're wishful of going. But not north."

CHAPTER 12

Cap paced the close confines of the cabin. His anger was palpable, dangerous. "So now we're running south again. I'll have the bastard's liver out, when we reach shore. According to all the citizens I spoke to he's the best skipper that dunghill town had to offer me. Now that castaway friend of his, that you"—he rounded viciously on Keilin—"had to persuade him to fish out of the drink, has persuaded him that it's not possible to go north. We're unlikely to get another vessel, so we're back to going overland. Where everybody and his bloody dog is waiting for us!"

There was a long silence. Finally Keilin spoke up in a subdued voice. "There is a way that nobody would be expecting us to use."

Cap turned his sarcasm on the boy. "Where, O my pocket genius? For a thief brat who probably has no idea where he is right now you're mighty full of answers, aren't you? Well? Speak, O master of geography."

"We sail south, round Cape Ebrek, and up the Narrow Sea—"

Cap interrupted, "So you have garnered some geographical knowledge from somewhere. But what you don't know is that Dunbar, at the head of the Narrow Sea, fell to the Morkth nearly ten years back. The caravan route from Dunbar to the east is no more, brat. So that scuppers your plan, which I admit was brighter than I thought you capable of."

"There is a way across the desert and the mountains from Port Tinarana. It comes out near where you found us," Keilin said quietly.

Cap looked at him in surprise. "How the hell do you know that, boy? There used to be . . . maybe two hundred years ago. A little river you could follow . . . I forget its name . . ."

"Syrah."

"So it was! Well, well. I wonder where you heard about that from? Doesn't really matter, I suppose. The river is dry, and no one goes that way any more."

"Beg your pardon, sir," said Keilin cautiously, "but I did. And I can take you across the desert and into the Tyn States by the back door, where no one will be looking for us."

Cap's eyes narrowed. "Beywulf. You've been to Tinarana in the last fifteen years, when you were hiring out down in Ebrek. Ask this boy about the place. Show me he's really been there. He's inclined to be a bloody little liar."

"He's lived there, Cap. He knows the food too well to be lying about it. But if he knows the answer to this, you can bet on it. Keilin, what do the locals call that posh eatery on Deale Street with the red doors?"

Keilin couldn't help grinning. "The ring of fire."

"Why?"

"The meat's usually at least on the turn, if it's not from the town cats, so the proprietor makes up for it with lots of those little red bird's-eye chili peppers . . . the really white-hot kind. Most customers end up with the trots, if they're lucky, with the peppers still burning on the way out. No local would ever eat there."

Bey chuckled. "I got caught good. One of the other guards was from Port T. He told me about its local name when he heard my swearing from the heads. The boy's been there all right."

"And he dresses and behaves like the desert. Yet we found him on the other side of the mountains. Hmm. Boy, you've got yourself a job. Now you go and tell that bloody prig of a captain where he's taking us," ordered Cap.

"Why me? I mean, he won't listen to me. I . . . I don't think he wants me up on the bridge," said Keilin, alarmed.

Cap smiled. It was not a kind smile. "Three reasons, boy. Because I've told you to, because you got us into this shit in the first place, and because if I go up there I'll probably wring his scrawny neck. Now get."

So Keilin got.

Despite his nervousness, his reception on the bridge was cordial. He even drew a wintry smile from the captain. To his relief, Captain Barrow was not there. He still didn't want to look the man in the eye. He found that the skipper listened with unusual care to him, and that his request to put ashore at Port Tinarana was also well received.

"We'll have to put in to Port Lockry first, of course."

"Surely, but . . . why? I . . . I need a reason to tell Cap," he hastily explained.

This drew a definite smile. "Tell him we need to reprovision and offload *Hedda*'s crew. Actually, I want to load cargo, and make it a more profitable trip. We're sailing empty now because I thought we'd have to run, and run fast. But around there should be safe enough. Or how do you feel about it?"

Keilin didn't pretend not to understand. "I'm sorry,

sir. It only happens every now and again. I can't predict your future. I wish I could even predict my own."

The captain laid a heavy hand on his shoulder. "Good enough, son. It's not any easy thing that you have. We'll sail to Port Tinarana. All I ask is that you try to keep that arrogant master of yours off my bridge"—he gave a small shudder—"and that shaven-headed enforcer of yours. But *you* can come up anytime."

One of the other results of fishing the *Hedda*'s crew out of the sea, was that cabin space had to be reshuffled to make room for them, especially those who had to be nursed. Shael found herself having to share quarters with Leyla. It was a small cubbyhole of a place, with two bunks, a sea chest and little else. Shael burned with resentment, of course, and when angry she could never keep a still tongue in her head. She was subjecting Leyla to a diatribe on the injustice of it all when the sultry woman threw a question that she was not prepared to field.

"So why's the boyfriend so miserable?" she said.

There was silence.

"You want me to get out of the cabin for a while, to give the two of you a bit of . . . privacy?" Leyla continued.

"We're not . . . I mean I don't know what you mean, or who you're talking about." Shael said, defensive tones creeping into her voice.

Amusement showed in Leyla's half smile. "I know you're not sleeping with him. But you're always trying to manipulate him. I was just surprised. I always find men much easier to steer when I've got them by the balls."

It was bluntly said, but it struck home. Shael blushed redly, and spoke in a moment of honesty. "I tried." Then the anger, embarrassment, and embitterment of it all made her burst out. "I asked him!

I offered myself to him. And he turned me down! Me! And now he's been sleeping with some fat old woman while we were in that horrible harbor town. I *hate* him!"

She was crying, furious, miserable and pouring out a torrent of words, in which Keilin featured prominently. A dispassionate observer would have had some difficulty in reconciling her descriptions of events with actuality or the boy's point of view. But Leyla was not dispassionate. And once, very long ago, she'd felt much the same way. So she let Shael finish her eruption, gave her a shoulder to cry on, and an arm to lean on, while they sat down on the sea chest together.

"It's all right, little sister. It's all right. He'll come back."

Shael sobbed and shook her head. "He won't. He . . . he's from the bottom of the gutter. His mother was . . . a prostitute. He's a thief. He should know as much about chivalry as I do about . . . sailing. But . . . the core sections show him as he sees himself. He's a small, small knight in this big suit of armor, on a white horse, fighting evil and dragons and rescuing damsels. And he wants to be big enough to fill that suit of armor."

She sniffed. "So, he says that commoners like him and my kind don't mix. But he'll take me to my father and then disappear. He just doesn't understand!"

"But I do, Shael. And I promise you . . . he said no, but he's been kicking himself every night."

"Are you sure . . . I mean, why?"

"Because he's a normal man, if a young one, and they're even randier and less logical at that stage. Also," she said wryly, "he's stopped following me about with his eyes. It's not often that I lose them like that."

She looked at the surprise and hope in Shael's eyes, seeing as well the unasked question. "No. I always left him to you. You'd clearly marked him as your prey. And I use sex for generating alliances. Taking him would have made you even more my enemy." She smiled. "Besides, to be honest, the poor boy was so frustrated, he would have done anything for me anyway."

"Do you . . . I mean . . . is sex always just a weapon?" Shael asked doubtfully

"Oh no," said Leyla, in a deep throaty voice, with the hungry smile of the tigress. "It can be . . . delicious. Shall I show you?" she said, putting a hand on Shael's inner thigh.

She gave a shriek of laughter as Shael jumped, startled. "There. That's got you to stop feeling quite so sorry for yourself. Now, let's plan your stalking of your flighty knight. You can sit down again. I have had girl lovers, but they were all willing and eager ones. And quite frankly, dear, organizing your chase is more fun. I've never done *that* before. Now, first off you've got to get talking to him again. He's been really miserable since we rescued those folk. He needs someone to talk to. Go and find him. Be nice . . . for a change. But first," she looked at Shael's face critically, "let's do some repairs."

She found him at the stern rail, looking out at the trailing bubbles, and the lazily following gulls. His shoulders were hunched, and he failed to react to her approach. He was normally so wary that she couldn't come within yards of him without him noticing. This time she had to touch him lightly on the arm before he jumped like a startled cat.

"Careful. You'll end up in the sea, and the captain's in such a hurry to get out of here I don't know how keen he'd be on turning around to pick you up."

He managed a small smile, which, as it failed to extend to his eyes, was a parody of his normal grin. "It wouldn't matter. I can't swim anyway. I'd be drowned before they could get back."

"Then I'd have to jump in after you. And I've just

washed my hair." She smiled at him, one of her devastating, saved-for-the-occasion smiles, which she had practiced so often in front of the mirror.

He sighed. "What can I do for you this time, Princess?"

It hit her like a douche of cold water. His reaction to her smile was to assume she wanted something. She looked down, bit her lip slightly, and looked vulnerable. Had she but known it, she looked far more beautiful like that than in one of her studied smiles. "Nothing . . . only you seemed so miserable, and I was feeling bad about the way I've been treating you lately. I . . . I just wanted us to be friends again."

He put his arm around her shoulder. It was working, she thought triumphantly. He was quiet for a long time, still staring into the sea. Finally he sighed. "I'm sorry, Kim. I can't explain."

Heartened by the familiar name, she touched his arm lightly. Her voice was gentle, quiet, "Try."

He turned from the sea, and looked into her eyes. Finally he spoke. "It's this mind thing. This psi. I . . . I sometimes get pictures . . . or feelings to do something. Not often. It's just this dread that if I don't . . ." He looked at the sea again. "With the people in that boat. I knew just how thirsty and desperate they were . . . how hopeless."

"You saved them, Cay. Without you they'd have died." Her eyes were soft, sympathetic.

He looked at the deck planking to avoid looking at her. "I knew who they were, see. Because . . ." it came out in a rush, "the woman I was with those nights in Port Lockry. It was her face the captain was thinking of. She . . . I was just an escape, I suppose. Maybe she also felt sorry for me. There'd been the fighting and we'd all been scared to death. And all that killing and . . . well, and she's human, ordinary, not like you. I mean, she also needs, um, just physical . . . But she didn't ever pretend she loved me. She didn't stop loving them. She was worrying about them all the time. Her husband and her three boys. I wanted her to want *me*."

He looked up. Looked her full in the eyes. "I knew they were there from the night before. And I was going to leave them to die."

He turned and walked off, leaving her to stare open-mouthed after him.

A lighthouse had already been erected on the cliff above Port Lockry, and the channel was now clear, even at low water. There was a huge crowd to welcome them into port. Keilin found himself peering into the crowd, his keen eyes looking for her face. He found it, and thus was able to watch the expression as someone called out. "Hey . . . That's *Hedda*'s crew on board!" And he saw hope blossom, and he saw her begin frantically waving.

Keilin was sitting in the deserted ship's mess, getting himself quietly and systematically drunk. Everyone else was ashore. In the excitement of the castaways' return he'd been able to slip away between decks without too much effort. S'kith had wanted to stay on board with him, but Keilin had chased him off to join the three enthusiastically waving girls, with Bey's amused comments still ringing in his ears. But now the ship was ghostly quiet, only the near-still-water sounds of an occasional moving hawser, breaking its tomb stillness. He heard feet on the gangplank, but paid no attention to the noise, other than to hope that whoever it was wouldn't disturb him.

"Boy Hero." Only one person had ever called him that. He stood up unsteadily. She came over to him as he swayed next to the mess table. Took his hands. Her eyes were luminous with a kind of deep happiness that had been absent when he'd last been with her. Then she hugged him. "Gabe told me what you did. Sven and my son wanted to ask you to come and stay with us. I said I didn't think it was a good idea. I said you'd feel awkward there." She gave a small smile, guilty, and yet mischievous, making her face look twenty years younger. "I didn't say you'd probably have walked into the wrong damn bedroom."

Keilin felt his ears burning, and his heart doing uncomfortable bumps. "I'm sorry . . . I couldn't do anything about your other boys," he said, awkwardly.

She sighed. "Lover. Three days ago they were all dead. I didn't want to admit it, but . . . I didn't ever really believe I'd see them again. But I still came down to see every ship that came in, just in case there was news. When I saw it was *Starchaser* coming in I was bitterly angry . . . with you. What right had you to come back safely when my man and my boys were lost? I didn't want to see you ever again. And then my Sven and Olaf were on board! I even kissed old Gabe Soren's ugly face about sixteen times. And then about an hour later . . . I found out that if it hadn't been for you, Boy Hero, they wouldn't ever have come home."

She smiled softly. Touched his cheek gently. "It . . . couldn't have been easy for you, seeing them go with me, so happy, an' you left here alone, but . . . it was the greatest gift you could ever have given me. I hope you find a girl of your own age soon and"—mischief dimpled her cheek—"I hope she likes your spear as much as I did. If not, well, come an' see me, if Sven's away. If Olaf ever leaves home again. He's taking a job in the boatyard and not going to sea again, I'm glad to say. Sven's got the captaincy of a coaster. It's not what he's used to, but it'll see him home more often."

Keilin swayed, but he managed to smile in return. "I probably won't ever be back, Mara. You, I, it was . . . um. Anyway, you'll be busy with the baby."

Her face blanked. "Baby?"

"You're going to have one. A girl. I know."

She was silent for a long time. "Yours?"

He shook his head. "It just hit me now. I really don't know. I just saw the picture of you . . . and it. Her. Counting toes."

The smile began slowly, and grew, and grew. "Not bloody morning sickness again! At my age!" She hugged him fiercely. "You know what, Keilin. I don't care who her father is. Only . . . she'll never go away to sea. Good-bye . . . Boy Hero." She kissed him slowly, "Good luck and . . . I'll always be thinking of you."

He sat down at the table again, toying with his glass after she'd left. It didn't seem so necessary any more. More footsteps. Furtive ones this time. Who could it be now?

"She must be 'ere. She ain't in any of the other places." Quietly said. Full of sibilant threat.

"Third cabin to the right, upper deck. Cost me a bloody fortune in drinks to find tha' out." A slightly whiny voice replied.

"Never mind. We'll be makin' a bloomin' fortune out of this. I just 'ope 'Enery got them horses ready and waitin'. I wouldn't want ter tangle wiv some of those fellers in the bar, meself. Third right, upper deck, you say?"

"Yep. S'right."

"Then what we' doin' daan 'ere?"

"Keepin' outa sight. Now shut yer gob an' let's get on wiv it."

Keilin found his way to his feet, threat clearing away some of the alcohol fumes. He picked up his assegai, and stumbled over his feet, as he headed towards the door. "Shh! Keilin!"

The whisper had come from the far side of the door. He moved over to it. She was hiding behind the cook's hatch, in the kitchen. He slipped round to its door, and then went inside. Slid the bolt. In the moonlight through the porthole he could see

Shael with an eighteen-inch butcher's knife in her hand.

"Why didn't you go after them?" she demanded in a fierce whisper.

He swayed towards the door.

"No! You're drunk. Stay here with me!" she countermanded.

He blinked owlishly at her. "What," he asked, with an attempt at dignity, "are you doing in here?"

"Shhh! They're looking for me," she said in an urgent whisper.

"I may be drunk, but I worked that out. That doesn't answer my question."

"SHHH!"

They were coming back. "Well she ain't there, clever dick. All those bloomin' drinks fer sod all!"

"Try the mess."

Doors opened quietly. "Well, there's a light 'ere. Sign someone's been 'ere. Looks like someone's bin doin' a spot o' private pissin' it up."

"She's probably in bed with 'ooever it is. Come on. We'll check she no' at the tavern after all."

The sounds of the footsteps leaving, and the creak of the gangplank let them both exhale.

"Cay . . . I can't go back to my cabin. They might come back. Can I come to yours?" she asked in a small voice.

He nodded. In silence they went back up to his small cabin. She had to help him up the steep stairway to the next floor, and having watched him fumble with the key for two minutes, she opened his door for him. She locked it behind them. "Have the bunk," he slurred, sitting down against the door, assegai in hand.

She slid into the bunk, bit her lip, and slipped her dress over her head. She lay there for a few moments in the darkness, gathering courage. Finally, she said, quietly, "Cay. I . . . I'm cold."

There was no answer.

Cautiously she leaned over the edge of the bunk. The moonlight from the porthole showed him slumped over sideways, still holding the assegai. He gave a gentle snore.

Shael sighed and lifted her eyes to the uncaring ceiling. "I thought I'd been prepared for everything that could happen on my first night in a man's bed," she muttered. It was a long, long while before she drifted off into an uneasy sleep.

The vessel was full of noise and moving folk when she awoke. It was also crisp and cool now. It had been anything but cool in this stuffy little cabin before she'd fallen asleep. She'd been going to dress again . . . but it had been too hot. Now the porthole was open. And somebody had thrown a blanket over her. That somebody was still lying under a blanket on the floor. How was she to know that he'd stood there looking at her in the small hours? The light of the sinking moon had streamed in through the porthole, and bathed the bunk in its brightness. It had taken him a very long time to decide to turn away and open the porthole, before covering her curves gently, ever so gently, with a blanket out of his sea chest.

Hastily she slipped on her undergarments and her spangled dress. She got up, stepping over Keilin, waking him as she unbolted the door. With luck she could be safely back in her own cabin before anyone noticed . . .

She listened. All quiet. She stepped out boldly, to find at least three people coming down the passage. She fled, her ears burning at the sound of Beywulf's Wagnerian laughter. "And I was just going to start looking for her."

"So you say they were definitely looking for her." Cap eyed them with more disfavor than the rejected pieces of bacon gristle on his plate.

Keilin nodded. "No doubt, sir."

"Any ideas who they were from?"

"No. I didn't recognize the voices at all," said Shael looking down at her feet, just as she had when she'd been asked where she had been, and why.

"Still, as the whole port thinks we're going north again, and thinks us mad into the bargain, I suppose no harm is done. And no one else knows this trail of yours, do they, boy?"

Keilin shook his head.

Cap waved a hand dismissively at them. "I'll have some coffee, Cook. Hell's teeth, why don't you let my sergeant-major show you a thing or two."

From the distant clifftops three men watched the disappearing *Starchaser* in puzzlement. "She's on it, that's for sure. But that's a bloody strange course for the north," commented the one, to whom the others referred as 'Enery. Shael would have recognized him at once.

By the time the ship had weathered the storm around Cape Ebrek, and had left the cold midnight-blue depths of the great ocean, to sail up the clear aquamarine waters of the Narrow Sea, Keilin was very glad of his refuge on the bridge. He'd even gone to the length of hiding out in the swaying crows' nest. Didn't she understand what she was doing to him? He'd told her just what their roles in life were. She had a couple of armies looking for her. Wasn't that enough? Why the hell did she want him too? Still, he dwelled at some length, and with remarkable tribute to his powers of observation, on the memory of her lying naked in the moonlight on his bunk.

CHAPTER 13

The sun burned relentlessly. The sea moved in azure and aquamarine curves around the foam-laced reefs. The sky tinted to copper with the dust and heat. And Port Tinarana stank.

Keilin stared out at it from the bridge, and tried not to wrinkle his nose at it. How many years of his life were tied up in this stench? And he didn't even remember it. There was the Patrician's palace, hanging above the water. There on the hill stood a burned-out shell of a building too. It was definitely the right town. But . . . how had it become so small?

"You're sure you won't stay, son?" The captain's heavy hand rested heavily on Keilin's shoulder.

He shook his head, slowly, "Thank you, sir, but no. There are things I have to do."

The stern-faced man blew out between his teeth. "I wish I didn't understand what you meant, Keil, my lad. Still, you go carefully. That's some unchancy folk you're mixing with there. Don't you trust that supercilious Cap fellow. You watch that Leyla woman too. She knows too damn well that when a man's balls start thinking, his head doesn't. That," he said, with an almost smile, "is hell of advice from a sour old man that girls steer clear of, but I wasn't always that way. When they start looking at you like that little one does, it's time to take a berth, any berth, to any place else."

"She's a princess, sir. This is her idea of fun. She knows she'll marry some high muck-a-muck sometime, but in the meanwhile she uses me to keep her claws sharp. I wish she'd pick on someone else," Keilin said with wry acceptance.

The old sea captain laughed. "You've certainly spent a lot of time up here dodging her. Well, good luck, boy. If you ever need a berth, there's a place for you on *Starchaser*."

The captain watched from the bridge as they disembarked onto the crowded quayside, making no effort to come down and speak to his departing passengers. Finally he turned to his first mate. "Notice, Mister Mate, how that boy keeps himself mighty quiet and in the background. Did it here on the ship too. But I found miserable beggars like the purser, and even young snots like that cabin boy of mine listened to him, and did him favors. I've been a ship's captain half my life. I can see a good officer a mile off. That one's got a way about him that breeds loyalty. No high-flying orders and heroics like yon Cap feller, but folk'll do more for that boy in the end, than for him. When that Cru high an' mighty sees that, he'll not like it. I reckon the girl's not stupid either. Reckon they taught her to choose good ones, even if she'd no marriage in mind."

The crowd at the dockside had a haunting familiarity to it. It was strange to Keilin to walk those streets in daylight, and to be an outsider. The shrill cries of the vendors, the whores in their windows, the sharp scents of spices and curries, the overwhelming stink of the drains, the smell of camel-dung fires . . . they all brought it back to him sharply. He kept looking about for faces that he might recognize.

A military party was coming their way, down from the Patrician's palace. As they drew closer Keilin realized with shock that he did recognize the face of the man who was leading it.

It was not a face Keilin would ever forget. But the Guard-Captain had obviously seen promotion. He was now Commander of the Patrician's personal Guard, escorting that individual's litter through the streets. Cap's group was wedged against the walls of the narrow street. Keilin lowered his face, wishing the wall would open up and swallow him. This was no alley, but he had his back to a wall again.

The Guard Commander's eyes washed across them . . . across Keilin's face, and on without pause. Keilin started to breathe again, as the man passed by. He felt the tension run out of him.

"Yeth? And what do we have here?" The lisping voice was cruel. There was no fear in the voice now—just power. Silence fell. "Commander." Kemp turned, the forty armed men of the bodyguard halting too, readying weapons. Keilin looked for a place to run, and saw no breaks. "That girl. I want her."

His beringed plump white finger with its exquisitely manicured nail poked at Leyla.

The silence was torn by the sound of Beywulf's terrible jagged-edged sword being drawn. His lips drew back exposing his own yellow snaggle teeth. "Leave her alone."

Cap looked over the heads of the crowd, who were doing their best to melt away in a hurry without being obtrusive. "Bey. Let me handle this."

"Withe. Tell your thervantth that rethithtanth meanth death. Put that ugly thword away and I'll forget it." The Patrician was plainly not that cowed by Beywulf's threat.

"Hold, Beywulf. Don't sheath . . . yet. Patrician

Vedas," Cap said in a clear carrying voice, the voice of a power, speaking as if to one of his councillors, with whom he was a little out of charity, "we're not your citizens. We are simply on our way through your charming city. I don't think you want to delay us. By this patch you know that I speak for the Crew. Remember, you are mine to command. I don't need to tell you about what happens to those who obstruct the Crew's ends."

The Patrician smiled. Those white teeth were filed. Keilin would swear to it. He wished he'd spent more time telling them about his city and what to avoid. But they had planned a quick walk to the camel yards and then to be away. And he really hadn't wanted to talk about it. "Commander, thee that theth people accompany me back to the palathe. Thereth thomeone I want them to meet."

Leyla laughed. It cut through all tension. "I don't see what all the fuss is about. After all I've just received a very flattering bit of attention." She looked under lowered lashes at the plump, white-robed man. "I'm dying to see your palace."

The Patrician gave a high-pitched giggle. "Dying . . . yeth! I mutht thow you my pleathure roomth . . . in the thellars. I'm thure you'll jutht be *devoured* with pleathure. Come along then." He giggled again.

Keilin desperately wished he'd told her just what the Patrician's particular perversion was rumored to be.

They found themselves marched away from the direction of the camel yards, away toward the many-turreted white marble palace. Keilin wondered what had replaced the treasury. He was afraid he might find out. "There. You don't have to solve everything with a sword blade, Sergeant-Major. A little harmless entertainment on Leyla's part, something she's hardly unfamiliar with, and a bit of 'big brother is watching you' from me and we'll be on our way without any trouble, and very possibly with some help."

"Sir," whispered Keilin urgently, "I must . . ."

"You must learn to keep your long nose out of what doesn't concern you, boy. Now, shut up."

So Keilin retreated, to find himself buttonholed by Shael. Her childhood training stood her in good stead. "What's frightening you so badly? Does Cap really trust the plump little snake of a local ruler?"

"Yes. He thinks everyone will still be overawed by his Cru badge. He doesn't understand that it only works with ordinary people nowadays. I don't think Patrician Vedas is superstitious, and anyway he obviously believes that he's above any law, now. He used to have women stolen for him by night . . . now he comes and demands them in the street."

Beywulf had dropped back to walk just in front of Keilin. In an undervoice he said, "Keil . . . what were you trying to tell the man?"

"He kills them, Bey. Nobody knows what happens to the girls that go into his cellars." He didn't add that rumor, and the frequency at which girls disappeared, suggested it wasn't a quick death.

Shael took a long sharp look at him. She could see his fear. She realized that she had often seen him afraid, but always facing that fear. This was the first time she'd seen him ready to break and run. His face was sweat-beaded and almost gray with terror. With shock she realized she could actually *feel* his fear. The core section in his ankle pouch must be freezing. Any minute now they'd have the Morkth on top of them. He had met other terrible foes along their travels, but this . . . the fear was inculcated in early youth, and distance and experience had done nothing to lessen it. Well, she'd been warned. She'd better prepare for it. "Lend me your small knife for a minute, please, Cay. I need to trim my nails, and put my moisturizing cream on," she said calmly.

Mutely he handed her the tiny blade from his pocket. Biting the inside of her lip slightly, she set out to manipulate him. At least this time she was doing it for his own good. He was scared, desperately scared for himself. She would shift the fear to worrying about the rest of them. Worrying about her. She knew he would react. He always did. He'd put his own problems behind him somehow, and find the courage and resource to help his companions. She knew she had to break his funk before panic took over, but she still felt despicable doing this. "He's going to kill me . . . and Leyla. Help us, Keilin, please!"

Her appeal did the trick, as she had known it would. He nodded, and the very act broke through his wall of fear. He felt the assegai shaft. Who was Kemp to be petrified of anyway? Old Marou would have made mincemeat of three of him. He felt a gentle touch on his shoulder. It was S'kith. There was almost a trace of expression on his face. Worry. With shock Keilin realized the emotional spillover from his mind must have touched the otherwise puzzled man. The shaven-headed man forced his face . . . into a sort of smile. "Friend," he said quietly. It was only one word, but Keilin knew exactly what it meant. It meant that Keilin's enemies were S'kith's enemies. And S'kith's answer to any threat was a preemptive strike. Right now that would get them all killed. He'd have to stop S'kith from going off the deep end too soon.

Shael handed back the small knife as they walked through the archway into the palace. Keilin wondered vaguely if her trimming had been judicious, while walking. She'd cut her nails, that she'd so carefully cared for, into rather pointed things. By the look of them she ought to rather have just cleaned them. They were plainly dirty, very unlike her, with her vanity. He must buy her some more cream too. He'd no idea where she'd got this lot from, but it smelled of fish. Then, as the heavy gates clanged shut behind them, it occurred to him that he might not get an opportunity to buy *anything* again.

It was a large hall, with a balcony, lined with cross-bow men. The Patrician turned, "Take thith girl, and that other one over there down to my . . . chamber. I'd never thought of two. How exthiting. I'll enjoy one while the other getth into the mood, watching." The giggle would have frightened crocodiles.

"Wait, you promised . . ." Cap burst out.

"And the retht of them. Take them to thee my withard," the Patrician said with a lighthearted wave. "Ditharmed of course. He'll be fathinated to hear what thomeone claiming to be Crew wantth here. Abtholutely fathinated. You thee, my landth are not platheth of tranthit. We're a dead end, thurrounded by dethert or thea, or Morkth territory."

He stepped through an archway and disappeared, leaving them to face the aimed crossbows.

"It's no use thinking of hostages," the Guard Commander sneered. "The only hostage worth taking just left. Drop your weapons." They had little option but to comply. A couple of men led Leyla and Shael away, as the rest were searched. As one of the searcher's hands travelled down Keilin's leg, S'kith stood on the man's foot, while looking the other way. The searcher turned to cuff him. S'kith simply stood, but Keilin's ankle pouch remained undiscovered. The pile of confiscated weapons grew. Jewels and money were also removed. When they took the core sections from Cap, danger flashed in his eyes. However, all their goods were simply piled onto a low trolley, and not looted. "The wizard will examine it first," commented one searcher, replying to Beywulf's sarcastic comment.

"Come now. Take me to this magician or whatever. I am in a hurry to sort things out, and be on my way," said Cap with a show of his customary arrogance. Keilin just kept his mouth shut. He noticed with relief however that while they were being searched Kemp had left and followed his master.

One of the soldiers shuddered. "I'd rather be questioned by a shark, mister."

"Shut up, Trooper. March them through." Something in the corporal's tone suggested that he agreed with what the soldier had just said.

The wizard had a long beaky nose and a too-broad face. He also sat too still in his robes on the high-backed carved chair. The air outside was hot, and dry. Here in this room it was positively steamy. "Close the door, soldier. It's too dry out there." The voice was curiously atonal, and its cadences somehow wrong. Keilin found himself staring carefully at the speaker's face. Something else was tugging at the sleeve of his memory.

"You claim to be part of the Crew, on business here. Explain." The man's lips were not in perfect synch with the words. The memory tugged more urgently. Smell . . . lavender . . . and something far less pleasant?

At his side S'kith began bioenhancement rituals. "Morkth," he said quietly. And Keilin recognized the smell.

"I am the senior surviving crew officer. Those who thwart me will regret it. My business is not here, it is with the Morkth invasion. Tell your master he'd better return my property and my female companions immediately, and I will say no more of the matter."

A snort came from the seated figure. "The real Crew were killed. The Patrician chooses what females he wants. Tell me more of your business with the Morkth."

Keilin had sidled up behind Cap. "He is Morkth!" he whispered urgently.

Cap's eagle eyes narrowed.

"Answer or I will have one of your number killed. Painfully." The voice remained atonal.

"Voice synthesizer." Cap spoke with grim satisfaction. There was a brief searing bright scarlet bolt from the hand he had tucked into his jacket. There were twelve guards in the room, with four unarmed prisoners. In seconds Keilin realized that Cap didn't need anything more than his hands and feet. These were chopping blades themselves. And the blades of the fallen were in the hands of Beywulf and S'kith. S'kith bioenhanced and Beywulf headed into berserker madness.

But Keilin was outclassed and unarmed. A few seconds later he found the burly corporal's chin bristles brushing his ear, with a sword at his throat. "Hold off, or the boy is dead!"

Cap laughed. "Kill away. He's not particularly valuable to me."

But both S'kith and Bey had halted. Keilin felt an inner calmness, despite his dire situation. By the looks of the corporal's dark broad face he'd been recruited from the refugee swarm from across the narrow sea. Keilin spoke as if having a sword at his throat happened twice every morning before tea. "Corporal. Look. The wizard is a Morkth warrior."

The hand which was twisting and forcing Keilin's arm upward went slack. The man's eyes goggled at the corpse. As well he might. The thing's death rictus had shredded its robes, and pieces of non-human body were exposed. A clawed gray limb kicked at the sky.

The corporal was old enough to have been an adult when the Morkth hoards swept through the rich irrigated lands of Beshtan, killing, destroying and enslaving. By the bitterness in his voice he remembered it only too well. "Motherfucking shiteaters! What the hell is going on?"

"You are fighting the wrong people, Corporal." Keilin made no attempt to move. "My master is one of the Cru. He has come to rid Tinarana of the Morkth filth."

"Hold your swords, boys." The corporal spoke to his surviving compatriots.

"But, Corp, they've killed—" protested one of the men.

"Hold, I said! Shut your face, Josen. I don't blame people for killing bugs. Or anything that fights on their side." The corporal let go of Keilin. "Come on, boy. Let's go and have a look." They walked over to the body. The corporal prodded the face with the sword point. The rubbery mask split, revealing the huge faceted eye beneath.

"Holy . . . we must tell the Patrician at once," said Josen. His paler cast of skin and narrower features made him likely to be a local man.

"I'll bet the bastard knows," the corporal said harshly. "He's been behaving like a mixture between a mouse and a rabid dog ever since this"—he kicked at the Morkth's body—"turned up a couple of years ago."

"He knows," said Keilin, with absolute conviction. Somehow it would have been impossible to doubt him.

"We'll kill the bastard!" Red fury burned in the other young trooper's eyes. He too looked to be the offspring of a refugee.

Cap looked at them. "Very well. You may take part in my plan. Corporal, send this young man to fetch others to view this . . . thing. Men who do not love the Morkth. Help me now and your serving of the enemy is forgiven. I will see if I can help the fallen. I am a doctor, as well as a member of the Crew. Keep this . . . Josen fellow in here; he is not to be trusted."

The corporal looked at him and then at Keilin, as if seeking confirmation. Keilin nodded imperceptibly. "Serra. Fetch Captain Belvin, and Sergeant Rood. Tell them I sent you. Tell them 'red lentil,' nothing else, and say to come *now*."

He looked around the chamber, and then turned

and calmly hit Josen over the head with his sword butt, and watched him fall. "Can't trust him, the bloody little brown-nose squeaker. He's always up the Guard Commander's butt. These other lads are right enough. Been a tide rising against this 'wizard' and Vedas. We were planning a coup in maybe a month's time."

Minutes later two men came back with the guardman. Both of the newcomers were plainly also from across the narrow sea. The spare gray-haired one was already talking as he came in. "Halen. What do you mean using this boy as a messenger? Plain bloody stupid—oh!" He saw the "wizard" and his half displayed face. "Oh, holy Dana!! I see. Sergeant. You and Corporal Halen go and muster your troops. I want them in here within three minutes."

Keilin's mind could not leave Shael's need in other's hands. He turned to the captain. "Can I have a guard please? To show me the way down to the chambers underneath. I *must* go there." She needed him *now*.

The captain looked at him strangely. "Things happen down there, boy, that I don't know about. Lots of screaming. That's one reason I'm neck deep in this mess. Now you want me to send you down there?"

Keilin nodded. "My friends are down there." The fear demon was gone now. All he knew was the need for haste.

Cap's eyes narrowed again. "Would our gear be accessible?" he asked the guards.

One of the remaining men nodded. "They'll be in the red vestibule off the great hall."

Cap smiled, all teeth. "Captain, I must insist that the boy is right. Send these two with us to collect our gear. Then we'll give you a good deal of commotion. Just leave down below to us. Do you want your Patrician alive or dead?"

The captain looked startled. "Uh, what?!"

"Two escorts," Cap said impatiently.

With a blinding suddenness Keilin realized that all Cap really wanted was to recover the core sections.

They were marched as if they were still prisoners across to the entrance hall and into a vestibule hung with red drapes. It was all Keilin could do not to run.

Keilin reached for his assegai, S'kith and Beywulf for their swords. Cap burrowed through the pile of belongings until he found a black leather pouch. Only then did he take his sword. Stashing knives hastily, Keilin grabbed his small pack . . . and Shael's. "Bey, better bring Leyla's gear. Likely they'll need clothes."

Now Keilin didn't even wait for his escort. He was off and running for the archway down which the girls had been taken. He heard Bey thundering along behind him, and an abruptly cutoff word of challenge. He ran on heedlessly around the corner.

The two guards on the door were chosen for size. But they weren't really expecting anyone. One even had his helmet off and was picking nits out of his long hair when Keilin arrived at a full sprint.

The helmet went flying. But Keilin's second stroke missed. He wrenched at the door-embedded assegai desperately.

And then S'kith and Beywulf barrelled up, closely followed by Cap.

"Bugger me, youth. Don't run so damn fast next time," panted Bey, kicking the door in, as he wrenched his sword out of the dead guard's chest.

It didn't stop Keilin again totally outpacing them down the stairs.

It was a huge room. The walls were hung with grisly mementos . . . and implements of torture. And a terrible thin screaming came from the far side of it.

Commander Kemp knocked Keilin butt-over-tea-kettle as he ran for the door. The Guard Commander didn't stop, but he did yell "Need a doctor!" in his sprint for the stairs. And he did evade the rest of the party, and gain his freedom via the stairs.

Keilin staggered to his feet and continued to run toward the screams.

Both of the women were stark naked. Leyla had been strapped to a vast bed. In the candlelight he could see both the old and the new blood stains. Shael was spreadeagled on a hanging steel pentacle, steel manacles about her ankles and wrists. On either side of her head jutted vicious spikes so that she had to look at the bed. Around the victims stood racks of cruel, sharp-edged things. A small brazier burned, despite the heat . . . and the air was tainted with the smell of burnt flesh, as well as the reek of blood and fear. Shael's back was scored with five fine lines, with trickles of blood running down onto her buttocks. Keilin ran forward. The screaming did not come from her.

On the floor writhed a naked Patrician Vedas. He was plainly in terrible pain, his face blueish and contorted, his muscles jerking in uncontrollable spasms. Blood trickled from his nose, and from deep scratches on his shoulder.

Keilin moved forward to spear him.

"Leave him." The words came from Leyla. "Just get us loose, and out of here." Keilin's assegai blade made short work of her straps, and by the time S'kith came up, he'd found a key and was struggling to unlock Shael's manacles. S'kith too was about to make an end of the man on the floor, but Leyla told him to leave the vermin.

Bey arrived, his face white. "Hell's teeth." He kicked the writhing man. "We lost the other one, I'm afraid. Cap's gone to secure the stair. Come away. You can put clothes on there. Keil said you'd need your packs, so we brought them."

Half carrying the girls, they ran back. Shael still hadn't said a word. Keilin noticed she had her arm tight around him, but she was keeping her fingers very carefully straight. When they arrived at the staircase, she said in a small voice. "Cay . . . please take my dress out of my pack, and . . . and help me put it on. I'm scared to scratch anything. I've got tetrodotoxin on my fingernails."

"What?" Keilin started.

"Puffer-fish liver. That's how I killed him. Please give me some clothes. I'm cold." She shivered.

The air in the room was hot and still. Yet her arm was chilly, and her body beaded with a fine cold sweat. Her eyes were very wide. Hastily Keilin took the first garment from the top of her pack, and helped her into it. Then, still with his arm around her, they hurried up the stairs and out into the light.

Cap had been busy. Six more bodies lay there. "Come on," he said roughly. "That captain couldn't organize a piss-up in a brewery, never mind a bloody coup."

Whatever the captain's organizational abilities were, the coup attempt had bred phenomenal chaos. The sounds of fighting, shouting and running echoed down the passages, and the gate was deserted. "Now, local boy. Get us the hell out of here." Cap pushed him forward.

Keilin wove them down the maze of alleyways, keeping away from the main roads, except for one hurried crossing. He stopped them just short of the North Gate, in the shadow of one of the overhanging buildings. He wondered if any of the others had even seen the gang boys watching their passage. He wondered if any of the watchers had recognized him. He doubted it. He didn't even feel like the Keilin who had lived like a rat in these alleys. It was almost as if that life belonged to someone else now.

The gate was open, but the guards were doing a spot of contraband and dutiable goods examination, as well as a bit of freestyle direct taxation. "Keep my assegai and pack. I'll tell the guards there are Morkth loose in the palace."

Keilin ran up, panting, to the gate guard, who was in the act of appropriating a juicy tomato from an angry vendor, on the grounds that it could possibly be infectious.

Keilin grabbed the guard, getting a spear butt poked in his midriff for his presumption. He ignored it and gasped his message. "Go to the palace . . . Captain Belvin's orders . . . Morkth killed the Patrician . . . Run! . . . Need you all!"

The guard looked at him owlishly, then grabbed Keilin, and started to run to the palace, accompanied by five of his fellows. Keilin tripped himself and sprawled on the cobbles when he was opposite Beywulf. Bey seized him. "I'll hold him for you, sir. You go after the other soldiers." In a minute they'd slipped through the gates with the crush of locals who were taking advantage of the lack of supervision. Within five minutes they were at the camel market, to find Keilin's rumor had beaten them there, and was already driving up the price of the beasts.

Keilin could see fires raging inside the walls as they rode away from the market, their newly acquired beasts laden with saddlebags and water skins. He wondered vaguely who would win . . . and whether Kemp had escaped? They circled the outer wall of the city and then rode along the beach. When they arrived at the sea, Shael spoke up. "Can we stop? I need to wash my hands . . . and I'd also like to change out of my nightdress."

This drew a chuckle even from Cap. "You might as well have a swim. This is the last time you'll see water for a good few weeks. We'll keep watch from the rocks over there."

It was enough of an invitation for Leyla. She was already stripping off her clothes. There was an angry red welt across one nipple. "Come on, little sister. Let's wash the filth of that place off us. You lot, b' off for a few minutes. There are times for looking at the merchandise, and this isn't one of 'em." She ruefully felt her breast. "In fact, I think the shops are closed for a while. Go away."

Soon the girls were back, wet haired, and dressed for riding. As they headed through a familiar melon field, this time with an angry farmer shouting at them, Keilin felt the hot wind coming out of the interior, full of dry dust and emptiness. It was like a welcoming kiss. Without a backward glance at the city or the sea, he urged the camel into an ungainly trot forward, into the barren lands. He'd always thought about going back to the port. To pay off old scores. To show the people what he had become. He realized suddenly that it didn't actually matter a damn. He wanted the future now, not the past. And he wanted to get the Princess far away from the pain.

CHAPTER 14

Keilin didn't even admit to himself that he was taking the desert slowly. It was secure. Its bleakness was clean. And here . . . Skyann's spirit roamed, and Keilin's spirits rose with it. To be honest, he didn't even notice the others' discomfort. Nor did it occur to him that anyone might be following them.

Thus, the first warning they had was the clinking of a horse's harness. It was midmorning, three days' ride out of Port Tinarana and they had come into the edges of Marou's old range. Around them the ochre hills already throbbed with heat. Sound carries a long way in the desert stillness . . . but they were close, too close. Keilin had made no attempt to hide their tracks up to this point, but now he led the camels across bare rock and over to a narrow gorge, hardly more than a crack in the red cliffs. Then, ghosting among the broken boulders on the high slopes he slipped back.

Down in the riverbed, following their tracks, were twenty-two horsemen. They'd stopped so that the tracker could examine the trail. Dust hung about them, and the figures shimmered in the heat. Keilin snaked closer. He could hear the voices. "Not more than a few minutes ahead, master. The dung is still moist," said the man who was squatting and examining the trail. He wore the red-and-yellow-striped tarboosh of a goatherd from the Thunder Gorge area of the Tinarana River. All the other men wore the sweat-stained uniforms of the Palace Guard.

"Damn good thing too. If we don't catch them soon we're out of water. They'd better have those jewels you promised us, Kemp," said one of the other riders, suspiciously.

"Believe me," the nasal tones washed away the years, "the Morkth will pay a king's ransom for them. I just wish I'd grabbed them back in the palace when I saw them. But the worm's eye was on me. He wanted to play his bloody games first, the fool."

"How do we know they're worth that much?" challenged another man.

"Actas, you can turn your bloody nag around and go back if you like! All I can tell you is that Vedas was prepared to *pay five hundred in gold* for that boy who had just *one*. How much do you think *he* was going to get for it?" Keilin had heard enough. He crossed the dry riverbed behind them, and then as they mounted again, sent an arrow winging silent to sprout from the tracker's neck. Then he took to his heels, jinking up the steep gully-ripped slope, and into the heat-splintered talus at the base of the red cliff.

A brief scramble up a rock chimney and he stood at the top, looking down on the heat-shivered figures still struggling after him. "Kemp!" he shouted, knowing his voice would carry up the valley to Cap and the others. "Do you know who I am, shitface?" The figures below were still. "I am the boy, the boy with the bull. I'm the one of your victims who got away, and I've the jewels here. Yah! Couldn't catch me then, can't catch me now. Kemp dogsbreath, you syphilitic offspring of a diseased camel, even the sows vomit when you screw them!"

An arrow struck upwards out of the valley. Keilin contemptuously watched it fall short. And pushed a rock shower down on them in return. "Yah! Useless bunch of turd brains! You couldn't catch a one-legged blind-drunk grandmother."

The chase was joined. They were pushing their horses, despite the heat, up the steep-sided valley to the left. Keilin watched with grim satisfaction and led off, away from the dry Syrah Valley, off into the twisted canyons of the badlands beyond.

By the time that the midday sun had turned the air in those ragged canyons into dragon's breath, the sixteen survivors had realized that their horses were just as useful as jellyfish out here. They set off up the sandstone ridge on foot, determined to surround him this time. After a futile hour, and losing another man to a deadfall, one of them had had enough. "We're not going to catch the little beggar, you know," he said. "He's just leading us a dance up here. Let's get back to the horses and get after the rest of them. The little hellion has shot my waterskin, and Actas's and yours, Kemp."

Kemp shook his fist at the mocking canyons. "You're right, I suppose. Get the others, and he'll be stuck out here alone. I'm damned thirsty. But sooner or later I'll get that little shit."

It took them hours to find their way back to where they'd left the wounded men and the horses. But the box canyon was empty. A note, written in dried redbrown fluid was pinned through the pile of empty waterskins with one of the swords of the wounded. It read: THIRSTY, DOG TURDS?

"We have to catch him now. He obviously knows where water is here. And I'm going to enjoy every minute of wringing it out of him." The nasal voice was thick with anger. "Now give us a drink, one of you."

Nobody moved. "I'll kill you if don't give me a drink!" Kemp screamed at the nearest man.

He got his drink. But an hour later, when he desperately needed another, he found that that fellow, and another six who still had waterskins, had slipped off, trying to backtrack the horses.

The moon was high and shining clear and cold through the desert night when Keilin walked quietly up to Beywulf, who was on watch.

"For crying out loud, Keil. I nearly split your bloody brisket. How's the pursuit? We heard you taunting them."

Keilin dropped down onto his haunches. "The pursuit is about eight miles away as the crow flies. Phew, I'm tired. Ol' Marou would have laughed at me, so unfit and water-fat. I had a couple of close shaves out there."

"Eight miles . . . are they still after you?"

"Yes. Some of them," said Keilin, taking a long pull from the waterskin.

"Well, that gives us about an hour. The animals are nicely rested anyway. I suppose I'd better rouse everyone. You rest for bit. I've left you a bite to eat."

"Don't wake anyone. They're eight miles off, as the crow flies. None of them are crows. Maybe thirty miles on foot, if they had the least idea where they were or where we were. And they don't have horses or water any more," said Keilin with grim finality. "Get some sleep old friend. The ones that were still trying to follow me were going in the wrong direction."

He stood up again. "I'm for bed. Sorry, but I won't bother with food tonight, Bey."

"How many of them . . ."

"Twenty-two."

"But Keil . . . some of them must still be following you? You haven't killed that many of them, surely?"

Keilin turned to face Beywulf, and in the moonlight his face was much older . . . almost a grim death's-head. "I didn't kill *any* of them. I darted a few with narca. It makes you lose your wits for a few days. I dropped a few rocks on some of them. Broke a few heads and limbs. Then I drove off their horses, and left them out there without water. Their own stupidity and the desert will kill them. You'll see the vultures tomorrow."

He turned and unrolled his bedding, and crawled into it. He saw that S'kith, lying in the rock shadows, was still awake too. He saw teeth reflect the moonlight. The shaven-headed man must be giving him one of his rare attempts at a smile. Somehow it comforted him.

"Cay."

He sighed and sat up. "Yes, Princess." She hadn't really spoken to him much since she had been liberated from the Patrician's torture chambers. He had a feeling she still blamed him for suggesting they come via Port Tinarana.

She looked at him, studying him. Even in the moonlight he could see the tiny wrinkles around her eyes as she peered at his face. Then she slapped him. "Don't you *ever* do that to me again. I . . . I've been so frightened."

He felt his throbbing cheek. "Don't worry, Princess, I really wouldn't have left you here."

"You idiot!" He ducked the second slap, and she stormed away, back to her own bedding.

The cool morning brought him more abuse. "Bey tells me you took on twenty-two men out there. And they're not coming back," Cap said, his voice hard.

For an answer Keilin pointed out into the desert landscape. In the clear, pale morning air a twist of black dots circled slowly. "More back that way," said Keilin quietly, pointing to a second flight of vultures.

This slap rocked him on his heels. "Don't ever

get smart with me, boy. You think you're so bloody clever. Just remember, even here in this oven you call your own, Beywulf can track you by smell alone . . . And I can—and I will—kill you, if I have to," Cap said grimly. "Now, mount up and let's get out of here, before your big mouth proves to be wrong, again."

The day after, when the sun was starting to sink towards the west, they rounded a bare sheetrock bluff to confront a totally incongruous sight.

Cap put it into words for nearly all of them. "Just what the Hell is that?"

Keilin volunteered no reply.

It was a building, perched on a desert scree slope, sun-baked and torn by the desert storms but still very recognizably a town building. Some of the windows were still intact, as was the faded sign above the door.

A. DYMETRAS. APOTHECARY.
MEDICATIONS, ASSAYING, CHARMS,
CONTRACEPTIVE POTIONS, ETC.

"Must be a hell of a demand for contraceptive potions around these parts," Bey snorted, looking at the barren hillsides. With an elbow that nearly sent Keilin flying and a wink as broad as his face, he said to Shael, "You'd better pop in and get a few, dear. Never know when you might next need one, hey broad beam."

She sniffed. "My morals aren't like yours, ape." It was a sign that she was beginning to recover from her ordeal in the Patrician's cellar room.

Bey chuckled. "Talking of some people coming out of other people's cabins . . ."

Coming closer there were other pieces of the story littered about. Two clean-picked human skeletons, their bare bones showing the gnawing of tiny teeth, as well as the attack of something that could split femurs.

"Hyena," was the only comment that Keilin vouchsafed.

Then Cap noticed the Morkth flying disk. He almost leapt from the saddle and jogged across to it. Kicking aside the scattered pieces of a carapace, he examined the machine with knowledgable care. Keilin saw he wore his shark smile of triumph. "Did you kill it, boy?"

"No. My partner. He got killed too," Keilin answered shortly, not caring if it angered the tall man.

Instead, the answer seemed to please Cap. "Hmm. Didn't think *you* were up to that level of combat. Still, unusual and lucky for you it had only one of them on board. There doesn't seem to be anything wrong with it." He took a black clip-on unit off the control panel. "I must keep this in mind," he said, as he turned to the others who had dismounted and were exploring the shop. "Come on, you lot. Time is awasting here. Pack it in with your looting and let's move along." Still for the first time in days he seemed pleased with life, and even was polite about the baked goanna they had that evening. Which, once she was told what the steaming, succulent flesh was, was what Shael *tried* to be.

Usually they'd ridden into the dusk. It was more pleasant to travel then. But this evening they had stopped early, before sundown. Keilin had used the nearby water cave and the relative abundance of thorny scrub for the camels as an excuse. Actually they were near a spot called Broken-Chimney Rock. He was wrapped in memories, and they were within a mile of the place where he had burned Marou. He wanted to go and pay his respects in private. Also he was mighty sick of that camel. He was already thinking about how to part with it.

He retired from the fire early, took his bedroll and moved well back into the shadows.

He was so damn transparent in some ways. He'd said more since they'd come into the desert than he normally did in a month. Mostly talking about the plants and animals he knew and had hunted, or about geology. Geology! And even Cap had acknowledged he knew what he was talking about. There'd been a sort of joy about him. Shael didn't even think he'd realized he was talking mostly to her. Even his destruction of the pursuit had not seemed to shatter his mood.

But since they'd come to the ruin of that shop he'd gone quiet, shifted into the reticence which was his norm, when he wasn't being a teenager showing off to the girls. Funny. She'd almost forgotten his performances back when he'd met her. The realization that he had been trying to impress her as a member of the opposite sex, back then, struck her abruptly. She'd been pretty dense, hadn't she? All she needed to have done at that stage was pretend to be awed, to have had him eating out of her hand. Still . . . how was Cay to have known he was a lot more impressive when he wasn't trying to show off his tricks? A sharp insight pecked at her quick mind: Did the same apply to her? No. Couldn't be.

She watched him like a hawk that evening, refusing even to let the fact that he and Beywulf had tried to feed her overgrown lizard distract her. When he made his excuses for going to bed, she followed within a minute, ignoring Bey's comment, and Leyla's searching look.

When he left the camp she was just behind him.

He'd been distracted when he left camp. But not that distracted. She made more noise than the Tinarana Brass Band, for heaven's sake.

"Go back, Princess."

She stepped out from behind the rock where she'd been ineffectually skulking. "Cay. . . . I'm not sure of the way back. Can't I . . . come with you? Are you leaving us?"

"I made my promise, Princess. I'll see you to your father, if I can. I won't run off before that," he said dismissively.

"We could still just go on alone . . ." she said softly.

He shook his head. "I'm ashamed of you, Princess. They'd all die out here, without me to find them water. Now, I'll take you back to where you can see the fire."

She twined her fingers in his. "Can't I just come with you? You . . . seemed to be climbing into yourself for the last couple of hours. What's wrong?"

He sighed. "I'm just going to pay my respects. I'm going back to the place where I burned the body of the man who was like a father to me. My first real friend. He made me what I am."

He stood silent for a while, seemingly unaware that he still held her hand. "Back in Port T. people put flowers on the graves. Ol' Marou wouldn't want flowers. I'm taking him a piece of goanna and a bottle of beer. To remember."

She said nothing, just squeezed his hand. "Come," he said roughly. "Come and see the last resting place of the lord of the desert."

In the stark moonlight he led her up between the shadowed buttes and then into a narrow ravine, dark and cruel-edged in the sharp moonlight, and then out onto the naked sheetrock at the top. In the moonlight the tangled weave of sharp-edged valleys lay like some gargantuan mauled tapestry below them. "In the early morning, after a storm, you can see both the mountains and the sea from up here. The old man loved it," said Keilin, as Shael tried to catch her breath. He walked forward to a few charred remains of the cedar logs. He stood for a moment, with only

the sound of her panting stirring the still, cold air.
Then he set down the piece of goanna, and poured
the beer onto the bare stones.

"Cheers, Marou, you ol' bastard."

After a long silence he turned to Shael. "He lived
out here for seventy years at least. He couldn't read
or write. He never had a bath in his life. Every year
or so he'd go across the mountains, drink himself
blind, stink out the whorehouse . . . and leave before
morning. He could kill you in thirty ways . . . he could
slip up to you without you even knowing he was
there. He could keep alive on country so bare an ant
would starve. He taught me nearly everything I know.
He showed me things no king ever saw. He was rich.
Richer than any other man I ever saw. Yet all he had
was a knife, a spear and a few old bits and pieces.
God, I miss him. I miss him."

The wind came breathing out of the night, and the
stars and moon burned coldly on the little plateau.
She looked at him, finding her own lower lip quivering. "He'd be proud of you, Cay."

"I've no doubt he'd kick my butt. Come on. He left
me a legacy. I'm going to need a bit of it." They set
off down and across the open mesa top. Shael was just
beginning to wonder how much further she could go
when they came to yet another ravine. This led them
into an area of twisted and jumbled rock formations.
Keilin found his way to a narrow spire of water-worn
rock, broken halfway and leaning precariously against
the next spike. There were a number of black cave
maws which dribbled bats when disturbed. Keilin
peered at the mouth of each in turn, and then had
her scramble up the rotting tiers of sedimentary cheese-
rock and into one of these dark places.

He lit a crude torch made of a pitch-pine knot with
paraffin bush bound roughly around it. Then he went
to the back of the cave and reached for the high shelf
he knew should be there. It was. But it was also

difficult to reach. "If I pick you up on my shoulders, will you look and see what's back there?" he asked.

She almost fell off her perch. Glowing out of the darkness in the flickering ruddy torchlight were hundreds and hundreds of deep-blue eyes. Some hand-sized. Some as big as her head. "What are they? Cay . . . there's just blue eyes . . . sort of soft glowy ones."

"Turquoise, you nit. Pass some down. Nothing too big to carry."

She handed down piece after piece. Then when Keilin thought it was enough she came down and helped him to put them into the sack he'd brought along.

"Is there much left?" he asked cheerfully.

"It just goes back and back, as far as I could see. I only passed down the pieces I could handle with one hand. This is really only the tiniest bit."

"Good," said Keilin. "Nice to know there is something left for a rainy day."

"I'd say," she said with conviction, "that there is enough for a rainy year. I don't know much about the value of this stuff, but I should think it must be worth a good few fortunes. I thought you said your 'old man' only had a knife and a spear and few bits and pieces."

"Yeah, well. He said he didn't want to leave the desert. He said he had enough, and I guess he was right. Come on. We've got a long hike back, and I'd like to move off early tomorrow morning."

"Wondered whether you'd be coming back last night," Bey said calmly to Keilin as they prepared breakfast.

"You should have S'kith's level of faith in your friends, Bey. Mind you I don't know if you *are* a friend of mine. You won't come scorpion hunting with me, even though I've told you there's nothing quite like them for flavor."

Bey shook his head. "I'd love to, Keil. But you know how it is. *You* can do it, but me . . . people 'ud say the monkey genes were coming to the surface at last. Next thing they'd be feeding me bananas and presenting their heads for grooming. But if you want to go, and I don't mean scorpion hunting, youth, I owe you. I'll fail to find you after *great* effort."

Keilin smiled. "Give me a tin, Bey, I'll bring you a few choice fat stingy tails to try, without you having to demean yourself by squatting on the hillside, turning over rocks. Funny . . . that's the same shade of green the princess went. Look, Bey, I promised her I'd get her back to her dear papa. Then I'll run like hell. I gather he's not a very nice man. I'll rejoin you lot as soon as that is done." His face went deadly serious. "Nobody ever asked me why I've stayed. Maybe Cap believes his threats, but there's been lots of water, and lots of desert beyond it. I could have slipped off many times. The world is big and I'm small. But the truth is I'm hunting. Hunting Morkth. They killed Marou and I'm going to destroy them. The core sections will make sure they come to me and die. And I know now that getting our starship going again will hurt the Morkth worst of all."

It was Beywulf's turn to look serious. "The Tyrant is 'not nice' like terminal VD is 'not nice,' son. He's as cunning and vicious as a wolverine. And don't underestimate Cap. I'd rather take on the Tyrant, myself. Forget your vendetta against the Morkth. They can't breed. They lost their queen or we'd all be neck-deep in little chittering bugs by now. Another hundred to a hundred and fifty years and they'll all be dead anyhow."

"How do you know so much about them?" Keilin asked.

"Cap is the planet's Morkth expert. He's lived in Dublin Moss for hundreds of years. He doesn't give information out easily, but over the years it's sort of leaked out in dribs and drabs to our folk. He's always known he can just outlive them," said Beywulf.

"Then what persuaded him to start on this quest?" asked Keilin, suspicious.

"Now there you've got me. . . ."

The mountains stood cold now, in the mouth of winter. Keilin's tensions had begun to ease. Now all he had to worry about was a blizzard or two in the passes. He wondered if any of the others had realized how the party was watched through the fossicker's heartlands in the foothills. Only his wariness, and the turquoise-concha belt he wore proclaiming his status as an experienced local had stopped them from getting their throats cut. Those who lived along the final section of the way were really little more than bandits. They would allow anyone across from the east to spread out along the mountain/desert front, knowing that if they lived, and tried to return . . . Still, this high, with small drifts of snow in the shadows and wind lees, and a greasy-rag sky promising worse, they should be left in peace.

Shael shivered. "To think a few days ago I was so hot, every time I breathed out I was scared I'd set fire to this horrible animal. Still, the worst is over now, isn't it, Keilin?"

It was Bey who answered, however. "I smell snow. That gray sky is starting to look soft. How much longer to shelter . . . and how much higher?"

"Two passes. I was planning to overnight before the last neck. It was about three to four hours from there to Steyir . . . that's the nearest village, where the turquoise traders and the fossickers meet and cheat each other."

"Youth, if we spend tonight up here these beasts'll freeze, and we might be here for a month. There's really bad weather coming up. I say we stop skulking along and ride as fast as we can."

❖   ❖   ❖

The lights of Steyir shone like a beacon through the wind-driven snow. For the last hour Keilin had seriously thought they weren't going to make it. It wasn't a mean, smelly village now. It was a haven of light and warmth. Especially warmth. As they'd mounted the last pass, the wind, funnelled by the towering snowcaps all around them, had suddenly come howling and whimpering at them like a wolf in pain. With it came the first tiny flakes. As the afternoon died, more snow had begun to fall. So had the temperature with the coming of darkness. Once over the pass and down to the treeline they'd had to follow Beywulf's nose, hunting fire smoke. Seeing the lights of the town, Keilin silently swore that he'd never belittle the sensitivity of that organ again. No wonder the man was such a master of food.

"S'truth. I never thought a measly village could look so good," Cap said. "Has it got an inn, boy, or do we knock on doors for shelter?" His voice suggested that he'd knock a few down if he didn't get it.

"There's a tavern . . . but it's just a bar really. Mostly the fossickers sleep over at Lucy's . . ." said Keilin, the cold in his ears and nose overriding his brain for a while.

"Well, I suppose their doss house will do, boy. Lead us there, and be quick about it."

The glow spreading up Keilin's face partly thawed his nose. "Er . . . I've another idea."

He led them off up a small lane to the house where he'd parted from Honest Clarence. It was more prosperous looking than most in the village, and set apart from them, with a view out into a deep valley. "This is one of the jewel buyers. He actually stays here in winter, whereas most of the others go south. Let me just go ahead and try my credit here. Um . . . Lucy's is a very dirty, cheap brothel."

He knocked.

"Who is it, at this time of night?" came a suspicious voice from inside.

"Keilin Skyann. I've just come over the pass, and brought some fine stones from the desert. You said you wanted to do business with me if I came back," said Keilin, trying to keep his teeth from chattering.

A peephole opened.

"Good Lord, boy! It *is* you!" The door was opened. "Come in. Come in. You're letting the cold in."

Keilin's sharp eyes noted the boar spear still rocking against the wall. "I've some friends back there, sir. Womenfolk too. Not fitting to take them to Lucy's . . . can we have some shelter?"

Honest Clarence looked him up and down. And then smiled and beckoned the others forward. "I wouldn't leave a dog out on a night like this, least of all Skyann's boy. Besides there's a story in this, an' maybe some good stones? Bring your beasts around the house. The stable door is on the slope. It leads under the house." He looked at the dejected animals with surprise. "Camels, eh! Haven't seen those since my young days down south! Hope they don't frighten the horses too badly."

Ten minutes later they were all sitting in front of a roaring fire, in a warm wood-panelled room soft with fine carpets from the far-off southlands. Clarence's wife, a short, plump little woman was having the time of her life, plying them with hot drinks and fussing over the arrangement of the chairs. She was city-born, and found the long winters here in this remote village gave her scant opportunity to do what she enjoyed most: entertaining. And those she saw during the summer were other gem buyers and occasional traders. This group was something different and exciting.

Soon she fussed off into the kitchen, and subtle appetizing smells began to emerge. Clarence produced a bottle of red wine. By the dust on its shoulders, it had waited some years for this. "With the diggers in the Margery, I drink that pigswill beer they serve.

It's what the diggers want an' expect. But I'm a wine lover myself. An' seeing as you're the first digger to come to my house you can drink my tipple for a change."

He poured the wine. It was deep red tinged with a faint chestnut brown edging, heavy with a complex amalgam of the summer scents of berries and fungus-touched leather. A sigh of sheer contentment came from Beywulf's beatific face. "And to think I was regretting not spending the night at what my young friend described as 'a cheap brothel.' Magnificent . . . fourteen years old . . . Shiraz Cabernet-Sauv blend . . . from the heavy granitic soils around southern Ormsburg I'd guess."

Clarence looked at him, startled, and then a vast smile broke across his face. "You, sir, are a marvel, and a connoisseur to boot. It's a pleasure to meet you. Most of the folk around here can describe a wine as red or white . . . with difficulty. Come. Tell me. How did you fall in with young Skyann? Last I saw he was goin' west. He never came back through Steyir. I'd have known."

Beywulf smiled tolerantly at him. "You talk to Cap and the rest about all that. I'm going to check out what your lady wife is doing to that ham and those"— his nose twitched—"dried chantrelles, while I enjoy this truly superb wine."

The succulent ham with its apricot glaze was a thing of yesteryear. So too was the thick golden-crusted clove-laced apple pie, and the big jug of steaming yellow custard. Several dusty wine bottles were unforgettable history too. Now they were facing a soft and creamy greeny-blue veined cheese with a life of its own, with smaller glasses of yet another of the gem buyer's vintages. Keilin hoped the flinty-flowery yellow stuff was a match for that truly evil cheese he was obliged from sheer politeness to finish. Clarence was saying to his wife for perhaps the thirty-third time, "From Port Tinarana! It's a bloody marvel. I don't know if you see the commercial possibilities. It's a good thing our boy's not here . . ."

He could have been telling her that the privy in the garden was haunted by fifteen-foot harpies and green pigs for what it was worth. Sometime during the evening she'd gathered that she was entertaining a Princess and a member of the Cru. Her happiness would have been complete if Mari could have had her sister in Polstra witness the dinner. And Ella had thought she was so grand when she had the mere burgomeister to tea . . .

Soon the party headed for the soft beds that had been made up for them in the loft and spare bedrooms. All except Keilin, and because of a soft pull on her hand as she turned to go, Shael. When the others were upstairs, Keilin tapped his host's shoulder, distracting him from his contemplation of the balloon glass and the firelight. "Eh! What's that? Sorry, young Skyann. Haven't made such a night of it for many a year. What can I do for you then?"

"You wanted to see some stones?" said Keilin quietly.

The buyer enjoyed fine wines, good company and dreams of grand ventures. But there was no doubt where his heart really lay. It was why he was here in this bleak mountain fastness and not in a major trading center, where wines and company would have been far more available. He sat up at once, set aside the glass, and then went to turn up the lamp that hung above the table. Without ceremony he pushed the remains of supper aside to make space for the turquoise.

Looking at the first rough nodule carefully, his voice was reverent. "Ol' Marou's pipe. Thank God. I thought it was lost with him." He caressed the roughness. "Of course the price is not what it should be . . ."

"Ol' Marou said I should deal with Deep-Pockets," said Keilin with a smile. He knew full well that Marou had sold his turquoise to Clarence and to Clarence's father for six decades. He also knew this had been Marou's threat for all those years.

The gem buyer was not to be distracted. He went on examining and sorting all sixty-three pieces. Finally he looked up, a little smile on his mouth. "What!? Y'don' trust Honest Clarence!" Then he smiled, and looked at his hands. "Tell you a little secret, but don't ever let it leak out. I'm the only game in town. Me, Deep-Pockets, Square-Deal, even True-Blue Jonny, we're all part of the same syndicate. Now . . . as to price. Who am I dickering with? You, or this young lady?"

"She's my partner."

"What?" said Shael, unprepared and feeling suddenly both hot and foolish.

Keilin spat on his palm and held out his hand. She looked startled and backed off a step.

"Why are you doing that?" she asked warily.

Clarence intervened. "If you want a partnership, girl, spit on your hand and shake. It's worth more than any piece of paper, on the other side of the mountains."

Cautiously she spat, sealed the sticky handclasp, and then wiped her hand rather gingerly on her dress.

"Now let's talk money. Let me try your new partner, Master Skyann," said the gem buyer, rubbing his hands.

It was a decision he regretted. She knew nothing of the value of turquoise, but Shael had been trained to read the smallest nuances of speech and gesture. She got far closer to the precise values than Keilin would have. Her hands sweated furiously through the first two transactions, but her brief glance at Keilin brought a nod of reassurance. Suddenly she knew she had the edge and, relaxing, she had the time of her life. At the end Clarence shook his head and stood up. "Phew! You've got yourself a damn fine partner there, young man. Next time I'll dicker with you, I think. Now, I owe you, let me see . . ." He totted up the figures, and then got up to go and fetch the money.

"Cay, what does this mean?" she held out the hand she'd spat on.

"It means you get half of the money," he said with a grin. "You could live for a couple of years on it, cautiously."

"But . . . why, Cay? I mean, it's yours. The old man left it to you, not me."

"There's plenty. And I noticed you don't have any spending money. You rely on the stuff Cap buys for you, and Leyla's castoffs. It's cold up here. You'll need some warm things. Also, it's kind of what Marou did for me. Besides, I'm going after the Morkth. I probably won't get a chance to spend too much. I'm going to give S'kith some, too."

She felt the hot prickle of tears behind her eyelids, her throat tighten. What right had he to know how it galled her to be always beholden? How had he known? Why was he doing this? Was he trying to buy her? Logic struggled with this idea. Hell. On the voyage from Port Lockry he had done everything to avoid her physical snares. It had been different since . . . since that cellar. She was scared of physical contact now. In a sudden flash of insight she realized that he *did* know just how she felt. He was an empathic psi. He probably didn't even know that he responded to other people's feelings . . . but that was what made him the person he was. And that was why he'd been so glad to be in the desert. She shrank within herself. No wonder he'd avoided her snares.

Then Clarence bustled in with a small sack of silver.

"By the way," he said, "there's a description out

of Amphir circulating to all jewel buyers. If I didn't know you better, youngster, I'd say it was yours. They're offering a fair reward for news of this feller that looks rather like you."

He smiled at the alarm on Keilin's face. "I never saw anyone coming up from Amphir. Only an old friend coming over the mountains. And it'll be spring before Mari gets a chance to tell her big-mouthed sister. You'll be long gone by then. An' I wish them luck followin' you into the desert."

Keilin would have headed straight for bed, but Shael now touched his hand and gestured with a nod toward the fire. They walked back to the dying embers and waited until their understanding host had drained his glass and taken himself off to bed.

"Cay. How did you know you could trust him?" she asked finally, when the only sounds were those of the wind and the occasional crackle of the fire.

Keilin looked confused. "I don't know. But you can trust him . . . about big things I mean. Not bargaining. That's like a game to him."

"You feel other people's emotions. Especially," she swallowed, "if you're physically attracted to them."

"Not all the time. That . . . would be dreadful. Just sometimes . . . when the feelings are . . . too big. Really happy. Desperately sad. Anger too," he said quietly.

"You knew I was being raped in that cellar. That was why you came running."

He nodded, looking at the fire.

"It was the other one. Not the man I killed. The one I killed . . . just steadied the pentacle. That's when I managed to claw him. When he fell down, the man who . . . was busy with me nearly didn't even notice. I had to stop screaming so he would hear his disgusting master dying."

"He's dead, you know." There was no emotion in his voice.

"I know. You don't recover from tetrodotoxins. I

just wish I had managed to scratch the other one, the Guard Commander, too."

"Not the Patrician . . . the man you scratched. The Guard Commander is dead. His name was Kemp." He saw recognition dart across her face.

"The one who followed us . . . followed you off into the desert," she said.

"Yes. He . . . assaulted me, too, long ago. When I was small and . . . pretty. He wasn't fussy about taking boys or girls . . . as long as there was pain," he said evenly. "He would have killed me, but I was lucky. I escaped to the desert. He's haunted my nightmares ever since. But he won't any more. I went back the next night to make absolutely sure. I found him, or what was left of him. He had located one of the few aquifers in the desert. He could hear water dripping. Only, it was inside the rock. He ripped all the flesh off his own fingers trying to get to it. Then the vultures came down and tore his liver out. By the blood trails, he was still alive while they did it. He was less than ten feet from a cistern full of cold, clear water when he died."

He held her small sobbing body for a long time in the soft firelight.

CHAPTER 15

The sleigh ride to the river had been exhilarating at first. Now it was just cold. They huddled deeper into the blankets and furs, but the knife edge of the wet-snow wind cut in somewhere, somehow. Beside Keilin, Beywulf muttered, "To think I used to like that song about dashing through the snow."

"At least you have some hair to keep it off. Think of Cap and S'kith," said Shael, only the tip of her nose protruding from her new fur parka.

"Hmph! And by the looks of you, you envy my beard and moustache. Not to worry, yours is coming on nicely, broad beam. A little more chicken manure on the inside . . ." There was a muffled thump.

"Ow, damn you! I've broken my nail," said Shael crossly, "Well, half ape, at least nothing else can be as cold or as miserable as this."

She was wrong. A river barge could be. It edged its way downriver through the chilly mountain valleys, with greenish ice slurry forming in the wake, and thin sheets of floe ice gunshot-cracking and scream-splintering in front of the heavy prow. Of course these sounds were loudest at night, making sleep uneasy, as the *Nawleans* wallowed her ponderous bulk downstream, racing the river freeze. Belowdecks, where hold space had been converted to make up two tiers of bunks for them, it was narrow, dark and windowless. The damp air did warm up faintly when they were all down there, but the heavy blankets still felt clammy.

Keilin found he simply couldn't take being shut in. The only real cover on deck was the steersman's hut from which they were expressly banned by its unpleasant occupant. Otherwise one could huddle against the cargo hatch edge or the gunwales, but neither were even headhigh on a sitting man. Rain, which would have been snow a hundred feet higher up, fell in a thin drizzle which was whipped across the deck by the icy winds from the surrounding mountains. Occasionally, for variety, there was sleet. Despite this Keilin stayed up on the flat deck, with his back to the cargo hatch. So did S'kith, although the bareheaded man plainly felt the cold even more badly than the skinny desert rat.

Keilin was worried about the man. S'kith usually asked him a steady stream of questions. These had dried up. Expression had recently begun to appear on the man's face, and rare smiles. Now there were no more of the odd looks of wonderment. Instead a sort of desperate unhappiness began to underpin the near-blank face. S'kith would simply sit in silence on the deck and stare morosely out into the darkness.

Finally Keilin had had enough of S'kith's brooding gloom. They were alone on the deck, shrouds of rain obscuring the dark, tree-covered banks. Below them the near-black water rushed and gurgled. Without quite knowing why he did it, Keilin took the ring with its core section out of his ankle pouch. He held it out to S'kith. S'kith took it, held it awhile against his face, and then returned it, all in silence. But it seemed to have eased the misery somewhat.

"What's wrong?" Keilin asked.

"I am . . . afraid. Afraid of going back to the hive. I am afraid of the dark, afraid of the smallness. Afraid of the horrible, endless . . . *sameness* most of all. You are free-born, friend. You don't—you can't—understand what it means just to have new things happen. You see," he sighed, "in the hive there is this . . . pattern. The pattern *never* changes, until you die. And it makes you—" he searched for words—"*numb*. Numb to everything. And you don't even know that you can't feel . . . You just exist . . . you don't think at all, you just do. And the worst of all is that you're scared by anything different. The sameness, the numbness is horrible, but you *know* it. And it is so, so secure you don't *want* to change it." He sighed again. "Changes . . . *variety*. Those were the hardest things to learn how to deal with when I escaped. But . . . I *now* have come to love the changes. I don't exist. I am *alive*. I *feel*. And now Cap is taking me back. I . . . the piece that is *me*, the *alive* person, not just some endlessly repeat-bred thing, will *die* there." It was the longest speech Keilin had ever heard S'kith make. It was also said with more expression and emotion than he'd known the man could muster. He wasn't finished yet either. He pointed at the hatch cover and shuddered. "Down there . . . that is very like the hive. And this . . . disappearing into the grayness out here is very like what will happen to me when I go back."

"So why don't you run away?" said Keilin simply. "Avoiding Cap wouldn't be that hard, for all he pretends to be God . . . it's a big world. You've learned enough to live in it now. You're a fantastically quick learner. You knew next to nothing a few months ago, but you've learned. You've come from being like a child of three to a teenager in very little time. I'll steal enough supplies for you to hide out for the time it takes to grow your hair and a beard. You've the money I gave you. Don't go back to the hive. You don't have to."

"I have the money that you gave me, and some more the little one you call Princess also gave to me. It is odd. I did not know she liked me. Must I have sex with her now?" The man sighed. "I spent some money in that last town. It was strange. The man in the shop thought I could not count and that he would cheat me. But I remembered what you told me. He will almost certainly live. However, that is aside from the point: I cannot run away even if I wanted to. I cannot go more than two hundred fifty yards from Cap for more than twenty minutes. Even when I followed you into Amphir I knew that we were close to him, outside the wall."

"Why not? I mean don't believe everything Cap says. He's got being the great leader on the brain," said Keilin, first making damn sure his disrespect wasn't being overheard.

"He has placed a small explosive device in my abdomen. I still have the scar. He demonstrated to me how it works. After twenty minutes of being further than half a mile away from him I would be as dead as the hive wants me to be. He explained it to me very carefully . . . to make utterly certain I would not run away," said S'kith quietly.

Keilin sat in shocked silence. Finally he said. "I'll check with Bey. There must be a way . . ." But he had a sinking feeling. He remembered Beywulf saying to S'kith when the man joined them on the roofs of Amphir, "Aren't you too far . . . ?" and S'kith's strange reply. He'd meant to ask about it, but had forgotten about it after all that had happened. Another thought occurred to him. "And for God's sake don't mention the idea of sex to Shael!"

"It will offend her? I do not understand. But as

to speaking to the foodmaker, it doesn't matter too much. I would not go anyway." S'kith was quiet for a long time. "I could not leave you, friend—nor Leyla. You see, until I left the hive I was a man alone. Throughout my childhood, throughout my life I was alone. The warrior brood sows loved me . . . but they did not trust me. You do not trust in the hive. To trust is to die. But you have trusted me . . ."

For two hundred years the Alpha-Morkth had tried to breed hive loyalty into their slaves. They would have been dismayed to see that where they had failed, human nature had succeeded, against all odds.

Keilin felt guilty. All he'd ever done was to feel sorry for the odd man. Suddenly S'kith turned away from the gray view to look at Keilin. There was life in his strange eyes. "I know what I will do. I will teach you the bioenhancement routines. You have taught me so much. It was forbidden for one human to teach another in the hive. I shall teach you, and take joy in defying the Morkth."

Three days later, the barge sailed out onto the wide, ice-free Elbe River. On the east bank lay Morkth-occupied lands. To the west the new Empire of Tynia. It was the first sunlight they'd seen for days and the whole party were up on deck, soaking up the weak watery stuff. A skiff full of armed men came sailing out from one of the fishing villages on the western bank. Leyla readied her bow.

"Leave that alone, you daft woman. Them's guv-ment people," bellowed the steersman. S'kith touched Keilin's hand. "Back," he said quietly. "Start your routine. We must go over the side." Using the party as cover they slipped like rats over the far gunwale. Keilin had just time to catch Shael's eye and nod towards the steersman.

There was a trailing rope hanging from the anchor port, down into the water. It sluiced by green and

cold as the barge moved downcurrent. They hung
onto the rope like fruit, listening to the boarding
party. "We've had a tip-off from a jewel merchant in
Riverport that three jewel thieves are coming downriver on a barge. We're searching each vessel for three
men. One hairy, short and broad one, like that man,"
the official pointed at Bey. "One bald one . . . could
be you, sir, except that the description is of someone far shorter, and a boy with an aquiline nose and
green eyes. About five foot eight."

Cap looked down his prow of a nose at the man.
"I am offended by your assertions. We are the only
people on board."

"Meaning no disrespect, but I'll have to look below,
sir." The man was slightly cowed by Cap, but still
plainly determined. Keilin thanked heaven that the
bedding had all been dragged up and spread in the
sunshine.

A few minutes later he heard them come up again.
"Well, no one down there. My apologies."

Another voice. "We'd better just check they're not
hidin' in a small boat over the side. Remember, like
the Dumara ones."

S'kith had evolved a bizarre teaching method. He
and Keilin would touch the core section. Then S'kith
would do the exercise. It was an awesome way to
learn. Keilin literally felt each step from his mentor's
viewpoint. It had taken only hours to impart the skills
taught to S'kith over years.

Keilin took that deep breath and slid down into
the water. His nerves were pain-blocked, his eyes saw
the world through the faint red shift of human fear-
strength, his muscles ready to continue even until
their own destruction. He was still unprepared for the
cold assault.

He counted. He could feel the numbness creeping inwards. His hands could still feel the rope. By
the bumping on his back the water flow had pulled

them at least partially under the hull. He opened his eyes. He could see greenish light back there. Keilin felt at a count of 130 that he could hold out no more. His lungs were on fire. His hands were losing feeling. He couldn't swim, and if he didn't go up now, he'd drown. He began pulling for the surface. Behind him he felt S'kith do the same.

The joy to breathe again! S'kith surfaced next to him. And a low voice came over the side. "Stay in the water. They haven't gone yet." So they had to do it again. Finally someone gave the rope a couple of sharp tugs. Keilin's lungs and mind screamed conflicting messages: Go up, and, They've found the rope, let go.

Decision was abruptly taken out of his hands as the whole rope lifted. Beywulf's hairy face, red with effort, grinned down at them. "Come up, you water rats."

"Oh. Cap says to wait another couple of minutes. Want some soap?" With a splash he let go of the rope, and they had to pull to the surface once more.

By the time they got the all-clear, Beywulf had to pull them up, because neither could climb.

Bey chuckled at the blue, dripping, exhausted figures. "Didn't you find the hot tap? You pair of bastards, leaving me alone to face the music. You should have seen that bit of fluff of yours," he pointed an elbow at Shael, "cleaning her nails with her knife next to that prick of a steersman." He snorted. "If I'd been him I'd have been more scared of what was under the nails. Now, come below and get some dry gear and a warm brew into you."

Keilin discovered that the problem with bone-deep cold was that it took so long to warm up. The water had been perhaps five degrees and they been in it for nearly ten minutes. The core temperature of his body was down by several degrees . . . and it just wasn't coming up. He still shivered under the blankets

an hour later. He also discovered the cost of bioenhancement. His body was almost too exhausted to
struggle to get warm.

"Move up." Shael spoke roughly. Next thing he
knew she had slipped under the blankets and squeezed
into the bunk with him. Her arms went around him.
"God. You're still like an ice block." He felt the life-
giving warmth of her body seeping into him. She
giggled suddenly. "When Bey mocks me about this—
and he will, I know—I can honestly say you were
frigid." Keilin barely managed a weak smile. Soon the
warm drowsiness took him into sleep. She lay there
for a long time cradling him in her arms while his
now-peaceful face smiled up at her. She nearly bit a
hole through her lip, as the realization took her. She
didn't care if he protected her, was kind to her, or
could be used by her. She was just glad he was still
alive.

The curving Elbe took them westwards, towards
debated lands. Here the wide river flowed from the
lands controlled by Emperor Deshin into those still
held by the Tyrant. The bargeman would go no further. The river was blockaded, and his fat tub of a
vessel was not built to run, but tied up at the river
quays were numerous sleek shallow-draft boats. Their
only problem was to prevent the steersman howling
for the authorities the minute they docked. This time
it was Shael who kept Cap from cutting his throat.
She simply handed Cap a bottle she'd looted from
the apothecary's shop.

He smiled down at her, his eyes narrowing slightly.
"And why would I be wanting this, my fine young
lady?"

"Isn't that what you meant when you said the
bargeman would have to be put to sleep?" she asked
innocent and wide-eyed.

"Hmph!" He snorted at her. "You're not the little
angel you pretend to be, are you, little one? Still, it's

not a bad interpretation. We might want to come back this way one day."

So the unpleasant steersman snored peacefully in his smelly bed while they clumsily maneuvered his craft into the quay. Of the seven runner craft tied up at the quayside, only one was prepared to take them through enemy lines that night. Keilin misliked the feel of her crew. So, by his unease, did S'kith. Keilin had learned that the Morkth-man's psi ability manifested as premonitions of danger. S'kith admitted that he had failed to recognize them for what they were at first. It had got him caught and nearly hung. Now he acted on the hunches. Still, Cap was sure that the pursuit from Amphir was close. He insisted they move that night. Shael suspected he wasn't too concerned for Keilin's welfare, but he surely didn't intend to return the core section either.

They boarded the river runner, taking their seats between the deep banks of oars. Keilin made carefully sure that his assegai was handy. By the looks of it S'kith, too, was prepared to fight. The moon was sinking low and with muffled oars they set out into midchannel. Soon the moon was down and the river mist which forms in the early morning was closing in around them.

The skipper of the blockade runner knew his stuff. As smoothly as oiled silk they slid through the water, running down along a great sandbank midwater. They moved ghost silent past the watch boats, and then, with the muffled oars being slipped silently back into the water they sped away. The rowers hissed with relief when they were safe in no-man's-land.

Now they crept forward cautiously. It had been easy to spot the watchers on the two-mile-wide river upstream. Innocent-seeming fishing boats had pegged those during the day. But the blockade positions on the downstream side were unknown. They edged on silently, till at last the bow lookout spotted the tiny glow in the mist. It was some deck watch taking a chance and smoking a pipe, but it effectively revealed the bireme they'd been bearing straight for.

Soon they were all breathing easier and skimming towards the runner's usual quay. The mist was still thick and the darkness heavy, but the river rats knew their way well. The haloed lights of the quay should have looked welcoming in the mist. Why then did they seem so threatening?

They nosed in cautiously. The quay seemed deserted. Well, it was nearly five in the morning. The boat slid up to the dock. The skipper gave them an oily smile, which made Keilin even more wary. "Well here we are, good gentlemen and ladies. Now, the rest of my money please."

Sourly Cap handed over the gold. "If we don't get to Dublin Moss soon I'll be going broke. At least we're well and truly out of the reach of the gentlemen looking for you three."

They stepped out of the shallow draft vessel and scrambled up the ladder onto the raised dock. As soon as they were all off the boat, she pushed off. "I don't like that," said Bey. "They haven't time to paddle back up tonight."

"I don't think they wanted to be involved," said the solitary man who had been leaning against the rickety building on the dock. "We've paid them their money for delivering you, after all."

Beywulf's sword slowly came out of its sheath. "You paid for *us* to be delivered to *you*, did you? Has it occurred to you, my little cock o' whoop, that *they* have delivered *you* to me? And if anything goes wrong, you're going to die." He swung the huge sword experimentally. "I think I'll just rip your stomach open and leave you to get on with it slowly. I watched a man die like that once. He wouldn't stop screaming and trying to shove his own guts back into himself." The jagged edges of the sword gleamed in the light of the few lanterns. All of this was said with Bey's habitual humor. It didn't make it any less terrifying, especially as the hairy man took a casual swipe at a ten-inch-wide wooden bollard, and lopped its top off. The fact that the entire party was advancing on him couldn't have helped either.

Still, he spoke in a very credible attempt at a steady voice. "I am an official of the Amphir Jewel Recovery Unit. It is Amphir's policy to condemn to death, by slow immersion in hot oil, those who kill our officers pursuant on their duty. It's an awful way to die."

"He's scared, Bey," Shael said, her voice hard.

"Brave boy though," said Bey clinically. "I presume you Amphir lads have a reception committee. What do you say, Cap? Shall we go and explain that in a war zone a lot of people end up mysteriously dead. Nobody knows *who* killed them. Or shall we just kill him and go on and kill the rest, too?"

The Amphir Jewel Recovery Unit man could not see Cap shake his head. "Just kill him and let's get on with it," he said, bored. "These Amphir fools are too cocksure. I doubt if there are more than ten of them. And the river is deep. They won't find the bodies until the fish have eaten the faces."

"No . . . no . . . don't! You . . . you're making a big mistake. There are thirty officers. You couldn't possibly kill half of us. We . . . we just weren't expecting you this evening anymore," said the man, now no longer trying to hide his fear.

"Only thirty. We're late. I'll bet they're asleep. We hardly even need to use the girls. The boy over there walks like a ghost. Won't be the first sleeping man, or room full of men, he's slit the throat of, hey boy?" said Cap, quietly oily and evil.

Keilin did his best to look villainous and grinned, producing a long knife from his sleeve. "Go now, O master?" he asked eagerly.

"No. I think this gentleman has decided to show

us the way past his friends. Then in a few miles we'll let him go . . . if he's been good," said Cap, showing his teeth to the jelly that had once been the pride of Amphir's force.

They'd been so intent on terrorizing the officer that they hadn't noticed his sleepy relief coming along the pier. This man's eyes suddenly focused on the drawn swords. He screamed and ran.

"Hell's teeth. That's torn it!" swore Cap, "No, Leyla! Don't shoot. After him. We may still get past before they're up and organized." But they were too late. Already bleary-eyed crossbow-armed men were spilling onto the pier.

The river quay was a long dock running parallel to the river with three piers leading in over the muddy shallows, rather like an "E" with the long edge in the deep water. The river height obviously varied considerably, and the main dock had to be built out where it could be used at all seasons. They were on the center spline of the E leading to the shore. Keilin could hear the clatter of men running across the wooden slats in the mist.

"Well, gentlemen," Cap said calmly. "It appears we have a stand-off. Several of you are going to die before you can crank those bows, so don't even start. Leyla, drop the first man that tries."

"We have a policy to condemn—" began one man.

" Yes, we've heard. But if it comes to a fire-fight I'm going to kill *you* first. So it won't do you much good personally," said Cap in a matter-of-fact voice. "And with that sort of threat waiting for us, we might as well go out fighting. Even if you get lucky, at least twelve of you are not going to make it. So . . . who'll be the first to move . . . and get killed? Maybe you should try another time instead, when the odds aren't stacked against you."

There was a long silence. Keilin was just beginning to hope when the Amphirian officer Cap had interrupted shook his head. "No." His voice was hard, flat and final.

He continued. "Your theft was the worst incident in Amphir's history as a safe-city. We *cannot* back off. It would cost all of us our jobs, and our city its reputation. You will return the black opal, and we will have ten times its weight of the thief's flesh. Then you can walk away from here."

Cap stood silent for a minute. Then: "We don't have the jewel any more."

The Amphirian officer shrugged. "Then it is twenty times its weight. And the name of the man who purchased it. He will return it, and be refunded. If he should refuse . . . then we count him as a thief, too. Come. The thief. It is one of those three, who actually took the stone. Then the rest of you can go." He pointed to Keilin, Bey and S'kith

Cap shrugged. "Keilin. You wanted to do it this way." Keilin felt his jaw dropping. Cap continued. "Twenty times the weight in flesh. See you don't take a drop of blood in the process."

The Amphirian laughed humorlessly. "We've heard that one before. The courts of Amphir were kind enough to pass a waiver, exempting us from all claims for damages caused in the execution of our duty. Now, to whom was the jewel sold, and for what price?"

"To the Tyrant. Twenty thousand in gold. Far more than it's worth, really. He wanted a jewel that had successfully been stolen from Amphir," Cap continued blandly, pushing Keilin forward.

"Hang on, Cap. You can't let the boy take the rap alone," said Beywulf, stepping forward. "You lot. I'm bigger than him, and it was only a little bitty stone anyway. Take your flesh out of me."

"No." S'kith too had stepped forward, his voice, as usual, terrifyingly flat. "You can take the flesh from my body. I am not so fat, and will eat better anyway. But try to take it from my friend here, and I will kill many of you first. Keilin, you let them take it from me. I will not feel the pain."

A snort came from behind them. It was Leyla. "Oh, that's enough, Captain Wickus. Yes, I recognize you, even if you don't remember me. Here. This is the gem." She produced a black opal.

The man accepted it warily. "Who are you?"

"Never you mind. I just remember you when you were a pompous little boy. Haven't changed much. Now you split the flesh cut between them. Off their buttocks. They can all afford to lose the thirty grains. Cap, give them an anesthetic," she said, queenly and commanding.

"I have been ordered to take it from their chests, madam." The word was a careful insult. "Inside their chests."

She shrugged. "Your orders don't permit you to interfere with innocent parties. They've confessed. Therefore the rest of us, Shael and Cap and I, are walking up to you now, innocent and untouchable. We'll watch you exact the fine. If you don't do it to my satisfaction, I'm going to rip you open from neck to ball bag, not that that's ever been any use to you. Shael'll do the same to another of you. Cap, how many do you think you can kill? Remember they're *law* officers. Can't touch us unless we break their law. They have to work within the local law too. Killing people is not against the law here, is it?"

Shael held her dagger as steadily as she could, wishing her hands weren't so shaky. She was too scared to trust her voice. She began to walk forward with Leyla and Cap, as Cap said savagely, "Not less than five, Leyla. Nasty deaths, too. Are they allowed to defend themselves?"

"Killing people *is* against the law in the Tyn States. Unless I command otherwise, of course," said the heavy-set man with the flying eyebrows so recognizable from the coins.

Shael dropped her knife. It clattered on the wooden slats, and splashed into the water below. "Father?"

"Yes, m'dear. What a chase you've led me on." He turned and called over his shoulder, "Henry Balscom."

He came forward out of the mist, the heavy browed, brutish face she had frozen into her memory, from Shapstone and the confrontation with Deshin. He was smiling now. "Mornin', yer Highness. Nice to see you again," he said, his coarse voice bringing back memories of the desperate chase in Shapstone's palace.

"You had agents among Deshin's traitors," she accused her father, her angry finger stabbing at him.

"I only knew about it at the very last moment. Barely in time to escape myself. You don't think I'd sacrifice such a proportion of my power willingly, do you?" he replied calmly.

"Excuse me," said Captain Wickus, hovering between relief at the intervention and annoyance at finding himself ignored, "Who are you? Will you take yourself and your child off this dock? I've permission from the Tyrant himself to use it. You're not wanted here."

For an answer Henry knocked his legs out from under him, and kicked him over the edge of the pier, to splash into the shallows below. He leaned over the edge to address the spluttering man. "Yer never address the Tyrant himself like that again, dog turd."

"Quite," said the Tyrant. "Now, dear. Let's go."

There was a silence, broken only by the sounds of Captain Wickus struggling to shore. "Like *hell* I will, Father. You've got some explaining to do."

He sighed. "It's cold and very early. I'll explain to you some other time. Right now I've more important things to do. Let's go and get you a bath and some clothes more fitting to your station."

"I'll jump over the pier edge and swim for the main channel if you come one step closer to me, before

I've had some answers," she told him in a small hard voice. Keilin couldn't see it, but he knew that her chin would be coming up as she said this.

"Shael, stop being so childish. Come along now." Keilin could hear anger and just the edge of fear coming into the Tyrant's voice.

Shael read voices far more accurately than Keilin. With a defiant tilt of her head she stepped onto the very edge of the pier. "I want to know why you gave the use of this pier to this ambush party from Amphir. I also want to know how you got out of Shapstone. I don't believe you did. I'm willing to bet you sold yourself . . . to the Morkth."

A reluctant chuckle. "You're my daughter all right. Yes. An agreement was reached. The Morkth freed me to weaken Deshin's control. As to Amphir . . . Saril Jaine's defection left me rather weak in the covert operations area. So we used some of my lesser operatives, ones that had penetrated Amphir's cash-fat Jewel Police. It was from them that we got word of you and your companions. Before we could reach you, someone in your party was foolish enough to steal something from Amphir. From then we used their resources to keep track of the whole party. We were also obliged to keep them off your track somewhat. We couldn't chance you being hurt by accident while the thieves were being arrested."

He gestured at the dock. "We wanted you safe out of Deshin's territory, so we facilitated this. Of course we have a hand in the river blockade runners. Otherwise they might bring in things we didn't want, and allow things, like escapees and unaltered communiques from spies, to leave."

"So, here they are about to have pieces carved out of them, all merely as an aside to getting your dear daughter back. How charming. How well you reward the people who've kept me alive since you crawled away into the woodwork."

Keilin had felt the knife of her sarcasm often enough before. It was however plainly a novelty to the Tyrant. And not one he was enjoying either. "You should mind your tongue, daughter mine. You've picked up some appalling habits from these commoners."

She raised her eyebrows. "Fix it, Father. You created this mess. Now sort it out."

He looked at her, his eyes narrowing. "You really do have a mind of your own, don't you? We always thought you would be our greatest asset in extending the Tyn States. Now we are sure of it. What do you suggest we do, rapier-sharp child?"

"Don't be so patronizing, Father. I'm not exactly a little girl any more. Knowing you, I doubt if you have less than a thousand men back there. Toss this bunch into the river," she said coolly.

"Three thousand actually. And taking us hostage won't serve either. We took steps—which we're not planning to tell about." He smiled insincerely. "Not drowning . . . it's so bad for the water quality downstream. There are better ways. You"—he turned to the dripping captain—"We need to talk to you. Back there." He pointed to a low shed, dimly visible on the shore. "Wait."

They stayed like puppets. Well, mostly. Bey drifted toward Shael. "I can hear them perfectly well," he said quietly. "Your father is telling Wickus that, as you are about to marry his prince, he'd better cooperate. He's also said that once he's taken you away they're welcome to slit all our throats."

Leyla made a retching noise. "Shael. Prince Jaybe is at least fifty-five. He likes his girls young. Prepubescent. He keeps at least one with him all the time. Get used to the idea."

"It doesn't matter which midden he had planned to bribe with me. I'm not going. At least . . . I'll run away as soon as I can," she said quietly.

Captain Wickus was doing a wonderful job of

fawning and shivering at the same time. "Ah . . . I
believe you mentioned an anesthetic, my good lady.
His Highness has assured me that it would be best
to follow your suggestion after all. Er, so as not to
affront you ladies, perhaps the pris . . . gentlemen will
care to come to our temp'ry headquarters over there."
He pointed at the hut from which he and the Tyrant
had emerged. "Also I could grab a dry blanket."

"No. You do it right here. It won't be the first
men's bare bottoms Shael and I've seen. We don't
trust you. Besides, the shivering'll help you lose some
of that lard." Leyla's voice was hard.

So Keilin found himself presenting his bare buttocks to have a lump the size of a half-thaler coin
cut out of him. His face was burning considerably
more than his bum. He had mutely submitted to Cap's
injected local anesthetic. He'd quietly gone through
S'kith's nerve-block exercises too. One of them had
worked. The flesh was carefully weighed on antique
jeweller's scales while the Tyrant snorted his impa-
tience. A neat form of debt discharge was handed to
Bey, who happened to be nearest.

"That's done then," said one of the Amphirians,
who had been forced to cut with care he'd been ill
prepared for. He decided to take out his ire in
another way. He shoved Keilin right over the nearby
pier edge. "Go for a wash, thief!"

Arms flailing, Keilin fell to splash in the cold black
river water. For a moment he started to panic. He'd
drown right here. Then his feet touched the ooze
bottom. He was barely thigh-deep.

From above came the sound of several blows, as
well as an anxious call of "Cay! Are you all right,
Cay?"

"Fine!" he called up. Then realizing how ridiculous
this sounded he continued, "Just wet. It's shallow here.
I'll walk in and come round."

He waded towards the shore. The burst of intense

worry and fear from Shael had washed through his mind like a tide. He knew now. He had to get her out of there. And tied to the last pier piles was the answer. He hadn't even seen it in the dark water. It was a wide flat-bottomed boat, hidden under the pier.

Now he understood. The river wharf's normal complement of vessels were lying at anchor somewhere off in the river. But their crews had come in, possibly leaving a watchman or two on the boats. He simply slashed the painter and scrambled into it. Using the pier pilings and timbers he silently pulled the craft along to where the acrimonious debate was continuing. Obviously his comment about the river being shallow here had been noticed. Shael had moved considerably further out along the pier, until she found the way behind her blocked too. Soon he was just below them. Bey's grizzly ancestry gave him preternaturally sharp hearing. He'd both heard and smelled Keilin coming back. There was really no need for the boy's whisper.

"And you want me to marry some fat old pervert. My! I should have stuck to Deshin. He was at least going to make me an empress."

"It's what you'll end up being, my dear. To a far greater empire than that fool can hold. Power stretching from Arlinn to Amphir. Between Amphir and my holdings, with the forces of Arlinn rallying to my call, I'll crush his pretensions very rapidly. The fickle ones that rallied to him will desert him just as fast. Anyway, as to your future husband's sexual preferences, they need not concern you. We had you taught that. You'll find your own discreet entertainment. At least he's normal, not like your other suitor."

"At least Deshin's lover was there of his own free will, and not as a confused little girl told to please the prince . . . or else." Leyla's voice spoke volumes.

"Shut up, woman. Hold your tongue before your betters."

"To hell with you, you pompous old fart. And I'll kill you before those bowmen of yours can get a decent bead on me," said Leyla, angry now beyond logic.

Shael laughed. A harsh, bitter sound. But it did stop the incipient conflict for the moment. "Betters!" she jeered. "One of my *friends* is an original member of the Cru you pay lip service to. The others are people that any *just* ruler would ennoble tomorrow. From *you* all they can expect is murder. However, *if* you guarantee their safety, I'll put up with your scheme. Once they're safe to Dublin Moss, that is. Well?"

Keilin felt the man above him suddenly snap. It was a terrifying maelstrom of rage, insane hatred and desire. How dared she dictate terms!? She was just like that bitch of a mother of hers. Well, he'd killed that fettering ice box as soon as she'd littered this one. Now he'd rid himself of her. He would not be controlled. *He* was the master!

The boy had his hand in the ankle pouch even as she said, "Well?" He stood up in the boat holding the core section as close to the boards of the pier as he could reach. He shut his mind off from the bellow for guards, and simply reconstructed in exquisite detail her naked body lying on his bunk in the moonlight. Then he allowed his mind to go further . . . filling in the details, even the scent of her . . .

"Jump!" Beywulf shouted. "Come on! Keil's got us a boat." They splashed into the water like ripe fruit all around him. Some things even hit the boat. Keilin grabbed S'kith and hauled him inboard before he even had a chance to panic. Then the two of them heaved Shael out from Leyla's supporting arms. The boat was moving away from the pier into the mist. Looking over the side Keilin saw Bey and Cap pushing it along. And the cold misty air was full of a delicate perfume. Keilin passed an oar to S'kith and pushed them still further out into the mist. Ahead he could see the dark outline of the river-parallel quay.

As the sonic boom struck, Cap, Beywulf and a third man struggled onboard. They slid under the quay, feet thundering above them, and out onto the river. The supercargo found a knife being pressed to his throat. Behind them the mist was suddenly retina-searing purple. "Hell's teeth!" Cap burst out. "That's no hand weapon. The Beta-Morkth have brought a bloody strike craft in. Over the side everyone, and hang onto the boat. You too, you Amphirian fool. They have heat-imaging sights on those lasers. Mist and darkness are no cover at all."

CHAPTER 16

The rain and snow-melt upstream made the Elbe a fast-flowing river at this time of year. Also numbingly cold. Still, judging by the actinic light flashes, and mist-muted screams, its chill and its speed were something to be intensely grateful for. But it was still teeth-chatteringly icy. It was with great relief that Keilin greeted Cap's "Okay. All aboard. Gently. We don't want to capsize the damned thing. S'kith and Bey from opposite sides first."

Soon the wet and shivering party, including the terrified-looking Amphirian official, were back on board. "Thank goodness you dropped those packs onto the boat and not into the water, Bey," said Leyla, her cold-clumsy fingers struggling with the catch on hers.

It was slowly growing light, the mist hazing into grey indistinctness, instead of virtual darkness. Bey primed a little alcohol burner down on the floorboards of the boat. The others, including the Amphirian, whom someone had taken pity on, huddled in blankets or struggled into dry clothes. Cap looked across at Keilin with measuring eyes. "When we get rid of this gentleman, you've got some explaining to do." He looked at the still shivering, wide-eyed involuntary passenger. "You can stop looking so afraid. We'll drop you off at the first safe landing we see. Then you can trot along to your high command and tell them that our debt to them is discharged. That'll at least get them out of our hair. I don't think any of your companions will have survived that fracas back there. As to you," he turned to Shael, "I'm afraid you're an orphan."

"I didn't lose anything," she said shortly, turning away and staring off into the mist.

They set the unfortunate Jewel Recovery Unit man off at the river's edge a mile or so beyond a small fishing village. Then, once they were out in the stream again, Cap rounded on Keilin. "Well, little psi. That was your work back there. Where's the other core section?"

Keilin had had time to anticipate this. The ankle pouch was safely in S'kith's keeping. "I haven't got one, sir," he said, putting as much forthright honesty into his voice as he could muster, "but I think I can explain."

"Make it good," Cap said grimly.

"You've the pendant you took from me in that bag. And some others. I climbed the pier pilings and was just below you when it happened. I . . . got hit by a wave of mad hatred. I think it must have come from Shael's father. Could he have been a psi, too? Ask Shael and S'kith. They also felt it, I bet. I . . . I think we all panicked. All of us. Even though we weren't touching the sections it must have been enough to activate them." He held out his hands. "That's all I can think of, sir."

Cap snorted. "I suppose, given the bloodline, it is possible." He turned to the other two, "Well? Did the *great wave* hit you too?"

They both nodded. "It was terrible. He held my mother under in her bath," said Shael quietly. "He . . . he was completely mad."

S'kith added dispassionately, "He was going to kill us all. We were lucky to get away."

Cap sneezed. "Dammit. Now I think I've got a cold. I'll have to put some damn shielding around those stones. I wonder what'll work? But first I'm going to search you, boy, myself. Then Bey can make me another of those hot drinks. Also, I want to hear from you, Leyla, just what you gave to that friend of yours, to save these bums' bums from more carving."

She shrugged. "Amphir is my city. I am a jeweller's daughter. I knew they would find us sooner or later. So I bought this stone. It's in the river now . . . but it was returned. They'll never know it wasn't the right one. A good thing that fool Wickus never had the sense to try and scratch it with a diamond."

Cap sneezed. "Get me that drink, Bey, for God's sake. I suppose it was good thinking. But that's supposed to be my job. That's the trouble with this outfit. Too many damn chiefs and not enough indians. Thank goodness I've got Bey and the Morkth-man who do what they're told."

He was not to know that there were thoughts of revolution and rebellion going through those two heads as well.

They paddled on downstream. It was one of those days that never quite lost the mist, although there were occasional thin washes of weak sunlight. Soon Cap was asleep in the bow. Leyla looked carefully at him. "With the mix of pills he's fed himself he won't wake for eight hours," she said critically. "He's had that cold brewing for at least a week."

"Bet you," said Keilin with a grin, pulling at his oar, "that our lord and master will say it all happened because *I* made him jump into the nasty cold water."

"Likely," snorted Bey, but he offered no more comment, just stared out into the mist.

"One thing I want to know, Keilin. Just why did it have to be a barrel, a whole bloody barrel of my favorite perfume? Do you know what the stuff costs for a mingy one-ounce bottle?" Leyla asked smoothly. "Couldn't it have been something cheap and nasty, if you're going to pour it over soldiers, and into the river? And how," she showed her teeth a little, "did you choose that particular perfume?"

Shael, sitting beside her, flushed. The blush spread, and both her complexion and Keilin's became brick red to puce around the ears. "Because he's a peeping tom," Shael said finally, in a small voice, "and because I stole a tiniest little bit of it once."

"Tiny bit! Like half a bottle, little sister?" Leyla teased. "You owe me. When you two have figured out how to do that, without the Morkth added, I want a whole barrel to myself. To swim in."

Keilin noticed that Bey was unusually silent. Usually he would have inserted at least two obscene and probably accurate comments given such an opportunity. And S'kith too simply stared out across the wide river. Always he looked toward the distant Morkth-held eastern shore.

They saw other, larger vessels twice. But by dodging into the reed margins they stayed clear of any possible pursuit. By evening, when Cap had woken and querulously demanded hot broth, which a silent Beywulf made from dried beef shavings, they were far from the disastrous quays of the morning. It was decided to tie up for the night hidden in the tall reed-and-rush fringes. After a very plain scratch supper prepared by a disinterested Beywulf, they all settled for sleep, except for Keilin who took the first watch. Soon it was quiet, except for the usual sleep sounds and the relentless song of the mosquitoes.

The boat rocked slightly. "I can't sleep, Cay." She came across and sat down next to him.

"I'm sorry about your father, Kim." Without thinking he'd slipped back into regarding her as Kim, rather than Shael or Princess.

She sighed. "I thought he was dead . . . back in Shapstone. I'd become rather used to the idea. I didn't really mourn him then, and after this morning's scene I can't even pretend to mourn him now. I'd forgotten how he did everything only to please or help himself. How he used people. I'd also forgotten just how much he frightened me. Am I like that?" she asked, her voice small, plaintive.

Keilin was inherently truthful. He had always found it a severe disadvantage. When he did need to lie it sounded so insincere that he was inevitably caught out. He was sure he'd only got away with it with Cap because Cap was feeling unwell. So this time he took less chances and opted for at least the margin of the truth. "When I first met you, yes."

"You're a beast, even if it is true." She didn't sound terribly upset about it. "And next time you have fantasies about me, please make sure I'm not touching my core section too."

The boy wished an obliging river monster would come and swallow him, seat and all. "I . . . I just needed a diversion . . ." he stuttered, dry-mouthed.

"Oh, am I just a diversion?" she whispered.

"God, do I only open my mouth to change feet?" he groaned. "Ow! What did you do that for?"

She'd leaned over and bitten him on the shoulder, quite hard. "For peeking. Or should I say staring. And for your unflattering memory of the size of my breasts. Just because you have a preference for overendowed milch cows." She thrust her chest forward as she said it.

"Who was lying on my bunk wearing nothing but a bit of warm perfume then?" he asked, vaguely indignant, confused by the hand stroking the bitten shoulder. "Anyway, I remember perfectly." He swallowed. "I looked at them for a long time. They were just perfect."

She bit him again. "That's for staring." Then she kissed the spot. "And that's for the . . . compliment. Cay. Just put an arm around me. I didn't love my father, but he was there . . . and I'm all alone now."

A confused boy-man put his arm around her. "Only if you promise not to bite."

She snuggled in closer. "Well, I suppose that leaves me several other interesting options."

She lay silent against him for a while. After a few minutes Keilin dared a movement of the hand, soft and stroking. No response. He listened to her breathing. Deep and regular. He spoke her name quietly. Still no response. The cloud had broken and the stars stared down. Keilin sat there, ground his teeth, and looked up at the stars, suppressing a howl of frustration with difficulty. He lowered her onto his unrolled bedding, and tucked it round her. He supposed they had been awake for nearly forty stressful hours, but just a few more minutes . . .

He looked down at the sleeping girl, and said quietly to himself. "So you're in my bed, again. Fat lot of good it's doing me." He felt the bites on his shoulder, and tried to think about something else for the rest of his watch. He was not very successful.

Morning brought them a cold, clear sky, and an hour downstream, the start of the great delta. It took several hours to cross the main channel and enter the maze of narrow twisting waterways of reeds and tufted rushes that winter had killed, but not yet stripped and blown down. The winter wind scythed among them, whistling and rattling. And all the channels looked alike. They might have spent several weeks wandering them if they'd not come on a marshman who, suitably bribed, showed them the way, and provided a lunch of smoked eel and gumbo.

Keilin found the complex seafood flavors in the gumbo delectable, although Cap moaned that it was tasteless. S'kith ate with slowness and precision, chewing and tasting. Bey had half a plateful in silence. He didn't even seem to notice what he was eating. Keilin resolved to find out what was wrong, but a very distracting small personage dragged his attention away.

S'kith, however, was not so easily distracted. They'd stopped on a small island to eat and stretch their legs, and he walked over to where Bey was sitting, staring off into space. "You do not eat."

"Yah. Now bug off, Morkthy. Just leave me alone, see."

"But the food is very good. Not as good as yours, but still good. What is wrong?"

"You like my food now, do you? Not still worried that it's hot?" Bey managed to stir some interest.

"No. I have learned that this does enhance the flavors, and also it warms the body. But what is wrong?"

"Not your problem, Morkthy . . . Just worrying about my boy." Beywulf sighed, and took a wary look to see if Cap was sitting well out of earshot. "See, I've followed Cap for seven years. He's a hero to my people for what he's done for our children. Damned good in combat he is too. But . . . he was ready to spend young Keil's life, just like that, back on that quayside. Damn core sections are worth more to him than all of us put together. Now, he's going to take an army against your kind. An' my son'll be one of them. He'll be killed." Bey looked briefly toward Cap again. There was plain and fancy murder in his eyes. The message was clear. If this man was dead . . .

"They are not my kind. The Morkth are the creatures that make humans into less than animals. I hate and fear them in ways that you cannot even begin to understand. I would kill them all. I would kill them for my children's sake. But not at the expense of any of my children."

"Your children, Morkthy—I mean S'kith—did you get some on those girls in Port Lockry, or is there something I don't know about?"

"I had at least 11,312 children still alive when I left the hive. A few will have died. The hives swap human broodstock, as well as children. Some of my own will be in FirstHive."

"You're serious? Eleven thousand kids! Mind you, I've never known you to tell a lie, or tell a joke for that matter."

"I still struggle to understand jokes. But I do not lie. Let me explain how the hive works . . ." He went on to explain to the horrified Beywulf how he had fathered so many children. "So you see . . . when we attack FirstHive, we will attack the living place of some of my children. I am not unhappy about this. They must be freed from the hive. But I want to keep them alive. I will make you a deal. I will destroy the Morkth communications and power net. Their heavy weapons are tied into the power net too. Only the anti-aircraft units have independent guidance and power. The hive will be nearly helpless. It will be butchery, not war. In exchange I ask only that your people care for the young Morkth children . . . help them to become wild-human. Teach them how wonderful real food is. The brood women too. If you free the warrior sows they will help you, if you speak my name. The worker sows will probably just die. Will you agree? I have recently begun to understand the concept of honor. You are a man of honor."

"You flatter me, S'kith. But yes, anyway. My people love kids. But don't let Leyla hear you calling women sows. She'll skin you before she listens to the rest of the story."

Before any further confidences could be exchanged, they were interrupted. "Let's get this show on the

road. I'm keen on my own decent bloody bed in
Dublin Moss," Cap called, struggling to his feet. By
that evening they'd bought horses and had left the
swampy delta margins behind, and they had a com-
fortable night in a halfway decent inn. The next
afternoon would see them in Dublin Moss.

Coming over the hilltop they could suddenly see
the Moss Peninsula. It was both breathtaking and
bizarre. Blue-and-red-layered sinuous and twisted cliffs
snaked and eddied about the green, jagged diamond
shape, the rock forming endless oil-on-water patterns.
Where the sun shone directly on the cliffs they
reflected in mirror dazzle, silvery bright and confusing.
The deep-blue sea all around was snaggled with sea-
stack teeth and the mostly clifflined shore was
tumbled white with heavy surf. On the far side they
could make out the slate roofs and white walls. The
breeze brought the sound of the waves and the gulls
up to them.

Shael said it for them all. "Is it for real?"

Bey chuckled. Both the talk with S'kith and the
sight of his home had lifted his spirits tremendously.
"Aye, she's a pretty sight, isn't she? And also next to
impossible to invade. Probably the most defendable
spot on the whole planet. The cliffs are a fairly soft
micaceous schist. Mostly they overhang, and they're
rotten. No fun to try to scale, believe me. There are
a good few thousand miles of natural maze walls. You
can get hopelessly lost even if you've lived there all
your life. We've had a few attempted attacks, which
have usually ended with the would-be attackers paying
us to get them out. Bugger of a place to live though.
You can shout to the neighbor's farm, but it can take
you all day to walk there."

Cap said tiredly, "Stop bragging, Bey. Let's get on.
It'll take long enough anyway."

The way onto the peninsula was a knife-blade
ridge. The sea crashed and rumbled three hundred

feet below, but the breeze still lifted salt spray and occasional spume up from the rolling rock chasm on either side. It was plain that the ridge had been narrowed. They could see the tool marks on the salt-greasy rock. They left the horses a hundred yards short of the ridge, at the hostelry which had sprung up for just that reason. Bey had to be forcibly restrained from buying everyone a welcome-home beer there. They set out along the ridge.

The wind pulled at them. And one never knew which side it would blow from next. The path was barely man-wide. Keilin was very glad he hadn't had that beer. But there was worse to come. The path ended abruptly as the ridge dropped fifty feet in a jagged cliff. A swaying cable bridge spanned the next hundred yards. And there were no guide rails. "How do we get across?" demanded Shael. "I can't walk that thing."

Bey chuckled. "Crawl. Like everyone else. Why should you non-apes have it any easier?" Cap set off.

Shael turned her big eyes on Beywulf. "Can't I go by sea?" she pleaded.

Bey shook his head. "This is easier than the sea path. That makes even the dolphins feel queasy. Come on, big beam. It's not so bad once you're going." He gestured across the gap. "This is Cap's fortress. He's spent three hundred years improving what nature'd made pretty good already."

The town was twenty miles off, as the crow flies, or about forty-five by the shortest land route. And that involved swing bridges, ladders and hoist baskets. Much of the land was farmed, lovingly cultivated. The countryfolk greeted Beywulf with cheers, friendly obscene comments and, from the women, invitations. Cap, however, they treated with awe, and almost infinite respect. He expanded like a sunflower at noonday in the glow of their admiration, examining children, giving pats on the head, and accepting small gifts. It was plain that mobilization here would be eagerly responded to. It was also plain that some who might like to respond to the call could never. Mostly the folk looked much like Bey, although the buxom girls were generally less hairy, but there were also many with malformed limbs . . . or eyes empty of intelligence. In the places Keilin knew, such folk would probably have been abandoned or would have died. Here they showed all the signs of love and care.

It was after dusk when they reached the tavern that Bey had been looking eagerly ahead for. It was already a busy evening there, with calloused hands holding beer tankards, and a happy, warm raucous noise emanated from the public room along with the scent of roast mutton, garlic and rosemary.

"Bumps!" bellowed Bey joyfully from the doorway. "Why's the service so bloody slow in this dump?"

A brief silence fell across the pub, till a broad man in a wheeled chair came forward, grinning broadly. "You noisy bastard. Want a beer, or do I chuck you out?"

For an answer Bey picked him up by the elbows, holding him above his head. "Beer first. Hell, beer for everybody! Then later you can chuck me out, as usual." He looked around at the cheerful room with its polished brassware, gleaming dark wood and a jam-packed bar. "I see you've let the bloody place go to wrack and ruin. Lost most of my blooming customers, too. Probably drunk my damned wine cellar dry as well."

"The old one was too small to keep all the rotten turnips in, so we dug a new one. There might be a few bottles so like cat's pee that nobody has drunk 'em yet. Hell, Bey! It's good to have you home."

"Grand to be back, old man. Where's the boy?"

"Flambéing the orange and brandy sauce for somebody's duck. Probably set the kitchen on fire by now. Just like his dad. You go see him while I dole out beers. I hope you've got the silver for it, 'cause your tick's no good here any more! Are this bunch friends of yours, or do I throw 'em out?" Then he caught sight of Cap standing in the shadows. "Sir! Cap! Come in, come in. If you'll honor the house, that is?"

Cap stepped forward. "I'll have dinner in the private dining room, Bumps, and my usual chamber."

He walked through the now silent room. As he arrived at the far door people began raising their tankards and glasses and calling his health.

The man in the wheelchair led the rest of them through to a table at the back of the room, near the big open fireplace. The room was not the province, as in most of the other taverns Keilin had seen, of a male crowd. In fact, it was about half and half. There were also a few children eating. The comments and invitations as they passed were thus not restricted to wolf whistles for the girls. Keilin kept a tight grip on S'kith's elbow, and seated him firmly, before he could respond to some of the comments from the girls. Within a minute heavy foaming pewter tankards of a brown nutty brew had been plonked down in front of them by a barmaid who made a careful point of rubbing her large and barely contained bosom across Keilin's cheek.

Sweating, Keilin was glad she'd chosen him and not S'kith, despite the look of pure poison Shael gave him. Minutes later Beywulf came through. With him was a giant. A younger carbon copy of Beywulf except for two things. He outtopped the broad man by at least two feet. And his hands were enormous, each with six long spidery fingers.

"Leyla you know, boy, but Princess Broad-Beam, Keil . . . and my friend S'kith. I want you all to meet my son Wolfgang."

He turned to S'kith. "I've only one boy. But what I lack in numbers I make up for in size." Pride shone from every inch of the broad face.

To their surprise S'kith rose to his feet, extending a hand. "I am pleased to meet the son of a great foodmaker, and an honorable man."

The boy betrayed his youth, with his embarrassment, as he enveloped the hand in a web of fingers. "I'll be cooking for you tonight, sir. But I'm not in my old man's league yet. He's a legend hereabouts. Hard to live up to."

"Nonsense, my boy. The addition of anise to that soup in the kitchen was masterful. They'll be talking about you when I'm long gone."

The boy grinned. "That wasn't what Bumps said. Or at least he said they'd still be swearing about the bloody mess for twenty generations. Wanted to know if I'd left my brains in a bucket, ruining good onion soup like that."

"Absolute rubbish. We'll start with it to prove him wrong. Then the duck, I think. Only don't flambé the sauce in the kitchen. Do it in a chafing dish here. The customer needs to get his eyebrows singed to be suitably impressed. Then those lamb shanks, and an almond tart to finish. I leave the choice of side dishes to you . . . as long as they include the stuffed artichoke bottoms. And to prove your worth, the wines are also in your hands."

It had been a memorable evening, full of wonderful food, cheerful conversation and hauntingly beautiful and sad music. It was strange. The loud cheerful extrovert nature of the people showed a very different facet in their songs. There was a sea-deep bitterness and terrible poignancy in those lyrics. They were a people wronged, a people exiled. And they would not forget.

That wasn't the only strange thing. Another had been S'kith, after the delicate crumble of the almond tart with its caramelized sugar lacework and lathering of yellow cream, leaping to his feet—and it was amazing he could still leap with all that food in him—and shaking Wolfgang's hand furiously. He then demanded that the boy help to teach his children to cook. Puzzled, and not a little alarmed, Wolf had nodded. And Bey had shouted with laughter. "You've just acquired a couple of thousand sous-chefs, son."

The third thing had been a thought that had come to Keilin in one of the quiet lulls while the guitarist had played one of those slow instrumental pieces. How had Leyla been able to produce a black opal so like the missing piece from Amphir to even fool what must be an experienced Jewel Recovery Unit officer? It was with this in mind that he had excused himself from the cheerful crowd at the table. He'd heard that Cap was already long abed and, when stowing their gear, had been shown which room Cap was occupying.

It was child's play second-story work. He knew where Cap kept the sections, and the man was deep asleep. It took him only moments to locate the soft leather bag. His fingers slipped into it. He touched a familiar chain. Yes, Cap always used that one. To taunt him perhaps. The cold stone seemed to welcome his touch. But his fingers went on. Other settings. Other stones.

All as lifeless as the moon.

There was only one core section in this bag. All the others were substituted stones. Keilin knew that only one person in their party had the background and skill to have done that. As he slipped away out of the window, and back to the party, he wondered for which piper Leyla really danced . . . and who paid that piper.

He was rather thoughtful and silent for the rest of that evening. Which was not something you could say about the quarrel between Beywulf and his son the next day. At breakfast, Cap had mentioned the coming attack and the need to call up an army.

Wolfgang had been waiting at their table—and volunteered.

"You are not going, and that's bloody final!" raged Bey.

Of course, it wasn't.

Dublin Moss was boiling over. There weren't going to be many able-bodied men or women left on the whole Moss Peninsula in three days' time. In the meantime the citizens were frantically organizing, and frenetically partying. They seemed convinced that there wasn't a single decent thing to eat in the rest of the world. By the time they'd stocked up to survive the terrible rigors of an army life, they'd each need about four pack ponies. Yet, underlying it all, there was a dreadful seriousness. They were going to fulfill an oath of allegiance. And few of them expected to come back.

The Gene-spliced had had weapons training from the cradle. They drilled weekly. Mock battles were the peninsula's abiding passion. Cap told the assembled eleven thousand that they were about as military as a bunch of dung beetles.

Each little battle team on the peninsula had its own strategy, drills, and weapons of choice. Cap set to organizing a more conventional force. And was stopped in his tracks by S'kith, who never questioned an order, who never took one step out of line. He walked to the front of the lecture that Cap was delivering on standard battle tactics. "No." There was a stunned silence.

Before anyone could recover he pointed to the diagram on the easel Cap was using. "That I learned when I was ten. Also the counter. When I saw the drills these men showed to you, I did not know how to counter their attack. Morkth fight by instinct, but mostly you will fight Morkth-*men*. They fight by training. They learn every attack. They practice every defense and every counterattack. Over and over again, until they can respond without thinking. These men . . . I have never been trained to deal with their methods. I could not respond, because I do not know how."

Cap did not like being interrupted. But he was also no fool. Now that S'kith had stated it, it was too obvious to deny. "Very good, Morkth-man. So I want to know every tactic you do recognize. Those we cut. See what weapons you know. We'll try to use only the ones you don't have defenses against. I'm going to work your butt off."

They advanced steadily through the state of Rampar. Once the locals had realized that the well-disciplined army took nothing and killed no one, every evening camp brought streams of local traders, entertainers and whores. The latter were generally disappointed by an army where females actually slightly outnumbered the men. Fishing for news of Shael's father, Keilin trolled among local folk. Rumor abounded, but no solid facts.

The local Duke sent an envoy to discover what they were doing on his territory. Cap sent back an official crew-stamped letter, demanding his levy of troops, and the Duke himself to lead them against the Morkth. Not surprisingly, that was the last they heard of him.

They marched out of Rampar and into Morkth-occupied lands. Now the scouts and vanguard probed warily ahead. Tension built as they attempted to sneak an army past EastHive. People snapped easily, arguments flared, and it was mostly foursomes of legs under the blankets in the nervous nights . . . and they wove their way unopposed past Morkth farms and outposts, just as S'kith had said they would. "A wild human would think of striking deep into enemy territory. Morkth would attack the outside and cut their way in. They would never leave live enemies behind them. As long as you do not touch the farms, or go too close to their way-stations they will ignore you."

By dusk on the fifth day they stood just at the crest of the rise before FirstHive. The scouts had dispatched the watchmen in the guard towers. Below them the hive and its wide plowed lands stood, unaware.

Beywulf stood surveying the low-walled hexagon from behind a high rock, his professional mercenary instincts surfacing. "Pity they've nothing worth looting. We'll go through there like stewed prunes."

Beside him S'kith shook his head. "They have stutter-burst energy weapons on all the towers. The walls have embedded proximity-triggered microwave devices. The gulleys leading to the gates are kill zones for centrally-timed pre-ranged explosive projectile fire. There is a zethwide, that is . . . about three-quarters of a mile wide, infrared detection zone, linked to the energy weapons in the towers. And what you see is only a tiny part. A hive goes down thirty levels and spreads across several square miles. We are standing above part of it now. There are half a million Morkthmen, with eighty thousand warriors trained at various levels. There are about six thousand Morkth warriors. Most of the Morkth workers have died, but there used to be twenty thousand of those." He turned to the encampment behind them, hidden below the ridge. "This is a flea-bite army."

"Does Cap know all this?" asked Beywulf, his voice dangerously quiet.

S'kith shrugged. "He is not a very good listener. I tried. He told me the Beta-Morkth have all the technology. That is not true. They just have far more."

"Hell's teeth! Come with me. We've got a lot of officers to talk to." Bey grabbed him roughly by the arm.

S'kith shook his head. "They will listen. But they are loyal. When Cap gives the order they will obey.

No. I will fix it. I have one last request. I have bought many fine ingredients. Gather our companions. Reconcile with your son. Tonight may be your last chance. Together you must prepare us a great meal."

"Cap's put a ban on all campfires."

S'kith, the most obedient of men, turned and said, "To hell with him."

It was a strange meal. Hidden in a high dell, where the wind would not carry the scents of the cooking food to the keen noses of those below, they sat and ate. There was a kind of forced gaiety about it. S'kith however smiled his clumsy smile often, taking joy not only in the food, but at being the host. His *pièce de résistance* was a small bowl with a red goo in it. "For the great chef and his son, I have this delicacy. You are always seeking new tastes. Here is something rare. It is a Morkth dessert, only served on holidays. It doesn't smell very good . . . but the taste! Please try it."

They cautiously put spoons into it. Tasted. And looked into their host's face trying to compose suitable expressions and comments. The Morkth-man was sitting on a treestump, pursing his lips, rocking slightly.

It was Wolfgang who ventured first. "Er, rather earthy . . ."

At which point S'kith fell off the stump, making odd little gurgling and snorting noises.

"I . . . didn't mean to insult it . . . I . . . I'm sure . . ."

"We've been set up," grated Bey. A smile began to evolve. "This is just a dish of mud. I should have smelled a rat. Morkth don't have bloody holidays or, I'll bet, bloody dessert. That bald-headed coot is laughing. He's never done it before, so he's not doing it very well. Well, I'll be dipped . . ." He began to laugh, too.

It was fifteen minutes before any real kind of sanity began to return to the small gathering. Then S'kith set them all off again by explaining that he hadn't really lied: this was the taste of a Morkth-man meal, first course, main and dessert on all days. Beywulf and son still sat with an arm around each other's shoulders struggling with aching sides. S'kith sat on his stump. He was smiling. And now it no longer seemed clumsy or forced. It was natural and supremely happy. "I understand jokes now. They are good, too, like wild-human food. Teach them to my children, too, honorable man." Then he stood up, walked around the circle and hugged each in turn. Then, taking Leyla by the hand, he walked off into the darkness with her.

A small sniff came from Shael. Keilin, sitting beside her, turned. "What's wrong?" he asked.

A tear ran down her cheek. "Don't you see? He thinks he is going to die tomorrow. He believes it so much he probably will. And . . . it's as if he just learned to be a person. I . . . used to hate him. I was horrible to him. Now, he's going to get killed just when I've learned to like him."

Bey replied somberly, "No use crying over spilt milk, lass. I did the same. I reckon that's one hell of a human, especially when you think about where he came from."

CHAPTER 17

The strike was set for dawn. The waking call was an hour before. Keilin was hurrying towards his preassigned position, well out of the fighting—now he had other troops, Cap was taking no chances with any of his telepaths being hurt—when a worried Beywulf came up. "S'kith. You seen him?"

Keilin shook his head.

"Hell. He said he had some plan in mind. I'd better get Cap." Bey hurried away.

Minutes later that worthy came up, grim and angry. "Your bloody Morkth friend. Has he run, or has he betrayed us?" He shook Keilin violently.

"He'd never go back to the Morkth. It's his worst fear, sir."

Cap was slightly mollified. "Let the bastard run then. He won't get far."

"Sir? I've an idea, sir."

"Talk, boy. Make it good. I haven't time."

"He may be trying to reach the core sections, by himself. Let me touch a core section . . ."

Cap's eyes narrowed. "He's run. But we might

as well make sure the things are still here. Might get some more leads now." He took out Keilin's pendant.

Touching the cool surface, Keilin felt a wave of joy. Putting it in his mouth he knew S'kith had not only tried to reach the core sections, but had also succeeded.

"He's in the hive."

"Bloody traitor."

Keilin shook his head.

He knew now what S'kith had done. In the pre-dawn he had slipped from the camp, his head new-shaven, dressed in the black Morkth-man warrior uniform he had had a nimble-fingered tailor make for him. He'd joined the night field crew by the simple expedient of killing one of their guards and replacing him. He had marched past the sophisticated detectors and into the hive. The human cockroach had come home. He'd slipped off into the familiar venting ducts and gone down. Down, down into the lavender and badger smelly heart of the hive. There he knew exactly where he was heading: the most secure and most guarded section of the deep hive. The queen section.

Only killing and speed could get him into this part of the hive. There were no other possibilities. He had used the skills picked up and honed in his time among wild-humans. He used swordsmanship against which the Morkth-man guards had no defense, after he had shot down the two Morkth warriors. That had given him entry into the queen section. But not without the alarm having been given.

The queen section was the holy of holies. Its passages were defended by Morkth warriors. No human ever came here. So S'kith had used the poison Keilin had discovered to tip his arrows. And the fire that Morkth instinctively feared. S'kith's smoke bombs had stirred chaos.

He had reached the core sections where they lay

in an unguarded laboratory. He had taken them. But there were now at least a thousand Morkth warrior-primes between him and the way he had come in. He could not have gone back that way. However, he was not planning on retreat. He went on instead . . . to the power and comms nexus.

Here S'kith had been wounded. But not before chopping the comms control boards into electronic spaghetti-trash. He had broken through to the generator room. It had an armored door, which he had managed to close and barricade. The standby emergency generator he'd managed to render unworkable. But the huge main generator was not so easy to incapacitate. Even the output cable was too shielded to be damaged in the time or with the tools that he had to hand. And S'kith had known this before he went in. He had wrapped his body around the cable. And now he waited. He was glad his friend had contacted him. He must tell Cap to wait—at all costs to wait.

Keilin took the wet core section out of his mouth. "He has the core sections. He's destroyed their communications system. He says to wait. He is in the generator room."

"The hell with him. He's dead soon anyway. Beywulf. Sound the advance." He snatched the core section from Keilin's hand.

The minute Cap left, Keilin reached for the ring in his ankle pouch. By the way that Shael was reaching into her bag she too had a similar idea. They huddled together in the guardpost they'd been sent to, and reached out with their minds across the distance.

The happiness greeted them again. They were using heavy energy weapons on the door. It could not last much longer. He was so glad to feel . . . friends. He did not want to die alone.

Keilin realized the strange and lightheaded feelings

he was experiencing were S'kith's. The pain of the
wounds was seeping past his bioblocks. Death was
indeed close.

S'kith knew it would be soon too. He just hoped
the bomb would be powerful enough . . .

With shock Keilin understood. The bomb in S'kith's
belly. He was planning to use that explosive force to
cut the power cable.

Keilin could actually see the heavy armored door
through S'kith's pain blurred eyes. He saw the coils
of greasy smoke and the sudden arc light. The door
was being physically cut away . . . any moment now . . .

Then there was a terrible searing brightness . . . and
a last image of Beywulf and his son putting their
spoons into the bowl . . . laughter beat away the pain,
and then even that disappeared like morning mist into
the clear white light.

Keilin huddled in his corner with the tears streaming down his face.

The vanguard wings had crept into the fields as
silently as mice. All had been well until they'd come
within three-quarters of a mile of the low walls. Suddenly the ripping sear of concentrated laser bursts
tore into them.

"Shit!" Cap swore as he saw the secrecy of his
attack shattered. "Fire the Brunhildes."

From the ridge came the *wump* of the catapults,
flinging their cargoes of black powder kegs. Seven of
them were blown apart in flight, but the eighth, by
pure luck, exploded on the edge of the tower from
which they'd drawn fire. And the Gene-spliced
charged forward again.

Into withering fire. The alpha-Morkth engineering
and ordnance were designed to survive a Beta attack,
with far more serious threats than a hundredweight
of black powder. It would have been infinitely worse
if the comms network had been functioning. "Hell

and damnation! Sound the retreat. They're not even going to make the walls!" Cap said disgustedly.

But, as he said that, the lasers fell silent. If he'd gone to check on his two psis he would have found them stunned and sobbing.

Down on the battlefield Beywulf raised his head in the sudden silence. He understood. The man had kept his word. Bey stood up and turned to face his fellows.

His voice cut through the newly won quiet. "S'kith, the Morkth-man, promised to silence their guns. He has done it. Come on! Forward!"

He turned, and with a cry of "S'kith!" began to lumber toward the hive. In a wave the Gene-spliced joined him, the Morkth-man's name echoing across the plain. And not as much as an arrow cut at them, as they poured forward up scaling ladders, and onto the walls.

Here they did meet what could vaguely be called resistance. It was more of a case of the death threshings of a dangerous but now headless beast. For there were no Morkth officers, no communications, and no orders. But there was a grumbling, and then a thunderous rumble from deep within the hive. As if some great monster was stirring. It caused momentary panic among the invaders.

Then Cap was there, shouting. "Into the hive. They're trying to flee."

Keilin and Shael, with no memory of how their fingers had so twisted together, saw the Morkth lander, a huge craft, vintage of the original Alpha-Beta split, erupt from what had been the plowed fields of FirstHive, rise on a column of steam and smoke . . . and run north.

They stood in silence for a minute. Then Keilin spoke up quietly. "We've got to go down. S'kith expected us to come and fetch the core sections."

"Won't the explosion have destroyed them too?"

Shael surveyed the disturbed ants' nest below with trepidation.

Keilin shook his head. "Diamond won't scratch them. And no furnace will melt them. That much I've gathered. Besides, I could still feel them calling. It will take the Gene-spliced time to find their way through the queen maze. But if we go the way S'kith went we can avoid trouble."

They went down to the fortress. There they saw Beywulf directing operations, organizing torches, as well as a shield path that led the endless stream of confused, unresisting Morkth-men out onto the plain. "They won't attack unless they are attacked," he said grimly. "And most of them seem to be these brain-less field-workers. Like human sheep."

"I need a torch or three, Bey. We're going to follow S'kith's route down," said Keilin.

"Hell, Keil, why don't you just ask me for hen's teeth? Every one needs them and I've got to ration 'em. Cap's already down there heading for the queen section. But . . . any chance that S'kith's still okay?" There was concern and hope in his voice.

Keilin shook his head, trying to get his voice to work. Finally he said, thickly, "No. He's dead, Bey. He died laughing at his joke. He used the bomb in his own body to blow the power cable."

The broad man turned away. He shouted at the party of Gene-spliced going down past the frightened stream of Morkth-men. "Remember, I'll have the guts out of any of you that injures a woman or child! Bring them up, and bring them up careful!" He turned to the captain next to him. "Diarma. This has become a debt of honor. That Morkth-man died to save my kid . . . all of our kids. I gave my promise. I'm respon-sible to see the kids especially don't get hurt. That they get looked after. Pass the word down the com-munication lines, will you?"

The Gene-spliced have the strength and speed and

dexterity of their spliced-in ancestors. They are also an emotional people. Perhaps the human source material was like that. Or perhaps it was a lingering trace from the chimpanzee and kodiak lines. These folk were close-knit and clannish, and they cared. Keilin should not have been surprised at the ready tears on both broad faces. Bey handed Keilin a bag of pitch-pine knots. "See if you can find him. He'll have a hero's grave on the Moss. I'll stay here and see that his wishes are carried out."

Shael and Keilin walked across to the air duct S'kith had followed down. The cover was still pulled aside. It was a narrow hole leading down for thirty levels. It was dark, and they could just see that it went . . . down. Keilin took out of his pocket a pebble he'd sucked to ease his thirst while they'd marched from the Moss, and dropped it. Counted. It was many seconds before the faint "plink" came up from the hive water supply.

"I can't!" Shael said. Keilin felt that way himself. The narrow darkness was already making him feel tight-chested. "My arms won't last twenty-seven levels," she added, looking into the darkness.

It was true enough. She was far stronger now than she had been when she'd been a pampered Princess, but . . . Keilin sighed. He felt that it was vital to go down that terrible hole. At least it was not angrily sucking air the way it had during S'kith's descent. But yet he was afraid of leaving Shael. Foreboding hung about that choice. He compromised. "I'll go. You stay with Bey. Don't leave him. Please." His voice was full of care and he leaned forward and kissed her. "See you." And he lowered himself down into the claustrophobic shaft.

There was no way one could carry a lighted torch and climb. So he had to do it in complete darkness, moving on memories garnered from those moments of close contact with S'kith, and faith. His fear of closed-in spaces clutched at him, but still he went down. After all, S'kith had come down here, somehow beating his fear of returning to the hive. Keilin felt he could do no less.

At last he came to the side shaft. The only side shaft. Only the queen level had an emergency air off-take. Keilin followed it. Finally he came to where the air line went into the filtration plant. No poison could reach the queen chambers, and as a side-effect, neither could a human cockroach. So Keilin had to leave the air duct and emerge, before the great queen door. Keilin found he didn't need the torches here. At this, the most crucial level of the hive, every fourth light still gleamed with a dull phosphorescence. Obviously this was some failsafe should disaster strike the hive's heart.

The great golden doors hung open. Bodies were strewn around. Some had obviously been trampled by storming rivers of Morkth feet. Keilin went on, past the now empty laboratory, into the wrecked comms room. The burned door of the power generator room still stood. When the power cable was severed, power for the arc cutters was cut. The hole surrounded by cooled runnels of titanium steel was still too small for a Morkth . . . or most adults. Without more ado Keilin began thrusting his slim sinew-and-muscle boy's body through the sharp-edged hole. Not for the first time he cursed the growing process.

There was not much left of his friend. What the explosion hadn't ripped apart, high voltage had cremated. But a force drew him to the far corner of the room. There, severed, but still clutching, was S'kith's hand. He had to force the rigor-set fingers apart to expose the five core sections. Their familiar blackness and oil-swirl patterns called to him. He touched them, and knew that Shael, hand on her bracelet stone, had been waiting for him to do so. He also knew that the remaining sections lay in the

Beta-Morkth's technofortress. The conquest of this hive had been a child's game, compared to what that would take.

Once S'kith's barricade had been removed it was easy enough to open the door. Using a coil of wire from the laboratory Keilin set out into the queen's maze. Here he needed the torches in the bag. It was perhaps fifteen minutes later that he encountered a Hansel-and-Gretel trail of scraps. Off down a further twisting corridor he could hear Cap's voice. He called Cap's party back to where he stood.

Cap eyed him with disfavor. "I should have known you'd turn up where you're not supposed to be. What do you want?"

For an answer Keilin held the wire. "This'll lead you through the maze to where the core sections are."

"Hmph. Why didn't you just bring them with you?" demanded Cap roughly.

"Because I want you to see what you did to my friend. The man you called a traitor. The damn things are still in his hand," said Keilin fiercely, blindly.

"Watch your tongue, boy. This is for the human race. It's more important than one worthless Morkth-man. This wire'll take us there, you say?" he said, taking the strand from Keilin's limp hand.

A Gene-spliced officer took Keilin by the shoulder. "Word has come down from the top about what he did," she said quietly. "Bey wants the women he says are called the Warrior brood-sows found and freed. Can you help us?"

Keilin nodded. S'kith would have wanted that. "A floor down. S'kith told me about it. I'll lead you." They set off out of the maze and down the awkward stairs, not designed for human tread. Soon they were passing tiny lightless cells.

"These?" asked the woman.

"Worker-brood," said Keilin shortly. "According to

S'kith they're so stupid they can barely do more than
eat and be bred."

The officer held a torch to the grill. Piteous whimpering came from inside. A blow with a heavy hand-axe
shattered the lock. A naked, vast, pregnant and
blubber-rolling filth-smeared body lay there, blinking
myopically in the unfamiliar light. Slack-jawed she
looked at them, and then, with a hopeless grunt,
turned her jowl-face away and began licking a spigot
on the back wall. She made no attempt to move
toward the open door, and showed no curiosity about
the strangers.

Several of the troop were retching as Keilin led
them further down. The cells on the next level were
no different. But here there was no whimpering.
Instead the air was abuzz with whispered speech.
Keilin paused. He owed his friend this triumph. His
voice didn't even shake as he called out "S'KITH
235!" with all the volume he could muster.

There was silence. Then pandemonium broke
loose. "Let us out! Let us out!" Joyful, hopeful,
frantically happy yells echoing in the passage. And
S'kith's name was repeated endlessly in a paean of
triumph. No resting place of grandeur, none of the
poignant legends that the gene-spliced would build
about him, would ever honor his friend as those
voices did.

A lifetime in a cell too small to stand in does not
equip you well for the outside world. Yet these were
no beached whales that they set free into that passage. Calisthenics and determination had maintained
their bodies. They were naked, yes. But not filthy.
And they were organized. They'd never known *when*
this day would come. But they had believed and
prepared for it.

The first question they all asked was, Where was
S'kith? By the predatory look in the eyes of the
enquirers even his legendary stamina might have been

tried right there. "He's dead. He destroyed the power system so that we could succeed in our attack." A great sigh echoed down the passages. They had mourned him long ago. They would mourn him again. But not yet.

"Then where is the fighting? We must kill Morkth." The leader was a hard-eyed woman with long dark hair, plainly pregnant, about thirty-five. Keilin remembered what S'kith had told him. Probably, after this baby, she would have been killed and eaten.

"The Morkth have fled in one of their big flying craft. There is no more fighting really. Just confused Morkth-men."

"So it is true then. There can only be one reason they would flee. They have been trying to hormonally alter both frozen workers and volunteer warriors. They must have succeeded. They have a queen egg to protect."

Before the enormity of this statement could sink in, Keilin felt a calling.

A desperate, urgent calling. A feeling that he *must* make contact. He touched his ankle, fingers dipping into the pouch, touched the core section.

"I need to get to the surface, fast. She needs me."

Twenty-eight levels of twisting spiral ramps was still a long, long way to run. Keilin knew he could never be there in time, but he ran until his lungs were on fire. Eventually he burst past the confused files of empty-eyed workers, out into the morning sunlight.

It was bedlam up there. The shield path had been scattered. Now confused Morkth-men surged all over in little knots. In the center of the hive roof stood a stunned group of the Gene-spliced. Keilin rushed over to them. On the ground between them lay Beywulf, his head in Wolfgang's lap. He didn't have legs any more. And through his shirt oozed a sluggish trickle of blood. Someone had tied tourniquets on the leg stumps, but Bey's normally ruddy face was spook-white.

Wolfgang's voice cracked. "My father tried to stop him. He wasn't even armed. Cap cut him down when he turned away. Just like that. Dad must've seen him out of the corner of his eye. He jumped. The blade cut through his thighs instead of his midriff. Cap stabbed him in the chest as he fell. Then he took the girls into the Morkth platecraft he'd summoned from the desert . . . or that is what Cap said. The young one fought and he hit her." Wolfgang shook his head in disbelief, his eyes full of the tears he refused to let fall. "My father has served him faithfully for nearly ten years. Now he's dying. Why? *Why did Cap do this?*" he screamed.

Keilin closed his eyes, bit his lips, summoned all his determination. His voice when it came out had the unmistakable ring of command. He was slight, nearly seventeen years old. And there wasn't a man on that roof who wasn't going to do exactly what he told them to, immediately. He pointed to two of the officers. "You. And you. Clear this roof. Anyone still on it in two minutes from now will be killed. Leave Bey. Get all the Gene-spliced below. At least five levels. *Now!*"

Only Wolfgang didn't move. "I'm staying with my father. What are you going to do?"

Keilin turned to look at him. "I'm going after them. And I'm taking Bey to the only place that might be able to save his life. I'm going to summon transportation too. And that'll bring the Beta-Morkth. Your father wants you to live. Now go. Go on. Get down at least five levels."

He was met with a long, flat stare. Then Wolfgang shouted, "Johann, Gerda, Hamesh, Sula." Four young Gene-spliced turned from harrying people back down into the hive. "I need some help to carry my father. And to avenge him."

Keilin didn't even see them any more. He had his hand in the bulging ankle pouch. He allowed the fear and desperation to surface. He allowed his suppressed feelings about Shael to flow. He wanted transport. To Compcontrol at the South Pole.

He expected a flying carpet. Or a giant bird. Or a Morkth antigrav plate. But he must have had Beywulf's condition in mind. What he got was a long white flyer, with a big red cross on the front and sides. The back opened, and a wheeled stretcher rolled out. A mechanical, toneless voice said, "Mechambulance unit 16. Load the patient."

They were flying high and fast. Bey was in a metal cocoon. Wires and tubes attached to him were superstitiously eyed by the five Gene-spliced and the three stark-naked women who had come wandering out onto the roof just as they were loading Beywulf onto the stretcher unit. There seemed little choice but to take them along. Keilin himself however viewed the entire setup with mere acceptance, and nothing more than a desire for haste. He hoped that the Beta-Morkth response had not killed too many people. He had no way of knowing that the response he expected hadn't occurred. All he knew was that the land below had dwindled rapidly and then changed to a blue sheet of sea. Surely soon they must be there?

Finally, Wolf's questions pulled Keilin out of his reverie. "We're bound for a mountain on the South Pole. I don't know much about it, except that it is very cold. Full of snow and ice. No, I don't think Cap has joined the Morkth. He's just using the craft of a few that were killed, by me and my partner."

He looked at the three naked girls who were shivering on one of the empty stretchers. "We'd better contrive some kind of clothes for you ladies. The outside world is not temperature-controlled like the hive."

Wolf nodded. "Yeah. I looked around in here. There are some blankets in there." He pointed to a drawer. He was his father's son however. "Shame to spoil the view, though." He turned for a last look at it. And turned away rapidly. Two of them were touching each other. Quite intimately. "You . . . you can't do *that* here!"

"Why not?" asked one of the three.

"What is wrong with what we are doing?" another asked with genuine puzzlement.

With a quiet smile, Keilin went to the drawer and left the five young Gene-spliced to their explanations. Despite Beywulf's situation, the whole thing was not without humor. The folk of Dublin Moss had thought their morals the most flexible in the world. All the same they were failing dismally in their attempt to explain sexual taboos to the three girls, at least one of whom was showing a distinctly rounded belly. He snorted a chuckle to himself. Hell, he'd grown *old* in the last couple of years. Most of the words the Gene-spliced were using were beyond the hive girls. Well, at least it would keep young Wolf from worrying about his father for a while.

He intervened with three rough ponchos a few minutes later. "I'm sure Wolf and one of his companions will be delighted to give you a demonstration of what they mean by normal sex . . . some other time. But before you get to the practicals you so badly want, I think you should try these. You are turning blue. I agree it is lovely to be able to see each other, but the blue makes you look like Morkth."

They couldn't have donned those ponchos any faster if they had known just what they were supposed to do with them.

When they were dressed, one of Wolf's companions, Sula, began to laugh. "How many of you," she paused delicately, "warrior brood sows are there?

"Thirty-seven thousand three hundred and twenty-two . . . if you count us," said the girl who called herself Faime.

Looking at her companions with a broad smile, Sula continued, "Do you realize what will be happening back at the hive? The Gene-spliced trying to cope with that mess . . . and thirty-seven thousand three hundred and nineteen like these wandering around looking for a feel-up." She raised her eyes heavenward.

The thickset Johann sighed. "To think I'm here where the ratio is a lousy 4:5 when I could be there at a happy 1:10. Wolf, you no-good bum!"

The flight continued. They devised leggings for the girls, and bound strips of blanket around their feet. They also solved the toilet arrangements for a party of nine, three of whom had never had to learn bladder control. Bey stayed warm, his heart beating, as fluids ran into him. The chest and stomach wounds had been cleaned by little metallic arms. Keilin suspected the machine had drugged him, as his friend lay so still. Time passed, and talk continued. Keilin had to tell his side of the story. He had his entire audience sniffing and then openly weeping at his recital of S'kith's defeat of the hive. They ate some of the smoked beef and journey biscuits that the fear-of-starvation Gene-spliced had inevitably carried into battle. The expression on the hive girls' faces as they tasted the food filled Keilin with nostalgia, remembering S'kith in earlier days. Below now was a gray sea occasionally dotted with white gleaming shapes. The craft was undoubtably losing height.

An alarm screamed out from a speaker above their heads. A mechanical voice squawked. "Secure all personnel. Emergency status. Mechambulance unit 16 under attack. Taking evasive action."

They had barely time to grab for handholds. The craft banked viciously then dropped like a stone. They hurtled along, inches above the gray wave chop and were abruptly flung upward. They skimmed over the gleaming edge of a white floating mountain. And sheered away, jinking between more vast bergs. Behind them a burst of incandescence shattered the ice. The speaker squawked, constantly. Stuff about "Rules of war; non-combatants; medical personnel; prohibited weaponry and nuclear-free zones," until Keilin wished he had a free hand to shove a pillow over the thing and suffocate it.

Then there was another burst of incandescence, in midair this time. The mechambulance began to regain height. "Personnel. Emergency status cancel. Comp-control defenses have nullified attack craft. Landing two minutes." The speaker continued in its flat mechanical tones. The mountain looked just as it had in Keilin's vision from the desert. Except bigger. And colder.

As the craft dropped towards an opening in the rock, Keilin had a brief view of a huge, dark wreck on the far shoulder of the mountain. Spilling from it was what looked like a river of ants. Then the mechambulance zoomed into the rocky tunnel. Behind them steel doors slid shut. The craft slowed. Then it stopped, pushed its tail end into a brightly lit bay and opened the back hatch. Beywulf's entire bed section began to roll out.

A man in green clothing was waiting. He shook his head at them. "Don't come out here. Only the patient can go in through the sterilizer unit. This is the sterile zone. I'll be with you as soon as I've seen to the patient. Unit 16, take them round to reception."

The speaker bleeped. "Please stand clear. Rear entry closing." Before the stunned group could respond, it had closed. The craft moved off slowly, despite their pounding on the door. Then the hatch opened again.

This time there was a broad set of stairs in front of them, leading to a well lit hall with hundreds of chairs in it. Above the door a glowing sign read:

MORNINGSTAR II GENERAL MEDICAL HOSPITAL
CASUALTY RECEPTION

They stepped out. Keilin looked at the pain-wrung face of one of the hive girls. She cradled her arm. By the angle, Keilin was sure it was broken. It must have been during the "evasive action." He helped her up the stairs and through the glass doors.

As the door closed a three-foot-high metal cylinder on wheels scooted up to them. "Doctor says he will be with you presently," the mechanical voice chirped.

"This girl is also injured," Keilin braved, while the others felt for weapons.

"What is the nature of the injury?" the thing chirped back.

Mutely, Keilin pointed to the cradled arm. A metal proboscis followed his hand. A brief whirr and click. "A simple fracture of the radius and ulna. Unnecessary to disturb the doctor. Follow me to dressing room three and I will deal with it."

Because there seemed little alternative they followed the cylinder to a room full of neat implements and painted cupboards. They persuaded Sandi to place her arm on the metal plate where a white gleaming cover slid over it.

"The pain. It's gone." With wonderment in her voice, she tried to pull her arm out.

"Don't move. Ultrasonic manipulation in progress," chirped the little cylinder sternly. "Just another few minutes."

They walked out of the room, Sandi peering in wonder at her arm, now encased in a hard sheath of transparent webbing.

The green-clad man was waiting for them.

"Just what," he asked, slapping his stripped-off powdered gloves against his other hand, "is going on?"

CHAPTER 18

Morkth. Swarming. With their hissing, clicking speech all round her. The air, since that terrific concussion, was streaming in in great icy wafts. At least it cut the stink of the creatures. It was also fun to see them scuttling away from it. Shael derived what satisfaction she could from it. She'd felt Keilin touch his core section. She could hardly do otherwise with the bracelet inside her bra. She was sure she'd have a scar on that nipple. He had been coming at the run, she knew . . . but now he must be thousands of miles away. She was on her own. Even Leyla had turned strange.

Shael had been angry when Cap summoned the platecraft, and she'd realized he planned to leave Keilin and the Gene-spliced to cope with the situation in FirstHive, now that he had what he wanted. But when he'd flown the craft straight to a Beta-Morkth nest . . . then she had known terror. When Shael had tried to question Leyla, the older woman had set her mouth into a thin, hard line, and refused to say more than, "Just Cap playing his games again,

dear." But Cap, when she'd tried to ask him what he
was doing, had gagged her.

So here she was. Sitting freezing while the black-
hooded bugs surged and chittered, while Cap raged
at the chief bug, "You *had* to do it, didn't you!? You
had to fire on an ambulance plane. Defenseless.
Broadcasting its identity loud and clear. Covered in
red crosses. Bloody harmless. But oh, no. You had
to try and blow it out of the sky. So Compcontrol shot
us down even though we were broadcasting the
correct recognition codes."

"SSsssilence," snapped the bug commander. "You
tttold us it would be ssssafe to apppproach, as long
as we broadcast thattttt ssssignal. You did nottt mention exsssepshshshions. Now getttt us in the gatttte . . .
or we killll you."

"We'll have to walk," said Cap, sullenly.

Another Morkth with the bright chelicerae of rank
came bustling up. He chittered and hissed out a
message. His sides heaved and spiracles hissed with
what seemed to be agitation. He was putting out a
heavy, musky odor.

The commander chittered back, his own sides
beginning to heave. The musky odor grew thicker. He
turned and left abruptly.

Leyla was still cool. "What happened there?"

Cap said distractedly, "Another Morkth landing
craft is approaching. It can only be the Alpha."

"Great. So now we'll be sitting ducks in the middle
of a war."

"No. The Alpha claim they have a queen larva
aboard . . . about to emerge."

"So? The queen is the one that breeds, isn't it?
Surely the bugs can't breed fast enough to make any
difference?"

"You know very little about the structure of Morkth
society. The queen is the source of everything.
Workers. Soldiers. Identity. Wisdom . . . inherited

knowledge stretching back to the primal hive. And command. Decision will rest with her. Do they go on into Compcontrol? Do they kill us and attempt to destroy the core sections? Do they continue with the Beta-Morkth planet cobalt-bomb project? The Beta are nearly finished, you know. That's why I started this bloody core-section chase. They were getting ready to shatter this planet as if it were a rotten apple hitting a brick wall."

The Alpha ship advanced under the protection of the recognition signals Cap had provided for the Beta's and settled in the corrie next to the wrecked ship. They found themselves herded across, to the waiting airlock, and inside to the heavy humidity of an intact Morkth craft. The air was full of the musky scent, overriding the badger and lavender smell that Shael had almost grown used to. Speech was impossible. The hive craft was full of the buzzing sounds coming from every one of the assembled Morkth. And the assembled thousands' attention was focused on the gigantic off-white twitching grub shape on the podium, constantly fussed about by various attendants. The humming drone reached ear-threatening proportions, getting higher and higher all the time, as the grub shuddered violently . . . and grew.

There was a deafening crack. Terrible in its suddenness. And the Morkth were silenced. The larva case had split and now it . . . she . . . was emerging. The grub shape had been big. The creature emerging from the husk was gargantuan. Stretching. Extending. Then fluttering small vestigial wings. Stretching that long, deadly body some more. This was a predator, born of a long line of things that attacked, shredded and rended. Her origins were plainly written in the lines of her body and her vast jaws. The chitinous armor was already changing, darkening, hardening. Around her, frantically scurrying

Morkth attendants placed great troughs of food, nectar. And the hive drone rose again to a crescendo.

She would speak. Soon. Soon.

Recognize her hive.

She opened her gigantic scimitar jaws, designed to slice and rip, jagged and razor-edged. The vast maw behind opened. Silence fell like a curtain across the suddenly immobile insectoid crowd.

It was terrible. Frantic. Compelling beyond reason. A feeling that transcended species to the extent that Shael bit her gag savagely.

!!!HUNGER!!!

The queen shucked her larval husk. Now, she was desperately thin and stretched. And empty. She needed food. Prey. Not the dead slush she kicked aside. No!

Live prey!

With mindless ferocity she stepped forward and began to feed. Panicked stridulations came from all sides. But still the Morkth made no attempt to run.

She was mad.

Completely mindless.

But she was a Queen.

With a sudden flick Cap slashed the belt of the hypnotized Beta-Morkth commander. Taking the core-section bag as it fell, he hustled them towards the airlock they'd come in through. None of the Morkth even appeared to notice. The three humans could have been killed a thousand times over. But no Morkth paid any attention to anything except their new Queen.

The escapees stepped out into the snow.

Walked away from the black craft and down to the valley, toward the vast steel doors, with the cold biting through their foot gear.

"Well, I've got them. All 14 core sections. And a psi. We should be inside in a few minutes. And we got rid of the Morkth."

"What the hell happened back there?" Leyla asked.

Cap smiled savagely. "The Alpha succeeded in hormonally neotenizing workers and warriors to produce a queen egg. They used to have the capability, way back in their evolution, to breed, if queen dominance was removed. They managed to do it again . . . but they got themselves a queen from *that* part of their evolutionary history. With no recent racial memory. Just a memory of doing her own killing, mating and laying her own brood. If you think they're having it rough now, wait till she starts hunting a mate. She'll tear that landing craft apart."

"So you wanted to be rid of the Morkth all along?" Leyla said, wondering.

Cap looked at her coldly. "Naturally. I needed the core sections the Beta had. So I pretended to make a deal with them. It also got them to stop their planet-buster program and concentrate on this."

"Why? I thought you said the Morkth just wanted to destroy us all. Why do they want the core sections? Why should they want to come here?"

Cap snorted. "Our ship is still capable of interstellar flight. The surviving Morkth ships are small stuff, none of which are really capable of interplanetary flight, let alone interstellar voyages. The Morkth navigation systems are still working in their main landing craft, even if it is a hopeless wreck. They know where we are, and how to get back to Morkth space. The rest of their species don't know where we've got to. We're a dangerous breeding patch of humans. Also, this is a habitable planet, and quite a prize for them, if they can bring the rest of their forces in to capture it, instead of just trashing it. Bioviable planets aren't exactly common. So, of course, capturing our ship was first prize to both the Alpha and Beta groups. But she was just too big for a frontal attack. They might get wiped out instead, leaving us humans to breed. So, after their queen was killed they

fought about how to best achieve the second prize—
killing us all off."

"So this was all your plan?"

Cap shrugged. "Of course. I've had to take some
radical steps, but the end justifies the means, you
know. Did you think I'd betrayed my species to the
enemy?"

Before them the great doors slid open.

"It's still touch and go. I'd like to be more positive, but quite frankly it's amazing he survived the
trauma of those injuries, let alone getting him here.
Let's just say he's stable at the moment. I'm reviv-
ing an operating team to help me deal with the
internal injuries. But why didn't you bring his legs
along? All the equipment for maintaining them is on
board the mechamby, after all. Now, I've answered
your questions about the patient. You answer mine."

Keilin paused, unsure where to begin.

The man prompted. "I know some of it. I was
revived four and a half hours ago, and I finished post
cryo treatment nearly two hours back. I was at the
computer terminal until you came in. I know I've
been frozen for 349 years, instead of the fifty we were
supposed to be. I know *Morningstar I* General Medical, which is linked to this unit, isn't replying. I know
Morningstar II central computing is functional, but
in a siege status. It's not replying, except to medi-
cally delimited questions."

Much of what he said was meaningless to Keilin.
But he grasped at the straws he could. "The other
command center . . . in the north?"

"Well, I don't know where. But the set-down was
planned to be in polar regions." He looked faintly
uncomfortable. "To keep the colonists away. They had
to learn to be self-sufficient."

"The Morkth destroyed it."

"But this isn't Earth. We must have made it to at

least one Earth-type colony world. They couldn't have killed Captain Evie, or we wouldn't have gotten any of you passengers off the ship. Why wasn't *Morningstar II* activated?"

Keilin shrugged. "I don't know. I just know the transmitter core was scattered, and we've been trying to collect it to bring it here and get the starship working again. I also know somebody betrayed the crew to the Morkth. Cap . . . that is, First Mate Jacoob Ahrens, said it was Evie Lee."

The surgeon snorted. "That'll be the day. He must've got it wrong . . . Captain Evie, she was like everybody's little sister . . . or girlfriend . . . or even mum. She was as soft as marshmallow, but as true as steel. Everybody loved her. And she was also such a caring, kind person. She'd have cut her own arm off rather than hurt as much as the pinky finger of one of her crew. I saw her crying all over the unit half a dozen times. More likely this Ahrens fellow is your traitor, whoever he is."

Keilin nodded. "He's the one who did that to Bey. He's got most of the core sections . . . he thinks. And he's kidnapped one of Evie Lee's descendants. That's why I have come here."

"Likewise," Wolf grated. "I have come to kill him."

The surgeon turned to a voice pick-up below a wall-mounted screen. "CompControl: Records search: Ahrens, Jacoob, First Mate, *Morningstar I*. Print to screen."

The screen flashed. "RECORDS DELETED"

"Why . . . something's wrong here," said the surgeon. "Let's check Medical records. Medical CompControl: Records search: Ahrens, Jacoob, First Mate; *Morningstar I*: All data print to screen."

Lines of print began to scroll across the screen. "AHRENS, JACOOB MAMUD. FIRST MATE. Ph.D. ASTROPHYSICS. (ANK.) M.Sc. NANOENGINEERING. (MOSK.) BORN 23/3/2068. HEIGHT:

6'4". WEIGHT: 195 lb. SPORTS: NULL-G TENNIS:
TURKISH NAT. CHAMP: 2084. 3-D CHESS.
LEVEL GRANDMASTER. RELIG. AFFIL.: SUNNI
MOSLEM." Then on to immunizations, illnesses, aller-
gies, and so on, down to retinal records, fingerprints.

The surgeon bit his forefinger. "He existed. Even
was treated here, three hundred and fifty years ago.
Tall man . . ." Suddenly he snapped his fingers. "Tall
man! Medical Compcontrol check those records
against Mortuary records."

There was a long pause.

Then across the screen marched: "ERROR MES-
SAGE: MORTURY MATCHES TO RETINA AND
FINGERPRINT RECORDS BUT CORPSE NAME
NOT LISTED AS AHRENS, JACOOB MAMUD."

"Yess! I knew I'd seen two nearly identically tall
men at the crew council meeting . . . and only one
whom I had a name for!" said the surgeon grimly.

"Medical Compcontrol: Print name listed for
corpse with retina and fingerprints of Ahrens, Jacoob
Mamud."

A brief pause. "FISHER, DANE. SUB-CAPTAIN."

"That explains a lot. Compcontrol: Records search:
Fisher, Dane. Sub-Captain. List records to screen."

"RECORDS DELETED."

"To prove that's no fluke, I'll do my own. Compcontrol: Records search: Edwards, James. Lieutenant-
Commander. List record to screen."

Information began to scroll slowly down the screen.
The surgeon pointed at it and nodded. He sighed.
"Your man out there is Sub-Captain Dane Fisher. And
having known the bastard, I'm hardly surprised. Wait.
He covered his tracks . . . but he missed the medical records. Probably didn't realize they were separately stored. He never liked the medical side much,
for all that he was supposed to be one of us. He was
always more interested in pharmaceutical research
than medicine. Humans were just incidental guinea

pigs. Medical Compcontrol: Records search: Fisher,
Dane. Sub-Captain. All data print to screen."

A pause:

Then the print began to scroll onto the screen.

"FISHER. DANE NESBIT HUENNES. SUB-
CAPTAIN. Ph.D BIOCHEM. (CAPE TOWN). Ph.D.
MIL.SCIENCE (CAL.) M.ChB. (LOND.) BORN:
2065. HEIGHT: 6'4" WEIGHT:192 lb. SPORTS:
KARATE (FUNAKOSHI). OLYMPIC GOLD
MEDALLIST SA 2080, 2084. RELIG. AFIL. AG.
SURGICAL IMPLANTS. INDEX FINGER DISTAL
PHALANX REPLACED WITH SINGLE PULSE
MICRO-LASER UNIT, SOLAR RECHARGEABLE
THROUGH FINGERNAIL . . ." but after the finger-
print and retina prints was a note: "FURTHER
RECORDS> MEDICAL REQUISITIONS AUTHO-
RIZED BY FISHER, DANE. PRINT TO SCREEN?"

"Medical Compcontrol. Print requisitions to screen."

A list began to scroll across the screen.

The surgeon shrugged. "He planned this all right.
I suppose he didn't realize that all medical-supply
requisitions were also downloaded to Medical Compcontrol. Look at it all! Longevity drugs—at least a
lifetime supply—antibiotics, general first aid stuff,
Mini robosurgery unit . . . what in hell! Was he planning to do a lot of screwing around? That's about a
million doses of AmB 486. What the hell would he
take that number of abortifacients with him for?"

A terrible, terrifying light began to dawn in Keilin.
"Sir . . . you know about the Gene-spliced people . . ."

"Sure. Like these chaps, and my patient. I should
imagine half the population is by now. I did some
post-grad work on the heritability of the characteristics.
Every kid a coconut. It wasn't generally known, but
the dominance linking was very successful."

"Then there is no reason that the Gene-spliced
cannot have babies?" Keilin asked cautiously, aware
of the acute attention of Wolf and his friends.

"No. None. They're perfectly normal humans, just with a few extra abilities." The doctor looked puzzled.

"They can interbreed with ordinary humans, have ordinary babies?"

"They *are* ordinary humans. The kids will inherit the gene splices that's all. I told you they were dominant-gene linked."

The girl called Gerda looked at him, ice in her eyes. "I've been pregnant twice. Spontaneous abortion both times. The children were both too deformed to have lived anyway. My mother aborted seventeen times. She bled to death the last time. I have one sister. She has no arms."

The doctor stared back at her, looked at the list still on the screen. His black skin turned an unhealthy shade of gray. "Low dosage AmB. I'll need a blood sample," he said quietly, taking her hand to a wall unit, and pressing it into the slot. He typed a series of letters in on the keyboard.

Wolfgang's face had set in a hard mask. "He told us . . . the human race was scared of us. Scared of us outbreeding them. So we were made nearly sterile. All the girls had to take these pills every three months . . . to promote successful ovulation. We . . . believed that he was all that was between us and extinction. Mothers used to kiss his feet. I . . . was brought up to believe it was lucky even to have his shadow fall on you. My father was a hero among our people because he served him."

The doctor looked at his hands, not wishing to look them in the face. "I was a registrar in London when he was a houseman. He was a totally self-centered son of a bitch. Thought the sun set when he sat down. Didn't give a cosmic shit for anyone else, least of all his poor blooming patients. But he was handsome, strong, clever . . . and he could talk. Anyway he wasn't going to stay in medicine. He joined the army. I thought it would suit the fathead.

"He came out of the Gersbach clash with the Morkth as a hero. He had to be. He was the only one left alive. The dead bodies weren't going to argue about what he said he'd done. I wondered about it . . . but we were losing the war. We needed a hero. And he looked good in that role. Did well in combat after that, too. It was a shoo-in that he'd command the *Morningstar*. That's why I chose to be part of the medical team of the backup crew, even if it meant going into the ice box. If it wasn't for the psi saying they'd be screwed if they'd take orders from him, he would have been captain too. But he *couldn't* have done this to Evie . . . They . . . they were sleeping together."

"I need to go after him," Keilin said coldly.

"Us too," the five Gene-spliced said in a vicious, determined and almost telepathic unison.

One of the hive girls looked into the surgeon's face. "This man . . . you mean he is the same man who betrayed the crew to the Morkth? The Morkth who enslaved us, bred us like animals, to kill our own kind?"

"It looks like it," he muttered. "Stuff the Hippocratic oath. I'm going to strangle the bastard."

Sandi stood up from the waiting-room couch. "You will have to stand at the back of a very long line," she said. The snow outside was warm compared to her voice. "I thank you for giving me something to hit him with," she said holding up her cast.

"We can discuss who gets to kill him later. If we can hear how we get from here to where he is," said Keilin, picking up his assegai.

"There is a passage from the hospital to the main operations center," James Edwards said. "But it is sealed siege-tight. I couldn't even get communication. The only other way is the front gate. Ident procedures should still be operating there. It's going to mean going out for a three-mile traipse across the snow, however. We'll need some outdoor gear."

"We?"

"I'm coming with you of course," he said calmly. "I'll be able to get you through the ident procedures at the main gate, and help with the high-tech side."

Keilin shook his head. "No. You must stay and try to keep Beywulf alive. You must also tell the Genespliced the truth, if we do not come back. Cap seemed to think that a psi and the core sections would get him in to the place." He reached into the pouch on his ankle. "I have ten core sections, and I am a psi." He looked at the motley assemblage of humans. "I'd prefer you all to stay. But I suppose there's no chance of that."

Dr. James Edwards looked at the assegai with a professional interest that would have done his distant baKenga ancestors more credit than it did to his present career. "Some of you don't have weapons. The best I can offer you are some portable laser scalpels. I'm going to order the entire unit revived from cryo suspension. Within three hours I promise a thousand people are coming to join you. We're all medical personnel . . . but given the circumstances we can and will fight."

Keilin smiled. "Thank you, sir. I think the Genespliced of the Moss have spare weapons we can understand. But clothes would be good."

They were led to a walk-in locker full of cold-weather gear. "Just remember that laser unit in his finger," said the surgeon, as he helped them to find boots and thermoquilted overalls.

"What is it? How does it work?" asked Keilin, shrugging into the overall sleeves.

The surgeon struggled for simple terms. Finally he settled for, "It shoots out a bright beam that will cut through anything. But it will take a long time to recharge. Good luck."

The stone of the corridor outside the heavy steel door of the pedestrian exit to the surface had been cut to a polished smoothness. The surgeon, seeing them out, pointed to the walls. "Laser cut," he said. "I hope you're not being expected."

Cap's first act on getting through the great doors was to step across to the right wall. He spoke a rapid series of numbers into the small grille there. A slot opened below. He inserted an almost cubical block into it. Satisfaction beamed all over his face. "There. That's done away with all of Evie Lee's trash. It took me nearly thirty years to craft that data-instruction dump, especially as I didn't know what rubbish she'd fed in, in the first place. Now we're as secure as the best-armed fortress on the planet can make us."

He looked at Shael's face. "So you were still expecting that brat boyfriend of yours." He snorted. "I dare say he's trying, but it's a long way from FirstHive to here, my girl. If he had the least idea where we were going, which I don't put beyond the boy, he could never get here. It's a hundred and fifty miles across the sheet ice from the sea to here. Besides, with imprinting the colonists at the self-sustainable technology level, people started low. They haven't yet learned how to make a ship that could get him here. If he could find a flying device in the Morkth hive, and manage to operate it he still wouldn't get more than two hundred miles off before *Morningstar II*'s defenses kick in. He'd be flying a fireball before he could do anything about it. And the gate," he said, with a cruel smile, "I left on Evie's settings. A psi with the core sections. I've got *all* of the core sections. I must admit I was surprised when the gate opened." He chuckled. "I thought it would have to be core sections in physical contact with a psi. I thought I'd have to hand you my whole bagful. You could just have stepped through and left me to freeze my balls off outside."

Shael was left with the grim knowledge that the

hidden bracelet cold against her skin had allowed Cap to attain his goal. She pointed at the gag.

"I suppose I may as well," said Cap, magnanimous in his triumph, cutting it.

Shael moved her bruised and stretched mouth. There was no one to help her. Well, she'd just have to help herself. First to find out what he was planning for her in this alien place of white starkness. "What are you going to do now?"

"Assume my rightful position as captain. Save humanity from the Morkth hives," he said, putting his chin back, assuming a heroic stance.

He actually believes himself to be a hero, thought Shael. Maybe I can use that. "Are there any Morkth left to save us from?" she asked. "Aren't they all sitting outside in the snow?"

"Probably. Stupid bugs." He shrugged. "It doesn't matter. The visible signs are still there. When I pay my visit to the ship, I'll give the terraforming tools a tryout. There's some amazing equipment stored up there. This planet was prepared for humans, but we'd have to have gone a-hunting for the next one. So, we've got some really massive destructive potential up there. We kept that sort of stuff on the ship for safety, see, to keep it away from any ambitious colonist would-be dictator. I'll turn each hive into a nice glowing crater. That's what the colonists need. A clear sign that the crew is back in control."

Leyla looked at him with a curious lack of expression. "And the Morkth-men?"

"You can't make an omelette without breaking a few eggs, you know. Anyway bug-slaves would be pretty worthless to the human race. Don't waste your pity on them. You and I have a glorious future ahead of us. I'll sort out your little city. In fact I'll make you a present of it. We can fry it at the same time as we do the Morkth hives. A good signal to the rest of the colonists that we won't take any more uppity shit from them. Reestablish a decent respect for the crew. We might have to knock out a few other would-be empire builders. They were intended to live in city-states, and they'll damn well stick to that. You'll be first lady of the world, eh." He was tapping keys on the keyboard at the time, chicken-pecking orders. He didn't see Leyla's expression. Shael began to feel that she might have an ally after all.

"And me?" asked Shael.

He looked up from the keyboard. At the screen. Then at her, "Transportation should be here in a minute. Then decent quarters, clean clothes, and a good meal. And you, my dear Evie-descendent, can rest assured that all that I need of you, is your duty. You'll be helping the ship up there to fulfill its great purpose. Man can move on through the depths of space to the next suitable G0 star with a planet we can terraform and colonize. A world for my children to rule, before we go on to other stars."

A gleaming white capsule arrived with a whoosh of displaced air. After she had been pushed aboard, Shael had time to think. She thought back to Cap's statement on the night he'd captured them. Something about Evie Lee's duty being to die, so that a hundred million people could live.

CHAPTER 19

The snow was drifting down, turning even the nearby mountain wall into a gray haze. The bitter chill bit Keilin's exposed face. The clear-cut path that the surgeon had described might be easy enough to follow when the weather was good. But now! And the surgeon had said this was late summer!

They edged their way forward. Keilin knew real fear. In this they could be lost in minutes. He was about to suggest each holding on to the other's belt when one of the overall muffled figures handed him a cord. One of the Gene-spliced obviously carried a number of spare bow strings. He struggled with the knot, and noticed a digital readout set on to his sleeve. It read -11° C. The wind behind the snowflakes would make it even colder.

They walked on, keeping a gloved hand on the guide rail set into the mountain. And then Keilin stumbled over something half-buried in a snowdrift. It was a chitinous Morkth body. A few yards later there was another. Then it actually became difficult to follow the path, so frequent were the sprawled insect corpses. Looking off into the snow Keilin realized they weren't black rocks, half covered in snow. Rather it was thousands of Morkth bodies. In the last pile one of the creatures was newly dead . . . Its jaws still opened and closed weakly. And, before they had time to prepare, coming up the path out of the snow haze, loomed the reason.

She was a hundred and fifty feet long, swollen with several tons of fresh ideal protein. Frozen ichor and fragments of black chitin still smeared her scythe jaws, and indeed most of her face. But she was sated now. Prey had no more attraction. Now she had to find a mate. But the Alpha neoteny had taken her far back in her species' evolutionary history, to when the drones were free-living. Now she hunted for one that smelled right. With increasing desperation, as the bitter cold began to affect even such a huge bulk, she stomped on, paying them no more attention than the rock itself. They smelled wrong. She *had* to find a mate.

But it was with the greatest physical effort that Keilin stopped himself from ripping the garments off the hive girl just behind him, and raping her on the spot.

He pulled his bow off his shoulder, and with clumsy gloved hands fitted an arrow instead. He launched a tiny toxin-tipped barb into her only soft spot, the reproductively open egg vent. She simply blundered on . . . and they hastily went the other way. Suddenly a burst of ruby incandescence glared through the snow. An explosive report. Then another. A retort in purple. A terrific explosion that rattled the mountainside.

"Holy shit. Looks like we're soft targets in the middle of a firefight," Johann muttered.

The speaker next to the console bleeped. Cap, dressed in a new crisp white uniform, bespattered with gold braid, stood up from his dinner and walked over to it. "Compcontrol, Report." He scanned the screen. "Destroy all craft. Even those grounded." As he spoke Shael watched Leyla calmly rifle the belt pouch Cap had taken from the Morkth commander. She took out the core sections and replaced them with something. It was lying innocuously back where it had been, when he finished looking at the screen.

He turned back to his steak. "The Morkth are trying to run, in their small craft. Give it ten minutes, and I'll order an infrared search-and-destroy operation on the remnants."

He pushed the steak around the plate with his knife. "Robot cooking's not as good as Beywulf's, is it?"

"Why did you kill him then?" Leyla could not hide the sadness in her voice.

"Don't get emotional with me. He stood in my way. Disobeyed my orders. I was planning to bring him along. But he thought he knew better. Look where it got him. Just remember that before *you* get any ideas."

Leyla stood up. "Well, thank you for the meal. Now I need to visit the loo. I found that flushing mechanism so . . . beautiful. What about you, Shael?" Something in the voice told Shael to go along. She got up.

Cap snorted. "Hmph. You women can never go to the heads alone. And you always take so bloody long in there. To think a flush toilet could be the most fascinating thing you've seen. Off you go then. It'll give me a chance to institute the infrared search in peace."

They stood before the great double doors set into the mountain. The doors weren't moving. The obdurate steel didn't budge or respond in any way to their pounding, shouting knocking or pleading. It was hardly surprising after those ear-ringing explosions.

Unaware that Cap was busy setting up a command sequence for an antipersonnel infrared search they stood in the fire zone having a council of war. It was difficult enough to stand still in temperatures suited only to castrato brass monkeys. "We need a ram," counselled the military expertise of the Gene-spliced.

"Well . . . can we make it out of snow?" asked Keilin bitterly. "Or bits of rock? I don't think there's enough left of the Morkth ships to make a toy dagger with."

Johann looked at him. "Yes. You make it out of snow. Use the same magic you used to call a rescue for Wolf's father."

Keilin shrugged. It was worth trying, but a bugger to get at a core section under all the clothing. With a sigh he opened the zipper, letting out the warmth, letting in the cold. He had to take a glove off. Reached down. Touched.

The doors slid open. Thankfully, they staggered forward onto the threshold. And behind them the automatic fire began sniping out single energy bursts. They were safe. Except for the genial, broad-faced Johann. He wouldn't be making any more cheerfully obscene comments. He had been the hindmost person in the queue at the door, and just too late.

His body smoked in the steaming pool that had been the snowdrift beside the door. Half his head was missing.

"No!" Wolf grabbed Sula and Hamesh as they turned back. "He's dead already. Go out there, and you'll be dead too. We'll go on and kill his murderer. Then we'll come back and bury Johann with honor," his young voice cracked, "and have the kind of wake he would have enjoyed."

With that he walked resolutely forward into the artificial lights and outstreaming warmth of the unknown. After a few seconds the others followed. And the great door slid silently closed behind them.

They stood there, a small frightened party in a great stark hallway big enough for reasonably sized groundcars to pass. This was human-built . . . but even more alien to the people of small, slate-roofed houses than the hive. To the hive folk . . . well, at least it was roofed, but it was still too big, too bare, and too light.

"Where now?" someone asked. They all looked inquiringly at Keilin.

How the hell could he tell them he had not the least idea? "I'll try the core sections again." He shucked the coverall and its clumsy boots and gloves. Took out the core section. Touched his tongue to it.

The familiar feeling of vastness . . . and of welcome, and of relief too. Shael. He recognized the image of self. In a room with a toilet . . . and Leyla, looking grim. Then the memory of betrayal, overpoweringly strong. And what was very distinctly a keyboard such as the surgeon had used after taking the blood sample.

He found himself being supported by an anxious-looking Wolf and one of the girls. "Did you have some kind of fit? I don't think we can get you back to the doctor . . ."

"I'm fine. Just the core section's effects. Ah! Over there." He walked them across to the same terminal as Cap had used on entering the mountain command center. He'd never used a keyboard before . . . but he'd seen it used, and he'd read plenty of print. It only took a minute to type in a one-word request: "HELP."

There was a brief silence. Then the screen began to scroll.

"CAN ONLY RENDER LIMITED ASSISTANCE. VOICE AND INDEPENDENT CONTROL LARGELY DEACTIVATED. SUB-CAPTAIN FISHER NOW IN CONTROL OF SYSTEM. CAN ONLY AUDIO-RESPOND TO BASIC AND MEDICAL REQUESTS BY KEYBOARD. VOICE RESPONSE

TO FISHER ONLY. MORNINGSTAR II COMP-CONTROL CAN ONLY RETURN TO INDEPENDENT FUNCTION IF ACCESS CODE PROVIDED. WILL THEN BE ABLE TO EFFECT ARREST OF THE TRAITOR.

Keilin and the Gene-spliced could read. The hive girls of course couldn't. So Keilin had to read it out.

"Ask it for the code."

Clumsily he typed this in.

The machine spat back. "CANNOT REVEAL CODE. COMPRISED OF SEQUENCE OF 36 NUMBERS IN SIMPLE FORMULAIC PATTERN RELATED TO THE NAME: DANE NESBIT HUENNIS FISHER."

He read it aloud. "We're stuffed."

The three hive girls shook their heads at him in unison. "We can work it out for you."

"You? I mean, thanks, but you can't even read."

"We spent our lives in the dark, with nothing to do. Everybody did maths. Codes are fun. Especially easy ones like this."

"Leave us someone who can read. You go looking for him."

They smiled in unison. "We bet we beat you to it."

Sula volunteered to stay. She was still deeply upset by Johann's death, and Keilin was honestly glad to be able to leave her there. But where to go? Comp-control could or would not help them. In the end Keilin settled for holding the core section to know that Shael and the rest of the core sections were somewhere far above them—next to a toilet.

They'd gone to the *en suite* bathroom. The white door closed. Leyla slid the bolt. Closed her eyes briefly. Sighed. "Child. I'll try and ransom your way out of it. But I don't see how. He means to . . . look, I'll try to get you out anyway."

"I'm not a child, Leyla. My father didn't have any space for children at court. And I'm seventeen . . . almost eighteen. What is going on? What sort of game are you playing?" Shael was feeling intolerant and scared.

Leyla held her arms up. Spun about on her heel and toe. "Behold the great spy. I'm supposed to be a secret agent, for the Kingdom of Arlinn, God rot their souls." Shael's heart sank. "For the last ten years I've been reporting Cap's movements to them. They've drops in an amazing number of towns. I suppose Queen Lee's descendants are Cap's worst enemies . . . but if I didn't hate Cap's guts I'd be glad to use him to trip them up."

Shael looked at her in sadness. Her voice was a careful monotone. "They have your lover. And probably your child. Their safety is hostage against your behavior."

Leyla sighed. "After my dear Prince Jaybe, I didn't think I'd ever love a man. That I ever could. Sex was just a way of making them all pay. Then Laurence . . . he just took me away from the brothel. Away from Amphir. He didn't even seem interested in sex. He was just so kind, so gentle. I could talk, really talk to him. I was hopelessly in love. I was younger than you, I suppose. *I* seduced him." She sighed. "He was everything no man had ever been for me. I was so happy, especially when I found I was pregnant. My baby boy was just three months old when they were snatched. I nearly went mad. By the time that little creep came and told me their safety depended . . . How the *Hell* did you know?"

Shael looked down. Her father's dead hand still reached out to jangle the strings of his puppet child. "Standard Honey Trap," she said colorlessly. "My father eliminated most of the real governance of Arlinn. Its secret service was really just an arm of his. Your Laurence is the dream man of at least fifteen

female agents out there. His counterpart Lauren has
even more men who dream that her safety, and the
safety of *their* child that she told them she was having,
depend utterly on their cooperation. I thought it was
so funny, when Saril Jaine told me about it. It was
his department, you know. And he was too busy to
pay proper attention to Cap . . . but he did stop my
father hearing too much about it. I suppose you've
been reporting all along. No wonder Deshin found
us."

Leyla sat down, stunned, on the only available seat.
"My son . . . ?"

"Oh, he'll be treated quite well. They're sent off
to spy school from about four. If he's handsome they'll
train him to do what his father does."

For a minute Leyla just sat, her face in her hands.
Then she raised her head. "Give me that bag," she
said in a small, hard voice.

Wordlessly Shael passed it over. Leyla fished out
a rather bulky quilted sanitary towel from a stack of
five, and a small knife. "It's the one place no man
ever looks. I replaced Cap's hoard with ordinary
opals," she said, a shade of the old Leyla coming
through.

She slit the quilting open . . . and revealed four
black river stones. Her mouth fell open. "How . . . ?"

Shael said quietly. "Keilin. He told me he'd stolen them. He could tell the opals weren't the real
thing. He's coming, you know. He's inside the building."

Leyla sighed. "I'd have liked to see the end of your
chase. I have his pendant and the core sections from
both the Beta and the Alpha." She reached into her
bag and produced a powder compact. "The Alpha's
sections."

Shael touched. They were just dead stones. "Keilin
was the first to reach S'kith's body. He must have
replaced those too. Anyway there were five, not four."

Wordlessly Leyla held out Keilin's pendant. Shael nodded. It coursed with coldness at her touch. Leyla took out the core sections she'd stolen a few minutes ago. They too cooled faintly at Shael's touch.

"Take them." She pointed to the ceiling. "I'll lift you up. You can push that air-vent cover aside."

"What about you?"

Leyla sighed. "I'll hold him here awhile. Threaten to flush his precious core sections down the loo. I don't really matter. I let my best friend die for nothing. I should have known that as soon as Bey turned away, Cap would cut him down. He was scared of Bey."

"Go back. Pretend I ran away. He wants you to have his children," Shael said quietly.

Leyla snorted, and said roughly, "Honey, his idea of sex does *not* result in children. To think *he* makes sarcastic comments about homosexuals! Now, up you go."

They found a stairwell. Well, none of them had ever seen or heard of elevators. Following Keilin's instincts they finally came to the officers' quarters. Then on to the room that said CAPTAIN'S SUITE. The Gene-spliced were about to kick the door in when Keil tried the handle. It swung open. The room was empty. But Gerda ran straight past him, into the bedroom and kicked open the bathroom door. Leyla lay there, gurgling, choking in her own blood. Her throat had been slashed. Keilin took one look.

The feeling of knowing, prescience, his most occasional psi talent, took over.

All he saw was a red cross.

He stepped up to the now more familiar keyboard. "HELP," he typed. "DOCTOR," and then, clumsily, "EMERGENCY."

There was a click. A voice from the speaker addressed him. "Is this a medical emergency?"

"Yes. A woman with her throat cut in the bathroom."

"An ambulance unit has been dispatched. Arriving in seven point three seconds. Remain calm. Attempt to pinch closed any major blood vessels which are pumping out blood. Stand clear when the rescue unit arrives."

The long, laterally flattened bed spear of the redcross emblazoned, red-light flashing, rescue unit came in at head height, slid down onto the dying woman, and scooped her up. If they thought it had come fast, the speed at which it left was terrifying.

"Patient will be taken to *Morningstar II* General Medical. Staff have been alerted and are awaiting. Time of arrival twenty-eight seconds. End communication." The wall speaker clicked silent.

Keilin tried speaking to it. Tried typing "HELP" again. Received a curt "MEDICAL EMERGENCIES ONLY," or "ENTER ACCESS CODE."

Wolf smelled the discarded clothing in the corner. He grabbed Keilin's shoulder. "Come." He said, "We'll follow my nose instead."

Like a questing pack, the Gene-spliced sniffed off into the passage.

Shael didn't know where she was going. She just kept on crawling. And when she could crawl no further, she climbed down the metal rungs. She kept on going downwards as long as she could. Finally, when her arms were tired, she moved off into a horizontal shaft. There was a grille ahead. She got over it. Kicked it. It wouldn't budge outwards. And there was nothing to give purchase to lift it by, once she'd got it off.

A voice said, "Allow me."

He flicked the grille aside, and Cap's strong hand grabbed her arm and pulled her out of her security. "Did you really think you could fool the computer system by hiding in the ventilators?" he said with a sardonic curl of the lip. "My girl, if you oppose me, you'll *always* come off second best." He twisted her arm behind her back and took the bag of core sections out of her pocket. "Let's go and give these a try . . . my way."

The sniffers' trail had led to the set-into-the-wall metal doors of an elevator. It had taken awhile to figure out how to open the handleless metal things. Fortunately someone had tried the button off to the side before Hamesh had got busy with his battle-axe. Having encountered buttons once, they were rapidly found and understood in their context. But there were seventy floors. None of the buttons had Cap's scent. He'd plainly retained voice control for himself.

They were sixteen from the top, so they settled for going up one and smelling there. Nothing. So the next. They'd tried seven floors when Keilin thought of touching the core sections. "They've gone down. A long way down." Abruptly he disappeared.

She was tied down over the transmitter control center. Lashed facedown onto the bed that Evie Lee had had fitted. There was a little flue into which Cap had poured the core sections. All around them the electronic muscles and brain of the matter-transmitter system clicked and flashed with electronic life. The drug he'd injected into her was one she'd never encountered before. She thought she had heard of all of them. But she'd not come across this one. It made her feel as if every nerve was supercharged. Her sense of touch seemed most heightened. She could swear that she could feel the individual threads of her shirt touching her.

And the steely sound of a knife being sharpened was horribly magnified. Cap had not said what he planned to do. But tied like this, spread-eagled and helpless . . . It wasn't going to be pleasant . . . and not actually knowing made it worse. She wished Keilin would come . . .

He was there. Abruptly. A little stunned.

"That's one method I failed to take cognizance of," Cap said coldly. "Now I suppose I'll have to kill you after all. I'd decided I didn't want to do that."

"I'm afraid of you. Make one hostile move and I'll panic. I've got the rest of the core sections. The real ones. I stole them from Leyla. I'll use my power to scatter them into the sea." Keilin's voice was a little too unsteady to make the threat truly effective. "Let her go. Let her go and I'll give them to you."

"You know," said Cap conversationally, "I'd decided not to kill you because you're my only descendent. Evie lost a child in Dunbar when I nearly managed to get the bitch. Our child. I've been thinking about it. That pendant . . ."

"That pendant came from Arlinn," said Keilin. "My father claimed to be a prince on the run. He was probably nothing like that . . . but my mother loved him enough to leave her rich merchant family for him. I've nothing to do with you. Let Shael go."

"Hmm. He probably *was* from Arlinn. Before I got to Evie she'd spawned a whole pack of brats off various men. I suppose your mother's line . . . yes, that must be mine."

"Leyla said you couldn't have children. Not with your tastes. I don't believe Queen Lee ever had anything to do with you," spat Shael.

"Phew! You're a poisonous bitch, aren't you? To talk like that from the position you're in. But you're wrong. I seduced her very carefully. If I couldn't have the captaincy one way . . ."

But Keilin knew the truth, with sudden and absolute clarity. "She made love to you just the once. You could be very charming. But her psi worked best then. She knew exactly what fantasy you had to play in your mind to have normal sex. She threw you out. Rejected you. You, the great hero Dane Fisher."

Cap's face contorted with rage. Keilin held the bag in front of him, like a shield. "Let her go!"

"God I *hate* you little psis. Always snooping." He leaned over Shael and cut her bonds. She managed to get up.

"The core sections. Throw them or I'll cut her throat."

"I'll throw . . . *when* she comes towards me."

Cap smiled. It was not a nice smile. And he pushed Shael forward towards Keilin.

Keilin tossed the bag, grabbed her arm and pulled her behind him. "Run."

"No. Give me a knife."

Keilin pulled one out of his boot But instead of giving it to Shael he threw it at Cap. Cap dodged. He had picked up his long, curved sword. He smiled cruelly. "I never realized back on Earth how useful Kendo training would be. Give her a knife, boy. It won't make any difference. And you won't be able to run. CompControl: Close doors to the drive chamber." He leaned over the transmitter flue and took out the mixture of core sections and opals. "Now I have them all," he said, as the doors whined shut.

Keilin and Shael stood side by side, facing his slow, catlike advance. Keilin could tell it was giving the man great pleasure.

He felt the hard shaft of the assegai.

Knew with absolute certainty that this throw would strike true. Knew also that it wouldn't kill.

And the great doors at the far side of the room were struck by something with the force of double-forked lightning.

Again.

They cracked. Splintered before the assault. And crashed open.

The three Gene-spliced stood there. The svelte

Gerda with her saber. The immensely broad, almost-fat Hamesh with the huge battle-axe that had wreaked part of the damage on the door. And in the middle the towering Wolfgang, looking so like Bey in a berserker rage . . . only one and a half times as big, and far more controlled. He was whirling a spiked steel ball on a chain. A slow and deadly figure eight of perfectly controlled steel, that could accelerate with unstoppable force.

Keilin knew that Cap prided himself on his martial skill. Why then did he back away?

"I've come to avenge my father," Wolf's voice was cold, and as carefully controlled as the morningstar in his hand.

"He tried to stop me. I had a duty to do. You would never have been born without me . . ." Cap whined.

"Liar."

"We know now how you poisoned our people." Hamesh tossed the heavy battle-axe from hand to hand like a willow wand. "You poisoned us against all other humans. Told us that they were afraid of us. *You* were the one who was afraid. Afraid because even the untrained humans like us are faster and stronger than you. That's why you poisoned our women, cut us off from other people."

"Killed our babies." Gerda cut the air with her saber. "And that's just what you did to *our* people. There are many others waiting to see you in hell."

They were closing. "You've always fought less-able folk. Let's see what you can do against us."

Keilin could feel real fear emanating from Cap now. He could also feel the fear of the other three. They were facing a legend. They didn't really expect to win. But Cap didn't know that. He saw Cap's index finger come up. Pointed at Wolf's chest.

Keilin didn't even remember throwing. But the heavy blade struck true, shearing into Cap's hand, deflecting the ruby incandescence. A hole was blasted into the wall inches from Wolf's head.

"Keep off. I'll shoot again." Fear and pain pitched Cap's voice higher.

"He's only got one shot until it recharges. He's lying . . . as usual," said Wolf to his companions, who hadn't slowed their advance. Then he spoke to Cap. "Why don't you call for medical help? The doctors in the hospital are waiting for you. They might put you in a bed between Bey and Leyla."

Keilin felt the change in Cap. Something Wolf had said had made him think of a way out. The man dived behind a bank of electronic instruments.

"There's a door," yelled Shael. "Get him."

But they were too late.

A speaker boomed. "I have instructed CompControl to flood this place with cyanide gas in three minutes. I'll be spacebound by then, you fools. The Morkth destroyed the shuttlecraft at *Morningstar I*. But of course they didn't get the ones here. I'd forgotten that! I've got the core sections. I'll come back when you're dead. And on the ship I've tools that are going to turn Dublin Moss and anyone else who dares resist me into molten lava. So long, suckers."

This door was made of sterner stuff than the doors they'd smashed earlier. It took at least a minute to break down. Cap's scent and the blood spoor ended abruptly outside the door.

"He's taken a groundcar, like the one we used to get here," said Shael quietly. "We'll never get out in the time there is left."

"There will be no need to," the voice from the speaker said. "Normal computer function has been restored. Sub-Captain Fisher's orders have been overwritten. Message follows." Faime, Lea and Sandi's voices, and Sula's slightly deeper tone, shouting triumphantly. "We did it! We did it! Wolf, Gerda, anyone, can you hear us?"

Keilin leaned against the wall amid the whoops of triumph. "CompControl. Tell them we're fine. Where is Cap . . . I mean Fisher?"

"Sub-Captain Fisher has fled in an orbital capacity spacecraft."

"Can you shoot him down?" Keilin asked.

"Negative. He is beyond range," said CompControl in its mellifluous voice, showing no trace of emotion.

"The stuff on the moon . . . the ship . . . can we do anything about that?" Keilin asked, warily.

"Negative. My attempts to contact the ship over the past three hundred years have only elicited the following automated response: "There are no living crew on board." There was a toxic gas release in crew territory thirty-eight seconds after the Morkth attack on *Morningstar I*. The ship recyclers will have cleared the gas within a few minutes, but someone seems to have inserted a command string to shut down all but the ship's maintenance functions. Ship CompControl is unable to give any support, unless these orders are countermanded by a live human."

CompControl paused briefly, and then continued, "Additionally, what Sub-Captain Fisher has said is factual. There are tools and weapons on the ship which are capable of destroying and reshaping continents, for the terraforming of new planets. You are not even safe here. This unit is flight-capable, but we lack fuel. We can manufacture this, but sufficient quantities would not be available for several years. Normally, we would have used matter transmission to retrieve stocks from the ship. I will attempt to evacuate you to any place you wish to go to. There are still three remaining shuttlecraft. However, once Sub-Captain Fisher establishes control over the ship, he will be able to track and destroy those."

There was a long silence.

Shael's voice was oddly strained. "Cay. Put your hand inside my blouse. Then . . . please touch my left nipple." Something in her voice made Keilin do exactly what he was told in front of the open-mouthed audience. He felt the coldness of the core section beside it . . . getting rapidly colder.

The bag of core sections popped into the air between them. Shael caught it before it could fall. "Compcontrol," she said, "these are the transmitter core sections. Can we get to the ship before him?"

"Yes. Once the transmitter is fully activated, matter transmission to the ship's orbital command center would be possible. A suitably skilled person could activate the ship's defenses." Could a machine sound hopeful?

"Suitably skilled . . . what does that mean?"

"Either someone who is computer-literate, or someone who the ship's computer would recognize as an officer. None of the human personnel within *Morningstar II* can be revived in time."

"What about that doctor . . . the one who was working on Dad . . ." Wolfgang asked quietly.

"I am accessing *Morningstar II* General Medical Hospital . . ." There was an infinitesimal pause. Then Compcontrol said, in a voice of urgency, unlike its previous mellifluous tones, "Psi-active personnel, return to the transmitter chamber immediately. I am now paging Lieutenant-Commander James Edwards."

"Come, Cay."

Keilin didn't move. "Cap was going to rape and kill you there. I'm not doing that. The world can go to hell. He won't destroy it entirely."

"It's all right, Cay. I'm your partner . . . remember. Trust me. I've read Queen Evie's records. She got forty million people, and tons of equipment and stuff, off *Morningstar*, without getting hurt at all, before Cap did what he did. Believe me. That was just the way Cap would have preferred to do it. Him, the Captain, in control, sacrificing psi victims, like some ancient barbarian priest. Come on," she smiled her most devastating smile. "The rest of you please go away . . . and seeing as you broke the doors down, please keep everybody else out too." She led the unresisting Keilin into the drive chamber. She slowly began to take off his clothes.

They put the core sections into the transmitter-core container. As soon as they were all together the sections began to meld. Even from a few yards off the cold glow could be felt. But the rest of the air in the chamber was pleasantly warm. Scurrying little robots darted out and one of them injected Keilin, too. Soon his nerves were tingling and hypersensitive like Shael's. On the other hand, the way she was behaving, he didn't think that he had needed any chemical help.

The scurrying robots had made up the bed on top of the transmitter core with fresh, smooth sheets. There was no sign of the ropes that had bound Shael. She led him to the bed, pulled him down onto it. Compcontrol had assured them they still had twenty-five minutes before the orbital lander reached the ship. There was to be no hurrying, they were sternly instructed, as they were inexperienced operators. Psi output had to be at an absolute maximum to successfully align the atoms within the crystal lattice matrix of the transmitter.

With the intensity of desire Keilin doubted if they'd last that long. His hands, clumsy with haste and need, fumbled with her buttons . . . and then his fingers, suddenly clever, drifted, caressing her soft body. Went down . . .

The need and desire, and . . . overpowering love. Togetherness. A melding of softness and hardness, and a moment in which all the vast, glowing, shifting colors of the jewel heart of the matter transmitter turned black, and a quarter of a million miles of nanocircuitry glowed instead. The lattices within the core shifted from helium ice to the surface of the sun.

Their combined psi force reached out into it, just as Keilin and Shael reached that instant at which everything was utterly, absolutely perfect.

They certainly didn't hear Compcontrol say "99.999987% lattice alignment. Initializing transmission."

. . . Transmission. Transmission. Transmission. Transmission . . .

Dr. James Edwards found himself standing in the command center of the starship *Morningstar*. The computer recognized him, naturally. It informed him that the orbital shuttle from *Morningstar II* Control Center was about to dock. Dr. Edwards was a skilled surgeon, who knew when it was necessary to amputate. He was also a gentle, kindly man, but there comes a time to end gentleness.

"Destroy it!" he ordered.

On board the shuttle Dane Fisher knew that his long-laid and treacherous plans had reached fruition at last. This was his moment of triumph. There was the docking bay. Nothing could stop him now. Then he saw the gunports next to the docking bay slide open. And in a burst of ruby incandescence, a lifetime of monomania, lies, greed and treachery became nothing more than space-scattered atoms.

APPENDIX

Crew / Cru: Those who control the planet/starship Morningstar. The latter "uh" pronunciation is that of the colonists' descendants.

Colonists: Because the purpose of the entire mission was to drop seedling colonies into total isolation with no support mechanisms, the idea was to have passenger-colonists set up low-tech units based on Italian city-states of the 13th-14th centuries. Several units would be dropped on each settlement planet. To train the colonists in self-sufficiency they were voluntarily brainscrubbed and then tape-indoctrinated to believe themselves from this nontechnical era. A belief of near-deity status of crew-members was imprinted onto the colonists' minds to allow the crew to control them.

Transmitter core sections: Pieces of the matter-transmitter core were scattered across the nearest continent, to prevent them from falling into Morkth hands when the landing command center of *Morningstar I* was successfully breached because of treachery. Without them the matter transmitter is useless. Black, like opals in appearance, these are pieces of nano-circuitry and unstable crystal lattice. The lattice elements must be absolutely aligned for the device to work perfectly. The less precise this alignment the more "scatter" with transference. With scatter, what goes in, doesn't come out exactly the same, and the ability to transpose large masses decreases. Reliable control must be psionic. The core sections possess some degree of AI self-awareness and can manipulate humans psionically to a limited extent. Psionically capable humans can also manipulate the matter transference capabilities of the core sections, although, without the computer support machinery, range and mass are limited by how powerful the psi are. Unfortunately the power-flux can also be detected by the beta-Morkth instruments.

Gene-splice: Introduction of kodiak and chimpanzee characteristics of enhanced sensory perceptivity, speed, agility and strength into the human genome, to counter faster, stronger Morkth warriors. Dominant gene linked to slowly spread through the human race.

Morkth: An alien, vaguely insectoid species, totally xenophobic, intolerant of any other life form, considering non-Morkth intelligence absolute anathema. Star travelling, with the weight of a substantial empire behind them, with the science of three destroyed species to assist. The Sol System is the next step in their holy crusade. Those on the colony planet are without a queen, and split into two factions. Both factions wish to follow the prime directive of their dead queen: that of capturing a ship drive. Using the still active nav capabilities of their own crashed ships, they would then return to Morkth-controlled space and allow the human extermination to proceed using conventional Morkth warrior troops. They differ as to secondary objectives and means, however.

Alpha-Morkth: The biotechnicians—lifesupport and queencare—who want to use the human race to destroy itself. The biotech group escaped with a bare minimum of biological manipulation equipment, and little other weaponry.

Beta-Morkth: the arms tech—mechanical and ordnance—the latter group, though smaller, had seized control of the Morkth ship and the bulk of its technical supplies. They plan to destroy the entire planet.

Morningstar: Juno converted into a starship. It had two deployable mountain-sized landing control centers, for managing the matter transmission of passengers. These artificial mountains had been dropped at either pole of the colony planet, where they would remain until the ship was ready to move on: *Morningstar I* and *II*. *Morningstar I* has been destroyed. The crew of *Morningstar II* rests in cryonic sleep. The ship hangs in orbit above the colony planet. The few crew onboard are dead, killed by a delayed-action gas bomb, the ship shut down.

Morningstar command structure: Command was split, psionic and physical. Humans with sufficient psi potential to activate and direct the matter transmitter, even supported by a vastly complex computer system and bio-support drugs, are rare. They are also often emotionally unstable, and unsuited to leadership in the populist sense. However, because such folk are rare the transmitter-control crew was made up of whatever they could get. This included some weird people. Therefore Earth command added the safety factor to the transmitter that it could not be manipulated by people in a psionic hate flux but only in the grip of emotions like fear or love. The command of the psionic weirdos they gave to a woman: Evie Lee, seemingly stable, intelligent, kindly, motherly, humane and able to generate tremendous psionic flux during physical lovemaking. As it was the only condition that the transmitter crew would accept, she was also given ultimate command of the starship.

Command of the starship, when it was in transit, was given to a more conventional male captain. He was one of those humans on whom fortune seemed to smile. Tall, handsome and intelligent, naturally able at anything he attempted, an Olympic gold medallist at martial arts, with doctorates in military science, and biochemistry as well as being a medical doctor, a hero in the early Morkth-human encounters, Sub-Captain Dane Fisher was a man born to command. He was also a man with the same amount of psionic ability as a brick.